Club Wicked:
MY WICKED MASTERS

Ann Mayburn

LooseId.

ISBN 13: 978-1-62300-847-5
Club Wicked: My Wicked Masters
Copyright © February 2015 by Ann Mayburn
Originally released in e-book format in April 2014

Cover Art by Artist Fiona Jayde Media
Cover Layout and Design by Fiona Jayde Media

All rights reserved. Except for use of brief quotations in any review or critical article, the reproduction or utilization of this work in whole or in part in any form by any electronic, mechanical or other means, now known or hereafter invented, including xerography, photo-copying and recording, or in any information storage or retrieval is forbidden without the prior written permission of Loose Id LLC, PO Box 170549, San Francisco CA 94117-0549. http://www.loose-id.com

Image/art disclaimer: Licensed material is being used for illustrative purposes only. Any person depicted in the licensed material is a model.

DISCLAIMER: Many of the acts described in our BDSM/fetish titles can be dangerous. Please do not try any new sexual practice, whether it be fire, rope, or whip play, without the guidance of an experienced practitioner. Neither Loose Id nor its authors will be responsible for any loss, harm, injury or death resulting from use of the information contained in any of its titles.

This book is an original publication of Loose Id. Each individual story herein was previously published in e-book format only by Loose Id and is a work of fiction. Any similarity to actual persons, events or existing locations is entirely coincidental.

Printed in the U.S.A. by
Lightning Source, Inc.
1246 Heil Quaker Blvd
La Vergne TN 37086
www.lightningsource.com

Chapter One

Rhiannon Mirga, known at Club Wicked as Goddess, struggled to keep from slapping the bitch out of Doll, one of the newer servers. A pretty enough blue-eyed blonde, Doll was a classic "mean girl," and Rhiannon had gotten into it with her more than once. Evidently Doll had her eyes set on a particular Master who wasn't interested in her, and Doll blamed Rhiannon. The older woman seemed determined to try and chase Rhiannon out of the club through sheer bitchery, but Rhiannon had survived much worse than Doll, and there was no way in hell she was letting that woman intimidate her into leaving.

Unfortunately, Rhiannon had been told she had to take anger management classes to deal with her hot temper, and she'd been doing her best to keep herself under control. Mr. Florentine, the owner of Club Wicked, and someone Rhiannon adored, had asked her as a personal favor to try and not fight anymore. So far, she'd managed to respect his wishes, but damn, Doll was begging for a beating.

The blonde woman looked over from her spot three mirrors over as she was putting her boots on. "I love that outfit, Goddess. It makes your ass look so…lumpy."

Staring into the mirror, Rhiannon pretended to be concentrating on straightening her long black hair and ignored Doll.

Her gaze flickered to the other woman as Doll spoke again, this time with a little more venom. "I guess the men you whore for here like it. Some guys just get off on cheap and easy trash."

Rhiannon's hand trembled just the faintest bit as she parted a new section of her hair. She could do this. She could keep her cool. Losing her temper wasn't worth it; this woman wasn't worth it. Since she'd started her anger management, in addition to her regular therapy, she'd been calmer, less likely to lash out like an abused animal at anyone who got too close to her. Her coworkers had noticed, and Rhiannon was even slowly, very slowly, allowing a few friendships to form.

So she ignored an increasingly angry Doll and continued with her routine. Tonight her job as a server would be a little different. She'd worked at Club Wicked for over three years now; she knew her job and was used to helping train new employees. But tonight she'd be working with one of the club members who, for whatever reason, wanted to be a server for the evening. Rhiannon just had to hang in here until Jessica arrived or another server came into the unusually quiet dressing room.

Doll stood and said in a voice oozing insincerity, "Did you hear that Master Hawk bought Sunny a new car?"

At the mention of the bartender who Rhiannon totally did not get along with, and the Master who was the reason for it, white-hot anger flared through her. Even though she knew Master Hawk was a negative trigger for her, even though she knew it was completely irrational because she didn't want Master Hawk as a boyfriend, jealousy mixed with her ire, and she found herself counting from one to ten first in Spanish and then Chinese.

That managed to block Doll's voice out, but when Rhiannon ran out of languages, Doll said, "Aww, what's the matter, Goddess? Your feelings get hurt that Master Hawk thinks you're nothing but trash? I've seen how he looks at you, like he's disgusted. Not that I blame him. You're nothing but a running joke around here, the bitch who thinks she's too good for everyone when the truth is you're nothing. Less than nothing."

Oh, she was going to kill that bitch.

Rhiannon turned and met Doll's smirking gaze. "I'm going to kick your fucking skank ass."

Before she could stand, a woman's soft voice said from behind her, "Goddess, don't waste your time on that bitter old bitch. She's so jealous that if envy were acid, the only thing left of you would be your earrings."

That unexpected defense managed to snap Rhiannon out of her anger, and she looked behind her, surprised to see Jessica, the club member she was supposed to train. At barely five feet tall and curvy, Jessica didn't exactly strike an intimidating chord, but the way she faced off against the much taller and bigger Doll made Rhiannon think of a kitten facing off against a tiger.

Doll glared at the other woman and opened her mouth, no doubt to say something nasty, but Rhiannon cut her off. "Doll, shut it. This is Jessica, and she's a club member."

Fury sparked in Doll's eyes, and the lines around her mouth deepened in anger. They both knew that while some fighting between the staff would be tolerated, Doll would be shit canned in an instant for mouthing off to a club member. While it would be nice to not have to work with the blonde, Rhiannon really didn't want to be responsible for Doll losing her job. Despite the fact that Doll was an überbitch, she had two teenage kids at home and was a single mother with Club Wicked as her only source of income. The poor kids probably suffered enough having the sharp-tongued and vain Doll as mother. Rhiannon wasn't about to add to their burden.

While Doll gathered her shit and left, Rhiannon took her seat again and returned to getting ready as if nothing had happened. After a moment, Jessica sat down next to her and placed her bag on the floor with a *thump*. The two women looked at each other in the mirrors, and Goddess was surprised at the rather shy smile on the pretty Asian woman's face. Gone was the feisty kitten who'd defended Rhiannon, and in her place was a woman who shifted uncomfortably beneath Rhiannon's gaze. She's spent some time with Jessica last night, going over the bar basics, but she hadn't been around the other woman long enough to really get a feel for her.

Visibly screwing up her courage, Jessica said, "So, you ready to watch me mess up?"

"I'm sure you'll be fine." When Jessica wilted beneath Rhiannon's cool tone, she had to remind herself that Jessica had just defended her, and that the comment had sounded bitchy. "From what I've seen you're a quick leaner, a hard worker, and you're pretty. You'll be fine. I know going out there the first time as a server can be scary as hell, but I'll be keeping an eye on you."

Jessica beamed at Rhiannon, then started to dig through her bag. "I don't know about all of that, but thanks for trying to keep me from freaking out."

Rhiannon tried to subtly watch Jessica in the mirror as they got ready, puzzled by the other woman. The whole situation was odd. If playing at being a server for the night was a sexual kink or some kind of thrill, Jessica should be excited, but instead, the woman looked ready to bolt for the door. Jessica was a member training to be a submissive with two of Club Wicked's Masters, Rory and Liam. Rhiannon didn't know the men well; they rarely came into the public bar where she worked as a server, but in her three years working here, she'd never heard of a submissive who actually wanted to be trained on how to be a server. She wondered if serving at the bar was some kind of punishment, but Jessica didn't seem upset by it.

"Goddess?"

She looked up into the large vanity mirror at Jessica and found the other woman staring back at her. "Yeah?"

"Can I tell you something?"

Frowning slightly, she leaned forward to check her makeup and shrugged. "Sure."

"I'm kind of nervous. Like really nervous. Like I don't know if I can do this nervous."

That made her stop messing with her lipstick and really focus her gaze in the mirror on the other woman for the first time. It was easy to dismiss Jessica as just another pampered club member looking for some kind of thrill from doing a stint as a server, for whatever reason, but to see the uncertainty in the other woman's eyes made Rhiannon want to reassure Jessica.

She shifted uncomfortably as she adjusted the straps of her glittering blue bikini top. Rhiannon had formidable walls around her heart, but she couldn't maintain her usual cold disposition when Jessica had such a vulnerable expression.

Rhiannon gave Jessica a small smile. "What are you scared of?"

Jessica swallowed hard and looked down at the makeup on the table in front of her. "I…I have a fear of crowds."

Out of all the things she'd expected Jessica to say, that wasn't one of them. "What? You have a fear of crowds, but you want to work in a very, very crowded bar?"

"It sounds crazy, I know." The other woman blew out a harsh breath. "I'm supershy, like to the point where I freeze up in public situations. That's why I'm training with Master Rory and Master Liam."

Trying to hide her surprise, Rhiannon turned to face Jessica. "I thought you were training with them for...you know...sex stuff."

Jessica flushed bright red, then met Rhiannon's gaze in the mirror. "That's part of it, but mostly I'm training with them so I can learn how to love myself. How to be brave and go after what I want."

Rhiannon knew all too well what it was like to hate herself, but it probably wasn't for the same reasons as Jessica. At least she hoped it wasn't. She wouldn't wish her nightmare past on anyone. Shaking off those dark thoughts, she reached out and gently touched Jessica's shoulder. "Hey, don't be so hard on yourself. You're a beautiful woman."

Jessica gave a surprised laugh. "Are you kidding? Next to you I feel like an ugly duckling."

"Stop that. Come here." She dragged Jessica next to her and turned them to face the mirror together. "Look at yourself. You have the loveliest skin and exotic eyes. The Doms will be falling all over themselves for your attention."

To Rhiannon's surprise, Jessica leaned her head against Rhiannon's shoulder and sighed. "I wish I looked like you. Perfect black hair, emerald-green eyes, and the body of a porn star. Except your tits are real."

Jessica's last statement startled a laugh out of Rhiannon. "Thanks, I think. But that's just the outside. I'm like a hollow diamond filled with coal."

She hadn't meant for her voice to come out so bitter, but because she wasn't talking with anyone other than her best friend about her feelings, she tended to be more open when she did let her guard down. Latisha, Rhiannon's best friend who was known at Club Wicked as Mistress Onyx, often said that she wanted to kick Rhiannon's ass for her distorted view of herself, but Rhiannon knew what she'd said was true. Yes, she was beautiful, but on the inside, she was so damaged no one would ever want her.

Lifting her head from Rhiannon's shoulder, Jessica gave her a serious look. "That is the stupidest thing I've ever head."

"What?"

"You heard me. You're beautiful inside and out. I don't know who told you differently, but they should be whipped for making you doubt yourself."

Disconcerted by the unexpectedly forceful tone in Jessica's voice, Rhiannon pretended to look through her bag for something so she could avoid Jessica's gaze. "I don't know what you're talking about."

"Bullshit." Jessica lowered her voice. "I want to tell you something, but it stays between us, okay?"

Rhiannon stole a glance at the other woman and nodded. It wasn't like any of the servers really talked to Rhiannon anyway, but she didn't tell Jessica that. "Okay."

"The real reason I'm so shy, so scared of dominant men is because my first Master was a real shithead. I met him when I was eighteen, and he was much older. He mind fucked me so good by the time I got away from him I was a pathetic mess. He made me believe I was worthless, *less* than worthless, that I was nothing." Jessica drew in a shuddering breath. "It took me a long time to get past the bullshit that he programmed me to believe, but I'm not going to let him win, even when I feel like the battle's already been lost. Can you understand that?"

Oh, Rhiannon understood that only too well; however, the ability to speak was beyond her at the moment. Part of her wanted to tell Jessica that she knew exactly what she was talking about, but she couldn't manage to get the words out, so instead she nodded.

Jessica gave her an understanding smile. "Mr. Florentine said you would understand, that I could talk to you. I thought he was crazy. You can be plenty intimidating when you want, but as usual he was right."

Shock followed quickly by betrayal burned through Rhiannon. The owner of Club Wicked was one of the few people who knew her dark history, and she trusted him. To know that he was telling people about her past hurt her deeply. "What did he tell you?"

"Oh, don't look so scared. He didn't tell me anything—just that I could talk to you and you would understand." Jessica gripped her hands together so tight her knuckles turned white.

"Please don't be mad at him. He didn't do anything wrong. I'm so sorry. I'm so stupid. I should have known not to say anything. I always mess things up."

Seeing Jessica hunch in on herself, hearing the fear mingled with self-disgust in her words, gave Rhiannon the strength to push aside her own demons. "Jessica, stop it. Look at me."

The other woman looked up, and Rhiannon's heart ached at the tears swimming in Jessica's eyes.

"It's okay. I was just a little shocked. I don't...I don't talk about my past. It gives me really, really bad nightmares if I think about it too much." She blinked back tears and turned back to the mirror. "So. You ready?"

Letting out an audible sigh, Jessica then said, "Yeah, I think so."

"Don't be so freaked out. We went over everything yesterday, and you have a great memory."

"Thanks." Jessica smiled at her with such joy that Rhiannon couldn't help but smile back.

"You'll be working in my section and Mistress Onyx's. Don't worry. She's supernice."

"What if I mess up?"

"Then you mess up. It's not the end of the world."

"I don't want to disappoint you."

Rhiannon looked at the other woman with surprise. "Why would you worry about disappointing me?"

Jessica stood and smoothed down the sheer black nighty she wore paired with a lacy black bra and panties set. "Because I admire you."

"You admire me?" The thought baffled her. "Why?"

"I've watched you work. You're so elegant and confident. The way you move, it's almost like dancing. I want to be like you."

Rhiannon burst out laughing and stood as well, then gave Jessica a hug. "I wish I could be like you."

"What do you mean?"

"You're so nice."

"I think you're nice."

Shaking her head, she then applied her glittering blue mask, once again slipping fully into her role as 'Goddess.' "Then you're in the minority."

"Well, maybe if you let more people know the real you they'd find out how nice you are. I admit I was intimidated as hell at being paired up with you, but Mr. Florentine was right. You are sweet once I got to know you."

"Mr. Florentine said I was sweet?"

"Yep. He really likes you."

She couldn't help her pleased smile. Not only was Mr. Florentine her boss, but he was also a father figure to her. God knew her own dad wanted nothing to do with her. That thought made her stomach cramp, and she placed a hand on her belly, taking a deep breath and calming herself.

Dark thoughts threatened to break free from her mental prison, and she shook her head, trying to get her mind off the past. "Come on. Let's get out there. If you don't mind me asking, why did you want to learn to be a server?"

Jessica didn't bother with a mask, so her blush was easy to see as they walked out the door of the dressing room and down the long hallway leading to the Hall of Mirrors bar. "Remember that being shy thing? Well, back in college before I met…him…I was a waitress. I was shy even back then, but while I worked, I found it easy to talk to men. Now I freeze whenever I try to talk to any of the single Doms, so Master Rory and Master Liam thought that maybe if I could meet some of the other members of Club Wicked while serving them, it might help me get over my fears."

"Wow, Master Rory and Master Liam really know their stuff."

"Oh, they do." Jessica practically glowed with happiness. "Not only are they amazing Masters, but they're really nice guys. And they give me multiple orgasms. What more could a girl want?"

Laughing, Rhiannon held open the door leading to the back section of the massive bar. "Sounds like they're quite a catch."

Jessica slowed down and audibly gulped. "Holy shit. It seems a lot bigger than yesterday."

After the quiet of the hallway, the voices of the crowd that filled the Hall of Mirrors bar was indeed intimidating. "Don't stress. I'll take care of you. We'll make sure you get the easy tables, and I'll handle any of the assholes."

Jessica licked her lips and looked over at Rhiannon. "Assholes?"

She nodded and motioned for Jessica to follow her. "There are some Masters here that don't like to take no for an answer or think that just because we work here they can paw all over us. Don't worry. You'll be fine. See those big guys in the suits on either side of the room standing against the wall? Those are our bodyguards, and they'll keep an eye on you. You're smart, and Mistress Onyx and I will help you out. All you need to think about is keeping track of what Masters or Mistresses catch your eye."

Two hours later Rhiannon was at the bar talking with Latisha, now known as Mistress Onyx, while the other woman filled her drink orders. The tall, black Domme wore a cherry-red PVC catsuit that suited her lean frame and dramatic bone structure. Though she looked intimidating as hell, Latisha was her best friend—almost like an older sister. Some people might find their relationship odd, but when Rhiannon had first started working here, Latisha had taken Rhiannon under her wing, and they were very close.

Latisha returned with the drinks and smiled at Rhiannon before leaning over the bar and saying in a low voice, "I'm proud of you."

Arranging the drinks on the tray, Rhiannon gave Latisha a questioning look. "About what?"

"For being so nice to Jessica."

Rhiannon tried to fight a smile and looked down. "She's easy to be nice to."

"I mean it, honey. I'm proud of you. I know it's hard for you to let anyone get close to you, but you're missing out on so much by isolating yourself from everyone."

Sighing, Rhiannon then took a quick glance around to make sure no one was listening. "I know you're always harping on me to make friends, but it's hard."

"It's only hard because you make it hard. If you didn't act like such a bitch all the time, you might be surprised at how nice people can be to you when you aren't pushing them away."

They'd had this discussion so many times Rhiannon could almost recite it word for word. "I'll try."

"Don't try. Do."

"Yes, Mistress," she said with enough snark that Latisha gave her a narrow-eyed look that would have sent most submissives running.

Rhiannon was so busy focusing on Latisha, she didn't even notice Jessica until the other woman stood at her side.

The Asian woman blew out a harsh breath. "That jerk!"

Immediately Rhiannon gave Jessica her full attention, her internal alarms going off at the anger rolling off the other woman. "What's wrong?"

Jessica set her tray down and clenched her hands into fists. "It's Master Curt. He's such a fucking dick. I swear if he tries to 'accidentally' grab my tits one more time, I'm going to deck him. Oh, and he wants a refill on his vodka tonic. Thank God it's the last one he's allowed to have tonight."

Rhiannon turned casually so she could glance over Jessica's shoulder at the man in question. Master Curt was a blond-haired blue-eyed middle-aged Dom who had been a pain in Rhiannon's ass the entire time she worked here. He liked to prey on new submissives, spoil them with expensive gifts, seduce them fast, then dump them just as quick. If that wasn't bad enough, he also got off on playing submissives against one another. She'd seen him manipulate women so skillfully that she didn't think anyone else noticed, certainly not the women involved.

He'd tried that shit with Rhiannon and another server, but Rhiannon considered him a total douche bag and didn't care if he dated every server at Club Wicked. He was all about the chase, and since he'd been chasing Rhiannon for years he was especially aggressive with her. She knew how to handle him and how to avoid his grabby hands. He never did enough to get kicked out, but his "accidental" gropes were infamous among the servers.

"I've got it, Jessica."

"Are you sure? Master Curt was asking about you and telling me about some rather yucky things he wanted to do with you. Gah, did you know he likes to pee on people?"

Rhiannon rolled her eyes. "Yeah, he used to try and shock me with that until I threatened to pee in his drink if he didn't shut up."

With a laugh, Latisha shook her head. "He's such an egotistical jerk."

Straightening her shoulders, Rhiannon then motioned to Latisha. "Give me his order."

Jessica chewed her lower lip. "I don't know if it's a good idea. He seems kind of drunk and obsessed with you. He kept on asking about you."

"I'll be fine. Go see if your Masters want anything."

After giving her an uncertain look, Jessica nodded and headed through the bar in Master Rory's and Master Liam's direction on the other side of the room.

Rhiannon picked up the tray with Master Curt's drink and the rest of her orders. She filled her other customers first, smiling and turning on the charm for her patrons. This job was her only source of income, so she'd gotten good at working the crowd, chatting and flirting with her regulars when they wanted her to, being polite and quiet when they didn't.

Turning to the seating area a few tables away from Master Curt, avoiding him as long as possible, she smiled at the sight of Master Jesse and his submissive, Dove. The pretty and buxom blonde woman had been a server for a brief time at Club Wicked. Dove was friends with one of the bartenders, Sunny, who Rhiannon did not get along with, but Dove seemed to go out of her way to be nice to Rhiannon. At first Rhiannon had been suspicious, wondering if the woman was trying to become friends so she could somehow help Sunny hurt Rhiannon, but she'd soon realized that the other woman was just genuinely pleasant and didn't have a mean bone in her body.

Tonight Master Jesse was wearing a brown leather vest with no shirt beneath, revealing his toned physique. He had a neatly trimmed reddish-brown beard and a nice amount of hair that covered his muscular chest. While he was a good-looking man in his own right, the way he looked at Dove with such open love and devotion always made Rhiannon slightly envious. It must be nice to have someone to trust and adore as much as this couple obviously cherished each other.

Dove leaned forward to take her glass of champagne and orange juice, the large diamond engagement ring on her finger glittering beneath the golden lights. "Thanks, Goddess."

"You're welcome." She handed Master Jesse his beer and glanced at her tray, not wanting to serve her last drink. "Is there anything else I can get you?"

Dove tilted her head, her blue-gray eyes watching Rhiannon intently. "Are you okay?"

Aware that Master Curt was within hearing range and not wanting to give him any power over her by the knowledge that he made her uncomfortable, she gave Dove a bright smile. "I'm fine. Just a long night."

Master Jesse shot Dove a curious look, and Rhiannon took a step back.

"Please let me know if you need anything else."

Rhiannon turned and took the four steps necessary to bring her to where Master Curt sat. As soon as their gazes met, he gave her a wide smile that reminded her of a shark baring its teeth. Tonight he wore his usual suit and tie, looking more like he was going to a business meeting than a BDSM club. His gold and ruby pinky ring flashed as he motioned for her to come closer.

"Goddess, my pet. Where did that delicious little submissive that was serving me go?"

"She had other things to attend to, Master Curt."

"So you came to see me instead." He stroked his lips with his fingertips and gave her a look that made her very uncomfortable.

He sat forward, crowding her as she maneuvered her tray to set his drink down. The reek of alcohol came off his breath, and she wondered if Jessica had been right and he was drunk. If he was, he must have somehow conned an extra drink or two out of a server at one of the other bars. Clenching her teeth, she quickly put his drink down, wanting to get out of his reach as quickly as possible.

From across the room came shouts; then a woman screamed, and Rhiannon looked for the source of the noise, her gaze landing on two Masters who were now duking it out with a horrified-looking female submissive trying to break them up. The bodyguards moved in on the scene, and she felt Master Curt grab her hips. Mad at herself for not being on her guard, for believing that she was safe here, Rhiannon tried to twist out of his grip.

Unfortunately she moved too slow. He managed to pull her down onto his lap, knocking over the glass in the process and soaking her bare stomach with the booze. She tried to push out of his arms, her heart racing as a stinging sweat broke out all over her skin. Fear flooded her. His restrictive hold triggered her terror even as she struggled to fight off both it and him. He fisted his hand in the back of her hair, pulling hard enough to really hurt.

"Fucking cock tease," he said in a low, dangerous voice. "I'll teach you to say no to me."

The words ricocheted in her head like a bullet gone awry, taking her back in time to a place where her kidnapper had said almost those exact words while he beat the shit out of her. For a brief, terrifying moment, she wasn't in Club Wicked but rather strapped to a bed with handcuffs that bit into her wrists while she tried to avoid the fists coming down on her unprotected torso, her chest, her face. Master Curt must have taken her lack of resistance as encouragement, because he shoved his hand beneath her bikini top and grabbed her breast in a punishing grip. Staring into her eyes with an evil smile, he squeezed hard enough that his fingernails dug into her skin.

Pain from her past and present merged, and she descended into a full-out panic attack.

Screaming, she clawed at his arms and face, trying to get him to release her. He probably only held her for a second, but by the time she'd managed to get free, his face was bleeding from where she'd scratched him. With a roar he stood and backhanded her, knocking her on her ass. She tried to scramble away, only to get picked up by a pair of strong arms while all around her male voices were raised in anger. Still shrieking, she kicked at the person holding her, making them drop her.

"Don't let him touch me," she begged in a broken cry. "Please don't let him hurt me!"

Overwhelming fear sent her running as fast as she could from the room, everything around her blurring, becoming indistinct as she ran with her breath searing her lungs and her heart racing so fast she became light-headed. Her fucked-up mind insisted that she was going to die if she didn't run and hide.

Everything went blank for a little bit. As awareness returned, she became conscious of a woman's gentle voice saying, "Goddess, honey, it's okay, please come out."

A hard shudder racked her, and she realized she was making a high-pitched, wounded noise. She stopped, confused as to where she was and what was going on. She realized she was beneath a desk and that Dove was kneeling a few feet away, mask off to reveal her face. Rhiannon's dazed mind tried to make sense of why the pretty young blonde woman was crying, but her thoughts were still too scattered.

Dove held out her hand again. "It's okay, honey. No one's going to hurt you. I promise you can come out."

Licking her lips, she slowly uncurled from the fetal position and glanced around. As the fear receded, humiliation took its place. It had been a long, long time since she'd had a panic attack like that, and she tried to think of what had happened. She remembered Master Curt grabbing her, then his bloody face, then...fear. Before the fright could drag her under again, she forced herself to focus on something mundane, and her gaze fell on Dove's manicure. The woman had her nails painted pink with a white pattern overlaying the pink that looked almost like lace. Focusing on a minute detail was a trick her therapist had taught her when she was trying to fight off a panic attack, to focus on something normal, something that had nothing to do with her triggers. In this case, Dove's soft hand and her lovely nails.

Pretty, feminine, safe.

She reached out and allowed Dove to help her out from under the desk. As she stood and looked around, she realized she was in one of the managers' offices. They were alone, and when she stood and tried to pull her hand away, Dove wouldn't let her.

"Are you okay?"

"I'm fine," Rhiannon murmured and looked away, so ashamed that she'd cracked in public. Everyone must think she was a psycho. *Fuck.* She'd worked so hard, had come so far, but no matter how hard she tried she couldn't escape her past. "Where's Latisha?"

"Who?"

"Mistress Onyx."

"Oh, she's with Mr. Florentine dealing with that fucking asshole Curt right now." Gently tugging her hand, Dove led her over to the small gray leather sofa on the other side of the room before making her sit down. "What happened back there?"

"I don't want to talk about it," Rhiannon whispered.

"Okay."

To her shock, Dove threw her arms around Rhiannon and hugged her. Rhiannon gasped. "What are you doing?"

"Just shut up and let me hug you."

The anger in the woman's voice startled her, and she tried to pull away again. "I don't understand."

"Look. Either you let me hug you and try to make it all right, or I'm going to go out there and kick Curt's ass."

The mental image of sweet, gentle Dove trying to kick anyone's ass just didn't work. "What are you talking about?"

Dove squeezed her hard enough that Rhiannon had trouble taking a deep breath. "I saw what he did to you. He's lucky Master Jesse held me back, or I would have given him a matching set of scratches on the other side of his face. I'm sorry we didn't get to you sooner. I was distracted by Master Kyle and Master Perry fighting."

Despair filled Rhiannon at the memory of what she'd done to the man's face. "Shit. I'm going to be fired."

Releasing Rhiannon, Dove then leaned back and shook her head empathetically. "Hell no, you aren't. I saw what he was doing to the new server girl all evening. I was about to have Jesse say something to him, but when you took over his table, I figured you had it handled. I mean, no one wants to fuck with you."

"What?"

Dove flushed. "I mean you're a badass."

She blinked, not quite sure what the other woman was

talking about. "I don't understand."

"I just mean that you can handle yourself. You have that 'don't fuck with me' attitude that usually keeps people in line." She frowned and looked down at Rhiannon's breasts, then back up to her face. "Did he bruise you?"

She touched her chest and lifted her bikini top, wincing at the sight of the purple crescent-shaped marks from where he dug his nails into her skin. "I'm okay."

"Let me see." Before she could protest, Dove wrenched her top to the side and made a disgusted sound. "That fucking asshole. We need to put some antibiotic on those scratches. No telling what kind of messed-up diseases he has. Do you know where the first aid kits are?"

"No."

"Hold on." Dove jerked open the door to the manager's office, and Rhiannon flinched at the sight of Mr. Florentine talking with Master Jesse.

Dove said in a commanding voice, "I need a first aid kit."

Both men looked over Dove's short head to Rhiannon, and she wanted to just disappear. No doubt she'd be fired, no matter what Dove thought. This was the third time she'd gotten into a physical altercation with an overzealous Master, but this time, she'd really hurt the guy. The memory of the blood dripping off Master Curt's chin made her nauseated, and she put her head between her legs, trying to keep from throwing up. Fuck. She'd tried so hard, given her all during her anger management therapy, and it still wasn't enough.

Mr. Florentine's deep, authoritative tone came from right next to her. "Rhiannon, are you all right?"

Tears welled in her eyes as shame filled her over her actions. "I'm so sorry. I'll gather my things and go."

Dove's voice rang out through the office. "You can't fire her! She didn't do anything wrong. She—"

When the woman's shout abruptly cut off, Rhiannon looked up to find Master Jesse had put his hand over his fiancée's mouth.

"No one is getting fired."

Rhiannon looked over at Mr. Florentine. "I'm not?"

He shook his head, looking as dashing as always in his three-piece suit and carefully styled silver hair. "No, you're not. Jesse and a few of your other friends who'd been watching stood up for you and told me what happened."

"My friends? I don't have any friends."

Mr. Florentine patted her cheek. "You may not realize you have friends, but you do. Like that little blonde spitfire over there."

Jesse released Dove, and she frowned at him before going over to Rhiannon and kneeling before her. "Gentlemen, can I have a moment alone with her, please?"

When the door had shut and Rhiannon was once again alone with Dove, she studied the blonde, unable to understand what was going on and why Dove was here.

Before she could say anything, Dove took a deep breath, then sat on the couch next to her. "I have something to tell you, and you might not like it, but you have a right to know."

Dread filled her as a million and one horrible things went through her mind. "What is it?"

Dove looked her in the eyes. "I know what happened to you—how you were abducted and abused."

If Dove had slapped her across the face, she couldn't have been any more shocked. "What? How? Who told you?"

The blonde flinched but continued to hold her gaze. "I swear I wasn't spying on you. It was months ago, before I went to Paris. I got lost while I was trying to find the conservatory, and I stumbled on you talking with Mistress Onyx."

She tried to remember when that could have been but came up blank. "What did you hear?"

"You talked about being kidnapped, but I left before I heard much more than that." She looked away, then swallowed hard and met Rhiannon's gaze again. "Please don't be mad. I really wasn't trying to spy on you."

Angry that the other woman had invaded her privacy, terrified at the thought that she may have told others about what she'd found, Rhiannon jerked away from her. "How dare you!"

"I know. I know it was shitty, but I swear I wasn't doing it to be mean." Dove's lower lip trembled, but she squared her shoulders. "I haven't told anyone what I heard. I swear."

"Yeah, right."

"I'm serious. I would never tell anyone." Tears streaked down Dove's cheeks. "I'm so sorry that happened to you, Rhiannon. Even though I don't know the details, I can see how it's affected you, and it hurts my heart."

Dread filled Rhiannon at the thought of Sunny finding out about her. Even worse, for Sunny to figure out that Rhiannon's obsession with Master Hawk, Sunny's kind-of boyfriend, was because he resembled her abuser. She'd learned through therapy that her attraction to a man who looked like the man who'd abducted her wasn't unusual—that it was her mind's way of trying to deal with the trauma—but she was still ashamed of it.

The thought of Master Hawk and Sunny made her stomach clench. Even though Rhiannon had legally changed her name after the trial, and she looked different now, she feared that if Sunny dug deep enough, she'd figure out who Rhiannon was or at least who she used to be. Deep down she knew Sunny wasn't a bad person, but they had a lot of negative history between them, and they constantly fought. The last thing she needed was Sunny bringing up her past during one of their public confrontations.

"Oh, God. You didn't tell anyone, did you?"

"No, absolutely not. It's not my place to tell anyone. I didn't even say anything to Jesse, and I don't keep any secrets from him."

"Please don't tell him. If you tell him, he'll tell Master Hawk."

Dove bit her lower lip, then released it. "Does Master Hawk know about your past?"

She flinched, the memory of the one night she'd tried to do a scene with Master Hawk flashing through her mind. Though at the time she didn't realize it, in her own fucked-up way, she'd been trying to replace bad memories from her abduction with good memories with Master Hawk. To have control in a situation similar enough to her abduction so that it would somehow banish the demons from her past. It wasn't a rational thought or one she was even really conscious of having, but after that disastrous night and some intense therapy sessions, she'd realized why she'd been obsessed with Master Hawk, and had been disgusted.

"I... Master Hawk tried to do a scene with me—just bondage, no sex—but it... I had a flashback to when...you know."

"That would explain a lot," Dove murmured with a distant look in her eyes.

"What do you mean?"

"He's very protective of you. It drives Sunny nuts, but I couldn't figure out why since you seem to avoid him completely and he—please don't take this the wrong way—he doesn't seem interested in you sexually."

A harsh laugh managed to escape Rhiannon. "I bet not."

Dove opened and closed her mouth a couple of times before sighing. "I'm so sorry you got hurt. I'm sorry I didn't send Jesse over there sooner."

Rhiannon's head began to ache, and she closed her eyes. Already they'd talked about her past to the point where she was sure she'd have nightmares tonight, which meant Latisha would have to spend the evening with her. "What do you want, Dove? Why are you here?"

"I want to be your friend."

"You what?"

Rhiannon watched Dove in confusion as the blonde lifted her chin looking adorable yet formidable at the same time. "I want to be your friend."

"Why?"

"Stop giving me that suspicious look. I want to be your friend because I think you'd make a good one."

"You aren't making any sense."

Dove stood and approached Rhiannon slowly before reaching out and putting her hand on her shoulder. "Is it so hard to believe that I think you're nice when you're not trying to shove people away? I think underneath your bitchy exterior you're funny, kind, and that I would be lucky to call you my friend. And it's not because I feel sorry for you, though my heart does ache for the pain you endured, but because my heart tells me it's the right thing to do, and I always listen to my heart."

Rhiannon studied Dove, trying to figure her out. Part of Rhiannon wanted, desperately, to believe the blonde woman, but the wounded portion of her soul shivered at the thought of trusting anyone. Then again, she was tired of being alone. Yes, she had Latisha, but lately, she'd been yearning for what Dove was offering: a chance at being normal again, at being able to go out and do fun things with other women. If she was being totally truthful with herself, she'd also begun to want a man in her life as well, but all her past relationships had left her both sexually and emotionally unfulfilled.

"I don't know if I'll be a very good friend, but I'm willing to try."

"Yay!" Dove threw her arms around Rhiannon and squeezed her tight. "I promise you won't regret this."

Relaxing just the slightest bit, she hugged the curvy woman back and let out a shuddering sigh. "Please don't hurt me."

Chapter Two

Three months later

The door to the dressing room opened, and Rhiannon winced at the sight of Brandy and Margo, two of the servers who hated Rhiannon, coming into the dressing room. She was already a nervous wreck because of what she was about to do, and seeing those bitches was not helping. Not wanting them to see, she quickly slipped the folded piece of paper she was holding into her top. For a moment, she considered fleeing the dressing room, even though she wasn't done getting ready, but if she showed any signs of weakness, those women would use it against her.

Sure enough, as soon as Brandy saw Rhiannon, she curled her lip in disgust. "Hey, slut."

Rhiannon's stomach churned, and she struggled to remain calm. Brandy had been one of Master Curt's favorites before he was kicked out of Club Wicked three months ago, and now the other woman hated Rhiannon. She tried to ignore the pretty blonde, but it was hard to do when Brandy came over and invaded Rhiannon's personal space, pretending to fix her makeup in the mirror but instead hip checking Rhiannon.

Margo gave a tittering laugh as Rhiannon stumbled. Margo's Master had been trying to get Rhiannon to do a threesome with them for months, but Rhiannon had absolutely zero interest in having sex with either of them. The redhead gave Rhiannon a nasty smile. "Why are you all dressed up? Your shift is over."

Brandy let out a mocking gasp. "Oh my God. Is the ice bitch

going to go get laid? Is someone going to defrost that nasty pussy?"

Rhiannon struggled with her anger. The other women were just trying to get a rise out of her, wanting to start a fight. If she got into an altercation with them, it would be their word against hers. She couldn't afford to get fired, and that was a very real possibility after her last public fight with Sunny. The other woman seemed to know just what to say to make Rhiannon lose it. Though Rhiannon and Sunny hadn't gotten to the point of trading blows, they had screamed at each other in public and broken a bottle of very expensive champagne by accident. That led to a two-week suspension for both of them, and now Rhiannon was on probation. Brandy and Margo no doubt knew that and were trying to piss her off so she would be fired.

Ignoring the women, she checked over her outfit and tried to gather her tattered self-confidence. Her golden harem girl outfit flattered her dark tan, and the glittering crystal mask she wore tonight looked like a bunch of daisies with their stems woven together. The green made her emerald eyes stand out, and the outfit flattered her hourglass shape. While she looked physically put together, emotionally she was as fragile as crystal glass, ready to shatter with one hard blow.

"Whose Master are you trying to steal now?" Margo sneered.

Normally she could handle these bitches, but tonight she was on edge and the other woman's words struck hard at her. In a way she was about to try to steal another submissive's Master but not really. The Masters she wanted weren't really attached to anyone, or at least they wouldn't be soon, but there was literally a waiting list for those seeking their attention. Tonight she needed to try and get at the top of their list, though it was a next to impossible task.

Margo gave that harsh, mocking giggle again that got on Rhiannon's last nerve. "You know that any Master that fucks you is just doing it for the prize money, right?"

That startled her enough to speak despite her best intentions to ignore them. "What?"

Brandy leaned against the counter and smirked. "Oh, you didn't hear? There's a bounty on you. First Master who manages to fuck you will win a two-hundred-thousand-dollar prize. You know how these rich guys are. They'll bet on anything, including your skanky ass."

"Bullshit," Rhiannon managed to whisper while shoving her things in her bag, needing to get out of here right now. She grabbed her bag and went to her locker, trying to keep her fingers from trembling as she entered the code to unlock it.

"Nope, it's true," Brandy said from behind her. "Nobody wants you. They just want the money."

Her words stung, badly, and Rhiannon shoved her bag into her locker before shutting it. She turned to leave, but Brandy and Margo were blocking her way. It was getting harder and harder to control her anger, and she struggled to keep it in check. She wasn't going to let these bitches get to her, wasn't going to give them the satisfaction of seeing her fired. She was at Club Wicked, she was safe, and after six years of intense therapy, she was finally at a place in her life where she was ready to move on, find love, and live the life that had been so viciously ripped away from her.

She wasn't a victim. She was a survivor and it was time for her to reclaim her life.

"Excuse me," she said in a stiff voice.

Brandy opened her mouth but the door leading out to the hall opened, and a couple of the other servers entered. One of the women frowned, a new server Rhiannon had begun to make friends with said, "You okay, Goddess?"

Lifting her chin, Rhiannon pushed past Brandy, ignoring their whispered insults, and nodded. "I'm good."

Before anyone could say anything else, she barged out into the hallway, sucking in deep breaths of air, trying to calm her racing pulse. Fuck. This was so not what she needed. Part of her wanted to just get her shit and go home, to go back to her quiet, safe, lonely house and shut the world away. She'd cuddle with her cats, maybe have some ice cream, and read one of her trashy romance novels where the heroes always saved the day and true love really existed. For a moment she almost turned back to the dressing room to gather her things and leave, but oddly enough, the jingle of the coins around her waist stopped her before she put her hand on the door.

She'd worn this coin belt at work once before. One of the

Masters she was going to talk to tonight had complimented her on it. While she was used to people trying to flatter her, it had been different when he'd said she looked beautiful. A warm, happy glow had blossomed inside her, and she'd practically floated for the rest of the evening. It was that memory that gave her the strength to go into parts of Club Wicked she normally didn't enter, the places where truly wicked things happened.

Before she knew it she was at her destination. She stared at the brass handles of the double doors leading to the Victorian-themed auditorium and made herself breathe. Now all she had to do was find the courage to go through those doors and plead her case to Master Rory and Master Liam. Surely they could do for her what they had done for Jessica. The beautiful Asian woman had been transformed by their training, turned into a woman confident in her own worth.

A delicate, soft hand slipped into her own, and Rhiannon flinched. She turned and found one of her new friends, the very pregnant flame-haired Lady Kira Sutherfield, smiling at her. Dove had introduced them one day while Rhiannon was over at Dove's house, helping the other woman with the six-year-old twin boys who were soon going to be her stepsons. At first Rhiannon had been nervous around Kira—the woman was so confident and beautiful—but she'd soon found herself laughing at Kira's naughty sense of humor and they had become friends. Dove, bless her heart, had been right. When Rhiannon wasn't busy trying to keep her emotional walls up, she had been able to make friends. Kira had insisted on being here tonight to give Rhiannon the emotional support she would need because, as she'd been told when she protested the other woman staying up so late, that's what friends did for each other.

Kira gave her hand a squeeze. "Want me to come in with you?"

"What?"

"Darling, you've been fretting about this night for weeks. Have some faith in yourself. If it's too scary to do this alone, I'd be more than happy to go in with you. You know Master Liam and Master Rory wouldn't do anything to hurt you."

"They're friends of Master Hawk...and Sunny. What if she's told them bad things about me? What if they laugh at me or call me names or—"

Kira gave her a hard look. "Look. I know you think Sunny hates you, and while I'll admit you're not her favorite person, I don't think she would bad talk you to Master Liam and Master Rory. Even if she did, they're not stupid men, and they don't listen to gossip. Have some faith in yourself, Rhian-er, Goddess."

A sour taste filled Rhiannon's mouth. She hadn't actually picked out Goddess for her name at Club Wicked. The woman who had trained her to be a server had because of Rhiannon's exotic beauty. While Rhiannon didn't have any formal education past the tenth grade, or much worldly experience, she was considered attractive by society's current standards, even though she felt like she was nothing special. She wouldn't have suffered if she'd been plain, wouldn't have wished for death if that pedophile hadn't found her beauty something to covet and destroy. And she wouldn't have become a media sensation when he had gone to trial if her looks hadn't sold tabloid papers. A harsh shudder ran down Rhiannon's spine. She had to fight back the panic that always came from thinking too much about her past.

Kira suddenly enveloped her in a hug. Well, as best the other woman could with seven months of belly between them. Pressed this tight to the curvy submissive, Rhiannon felt the kick of the baby in Kira's belly against her own stomach. The faint pressing made her giggle and helped wash her mind clean of the past. She needed to treasure the blessings in life and not take the small things for granted.

Drawing in a deep breath, she gentled her hold on Kira and pulled back enough to see her face. "Sorry. All the stress is dredging some things up from the bottom of my mind."

"It's okay, sweetheart." Sympathy filled Kira's expression. While none of her new friends knew the details of what Rhiannon had been through, they knew something bad had happened in her past but respected her wish to not talk about it. Kira took a step back, then wiped away a tear that Rhiannon pretended not to notice. "Did I ever tell you how proud I am of you?"

"What?"

Rubbing her swollen belly, Kira softly smiled. "You're one of the strongest women I know, and I pray that my daughter has your strength someday."

A flush heated Rhiannon's cheeks, and she looked away. "I don't feel very strong. The thought of going in there terrifies me."

"Then why are you doing it?"

"You know why."

Kira cleared her throat. "I do know what you're doing, but you need to tell me again."

"Why?"

"Because I think you need to remind yourself."

"Did I ever tell you that you sound a lot like my therapist?"

"Your therapist knows her shit. She sure as hell has helped me out with dealing with my adrenaline junkie issues, so I'll take that as a compliment. Now, tell me."

"You're awfully bossy for a submissive." Kira crossed her arms and gave Rhiannon a pointed look. Rhiannon sighed and continued, "Fine. I'm doing this because I'm in charge of my destiny. I cannot change my past, but I can change my future, and if I really want love in my life, I have to first learn how to love myself. I'm a survivor, not a victim."

"Excellent. And why do you need Master Rory and Master Liam to train you?"

"Because they're the best."

"Yes, they are, and you deserve the best."

The pulsing beat rumbled from beyond the door. A second later the crowd inside began to cheer. Evidently Jessica had just finished her graduation ceremony. The other submissive who had been training with Master Rory and Master Liam, Gloria, had graduated two weeks ago. The men were finally free to take on a new submissive to train, and Rhiannon couldn't waste any time asking them before they selected a new submissive from what Jessica had said was a long list of women.

She needed them to take her on because they were the only Masters she could even vaguely imagine trusting.

She hadn't said this to Kira, but while she did want to train with Master Rory and Master Liam because of their reputations, that wasn't the main reason. They were the only men she'd fantasized about. They were the only Masters she thought might be able to touch her without making her ill with fear. And unlike the nice, kind, polite, safe, and boring men she'd dated, they actually made her want to have sex. It still surprised her that arousal could spin through her body at the thought of the two big, intimidating, and totally dominant males ordering her to do things that made her wet.

Really wet.

Both women stepped back as the doors opened and the crowd began to filter out. On the small stage, Jessica was being hugged by both Master Rory and Master Liam. The men looked so proud of Jessica that it made Rhiannon's throat ache with longing. She wanted someone to be proud of her like that, to hold her like she mattered to them.

Jessica gave each man a soft kiss as they embraced her from the front and the back, surrounding her with their heavily muscled bodies. On the right, Master Liam wore his customary black leather kilt and big ass-kicking combat boots. His legs were unbelievably muscular, and Rhiannon wanted to sink her teeth into him. Unlike fair-haired redheads that people stereotypically thought of as someone looking Scottish, Liam had mocha-brown skin and hazel-green eyes that made most women swoon, including her. He kept his curly black hair in a buzz cut and looked as intimidating as hell, but Rhiannon knew from her conversations with Jessica that Master Liam had a tender heart beneath all those fine muscles.

On the left stood Master Liam's partner and best friend, Master Rory. The man had the solid bone structure of a male supermodel and was almost unfairly handsome. His nose had been broken a few times, and a nice scar went across his forehead from some injury he'd sustained on the rugby field, but they only gave him a rugged beauty. With his light bronze hair and amazing blue eyes, he reminded Rhiannon of a movie star she'd had a crush on while growing up. He wore his customary black leather pants and tight black T-shirt. When he grinned at something Master Liam had said, a dimple appeared in his cheek, and she had to stifle a sigh of appreciation.

Separate, they were amazing, but put them together, and they were devastating.

Kira let go of her hand and gave her a little shove. "Stop mooning over those hot pieces of man candy and go talk to them before some skank beats you to it."

Rhiannon stumbled forward, then straightened her spine and put some slink into her step. She shot Kira a warning look, but the other woman merely rolled her eyes. Hoping the men hadn't seen her clumsy entrance, she threw her shoulders back and began to walk down the aisle toward the stage. With a sway in her step, she used that knowledge of how to make even a simple act like walking look like an erotic dance even if she was coming apart at the seams on the inside. She'd learned early on to never show fear, to never show weakness, and she relied on strength to carry her down the red-velvet-couch-lined aisle toward the raised stage.

She could do this.

She *had* to do this.

Jessica saw her coming and smiled, the encouragement in her expression warming Rhiannon a bit. Her friend had been the first to suggest that Rhiannon train with Master Rory and Master Liam, and Jessica had worked hard with Rhiannon to help her find the courage to approach the men. In what seemed like a heartbeat, Rhiannon found herself standing at the base of the stage with Jessica motioning for her to come closer. Master Rory and Master Liam gave her a curious look as they glanced down at her from the slightly elevated platform.

Before she could speak, Jessica stepped back from the men, nude as the day she'd been born. Rhiannon averted her gaze to the deep red carpet beneath her feet. It felt weird to see a friend nude, no matter how comfortable the other woman seemed. Especially when marks from being spanked reddened her breasts and thighs.

Jessica smiled at Rhiannon before turning back to the Masters as she said, "Thank you so much, Master Rory and Master Liam, for everything you've done for me."

The smack of hands hitting flesh echoed in the room as Master Liam spanked her butt. "It was our pleasure, Jessica."

Giggling, the other woman rubbed her rear end and gave Master Liam a mock scolding expression. "Be nice or you'll scare Goddess away."

That brought both men's attention back to Rhiannon, and she swallowed hard, all the saliva in her mouth drying as their gazes caught and held her immobile.

Jessica took another step back. "I'm leaving, Goddess. You can't chicken out now."

Anger churned her stomach, and Rhiannon was tempted to flip the other woman off, but she was afraid if she unclenched her hands, they'd shake so much that her fear would be obvious.

"Travel safe, love." Master Rory smiled at Jessica's departing figure although Master Liam's gaze never left Rhiannon.

Master Liam's mellow Scottish burr rumbled from the stage. "Did you need something, girl?"

His tone wasn't unkind, but she didn't like that he wasn't using her name. It made his question seem impersonal. Even worse, she wanted him to call her by her real name instead of her work name. Well, sort of her real name. She'd legally changed her name from Crystal to Rhiannon after the trial in an effort to disappear from the tabloids.

"Masters, would you mind going someplace quiet so we could talk? Please?" Her voice cracked on the last word, and she swallowed hard, hating how pathetic she sounded.

Now it was Master Rory's delicious English-accented voice gliding over her skin like a cool wind. "Can it wait until tomorrow?"

Panic seized her, and she looked up, meeting his gaze for a brief moment, willing him to see how much she needed him to listen to her.

Master Rory shook his head, his expression unexpectedly kind, then said in a soft voice, "No, I guess it can't."

Master Liam jumped off the stage, startling her. She started to raise her hands in a defensive gesture but managed to stop them at the height of her hips and pressed her hands at her sides. He paused and stood a bit taller, becoming more...there. The flecks of amber in the ice green of his eyes mesmerized her as he took a step closer. "Easy, lass. I'm not going to harm you."

"I know that." Her voice came out with an unattractive stutter, and she flushed. "I'm sorry, Master Liam. I-I don't know how to handle this. This was a mistake. I'm sorry for wasting your time."

Master Rory came off the stage and stood next to Master Liam, two big men who radiated the kind of dominance that made her knees weak. She yearned to touch them, to be touched, yet part of her also wanted to run away. This was too real, too intense.

The men looked at each other, then back at her. Master Rory held out his hand at the same time that Master Liam did. "Come with us."

Dazed by being so near to the men, she took their offered hands with barely a thought. Master Rory grasped her left hand, Master Liam her right, and she found herself floating between them as they led her backstage. She couldn't help looking from one man to the other, having only admired them from afar up to this point. Their colognes mixed together into a surprisingly pleasant blend of cedar and bergamot. Mixed with their natural scent, the combination made her hungry for them even as she wondered what the hell she was doing.

After leading her across the room, they paused before the first door to the right. Master Rory opened it while Master Liam ushered her through. She found herself in an exquisite Victorian sitting room complete with a blue velvet fainting couch. A lovely vanity took up half of the room along one wall. The mellow golden lights from the stained-glass lanterns on the walls instantly soothed her. She treasured beauty in its many forms and enjoyed surrounding herself with lovely things. One of the parts she liked the most about working at Club Wicked as a server was being around such opulence.

She took a seat on the fainting couch and made sure her posture was correct and her legs demurely crossed. After flipping her long hair over her shoulder she unnecessarily smoothed the fabric of her harem pants. The men took a seat in dark brown leather wingback chairs that faced the couch. Each of them more than filled up the space with their toned frames. Another rush of heat went through her, and she drew in a deep breath in an effort to steady herself.

Master Rory was the first to speak. "What is it you wanted to talk to us about?"

"I'd like you to train me, please." They both gave her startled looks, and she rushed on. "Jessica said you don't have anyone lined up yet. I'll pay you forty-eight thousand dollars to train me for three months. I know that's not enough, but it's all the money I have saved up. Please—"

Master Liam sat forward, his hand going up. "Wait. You want to pay us to train you?"

The question threw her off-balance enough that she forgot to be nervous. "Of course."

"Goddess, we don't charge for our training."

"You do it for free?" She couldn't help the shock in her voice. It didn't make any sense. While she never asked Jessica how much the men charged—that would just be tacky and rude—she'd assumed they required some kind of monetary compensation for their time.

"We do it for free because we love to help submissives." Master Rory cocked his head and examined her. "I must say this is a bit of a surprise. I thought you didn't like any Dom near you."

"Besides that, we're taking some time off from training." Master Liam gave Master Rory an almost frustrated look that Rhiannon didn't understand.

She started to protest, then remembered how Jessica had said the men demanded her complete honesty. If Rhiannon wanted them to consider her, she had to convince them of her sincerity. Jessica had also said they had applications from hundreds of women to be in their next training session. Rhiannon had to somehow make them pick her over all those women who were already waiting. But she really didn't want to talk about why she didn't like men touching her—now or ever.

She could feel the opportunity slipping through her fingers. The one thing a Dom valued above anything was trust. So she'd seduce them by trusting them. With a soft sigh she removed her mask and quickly brushed her hair back before looking up at them. They wore almost identical looks of shock and confusion. "My name is Rhiannon. I'd prefer if you call me that, please."

Master Rory rubbed the space between his eyebrows. "Rhiannon, what is it you think we can do for you?"

She opened and closed her mouth a few times before she could force the words out. "I want you to help me be someone a Dom could love."

"We can't make anyone love you."

Frustrated, she gripped her hands into fists. "I know that. But you can help me get the skills I need to make my Dom happy. I want to be whatever my future Master desires, and since I don't know who he is yet, I want to learn everything I can so when I do meet him, I'm ready." She took a deep breath and forced herself to meet their gaze in turn. "Right now I have no idea how to do any BDSM stuff. I mean I've seen it, I've read about it, and I've talked with other submissives. But I haven't actually done any of it."

"You've never had a Master?"

She swallowed hard. Well, she'd had a guy who called himself her Master, and for a while, she'd actually believed it, but in the end, all he'd been was a monster. Certainly not the man who held the key to her submission and her heart.

"No."

Master Liam rubbed a hand over his hair. "We don't usually train submissives totally new to the scene. Maybe you should talk to Master—"

"No, it has to be you!" The words came out louder than she intended, and she tried to do some damage control. "I mean, you and Master Rory are the only ones who can help me."

Master Rory sat forward so his elbows were resting on his knees, drawing her eyes to his strong, capable hands. "I don't think we're a good fit for what you need, darling."

His rejection crushed her. She somehow managed to lift her chin, then picked up her mask. "I'm sorry I've wasted your time."

Her throat closed up, and she started to stand, wanting to be away from them before the tears fell, instead schooling her features into the familiar icy mask she used to protect her heart. She'd tried to not get her hopes up, knew how badly the odds were stacked against her, but dammit, she thought that for just once things were going to go her way. But yet again it seemed like the universe was against her. Before she'd taken her first step, both men looked at her and said in stern voices, "Sit down."

Her ass made contact with the sofa so quickly that her teeth clicked.

If these men could command her with just their voice, maybe they were strong enough to actually dominate her. The thought at once scared and excited her. It had taken many talks with her therapist to not see her submissive nature as a bad thing. Now she was ready to move on with her life, and she wasn't going to let anything stand in her way.

Even herself.

Master Rory stood and began to pace. "What do you want to learn? 'Everything' is a rather broad term."

The way he moved, his thick leg muscles pressing against the leather of his pants with each stride, made her totally lose track of her thoughts. Fortunately she followed Dove's and Kira's advice and had written a list of what she'd like to cover. She pulled a folded piece of paper from her top, and Master Liam snickered. Being laughed at was one of the things she hated more than anything in the world, so she gave him a nasty glare.

Almost immediately Master Liam got up and strode over to her, his teasing expression gone and a cold, demanding look in its place. His hard look sent a little thrill through her, but when he reached for her, she knocked his hand away. She babbled out an apology. "I'm sorry. I didn't mean to hit you. Please don't send me away."

His expression gentled, and he slowly held his hand out. "Did I startle you?"

"Yes."

Her fingers trembled as she took his. She felt tiny next to him, like he could squish her if he wanted. Instead of gripping her hand hard, he lightly held her fingers in his grasp like she was made of glass. The kindness in his gaze settled her further until she found herself mesmerized by him once again. Master Rory joined them and looked from her to Master Liam. "What's on the paper?"

Master Liam pulled her up and scooped her into his arms. She squealed, but her panic stayed at a controllable level. It helped that she'd been fantasizing about him on a daily basis and had a rather embarrassing crush on the man. Almost as bad as her crush on Master Rory.

He turned them around and sat on the couch. Master Rory sat on the other end, and the men arranged her between them in a way that made her feel almost like a rag doll. Her temper flared, and she squirmed. "What are you doing?"

Master Rory stroked her leg in a soothing manner. "Rhiannon, do you know what a safe word is?"

She stiffened her spine even as Master Liam curved her into his chest, and she found herself relaxing against him. "Of course I do. Just because I don't play with anyone doesn't mean I don't know anything about BDSM."

"Good. What is your safe word?"

"Mercy."

Master Liam began to slowly trailed his big fingers over her exposed ribs, the touch light and teasing. The sensations threw her further off stride until she found herself snuggling into Master Liam. She hadn't been held by a man in a long time, and her affection-starved soul soaked up their gentle touches. When Master Rory plucked the paper from her hands, she protested. "Hey, that's mine."

He ignored her and scanned the list, his eyes growing wider by the second. "Bloody hell, girl. Is there anything you don't want to learn?"

The way he said it made her feel embarrassed by her desires. She'd only had three vanilla lovers, so this was the first chance she'd had to experience all the things she'd been craving but had been too ashamed to ask for. Now they were ridiculing her for being honest?

Well, fuck them.

She tried to sit up, but Master Liam tightened his grip. "Maybe it would be easier if you told us what you don't want to do."

Trying to wiggle out of his hold wasn't happening. To her shock, she felt him harden beneath her ass, and she froze. He chuckled and continued to stroke her, but now he was playing with her belly button in a way that made her body tingle. It was hard to think with them surrounding her like this. "I don't like humiliation. Ever. I don't like being yelled at or debased or hurt. Or laughed at. I hate that."

Master Rory looked up from the list with a slight frown. "But you put down that you wanted to try all types of impact toys and other things that could potentially hurt you."

Unable to meet his gaze, she looked at the lovely stained glass lantern behind him. "I meant abuse. I don't want you to abuse me."

Master Liam stiffened. "Has someone done that to you, lass?"

She was tempted to tell them no, to laugh it off, but if she did, her therapist would kill her. "I-I had an incident that I would rather not discuss."

"How long ago?" Master Rory folded up the paper and put it in his pants pocket.

"Six years." She took a deep breath, afraid they wouldn't want her anymore when she told them one of the conditions of her training, but Latisha had made her promise she would at least mention it. "Please. Don't ask me anymore. If I talk about it, I have terrible nightmares, the kind that make me afraid to go to sleep."

Tilting his head, Master Rory examined her face. "Are you sure you're ready for something like this?"

"I am." She firmed her chin and met his gaze. "My therapist and I have been working hard to get me to where I am right now."

Master Liam's grip on her eased, and Master Rory gently turned her, then set her feet on the floor. "Rhiannon, we're not qualified to act as therapists in any way."

Stung by their sudden physical rejection, she stood quickly from the couch and turned to face them, anger and hurt boiling over. "I don't need another fucking therapist! I've been in therapy for five goddamn years. I've talked about it, I've journaled about it, I've done everything I can to make myself whole again. But you know what? None of us are whole. Every single one of us is a work in progress, and I refuse to accept that I'm so fragile, so damaged by what happened to me that I have to be stuck in vanilla relationships for the rest of my life. That's bullshit. I don't need you to sit around in a circle with me and talk about my feelings. I need someone to Master me!" The words rolled around in her mind, and she quickly tried to clarify herself. "I mean, I need someone to teach me how to submit so I can find a Master."

Steepling his fingers beneath his chin, Master Rory contemplated her while Master Liam shook his head. "Lass, we just don't want to add to any damage that's been already done."

"Please." The word tore from in an anguished whisper. "I'm not damaged, dammit. I'm not broken. Please help me. I need this. I need your help. Please."

Master Liam started to say something, but Master Rory cut him off. "Rhiannon, go kneel in the corner facing the wall."

Confused, she nodded and clumsily made her way to the corner. As she knelt and faced the wall, she tried to listen to what they were saying. All that reached her ears was a low rumble of male voices that reminded her of the ocean. It was a soothing sound, and she slowly relaxed.

She had no idea how much time passed, but she eventually closed her eyes and just breathed. Yoga had become a big part of her life, and she used the techniques she'd learned from the classes she took to center herself. Bit by bit, she relaxed the muscles in her body until she was in a state where she could remain kneeling for hours. Sure, her legs would be on pins and needles, but sometimes beauty was pain, and she'd endure it in order to be as lovely to look at as possible.

Despite everything that had happened, she still had her pride.

Chapter Three

Liam stared in disbelief at his best friend and business partner for the past twelve years. He leaned closer to Rory, almost close enough to kiss the other man. Why he tormented himself with what he couldn't have he didn't know, but for Liam, Rory was the ultimate forbidden fruit. The one man in the world he wanted to take as a lover but was completely hands-off.

And right now, he was trying to figure out what the fuck his best mate was thinking.

"Have you gone daft? Yesterday you were going on and on about how much you were looking forward to vacationing in a tropical paradise. Now you want to take on a submissive trainee who is an emotional minefield?"

With an unusual intensity, Rory leaned farther forward and whispered into his ear, "Can't you see how desperately she needs us? I've been watching her for a while now since she became friends with Jessica. From what Jessica's told me—"

"Wait. Jessica talked to you about Goddess, I mean, Rhiannon?"

The warmth of Rory's breath on the sensitive skin of his neck made Liam suppress a shiver of desire. "Jessica has a kind and good heart, and she says Rhiannon is hurting badly."

More confused by the second and angry at how aroused he was becoming, Liam shook his head. "Which brings us back to her psychological state. We help submissives who are shy and don't know their own worth. Not women who are in the care of professional therapists for what I'm pretty sure was some kind of abuse. What if we fuck her up even more?"

Rory pulled back the slightest bit and smiled at him. "We'll make sure we talk with her therapist and try to find out the key to unlocking Rhiannon's inhibitions. I think she's a lot stronger than you're giving her credit for, and she obviously wants to train with us. Besides, I'd love to see you fuck her." His voice took on a rumbling tone that went straight to Liam's cock. "Did you see that glimpse of submission from her? When we held her in our arms, she relaxed completely, and a peacefulness entered her that I've never seen before. I want to help her, Liam, but I won't do it without you."

Groaning, Liam rubbed his eyes. "You are a master of the guilt trip."

"So you'll do it?"

Unsure of how he'd lost the battle so quickly, Liam nodded. "I'll try. I'm not promising anything until we talk with her therapist. I mean what I said about not wanting to damage her any further."

Rory gave him a brief hug that left Liam aching for the feel of the other man's arms. Over a dozen years was a long time to deny his feelings, and Liam was getting tired of fighting to hide how much he wanted Rory as his lover. But the thought of anyone finding out that he desired Rory as more than a friend still sent him into a panic no matter how many times he tried to tell himself that the rest of the world wasn't like the place where he'd grown up. That he wouldn't be beaten to death for the sin of being gay.

"Thank you."

Almost as one they looked over at Rhiannon still kneeling in the corner. She wasn't fidgeting and kept a lovely form. Her back was perfectly straight, and her round ass was perched on her heels. Even from behind, she was amazingly beautiful, but Liam was having a hard time understanding why she wanted to train with them.

Everyone knew Goddess was a pain in the arse of the first order, so it had baffled him that she and Jessica had become friends. Only a couple of months back, Liam had to break up a fight between Goddess and Sunny, a pretty little bartender who worked at Wicked. The snarling female he'd dragged away by the scruff of her neck didn't resemble the composed woman looking at the wall in the corner of the room.

"I have one thing I want to ask her first."

"That's fine. I don't want to agree to anything tonight but just keep an open mind." Rory raised his voice. "Rhiannon, come here."

She gracefully stood, only the slightest tremble of her legs signaling that she had any discomfort. Liam found himself stunned by her beauty as she sauntered across the room toward them. There was an almost predatory look in her eyes he'd never seen before. A kind of sexual challenge that resonated in his bones. His already semihard cock filled to full mast and tented the front of his kilt.

Rhiannon glanced down at his crotch, and then a blush heated her from the center of her chest all the way to her hairline. He had to suppress a chuckle and wondered how long it would take to make her wet at the sight of his arousal, knowing the kind of pleasure he would give her. When her gaze met his again, it was with a defenseless uncertainty that tugged at his heart rather than his loins. She looked so vulnerable. Damn. Her normal ice-queen persona was an act, and a very good one. If someone had asked him ten minutes ago if he thought Goddess—no, Rhiannon—would be giving him the cutest puppy-dog eyes he'd ever seen, he would have told them they were daft. And yet here she was, an innocence projecting from her that had him receiving all kinds of confusing reactions from his heart and body.

On one hand he wanted to reach out and touch her again, knowing that it would reassure her. If he'd had any idea she had abuse in her past, he never would have been so hands-on with her when he picked her up. At the time it had just seemed like the right thing to do, and he hoped he hadn't broken any trust with her. Regardless of what his and Rory's decision was, Liam would rather cut his arm off than ever harm a submissive. Rhiannon's trust—any woman's trust—was a sacred thing, and he needed to acknowledge that, regardless of his mixed feelings about her.

She dropped to her knees when she was close enough to touch, the heat of her body pressing against his leg like an ethereal caress. On Rhiannon's other side, Rory watched her with a guarded expression, but Liam knew him well and could see

Rory's fascination. For a second, Liam was jealous of Rhiannon, then scolded himself for being such a dick. He needed to get his head on straight and deal with this situation like the Dom he'd been trained to be, not like some immature wanker.

Speaking of wankers, his friend Hawk had been with Rhiannon before. While Liam couldn't remember what exactly had gone down, it had ended up with Rhiannon getting hysterical and sent Hawk straight to the nearest bar. Hawk had gotten blind, stinking drunk that night, something Mr. Florentine normally didn't allow but had in this case, which was another oddity. Hawk wouldn't discuss what happened, but from that point on, Hawk had been very protective of Rhiannon, just not in a sexual way. Something bad occurred between them, and Liam needed to find out more before he even considered training her.

"Lass, I have a question that I need you to answer truthfully before I can agree to do anything with you."

She glanced up, her stunning green eyes capturing him. "Yes, Sir?"

"Do you still love Master Hawk?"

Gaping at him, the color drained from her face, and she looked like she might be ill. "No. I never loved him."

Rory reached out to touch her, but she jerked back, almost falling on her side. "Rhiannon, it's all right. I'm not going to hurt you. But Liam has a legitimate question. If you're in love with someone else, our training won't go well because you'll resent our domination."

She shook her head. "I don't love him."

"Then why are you always fighting with Sunny about him?"

"I don't want to talk about it."

Liam exchanged a look with Rory and could see his own worry reflected on his mate's face. "Did he do something to you?"

"No!" She covered her face with her hands. "It's so damn embarrassing."

Liam could read his best friend like a book, and right now Rory didn't know what to do. That threw Liam for a loop because his best mate always knew how to approach a submissive. There wasn't a woman alive who stood a chance when he decided to seduce them. That was Rory's specialty. He was the one who got the submissives to agree to do things they normally wouldn't, out of shyness. And his methods were very physical—something he obviously wasn't going to use on Rhiannon right now.

That left Liam, who usually took on more of a friend role. But he didn't know if he could be buddies with Rhiannon. She was as polite as could be with him, but Liam had never felt any hint of interest from her. Despite the sexual nature of the training he did, he knew that becoming friends with a submissive, earning her trust, was more important than any orgasms he might give her. And with some women, without that trust, they would feel no arousal, making training impossible.

He crouched down on the floor in front of Rhiannon, trying to get her to look at him. She glanced up, her jaw went slack; then she erupted in giggles and covered her eyes. "Oh, God, Master Liam. Please close your legs. I can see everything!"

Behind Liam, Rory began to laugh. A hot flush moved through Liam when he realized he was giving Rhiannon a rather good view of his cock and balls. With a chuckle, he shook off any traces of embarrassment and knelt in front of her. "There. Now I'm decent."

She peeked through her fingers, and when she lowered her hands, he wanted nothing more than to take a picture of her. The smile she gave him was filled with light and laughter, an almost tangible warmth radiating from her. Then her face closed down again, and she stared at her hands. "If I tell you, will promise not to tell anyone?"

Balls. When she said that, she sounded so young. He wondered how old she really was. If the abuse had happened six years ago, it had to have been when she was in her teens. Maybe early teens. The thought made him sick. "Of course."

She looked up, an unexpected hardness entering her gaze. If she hadn't been so submissive during their meeting, he would have never known that she even had it in her. He watched as the persona of Goddess came over her, and she gave both him and Rory an aggressive glare. "I want your word on it, as men."

Both Rory and Liam said in unison, "You have my word."

Lately he and Rory had been butting heads, leading to a

discordance that he wasn't used to in their relationship. Rory seemed filled with a restless energy, and he'd often stay awake late at night playing his guitar. Liam knew this because Rory's bedroom was on the other side of the wall from Liam's bedroom. They shared an old mansion in DC that had been split down the middle and converted into two separate residences. Tense silences would fall between them for no reason, and Liam had begun to fear that he was losing his friend and the man he loved.

Yet when their gazes met, Liam felt that familiar perfect understanding of each other fall back into place. And it was because of the girl kneeling before him. While Liam and Rory had worked together with their old trainees, Gloria and Jessica, it wasn't the usual harmonious melding that it had been in the past. Rory didn't like to do aftercare with Liam anymore and would often leave Liam alone with the submissive. Liam wondered if Rory would do that with Rhiannon if they took her on, or if whatever so attracted Rory to this woman would bring the men back together.

Rhiannon remained silent, and Liam turned his attention back to her. She was looking at the floor again, and her chest heaved as she struggled to take an even breath. He almost grasped for her, then remembered her negative reaction. Instead, he reached out to her with his voice. "Come on, lass. Trust us just a little bit. I promise you we won't betray you. I swear that whatever you're going to say, no matter how embarrassing, Rory and I have done worse."

She laughed, but this time it was a painful sound. "I highly doubt that. The reason I am the way I am about Master Hawk is he looks like a man from my past that was...very bad to me. I don't want to discuss it any further. Just believe me when I say I have no romantic feelings for Master Hawk."

Big tears rolled down her cheeks, so Liam stripped off his shirt, startling a squeak out of Rhiannon. He handed it to her. "Here. Blow."

She grasped the backs of his hands and made him lift the shirt to her face. Then she placed her cheek against the cloth in his hands and let out a long, watery sigh. "Thank you."

Rory shifted, then joined them on the floor. The sight of both himself and Rory on their knees before Rhiannon struck him as funny. Here they were, two powerful Dominants kneeling in front of a slip of a girl who desperately grasped his hands and held him still while she rubbed her face on his shirt. He could hear her deep inhalation as she took his scent into her lungs, and it pleased him on a primal level.

Then Rory touched her shoulder, and she scrambled away. Fuck. If she reacted like this every time they touched her, this would never work. They needed to talk to her therapist and find out exactly what was going on before they did anything else. Liam had the urge to grab Rhiannon and hold her until she calmed, but for once, he didn't give in to his instincts. His fear of hurting her had him paralyzed with indecision, the state Rory seemed to currently be in as well.

Rhiannon quickly came back to herself, and she wiped away her tears. "I'm sorry. It's just…talking about…him… I don't like it. He's ruined enough of my life, and I don't want him to take any more of it away from me." Her look became fierce, and she leaned forward. "I don't want to be like this anymore. I want to be loved, I want to love someone, and I don't want to be alone anymore. Please, please help me."

Rory sighed and ran his hands through his hair. "Rhiannon, I can't even touch you without you flinching."

"I'm sorry about that, I really am, I'm just so nervous." She chewed her lower lip hard enough that Liam was afraid she'd draw blood. "I-I have a friend here who can help me with that."

Confused, Liam examined her face closely. "What are you talking about?"

"It might be easier for you to touch me if I had someone in the room I trust. Not always, but just for now."

"Who?"

"My best friend."

No matter what was going on in his head, his body wasn't conflicted. It wanted to fuck Rhiannon until she screamed his name. Mad at himself for allowing his lust to distract him, Liam stood and went over to the small bar next to the vanity. He took down a bottle of gin and poured a tumbler.

Rory's voice came from behind him as he said, "Please go get her."

"Yes, Sir."

She put the mask back on, and her whole body language changed. Her shoulders went back, her spine straightened, and her lips set into a sensual pout. The change was startling, and Liam wondered how much effort it took Rhiannon to keep her ice-queen persona in place all the time. The attitude she now projected was one of "don't fuck with me." Liam wondered which one was the real Rhiannon: the scared young girl or the warrior woman who now faced them with her chin held high.

Rory looked up. "Rhiannon."

"Yes?"

"Thank you for trusting us enough to be honest. I'm proud of you."

With a visible bounce in her step, Rhiannon beamed at Rory, that bright and joyful smile that affected Liam so deeply. Evidently it did the same thing to Rory, because he grinned back at her in a way that Liam hadn't seen him smile in a long time. His heart gave a solid thud as he wished Rory would look at him like that, but he wasn't holding his breath. Things had changed between them, and Liam didn't know how to fix it. He could only hope that if they took Rhiannon on as a trainee it wouldn't tear apart what remained of their relationship.

Chapter Four

Rory stood the moment Rhiannon closed the door behind her, then strode across the room to Liam. The other man filled a crystal tumbler with a healthy pour of gin from one of the decanters arranged against the wall. After giving Liam a brief nod of thanks, Rory took the drink and slugged it down in one gulp. The liquid fire racing down his throat made him wish he could have another, but he didn't dare. Not with Rhiannon's happiness in their hands.

Yeah, it sounded crazy even to him when he thought about it, but bloody fucking hell, everything inside him that made him a Dom was screaming that Rhiannon was in danger. While he didn't think she was suicidal, he'd never seen someone so sad hide it so well. It physically hurt him to know how much pain she'd been in this whole time, and that he'd been oblivious to it, fooled by the confident and almost intimidating persona she put on in public.

Goddess was the unapproachable ice queen. The uppity bitch many a Dom wished they could spank. Feeling like an asshole, Rory admitted that he'd been blind to Rhiannon's inner turmoil because of her beauty. She was stunning to the point where her attractiveness had become all he noticed. But now he'd seen her need, and he had to admit, she intrigued and worried him.

Looking up at Liam, Rory caught the mixed emotions of anger, confusion, and lust flashing over Liam's face. Just the sight of his best mate looking equally befuddled by Rhiannon made Rory want to get drunk. Even now, when his thoughts were spinning from the beautiful mess that had landed in his lap, he couldn't help but admire Liam's square jaw and full lips. Maybe if he got drunk, then he'd finally have the courage to kiss Liam. Everything inside Rory demanded he tell Liam that he loved him, had loved him for twelve years, but he just couldn't. No doubt if he admitted his feelings, Liam would leave, freaked out by the thought of being attracted to another man.

Rory understood why. Liam had been raised in a very small, very conservative, rural village in Scotland. To say his hometown was anti-gay was like saying a few people got asked questions during the Inquisition. Rory's gut tightened in anger as he remembered driving past the burned-down home where a gay man had used to live before he and his family had been run out of town.

In the backward village where Liam had grown up, gay men were demon-possessed sodomites who brought evil and AIDS into God-fearing homes. Liam had somehow managed to come out of that toxic environment relatively unscathed. The other man had a big heart and was a genuinely happy person, but the thought of anyone thinking Liam might be gay sent him into a blind panic. Seeing Liam's worry and confusion made Rory want to comfort the other man, to take away the frown lines deepening around Liam's mouth.

After setting his glass down, Liam grasped Rory by the shoulder. "You okay?"

Rory sighed and pushed his never-ending battle with himself about Liam to the side, focusing on Rhiannon. "Yeah, I'm kind of mad at myself. Now that I think about it, Jessica has been trying to hint to me that Godde—I mean, Rhiannon—could use our help. Jessica would always try and get Rhiannon to hang out with us. I thought it was just because she liked the female companionship of someone not in training, but I think there was more to it. Jessica is remarkably astute at seeing through people's bullshit to who they really are."

Liam snorted. "How the hell would we even know? Rhiannon walks around with a stick up her arse. Are we really considering this? What about our vacation? We own the damn island, and we've only been there twice. I was looking forward to spending some time away from all of this."

At the mention of their private island in the Caribbean, a

pang of longing went through Rory. He'd planned on laying it all on the line with Liam at their vacation home. On the island, there would be nowhere for Liam to run. Then they'd no longer have to hide their love. Not that they did a very good job of it anyway. There was heavy speculation at the club that Rory and Liam were lovers behind closed doors, but he didn't think his friend knew that, or if he did he'd never mentioned anything to Rory about it. If they had sex at Wicked, it was always with a submissive female between them.

Like Rhiannon would be if they took her on.

He had a vivid fantasy about Rhiannon in a sex swing with her undoubtedly beautiful pussy spread wide. Liam would be at the front, and Rory would have the pleasure of watching Rhiannon suck off Liam while he fucked her. Then an even more vivid fantasy filled his mind of both of them making love to Rhiannon at the same time, of the exquisite sensation of Liam's cock rubbing against his as Rory took her pussy and Liam her ass.

A hard surge of blood tightened his pelvis, and Rory tried to claw back his arousal. Now was not the time to be thinking with his dick. Then again, perhaps it would be better if they brought a woman to the Caribbean so if Liam did freak out and leave at least Rory would have someone to hold at night. Liam had been acting so odd lately that he felt like his best mate was one step away from ending their friendship. It was incredibly selfish of him, but Rory was really tired of falling asleep alone, of waking up alone, of not having someone to love.

"We have some time until we leave for the island. If we decide to train her...well, I don't see why she can't come with us."

Liam stared at him, hurt tightening his features. "I thought we were going there to get away from the stress, not bring it with us."

If Rory didn't know better, he'd say Liam was jealous of Rhiannon. "I know, I know. I want time to relax, to get away from everything. But I can't turn my back on her, Liam. I have a feeling that if we turn her down, it'll be a huge blow to her self-esteem. I'm sorry, but to me that's more important than sipping a frozen beverage while tanning my ass."

"You make it sound like I'm some kind of fucking asshole."

It took a great deal for Rory to keep his leash on his temper. They'd reached the point where they were either going to fight or fuck, and since they'd never even kissed, it seemed all they ever did when they were alone was fight. He didn't want it to be like this between them, but he also didn't want to fail Rhiannon. The instinct that had told him Liam was going to be someone special in his life said the same thing about Rhiannon.

"I'm sorry. I really am." He set his glass down and grasped Liam by the back of his neck, then jerked him closer until their foreheads touched. "I feel it in my bones that if we let her go, it is something we'll regret for the rest of our lives."

Liam tried to pull back, but Rory held him firm. Their breaths mingled as Liam said, "You sound like some old fortune teller."

"Are you with me on this? I need to know before we talk with her therapist."

A few tense seconds passed before Liam nodded. "Yes."

"Thank God, because I couldn't fucking do it without you. Rhiannon is going to be high maintenance. That means no secondary trainee."

"I agree. We need to hear what her therapist says, but I haven't decided yet. I'm still not sure if this is a good idea."

Liam adjusted the way his kilt hung on his hips, drawing Rory's gaze to his groin. God, it would be so fucking easy to just slip his hand beneath Liam's kilt and touch him the way Rory wanted to. Maybe Liam was right about this not being a good idea. Truth be told, Rory wasn't sure if he was in the right headspace for taking on another submissive trainee. He was too focused on Liam and their imploding personal relationship. Bloody hell, when had his life become so complicated? And why was he driven to complicate it further by adding Rhiannon to the mix?

A light knock came from the door leading to the hallway, and a moment later, the door opened, and Mistress Onyx strolled in. Behind her trailed a meek Rhiannon who kept her gaze on the floor. To the casual observer, it would appear as if Mistress Onyx was Rhiannon's Domme with the way Rhiannon obediently followed the other woman—except there was no sexual chemistry between the women.

Mistress Onyx gave each man a brief nod before sitting on the fainting couch and crossing her long legs. Today she wore a skintight navy-blue latex catsuit with matching boots decorated with silver buckles. Tall and solidly built, she'd always reminded Rory of an Amazon.

Mistress Onyx looked over at Rhiannon hovering by the door and sighed. "Come here, girl, and take off that mask."

With a humbled look, Rhiannon did as she was told, removing the mask and setting it aside before kneeling next to Mistress Onyx's feet. She stole a glance at Rory and Liam before looking back down at the ground, her expression indecipherable. Fuck. She had to be the hardest woman to read when she had her shields in place.

"Thank you for joining us, Mistress Onyx."

"Please, call me Latisha." She ran a soothing hand over Rhiannon's long hair. "Rhiannon tells me she needs some moral support while facing off with you two big, badass Doms."

When Latisha put it that way, Rory could see how it might be a bit intimidating for Rhiannon to face them both. In fact, given her history, he was rather surprised at the inner strength the beautiful woman had shown in approaching them in the first place. Rory didn't move from Liam's side by the bar. He wanted to keep some distance between them and Rhiannon to try and give her breathing room.

"Is this a good idea?" Liam blurted out in an uncharacteristic display of nerves.

Rhiannon tensed, curling her hands into fists at her sides, but Latisha ignored her. Or at least appeared to. Rory had a feeling that not much got past Latisha. "That is not my call to make. Rhiannon has to decide for herself what she wants. I'm here as moral support."

Confused, Rory and Liam exchanged a questioning look before Liam said, "I don't understand."

Mistress Onyx glanced down at Rhiannon. "Have you tried kissing them yet?"

"No." Rhiannon's voice came out small.

Liam shifted and took a small step forward. "There's no need to rush her."

Rhiannon stared up at Latisha with a pleading look, but the other woman shook her head. "No, Rhiannon. This is your decision, your choice. I can't and won't do this for you."

Blowing out a frustrated breath, Rory had to resist the urge to grab another slug of gin. Rhiannon appeared about as excited at the prospect of kissing them as getting shot in the leg. "I'm not kissing anyone who doesn't want to be kissed."

Giving Rhiannon a small smile, Latisha then leaned forward and smoothed back Rhiannon's midnight silk hair. She said in a low, soothing voice, "You've come this far, and I'm so proud of you for everything that you've accomplished. Now use that formidable strength of yours to decide what you really want."

Rhiannon shuddered, then quickly stood. Without looking at either Rory or Liam, she swiftly crossed the small distance to them. She reached Liam first and leaned up on her tiptoes, pressing a brief kiss to his mouth that was about as nonsexual as possible. Before she could move away, Liam caught her about the waist with his arm, gently pulling her closer.

"You call that a kiss? I've had more passionate kisses from my grandmother."

He said it in a teasing tone, but Rhiannon reacted as if he'd slapped her. Both men stared at her in shock when she yelled, "Fuck off!"

"Rhiannon." Latisha's voice snapped through the air like a whip. "Do not take out your fear on him like that. He doesn't know, and that's not fair. How would you feel if your positions were reversed?"

Rhiannon sighed softly, then rested her forehead against Liam's chest. "I'm sorry."

Mistress Onyx caught Rory's gaze, and she tilted her head in Liam and Rhiannon's direction. It took him a second to realize she was indicating that he needed to be over there as well. Damn. His head just wasn't in the right place for dealing with a potential new trainee, especially one who was a maze of dangerous emotions and hazardous pitfalls. Usually by the time he and Liam met the submissive, they'd been in contact via phone and e-mail, having long conversations about what the submissive needed. Now, he was flying blind, at night, through an emotional hurricane named Rhiannon. But maybe he just needed to follow his instincts. They hadn't steered him wrong so far, and his soul's need to help the girl far outweighed his rational mind's fear of screwing her up even more.

Without giving himself time to overanalyze, Rory shifted to stand behind Rhiannon and moved close enough so that he could hug her at the same time as Liam. She remained stiff only for a moment before melting against them with a long sigh. Liam met Rory's gaze, and Rory mouthed the words *seduce her.*

Liam gave him a hard, searching look, then nodded. "Lass, look at me."

She immediately did as Liam asked, her soft hair brushing against Rory's lips. He tightened his hold on her, letting her feel them surrounding her. It seemed like she reacted better to a slow, firm touch than to small and light ones. If she had been abused, it would make sense. Punches and blows came at a person fast, while affectionate touches were generally slower and lingered.

"There we go." Liam's voice took on a seductive purr, and Rory wished he could see the way Rhiannon was looking at the other man. Something in her expression must have touched Liam, because he gave her a gentle smile as his gaze softened. "I promise, I'm not a bad kisser, and I did brush my teeth this week."

She gave a choked, almost painful-sounding laugh. "This seems a lot easier in books."

Liam tilted his head down with a smile. "Kissing?"

"Yeah."

"You've never kissed anyone before?"

"Oh, I've kissed guys. I just don't think we were doing it right."

"Why do you say that?"

"Well, isn't a kiss is supposed to make you feel good? With those guys, the only thing I felt was nervous and slightly icked out. I mean, with some of them, it wasn't bad, but there were certainly no fireworks."

"Icked out?"

"Yeah." She cleared her throat. "Tongue kissing someone is like having a big, fat, wet worm squiggling around in your mouth with some guys."

Both Rory and Liam burst out laughing, and Rhiannon tried to push her way out from between them. "Don't laugh at me."

"Oh, come on now, darling. You have to admit that was funny."

She huffed, then settled down. "It's not funny when it happens to you."

"No, I suppose it isn't."

Rory snuggled her closer, enjoying the way she fit between them. She seemed to be the perfect height for both men to hold but wasn't squished between them. "I may not know what I'm doing exactly, but I'm willing to learn."

The way she said those words, the uncertainty beneath her snippy tone, made Rory want to show her exactly how good sex could be with the right person...or in this case persons. But he couldn't have her, not yet, so the thought was driving him crazy. She was so fucking beautiful, and he wanted the pleasure of slowly disrobing her, seeing her body inch by agonizing inch. He bit his inner cheek and tried to distract himself from his own needs and focus on her.

Rory brushed her hair over her shoulder and whispered into her ear, "Are you sure?"

She bumped against his erection, and she froze, then hesitantly leaned back into him. She was as stiff as a board, but Rory hoped Liam's kiss would warm her up so by the time Rory got to kiss her, she'd be ready for whatever he had to offer. At least he hoped she would. While he didn't want to push her, he had to know if she could take their intimate touch.

"Easy, sweet lass. Just relax and let me pleasure you."

Liam cupped Rhiannon's face in his hands, making Rory aware of how small she was. He took a slight step back and tugged Rhiannon off-balance, forcing her to fall into him, to let him support her. She gasped, then moaned as Rory began to gently brush his lips over the side of her neck. He'd found that women's necks were much more sensitive than men's, and a light caress would often drive their arousal higher.

He wanted to let his hands drift to her large breasts, but he needed to tread carefully with her. He didn't know what turned her on yet, what her arousal looked like, or what she craved. Would she be the kind of sub who liked a light spanking, or would she want the hard stuff? Even more importantly, what were her turnoffs? The last thing he wanted was to trigger her bad memories in some way.

Rory could tell the moment Liam began to kiss Rhiannon, because she tried to go stiff again. In an effort to bring her arousal back, Rory gently set his teeth into her shoulder, and she moaned, going limp. He experimented with the pressure of his teeth, alternating between hard and soft nibbles. Soon she was squirming between them, making both men grunt.

Bloody hell, she was a hot piece of arse.

She began to touch them, running her hands over their bodies as best she could in her confined position. Groaning deep in his throat, Liam broke their kiss. Sexual tension radiated from Liam, and it made Rory hard as fuck. When Liam looked up at Rory, he was surprised to see a look of almost jealousy on Liam's face. Before he could question him, Liam turned Rhiannon around so she faced Rory.

At the sight of her glazed eyes, her lips swollen from her kiss with Liam, and her hard nipples pressing against the thin fabric of her top, Rory had to once again pull himself back in an effort keep from devouring her. Liam faded into the background as Rory slowly closed the distance between his lips and Rhiannon's, savoring how she softened for him. An electric tingle went through Rory like a pleasurable shock of static.

He took his time, learning her responses, tasting her mouth but not seeking entrance yet. She started to become more aggressive, licking against the seam of his lips. Rory hesitated, then grabbed a handful of her hair and pulled her back enough so there was the tiniest bit of space between them.

"You are so fucking sweet. Kissing you is like eating candy."

She smiled and wrapped her arms around his neck. Then she jerked, and her eyes went wide. What had startled her became apparent when Rory looked down to see Liam had cupped her breasts. He wasn't doing anything more than holding them, and her tits were more than a handful even in Liam's big grip. Her breasts were absolutely luscious. Rory was dying to touch her, but she was starting to become a little panicky.

Before she could get too tense, he pulled her back to him for a kiss, tightening his hand in her hair. She sighed into his mouth, and Rory took advantage of the moment to stroke just the tip of her tongue with his in a slow, controlled slide. Then he just focused on kissing her lips until the first hesitant stroke of her tongue against his mouth. He let her explore the pleasure of taking the lead in the kiss for a few moments, enjoying the way she melted once again. He'd never felt a submissive relax as quickly as she did.

Her moan vibrated through his mouth as Liam began to lift her breasts and rub her hard nipples against Rory's chest. Rory wished he'd stopped to take his shirt off, but maybe having the clothing barrier between them was a good thing. He was extremely tempted to take this further, to taste Rhiannon, to fuck her and watch her get fucked until none of them could move. In his current state, that might be for hours.

The thought of her wet, slippery flesh sliding over his body while Liam fucked her in the shower wasn't helping him calm down.

He unwound her arms from around him and took a step back. For a long moment, he looked from Liam holding her breasts, to Rhiannon, still looking like she needed a good fuck in the worst way. This had gone better than he'd expected, but he wasn't sure how Liam felt. The last thing he wanted to do was mislead Rhiannon if his best mate wasn't keen with taking her on as a trainee.

"Rhiannon, you will go home and get something to eat, then get ready for bed. Next I want you to go to your bedroom where you will masturbate for me. I want you to think about Master Liam and myself while you do it. The next time we meet to discuss the possibility of taking you on as a trainee, you will tell us what you fantasized about."

Her cheeks burned bright red, and she brushed Liam's hands from her chest. "I can't do that!"

He grinned at her, loving the indecision in her gaze. "Why not?"

"Because...because it's not decent."

Latisha laughed from the couch and startled Rory. Shit.

He'd forgotten about the other woman. It wasn't often that he became so lost in a simple kiss that he overlooked there were people in the room with him. Come to think of it, he couldn't remember the last time a woman had taken his total attention like that.

Liam gave Rhiannon a brief hug before letting her go. He walked to Rory's side, presenting a united front. She immediately dropped her gaze and clasped her hands together. "I'm sorry."

Rory smiled at her. "Don't be sorry. I'd rather have you speak your mind than feel like you have to hide things from us. That doesn't mean you get to be a bitch, but we'll discuss things with you. We aren't even your training Masters yet, so don't censor yourself."

"Yes, Sir." She began to toy with the coin belt around her waist, drawing both men's attention to her smooth belly. "Could I like e-mail or text it to you instead? I don't know if I can talk about...that stuff with you face-to-face."

The men exchanged a glance, and Rory easily read Liam's capitulation to her terms in his friend's gaze.

Rory smiled at Rhiannon. "Yes, you can text us, but there is a price."

She lifted her gaze, and that subtle shift happened where she went from Rhiannon to Goddess. It was amazing how she put on that persona like a cloak. No, not a cloak. More like she was putting on her armor. "What price?"

"You have to text us while you're touching your sweet little pussy."

"What?"

Rory shrugged. "It's either that or tell us your fantasy face-to-face. Think of it like homework. We all know that our training will be of a sexual nature, and we need to see if you have the courage to be honest with both yourself and us about what you want. While we can work with you on getting over your shyness, we can't work with lies—either to yourself or us."

"Oh. Well, okay then." She tossed her mane of dark hair over her shoulder, the long strands framing the sweeping curve of her tiny waist. "Are you sure you don't want to do this tomorrow? I mean, it'll be three a.m. by the time I get home. I don't want to keep you up."

Liam chuckled. "Too late for that, lass."

"What?"

Liam gestured to his rampant erection tenting his kilt, and she flushed.

"Yes. I see." She stole a glance at Rory's hard cock pressing up against his leather pants and began to giggle. "Guess I won't be the only one touching myself when I get home."

Oh, she wanted to be a brat?

Rory took a slow step toward her, capturing her gaze and signaling his intent way before he reached her. His world narrowed to her as he took in the dilation of her pupils, the way her breath hitched, and the slight softening of her lips. All inviting him to do with her as he wished.

Gripping her world-class ass with both hands, he then shoved his thigh between her legs and forced her to straddle it. The nice thing about leather pants was it almost felt like bare skin, especially against the barely there cloth of her harem girl outfit. He swore the heat of her pussy as it met his thigh muscle burned him. She was so hot and soft. His imagination ran rampant as he tried to imagine what her pussy looked like. If she shaved it bald or left the soft, downy hair he loved.

He rocked his hips and slowly slid her over his leg, then tilted her hips until he hit the sweet spot that made her gasp. Movement caught Rory's attention as Liam edged closer and took a seat on one of the leather wingback chairs, watching them intently. A growl of satisfaction vibrated through Rory's chest. Being watched by Liam always did it for him, and his cock ached for relief. Rhiannon was now grinding herself on his thigh muscle with a sexy fucking wiggle that reminded him of the way belly dancers moved.

The thought of having her ride him and move like that nearly undid him.

Liam must have noticed because he spoke up. "There. Now we're not the only ones that will be kept up tonight."

Rhiannon shivered as Rory gripped her ass tight, giving her a good squeeze before he released her. She stumbled, and Liam was up in an instant, supporting her in a courteous gesture.

"Easy."

A pretty flush painted her cheeks red, something Rory found both sexy and adorable. "Oh my. You really know how to overwhelm a girl."

Rory laughed. "Darling, you haven't seen anything yet."

Chapter Five

Rhiannon turned down the Pink Floyd blaring from the speakers of her beloved white Mustang Cobra. Though it was over twelve years old, the car had been the first thing she'd ever bought for herself of any worth after she started working at Club Wicked.

A year into her job at Club Wicked as a server, she went from her modest apartment to owning a beautiful old farmhouse two hours outside DC on land owned by Latisha's grandmother, Ms. Althea. Latisha lived about a mile down the road, and several of her family members lived nearby as well. They'd pretty much adopted Rhiannon and made her feel like kin. Well, maybe not exactly like kin. They actually respected *her* privacy. While Latisha might be a formidable Domme, she was also a little sister to four overprotective brothers with no sense of personal space.

Rhiannon's home, built in 1909, still occupied its place of honor on a small rise looking out over the pastureland. Running a farm was hard work, and she knew she couldn't do it on her own so she let the fields around the house grow into meadows that fed deer instead of cows and horses. While she'd love to have horses someday, she didn't have the time to do it or the trust necessary to hire someone to come onto her land and into her home to care for any livestock.

The depressing thought dimmed her good mood as she drove up the freshly paved driveway to the quaint two-story farmhouse. Her headlights reflected off the decorative stained glass of the front door, and her security lights came on, flooding the yard. One of the first things she'd done when she bought this place was to install a state-of-the-art security system. Sure, at the time she didn't have furniture to fill it, but she had her peace of mind.

She pulled into her garage and before she shut the door she called out, "Kitty, kitty, kitty, kitty."

Less than a minute later two cats came at her from different directions. They were white and tabby Maine Coons. With their long hair and multilayer coats, they were excellent outdoor cats and very self-sufficient. They split their time between Rhiannon's home and Ms. Althea's, shamelessly sucking up to the old woman who fed them choice tidbits from her kitchen. Rhiannon had to admit she pampered them as well.

The different-toned chimes of the bells on the cats' collars filled the air as the cats bounced to where she stood. Smiling down at them, she closed the garage door before opening the door leading to the mudroom off the kitchen. She hit the switch for the lights and relaxed as the familiar sights of her home filled her with joy. Beautiful, clean, and safe—this home was her haven from the terrors of the world.

Tossing her keys onto the cream-and-gray marble of the kitchen counter, she then set about getting the kitties their midnight snack. Or their three a.m. snack now. She hadn't meant to stay at Club Wicked that late, but tearing herself away from Master Rory and Master Liam had been next to impossible. Thankfully having Latisha there kept Rhiannon from making an ass of herself by begging the men to touch her more, to kiss her more, to hold her between them and never let her go. Her thoughts drifted to the kiss she'd shared with the men, and she tried to remember every detail.

A chorus of impatient meows came from her feet, and she laughed. "Take it easy."

After making sure the cats were happy, she grabbed a banana and scarfed it down. Master Rory had said for her to eat, so she did. If she was going to train with them—if they didn't reject her—she needed to get used to following their instructions. She wasn't sure what their choice would be. Their meeting hadn't exactly gone as she'd planned, but hopefully they were at the very least intrigued.

The good Lord knew she was certainly intrigued by their kisses. The memory of their mouths moving against hers, each man with a slightly different but equally effective technique, made her body tingle with sensual awareness. They'd tasted wonderful, and the combination of their colognes had left her heady with desire. It was as if the men had been perfectly made to appeal to her on all levels. For a moment shame filled her at the thought of how wanton she'd been with them, but she pushed that emotion away.

No, no dark thoughts now.

Master Rory and Master Liam would probably want her to drink some milk as well, so she poured herself a glass and quickly finished it. After washing and putting the glass away, leaving the kitchen once again immaculate, she blew her cats kisses and turned off the light. All throughout her house she had different crystal nightlights that threw rainbow patterns against her walls. She didn't like the dark, and because she lived alone she saw no reason why she had to deal with it. Besides, the ethereal lighting was perfect for her fairy collection that filled the house. Everywhere there were different and beautiful fairy statues and pictures. Her father used to call her his fairy princess, and she'd been collecting fairies for as long as she could remember. A pang of homesickness cramped her stomach, and she pressed her hand to her midriff, then massaged the muscles into relaxation.

Trying to banish those negative thoughts, she focused on the giant fairy and butterfly mobile that hung in the two-story entrance of the foyer. She'd spent half a month's wages on it and never regretted it. As she climbed the stairs the delicate figures in the mobile spun and danced with the faint breeze of her passing. When she opened the front door they would whirl into life in a symphony of glittering color.

She'd almost reached the top of the stairs, and she stretched out to brush one of the butterflies, setting off a chain reaction of motion. That was kind of like her experiences tonight. One action that could be a great catalyst for her life, sending her spinning in ways she'd never imagined. At least her meeting with the Masters was over with, and she could stop worrying about it. She'd been so tense for the past month, fretting about how this evening would go. Every terrible, horrible scenario had gone through her mind until she could barely sleep at night.

The hardwood floors of the landing creaked beneath her

weight while she made her way to her bedroom. Once inside she removed her clothes and took a quick shower, tempted to give herself an orgasm with the showerhead before she texted Master Rory and Master Liam. But she was pretty sure they'd want to control her orgasms and didn't want to start off her potential training by disobeying them. She knew they forbid Jessica from touching herself without them present. It had irritated her friend to no end, and now that Rhiannon had a taste of how being left aroused and wanting felt, she agreed it was really irksome.

Toweling herself off, Rhiannon quickly rubbed some of her honeysuckle body lotion on before grabbing her phone off the antique white dresser. First she jumped onto the lush mattress of her king-size canopy bed; then she lay back with a sigh. The towel was still knotted around her chest, so she didn't bother to get beneath the covers. In the nightstand next to her bed she had a variety of vibrators and dildos. Maybe she should text the Masters first to see what they wanted her to play with. A flare of nervous energy churned her stomach, and she had to resist the urge to pretend the battery on her phone had died or some other stupid thing. She'd already done the difficult part and approached them, so she wasn't going to throw away all her hard-earned bravery now.

It was time to put on her big-girl panties and take the next step to the life she wanted to live.

As she texted Master Rory's number, excitement began to push away her apprehension. She'd been dreaming of a moment like this for such a long time. Finally she was going to get a taste of what she'd been craving, what she'd been needing. A firm male hand to guide her and protect her. True, they were only her trainers, not permanent Masters, but oh, did it feel nice to have someone else take charge.

The canopy above her wasn't made of cloth, but rather a specially crafted collection of strung crystals that went from post to post. In the golden light from the small nightlight on the far wall, the crystals sparkled like stars. Her phone beeped, and she picked it up, grinning as she saw Master Rory and Master Liam had joined the chat.

Master Rory: Are you naked?

Master Liam: And are you touching yourself yet?

She giggled, glad they couldn't see her because right now she had what was no doubt a goofy smile.

Rhiannon: Yes and no.

Master Liam: I want your hand between your legs, girl.

She did as ordered, then stared at the phone. How the hell was she supposed to text and touch herself? Texting one-handed took concentration and made it hard to focus on arousing herself. Chewing her lower lip, she tried to stroke her pussy and type, but it was like patting her head and rubbing her tummy at the same time.

Master Rory: Are you there?

Rhiannon: Yes, sorry, Sir. I'm having a hard time doing two things at once. I forget which hand I'm supposed to be texting with.

There was a pause, and she took a deep breath, trying to get into the moment, but it just wasn't happening.

Master Liam: I have to say, that was a rather entertaining mental image.

She grinned. Master Liam was the quieter of the two men, and she was comfortable around him. Master Rory, on the other hand, made her feel like she was dealing with someone far out of her league. Master Liam had a rough form of good looks that she found extremely appealing, but Master Rory was the unattainable movie star gracing the cover of a magazine.

Staring at her canopy, she debated what to do next. She could always fake masturbating, but she felt like she'd be cheating herself if she did that. The memory of their bodies pressing into hers as they kissed tingled through her, and she decided to confront her fears and see if her trust was well-placed.

Can I call you?

There was less than a ten-second pause before her phone began to ring. With a giggle that was part nerves and part excitement, she picked up her phone and looked at the screen. One Mr. Rory Stone was on the line. After taking a deep breath, she accepted the call.

"Hello, Rhiannon." Master Rory's smooth-as-whiskey voice melted her bones.

"Hi, Sir."

Then Master Liam spoke up. "Hello, lass. Hope you don't mind, but we were already talking to each other while we were texting with you. Figured it would just be easier to conference call you in."

"That's fine."

Silence stretched for a moment before all three of them started talking at once.

Both men laughed, and Master Rory said, "Beautiful girl, where are you right now?"

The sudden dip in his tone gave her a little shiver. "In my bed."

"Have you already showered and eaten?" Master Liam asked in his deliciously deep voice.

"Yes, Sir." After putting the phone down on her bed, she cleared her throat. "Okay. I have you on speakerphone so my hands are free for the touching."

"You make it sound so clinical."

Master Rory laughed as she scowled at the phone. "Why don't you put some music on?"

Music? She could do that. "What would you like me to play?"

Master Liam said, "Something that makes you feel sexy. A song that always makes you want to dance."

"Okay. One second please."

She quickly flipped through the music on her iTouch next to her bed, scrolling past her two thousand songs until she found the one she was looking for. The first time she'd heard this song, it had grabbed her by the heart and sunk its claws into her soul. Dancing was a part of her life, and this melody made her want to soar. She'd never considered formal lessons, for her dancing was a private thing, a release that lifted her in the way reading poetry or experiencing beautiful art did for others.

The first few heavy beats of the song came on, and she adjusted the volume.

"Nice," Rory said with surprise. "'Personal Jesus' by Depeche Mode. I would have pegged you as a pop girl."

She lay back on her bed and lifted her hair, then spread it out on her pillow. "I like anything that has a good beat."

"Perfect. Now close your eyes and start to stroke your arms and your chest but do not touch your breasts."

A blush heated her until she was afraid they could hear her pounding heart it in her voice. "Okay. I'm touching my arms right now."

"How does it feel," Rory asked with a soft growl in his tone.

"Good. A little tickly."

Liam cleared his throat. "Now imagine it's our hands touching you, lass."

The command in Rory's tone was evident as he said, "Tell us one of your fantasies."

She took a deep breath through her nose and tried to release her tension. They were so sexually experienced, they'd probably think her fantasy was tame and dumb, but to her it was almost too scandalous to even say aloud. While growing up, she was taught by her family that only bad women thought about sex and certainly never had fantasies like the one she would tell her Masters. Old shame tried to surface, tried to kill her hard-won courage.

"I-I don't want to sound stupid."

"I promise you, nothing you say could possibly sound dumb or strange or perverted to Liam and myself."

"Besides, we'll reward you next time we see you for your efforts to please us. Now just relax. You're alone, safe, and we would never do or say anything to abuse your trust."

Closing her eyes, she began to touch herself again. "I like to imagine that I'm a princess living back in the 1700s. It's nighttime, and I'm trying to find the groom who keeps telling on me for going off on rides without my parents' permission. I'm going to find the groom and yell at him for ratting me out."

"Sweetheart, you can start touching your breasts now. Play with your nipples harder than you usually would."

She couldn't help the sigh that escaped as she pinched her very hard nubs, squirming slightly when a pleasurable sensation shot through her and settled into her rapidly swelling clit. "As I'm storming down the hall, someone reaches out and grabs me, then pulls me into an empty room. I can barely see in the dim light, but as I struggle with him, it soon becomes apparent that it's the groom. Especially when he grabs a handful of my hair and jerks my head back. He stares into my eyes, and it makes me so hot, the way he's stern with me, how he isn't going to take any sass. Then he kisses me until I can't breathe, until I melt against him, until I submit."

Rory's voice made her moan as he said, "Touch that pretty pussy, girl. Tell us what you feel."

"I'm wet and very soft down there right now."

Liam muttered something that sounded like swear words. "You're killing me."

A sudden sense of power moved through her, and she smiled as she stroked her hard clit. "Mmm, I wish you could see me right now. I'm on my big canopy bed all stretched out on my white lace comforter, and I'm *so* wet."

"Bad girl, teasing us like this," Rory said in an amused tone. "Continue with your fantasy."

"Well, we have to be quiet because there are guards walking by all the time. And even though I know I shouldn't be doing this with him, I can't help myself. He takes control of me and makes feel him through his pants while he kisses me."

She paused and let out a small moan as the first gentle tensing of her stomach muscles before an orgasm happened. Normally it took her a long time to work up to a climax while masturbating, but now she'd been playing with herself for less than five minutes and was ready to go.

"He slips his hand beneath my dress and rudely shoves his fingers between my legs, like he owns me. I try to protest, but the feel of his rough fingers teasing my pussy steals my will to resist. I want him, but I shouldn't, so I try to feebly push him away. To my secret delight, he easily overpowers me. His dick jumps against my hand, and I want him, deep inside me."

Master Rory said, "Do you like that? Having a man take control?"

She nodded, then realized they couldn't see her. "Yes. Very much."

Rory cleared his throat, but his tone still came out gruff as he said, "Lass, don't stop telling us about your fantasy. I want you to continue, and I want you to make yourself come."

The way he said it, all strong and demanding without raising his voice sent a shiver through her. Authority just seemed to roll off the men, and it made her want to give herself to them in the worst way. The mental image of kneeling before Master Rory and Master Liam while they made her suck their dicks at the same time had her rubbing her clit in a hard, fast circle.

"While your moans are lovely, we ordered you to talk."

"Mmm. Yes, Master. I'm thinking about the feeling of you sliding into my mouth, of the sensation of being on my knees in front of you with both your hands on my head, guiding me as I suck you off. I can taste you on my tongue while I try to swallow down as much of you as I can. The sight of your cocks all shiny with my spit makes me so fucking turned on."

"Do you want us to come all over you, Rhiannon? Do you want to feel us covering you with our seed, claiming you as our submissive?"

It was like he'd tapped into her deepest desires. She slipped two fingers into her pussy, moving them in and out while she chased her orgasm. The thought of them climaxing on her, of having the evidence that she'd pleased them, aroused her like nothing else. Her pulse raced, sending her hormone-rich blood flooding into her body, sensitizing every inch until she was squirming and raising her hips, seeking her release. Her breasts trembled as she panted, and she was so wet her arousal had dipped down the crack of her bottom. Pleasure stole her thoughts, robbed her of her dignity, and turned her into a creature of pure need.

"Please, Masters. Please give it to me." Her words came out unsteady; her panting breaths were loud enough to be heard over the stereo. She had no shame right now, only the need to give them everything she had. To satisfy them and make them happy with her. She wanted to be their joy.

"Come for us, lass. Be a good girl and give your climax to your Masters."

Her body froze, locked in an agonizing clench of muscles tightening as her arousal built and built. With one last rub of her clit, she began to orgasm. Twisting on her bed, she then eased her fingers in and out of her grasping pussy, wishing it was their cocks instead of her hand, wishing their weight pinned her to her bed, wishing she wasn't alone. At this moment she wanted them more than she'd ever wanted anyone in her life. The power of her need for them scared her, and she prayed she wasn't setting herself up for more heartache.

Master Liam chuckled, but his tone held no malice as he said, "I'm so fucking pissed at myself right now for not being there to watch you. That sounded like a really nice orgasm."

All she could do was moan in agreement as she removed her fingers from her pulsing sex and closed her eyes, then said, "It was wonderful."

Rory replied in a warm voice, "Thank you, Rhiannon, for trusting us enough to talk with both of us tonight. Are you working tomorrow?"

She put the phone on the side table next to her bed and scooted under her sheets. "Yes. No, wait. Do you mean today tonight or tomorrow night?"

"I mean tonight. Bloody fuck, it's late, isn't it? I do hope you don't have any early morning engagements tomorrow...I mean, today."

Since today was Saturday, she was due at her neighbor Ms. Althea's house for their weekly brunch and then had to work tonight, but that was about it. Ms. Althea was always trying to set Rhiannon up with one of her eight grandsons. They were all nice guys. Too nice. They practically screamed vanilla, and Rhiannon had found out the hard way that vanilla lovemaking just didn't do it for her. There had to be some type of BDSM involved, even if it was just a hard bite or having her hands pinned while they had sex, or she was lucky to get wet. She used to think she was just a freak for needing a little bit of hurt and the feeling of being restrained during sex, but after working at Club Wicked and listening to the servers talk about their sex lives and watching the interactions between the Doms and the subs, she realized that she was submissive.

For a long time she'd condemned herself for being this way, for needing that domination and kink in order to become aroused, but with the help of her therapist she'd claimed that part of herself as much as she could. No matter what anyone else said, she was sure that she was born this way. For as long as she could remember, she wanted to be owned by a man worthy of her heart. Her need to submit was something that had been a part of her before she'd been kidnapped. The fucking bastard who had hurt her had tried to force her submission, but he couldn't. No matter what he did, no matter how much pain he caused her, he could never get her to truly submit, and he knew it. He hadn't been her loving Dominant; he'd been a sadistic monster, a man who inspired fear, not worship.

Rory cleared his throat. "Rhiannon? You there, girl?"

She took a deep breath, focusing on her bedroom. Beautiful crystals, clean floors, the light scent of lemongrass and honeysuckle. Delicate fairy sculptures were scattered about here and there with a beauty that lifted her from the nightmares of her past. No dank basement smell, no pitch-black darkness, no cold concrete floor. Grasping a handful of her soft comforter she grounded herself in the present. "Yes, sorry. I do work tonight, but the early shift. I'll be done by nine p.m. if you wanted...I mean...never mind."

"If we wanted what?"

An embarrassed flush heated her face. Why were they making her say it? She knew how out of her league they were. She had no illusions about being anything more than yet another eager sub begging for their time and attention. Master Liam and Master Rory were legends at Club Wicked while she was the bitchy server who kept hitting Doms. She didn't deserve them, and she knew it. They were probably just being nice and looking for a way to avoid her.

"I know you're busy, so please don't feel like you have to see me or anything. I know you have thousands of beautiful, talented, and worthy submissives that are begging for your time and I'm just a server but—"

"Rhiannon," Rory said in a sharp voice. "Stop. Now."

Confused, she curled onto her side and looked at her phone. Feeling incredibly exposed and emotionally open to the men, she did what she usually did when she was confronted by a situation that could potentially emotionally hurt her: she went into icy-bitch mode. "Stop what? Stop saying the truth? Well, excuse the fuck out of me for trying to be honest."

She slapped a hand over her mouth, silently cursing her need to protect herself even when there wasn't a real threat, tears gathering in her eyes as she waited to hear them tell her they weren't going to train her.

Master Liam's Scottish burr thickened as he said, "Why do you do that?"

"Do what?"

"It's like you're two different people, lass. One is a sweet, shy, but very loving woman. The other is an utter bitch. Why do you do that?"

She'd had this discussion with Latisha before, so she knew why she did it, but admitting her weakness to the Masters left a bad taste in her mouth. Even though she was pretty sure they wouldn't hurt her, letting them into her life was hard. "I don't know. I just..."

Master Rory sighed. "Darling girl, you can trust us. Please let us in just a little bit. I swear we won't hurt you but we need to know why you hide your light from the rest of the world."

"My light?"

"Yes." Master Rory sighed again. "We all know that you have quite the reputation at Club Wicked, that you've gotten into more than your fair share of fights. And just now you went from Rhiannon to Goddess. Why?"

"I... Shit. I get hurt easily, and that hurt stays with me. When I first started working at Club Wicked, I made friends with a couple of the servers who turned out to be backstabbing bitches. I don't want to go into it, but they made my life there hell until Mr. Florentine got wind of it and fired them. But I didn't tell him. I know they needed the jobs, and I felt bad when they got fired. So I decided it would be better for everyone if I just didn't make friends. That way I couldn't be hurt, and no one else would get fired." She took a deep breath and let it out slowly. "Sometimes I feel like an abused dog, snapping at any hand that gets near me, warning them away before they can touch me even if all they wanted to do was pet me. I can't trust them not to hurt me."

"Let me see if I understand this, lass. If you're feeling threatened, you strike out before they can hurt you? That sounds like a very lonely life to lead."

"Yeah." She curled into a tighter ball. "I understand if you don't want to train me. I don't deserve you."

Rory said in a husky voice, "And if you can't push someone away with anger, you then turn that anger on yourself?"

Startled by how quickly they'd figured her out, she nodded, then realized they couldn't see her. "Right."

"First, your estimate of us is highly overrated. We're two miserable old bastards while you are a gorgeous young woman who is surprisingly interesting and kind when you allow your true self to show through." Master Liam's tone had a snap to it that made her take notice. "As it happens Master Rory and myself are without a submissive at the moment. We still have to talk about any formal training, but I'd cut off my left bollock to watch you orgasm in person, preferably around my cock."

"Over and over again," Master Rory added with a dark purr.

Master Liam laughed. "The cutting off of the bullocks or watching her orgasm?"

A giggle escaped before she could help it, and she clapped her hand over her mouth. Great. She sounded like a silly teenager to these two sex gods. A mental reminder of her uncertain future with them tightened her stomach with anxiety, but she consoled herself they hadn't said no yet. And they understood her, knew what a bitch she could be yet still liked her. In fact, other than her small group of friends, they were the only people who saw past her Goddess persona. She really, really wanted to spend more time with Rory and Liam. Not only for the wonderful way they made her feel on the outside but on the inside as well. She'd just have to figure out a way to make it impossible for them to turn her down.

"Rhiannon, we'd like to meet with you after you get off work tomorrow."

She grinned and bit back an excited squeal. "Yes, Sir."

"Once again, we're not promising you anything, but we'd like to explore the possibility of taking you on as a trainee."

"If it doesn't work out, lass, for whatever reason, we will work just as hard to find you the right Master to train with. Not because we don't want you, but because we want what's best for you."

"Yes, Sir. And thank you for...well, for tonight. It was

lovely."

"Such a darling girl." Master Rory yawned. "Fuck, I need to get to bed."

Master Liam laughed. "Is that the bloody birds I hear singing? I'm too old for this shite. Ah well. Good night, you miserable old bastard, and good night, beautiful girl. I'll see you tomorrow night."

"Good night, Rhiannon. Thank you for being honest with us, and I must say, if we decide to train you, we will make that fantasy of yours come true. I promise."

She made her good nights, and as she got comfortable with her pillow, she let out a happy sigh and wondered which fantasy Master Rory was talking about. The one with the groom or the one with them covering her in their cum.

Chapter Six

Liam glanced over at Rory as they drove together to Club Wicked. It had been a silent ride so far. They hurtled down the freeway in Rory's red classic Jaguar convertible, and Liam tilted his head back, then took a deep breath of the still warm night air.

At this speed, he'd catch hints of different scents tickling his nose while the world rushed past. Cut grass, a river, exhaust from a semitruck, then the faintest hint of fall. It seemed as if the summer had gone by in three days. Weariness settled down on him like a smothering blanket. All day he'd been battling with himself over this and had looked forward to talking with Rory about training Rhiannon. He honestly didn't know if he had the energy left to train even one more submissive.

Usually when Liam couldn't make a decision, he'd listen to his friend's advice and follow it, but he wasn't sure where Rory stood with Rhiannon. He hoped that Rory would insist on training Rhiannon so he could just go with the flow instead of having to confront his own unusually strong feelings for the woman. But Rory was strangely quiet too.

Rory wore his black leather pants with chain loops around the waist. Those pants also tended to ride low, so Liam would have the torturous sight of Rory's rock-hard arse muscles working as he moved. Fucking hell. Liam wanted to bugger the other man so badly it had gone past desire to obsession. This was the main reason they shouldn't—couldn't—train Rhiannon. They had to project strength and confidence at all times and would need all their wits. Any submissive they bonded with would be able to sense the disharmony in their pairing, and he wasn't sure if Rhiannon could handle that additional stress or would even realize that it wasn't because of her but rather their own supremely dysfunctional relationship.

He so wasn't in the right headspace for Rhiannon. She needed slow and easy while all he wanted to do was devour her and slay whatever demons haunted her.

The way she'd followed their directions, that bloody hot fantasy of hers, and the sweet sounds she'd made when she came had given Liam a raging hard-on. After they'd finished the call, he'd had to jerk off twice before he could get any sleep. When he finally went to sleep, he had an intense, erotic fantasy about fucking Rhiannon while she was dressed like a princess. It had surprised him because his dreams lately had only been about fighting and fucking Rory. In his daydream, her pussy had been so wet for him, and she'd come hard with her pretty dress bunched up around her hips and her tiara askew from his hard thrusts.

Who knew he'd find the idea of defiling royalty so appealing?

They'd passed the guards hidden at two different turnoffs from the road. He knew security cameras had tracked their movements since the moment they rolled through the intersection in town. He'd bet their play bags were being pulled from storage. The contents would be checked, and any damage done to their gear during previous play would have been repaired by the master craftsman at Wicked.

An image of Rhiannon stretched out in a bondage frame, her hands and feet bound by thick leather cuffs lined with black rabbit fur, flashed through his mind. She could struggle all she wanted, but she wouldn't be able to get out. How he'd fucking love to peel her clothes off that bloody hot little body. She had the muscles and frame of a dancer, but somehow she'd been blessed by the gods of genetics with a big pair of tits. They made her waist look tiny enough to circle with his hands. He could almost feel what it would be like to lift her by that trim waist and shove her down on his cock.

"Liam!"

He gave Rory an irritable look. "What?"

"Don't glare at me. I said your name three times, and you continued to stare out the window."

Now his irritation morphed into embarrassment. "Sorry 'bout that. What's up?"

They turned into the small drive leading to the main gate. It wasn't until after they'd pulled through that Rory responded. "So, do you think we should train Rhiannon?"

"I was going to ask you the same thing."

Rory let out a sigh, and he flexed his hands on the steering wheel. "I-I'm fucking not sure, and that tells me right there we shouldn't."

A new ache pinged through Liam's heart. "Yeah, God forbid you do something you're not sure about."

Rory gave him a sharp look that Liam ignored. "Now you don't want to train her?"

Liam was tired of ignoring him. He wanted to argue with Rory, to yell at the other man until some of the tension between them disappeared. It had been a long time since they'd just hung out together, and he couldn't remember the last time he'd been over to his friend's house or vice versa. Considering they were neighbors, there really wasn't any excuse except than that they'd been avoiding each other. If they took Rhiannon on, it would at the very least bring them physically closer together. He'd missed that.

But how fucking selfish would that be?

It made him feel like he was using Rhiannon as something to bind them rather than as a woman who needed his help. No, they could not do this.

He opened his mouth to tell Rory just that, but the other man spoke first. "I'm not sure we should, but I think we may be the only ones who could try to help her."

While part of him wanted to shout at Rory that they couldn't help her until they helped themselves, he managed to choke the words back. They'd pulled into a parking spot, and Liam got out of the car as soon as Rory turned the Jag off. His legs were sore from a rugby match they'd played in two days ago, and he tried to get the blood flowing through his muscles to relieve their stiffness. Ten years ago, he wouldn't have felt a single ache from playing, but he was getting older, and so was Rory.

They weren't green boys anymore, and he couldn't help but feel like they'd entered a new phase in their lives. Or at least he had. Liam was tired of going to sleep alone, tired of not having someone to love, and tired of being in love with a man he hated himself for loving. Last year after consuming way too much whiskey he'd tried to land a kiss on Rory, but the other man had pushed him away with a forced laugh that had shredded Liam's self-confidence and made him all too aware that Rory would never accept him as anything other than a best friend. Well, bloody fuck. He was tired of being a friend.

He wanted to be a lover, a husband.

After Rory got out of the car, he gave Liam a visible once-over and grinned. "Nice shirt. Looks like something a medieval groom would wear."

Liam glanced down and allowed Rory to distract him from his dark thoughts. Paired with his brown leather kilt, the white shirt did have an antique look to it with the way the leather strap laced the shirt up to his throat. When he realized he'd subconsciously dressed the part of Rhiannon's fantasy, he laughed.

Looking up at his friend, Liam said, "Thank God she didn't have a fantasy about a doctor. Scrubs and a leather kilt just don't work well together."

Rory laughed, and just like that things became easy between them again. Instead of fighting it and hanging on to his ever-present anger, Liam refocused on the here and now. A very tempting reality that included a lovely young woman who needed their help. In an odd way, helping shy submissives embrace their sexuality made him feel like a knight in shining armor. While he enjoyed the hell out of the sexual aspects of training, his real reward was watching a woman in their care blossom into the kind of submissive she was meant to be. Over the years, the dozens of women they'd trained had all found their true loves, and he couldn't help but wonder if he'd thrown away some really good potential relationships for his fucked-up nonrelationship with Rory.

For the first time he thought of training a woman not for someone else but for himself. Yeah, he was getting way ahead of the game, but the idea of being the one to win Rhiannon's heart appealed to him. Beneath her tough-girl persona was a treasure waiting for the right man who had the patience and fortitude to reveal it. Last night he'd come to the conclusion that the real Rhiannon was a gentle and compassionate woman who'd closed herself off from the world in order to keep her delicate feelings from being crushed. She was at once vulnerable and very strong, an interesting combination that when paired with her sensuality and beauty made her a prize any man would cherish.

Shaking his head, he tried to bring his thoughts out of the clouds and back to earth. Right now the reality was that he wasn't going to be training her alone, if they decided to take her on at all. And no matter what happened in the future, she'd come to both of them for training. Rhiannon had issues, and there was still so much they didn't know about her. He'd need Rory's gift for being able to read people, for figuring out what went on in their heads.

Rory pressed his fists into his lower back and stretched with a small grimace. Seems like Liam wasn't the only one that was feeling the effects of the rugby game. "We're a little early. Let's head for the Hall of Mirrors bar and watch Rhiannon work a little bit. I want to see how she reacts to us in public."

Liam sighed. "You know she's going to expect an answer from us eventually."

"Yes, I'm aware. Thank you, Captain Obvious. I just want to be sure before we commit one way or another." He grimaced and ran his hand through his hair. "She's so fragile that I'm afraid if we mess this up, we could really hurt her."

"I know." Not liking the already defeated look on Rory's face, Liam slugged him on the arm. "Come on, lighten up. Rhiannon's a lot stronger than either of us are giving her credit for. I mean, when she came to us after Jessica's graduation, I thought she was going to bolt or faint from fear, but she not only stood her ground, she also did everything we asked of her."

"True. Let's get inside and see what our girl is up to."

They made their way into Club Wicked and walked toward the public bar. When they reached the huge bronze doors that made up the entrance, one of the guards standing in front of it gave them a congenial smile. As usual, the bar was packed, and the room with its high-vaulted ceilings echoed with laughter and conversation, instantly relaxing Liam as he took in the atmosphere and allowed his dominant personality to rise to the surface. They'd been members of Club Wicked for seven years now, and it felt like he'd come home every time they stepped through the front doors.

Dressed in an impeccable black suit that hid the guns Liam knew every guard carried, the man holding the doors open for them said in a cultured voice, "Good evening, Master Rory and Master Liam. Mr. and Mrs. Florentine have requested a word with you."

Unease pinged through Liam. The Florentines owned Club Wicked, and they were without a doubt one of the most powerful couples in Washington, DC. Mr. Florentine had been a top prosecuting attorney for the state of Virginia before he'd done a stint as a senator. Mrs. Florentine was originally a cultural ambassador for France before she'd met Mr. Florentine. There were even some rumors that at some point she'd been with the CIA. That was purely speculation, but the woman intimidated the hell out of everyone who met her, Dom and sub alike. Now both Mr. and Mrs. Florentine were retired, but they had more connections than God.

Liam considered the Florentines his friends, but usually if they wanted to talk to him, they called him first unless it was an emergency. To be summoned like this was disconcerting since he was impatient to see Rhiannon, even as he worried about what the Florentines wanted. He found himself scanning the slice of the room, hoping for a glimpse of Rhiannon.

Rory recovered first and straightened his back. "Of course. Where would we find them?"

"If you'll please follow me, I'll take you to them. It's a full moon tonight, so Mrs. Florentine has arranged a small garden party on the roof."

Liam's unease melted away. If it was something bad, the Florentines would never air their grievances in front of other members. They had more class than that. If it was just a party, they'd stay long enough to be polite, find out what the Florentines wanted, then go find Rhiannon.

They were quiet as they took the elevator to the roof. Once the doors slid open, the guard smiled. "Enjoy your evening, Sirs."

Stepping out into the enormous rooftop garden always made Liam's mood lift. This was a private place for the Florentines, and they allowed only their most trusted friends up there. Small white lights had been strung through the trees, giving more than enough light to see by when combined with the full moon shining down through the glass panes high above.

Laughter and conversation came from their left, so the men made their way over a stone-paved walkway and over the grass. When they passed beneath a climbing-rose-covered archway, Liam could only grin at the sight before them. Two beautiful submissives, one male and one female, stood in the middle of an enormous table in the center of the clearing. They were tethered together by clamps on their nipples, and if he wasn't mistaken, the male submissive was buried up to his balls in the female's cunt.

Arousal punched him as the sound of a woman having a very nice orgasm came from the shadowy area to their right.

Seated around the table were some of the more senior members of Club Wicked, and at the end, Mr. and Mrs. Florentine held court. Both in their seventies with silver hair, they radiated power and sophistication. Mrs. Florentine smiled at Rory and Liam, then stood, smoothing down the blue linen of her dress. Though she was a submissive, Liam had never seen her do a scene. He had a hard time imagining the regal woman submitting to anyone. Not that he really wanted to watch Mr. and Mrs. Florentine play. It would be like watching his aunt and uncle have sex.

Shaking his head to clear that unholy image out of his mind, Liam made his way to where Mr. and Mrs. Florentine now stood. Mr. Florentine wore an impeccable suit with a tie and handkerchief in the breast pocket that matched Mrs. Florentine's dress perfectly. Mr. Florentine's still thick hair gleamed in the low lighting, and his smile was warm and genuine.

"Liam. Rory." Mrs. Florentine gave them both a kiss on the cheek. The scent of her floral perfume teased Liam's senses. She wasn't one to call anyone Master except her husband. "Thank you for coming to see us."

Mr. Florentine offered his arm to his wife. "Gentlemen, let's walk."

Liam could almost feel the curious gazes on their backs as they walked down a path of the garden he had never been on. Soon they came out to another clearing, but this one had the most amazing hedge animals he'd ever seen. A rabbit stood on his hind legs to Liam's left, a curious tilt to his head. The sculpture was so well done that Liam could almost see an inquisitive expression. Gas lanterns circled the garden, adding to the effect of making the animals look as if they were moving.

Rory walked over to a fox and inspected it. "Wow, this is amazing."

With a soft laugh, Mrs. Florentine gestured to a grouping of black wrought-iron furniture covered with comfortable cream padded cushions. "Please, have a seat. We won't take long as we know you have other obligations tonight with Rhiannon."

Rory and Liam exchanged a glance. Liam could easily read his friend's surprise, and he tried to keep his tone bland as he said, "How can we help you?"

Mr. Florentine leaned forward and clasped his hands together. "What I'm about to say is strictly between us. If you ever breathe word of it to anyone other than Rhiannon, I'll have your balls in my trophy case."

Damned if Liam didn't feel intimidated. That happened so rarely, it caught him by surprise. "Of course."

With a low sigh, Mr. Florentine sat back and sought his wife's hand. "Let me just start out by saying that Rhiannon has given me permission to share this with those I deem necessary. If you two are going to take her on, you fall into the need-to-know column. Seven years ago, during my last year as a practicing lawyer, I helped to put one of the biggest child pornography rings in the world out of business."

Mrs. Florentine gave an audible swallow. "It was terrible. I still have nightmares about those poor children."

"One of our key witnesses was Rhiannon."

Rory glanced over at Liam, and the sorrow that Liam saw in his friend's eyes mirrored his own. "What happened?"

"Long story short, she met a man on the Internet when she was fourteen. You have to understand that Rhiannon dropped out of school in the tenth grade. In the environment she grew up in, her life's goal was to get married and have a family of her own by the time she was sixteen."

"What?"

"It's part of their culture in the American Roma family that Rhiannon was born into," Mrs. Florentine said. "I know it sounds strange to us, but for hundreds of years, that's how gypsy girls were raised. They grow up their whole life looking forward to getting married. For some it is the consummate moment of their life. I'm not saying all gypsies are like that, but in the insular community that Rhiannon grew up in, they were, and she was very, very sheltered by her family. Everywhere she went, including school, she had male relatives who would in effect chaperone her, giving her no chance to do all the normal flirting and talking with the opposite sex that young girls do in order to learn how to interact with men. This left her more vulnerable than most girls her age to the manipulations of an older, more experienced man."

Mr. Florentine patted her hand. "When Rhiannon was a week shy of her sixteenth birthday, she decided to elope with this man she'd been talking to on the Internet for two years. They met in an online forum where teenage girls got together to talk about books. Her parents thought her computer was safe to use because they had all those child-lock programs on it. Rhiannon believed the man she was talking to was in his late teens, and when he began to groom her, to manipulate her into trusting him, he couldn't have picked a more naive girl."

Liam swallowed his anger and tried to keep calm. "How old was he?"

"Thirty-eight. He was a computer programmer living outside Richmond, Virginia."

"Fuck."

"Indeed. I'm not going to go into the details of what happened, but I will say that he convinced her to run away, and that he had her for three days before he was caught. In that time he did some terrible things."

Rory reached out and clutched Liam's wrist. "Is he in jail?"

"Yes. For a long, long time. It was Rhiannon's testimony that put him away."

"Why are you telling us this?"

Mrs. Florentine scooted forward and looked them both in the eye before she said, "Because we're begging you to take her on as a trainee."

Rory and Liam exchanged a startled look. "Why?"

"Beyond the tragedy of her past, we've talked to the girl in-depth, and we believe Rhiannon is a born submissive. Whatever it is that makes certain women crave dominance, it has been a part of Rhiannon before she ever met that bastard. We know that she's approached you for training, and we hope that you will really consider taking her on."

Liam's stomach churned as he imagined all the terrible things that could have happened to Rhiannon when she was being held captive. Mrs. Florentine watched him with a compassionate gaze as he struggled to compose himself. "With all due respect, Mr. and Mrs. Florentine, are you sure she's ready for this? For us?"

Mr. Florentine met Liam's gaze and held it. "Yes, I do. Rhiannon has worked very, very hard to not let her past destroy her future. Women since the beginning of time have been hurt in one way or another but still managed to fall in love again. Rhiannon is ready to move on to the next phase of her life, to find love and a Master deserving of her and able to give her what she needs."

Mrs. Florentine sighed. "I believe that Rhiannon's one of those old-fashioned women who is happier letting a man make the decisions in her life. I'm not talking a Total Power Exchange relationship. More like she needs someone to be her John Wayne."

Liam cleared his throat. "I'm not quite sure of your meaning."

A soft breeze blew through the garden, and he briefly wondered where it was coming from since they were enclosed by glass. Mr. Florentine crossed his leg, while Liam tried to not fidget as Mr. Florentine closely observed him. The other man may have left the courtroom behind, but he still had that eagle eye that made Liam feel like Mr. Florentine could read his mind. "It means she needs a Master worthy of the gift of her submission, because she is going to do everything in her power to make him happy. We want to make sure she finds the love she needs with a man that deserves her and recognizes Rhiannon for the priceless treasure that she is."

Mrs. Florentine nodded at her husband, then turned back to look at them. "And you, gentlemen, are what she needs to do that. We understand that you need a break, we really do, and you very much deserve it. You've done brilliant work with the submissives that have come into your care. But we are certain that you can help Rhiannon. Over the years that you've been training submissives for us we've seen how kind and compassionate you are, but at the same time you are Masters in every sense of the word. You've performed miracles with shy submissives, given women who don't believe they're worth anything a self-confidence that is a joy to see. While Rhiannon isn't exactly like the women you usually train, she needs someone to believe in her, to make her believe that she's worth loving."

Mr. Florentine took a deep breath. "If you do this for us, we will make you members of the board."

Rory made a choked sound, and Liam said, "What?"

"We are expanding the board to thirteen members. Club Wicked is ever changing and evolving, and our board members are being stretched thin. We'd like you on the board as a representative for the submissives."

"You would be their advocate," Mr. Florentine quickly added. "The club submissives love you, and we know you will always do what is right for them, even if it's not easy."

Liam ran his hand over his head. "Can we discuss that at a later date? To be honest, we've got more than we can handle already between work and training."

"Yes," Mrs. Florentine said with a purr in her voice that didn't bode well for Rory and Liam. Mrs. Florentine never gave men that sugary smile without there being trouble. "Let's discuss your training. For three years we've been begging you to take on an apprentice or two, but so far, you've managed to avoid training another Dom or Domme to help you out. You are overworking yourself. I don't care what your excuse is. You need to approve some more trainers."

Looking between Liam and Rory, Mr. Florentine said, "We

have a great many Masters and Mistresses that would love to take on a more official training role at Club Wicked. You wouldn't have to worry about teaching them, just mentor them until you feel they are ready to take on more responsibility. Let's face it, we've had to turn away too many submissives that need help because your schedule is already full. It's not fair to them or you."

Guilt settled into Liam with a sickening clench of his muscles. The real reason Liam didn't want to train another Dom was he didn't want to watch Rory interacting with the other man. He got crazy jealous anytime Rory did a scene with another Master. Not that Rory was ever sexual with another guy but just watching someone touch him as they worked a submissive over together made Liam grit his teeth.

"We'll think about it," Rory said in a neutral tone, but Liam could tell he'd been thrown off stride.

Mrs. Florentine stood, and all three men followed suit. She tilted her head while giving Rory and Liam a measured look. "Please really do consider training Rhiannon. We will give you the run of Wicked. Anything you want, any fantasy you want to provide her, let us know, and we will make it happen. We care deeply for her and want only the best."

The fondness in Mr. Florentine's gaze when he looked at his wife made Liam slightly envious of their open affection. "Though if Rhiannon claims to have a pirate fantasy, make sure it isn't really Mrs. Florentine who wants to sail around on a replica pirate ship while being ravaged by the scurvy crew."

"Gary! Behave yourself," Mrs. Florentine said in shocked voice.

Mr. Florentine waved a dismissal as he gave his wife a heated look. "Off with you now. I need to ravage my wench."

Normally Liam would have chuckled at seeing the impeccable Mrs. Florentine so flustered, but his mind was overflowing. Between the revelations about the abuse Rhiannon had suffered to basically being ordered to find some new trainers to lighten the load, he couldn't think straight.

"I need a bloody drink," Rory muttered.

Liam nodded in agreement. "Me too. How much time do we have before Rhiannon gets off?"

"I'm not sure, but I think we can take ten minutes to get our shit together."

"That'll give us enough time to chug a beer."

They quickly made their way to the Viewing Room bar. Once inside, they had to pause to let their eyes adjust to the odd lighting. The floor was completely transparent to reveal the dungeon situated below. Inside the large space, several couples made use of the BDSM implements. They hooked a left and went to the bar set at the back corner. After ordering two beers, they selected a pair of chairs above a woman getting paddled by her Mistress while secured with hot pink bondage tape to a spanking horse. Her round arse jiggled as her Mistress struck her over and over.

Liam took a long drink of his beer, enjoying the silence of the room. This was a space that Dominants used as a place to unwind and relax. Conversation was kept low and to a minimum, which allowed Liam a chance to try to organize himself. Clasping the cold bottle of his beer between his hands, he stared at the room below them.

"We can't turn her down," Rory said in a low voice.

"Who? Rhiannon or Mrs. Florentine?"

"Rhiannon."

The affectionate way Rory said her name made Liam look up. Sure enough Rory had a small smile tilting his lips, and his tense posture had relaxed. "You sure about this?"

"Absolutely."

The knot in Liam's gut began to loosen at the confidence in his friend's voice, and he took a deep breath. If Rory thought they could train Rhiannon, then they could. "This is going to be hard."

"It is."

"I don't want to mess the poor lass up."

"Neither do I."

"You do realize that we're taking on a sub here who will need our complete attention."

"Yes."

"You also know that we're going to have to somehow treat her very gently but give her the sense of domination she needs.

And I doubt she'd be happy with either of us having sex with another woman. So we'll be going through a dry spell until she's ready for us."

"Yeah." He took a long drink of his beer. "It's going to be a pisser."

"I'll need to stock up on lube."

Both men sighed, then softly laughed. Liam clasped Rory's shoulder, needing to establish some kind of contact between them, even if it was platonic. "I can—"

He suddenly found himself surrounded by three very determined-looking submissives. Kira, Dove, and Kitten stood before him. The pretty auburn-haired Kira was heavily pregnant. Dove had her long blonde hair pulled back in a braid, and she seemed to be wearing some kind of sexy farm-girl outfit. She'd tied a blue plaid shirt under her breasts and had it unbuttoned until her large tits almost fell out. He'd done a scene with Dove and her Master that had been hot as fuck, so his cock gave a stir at the sight of all that creamy cleavage.

The lovely Latina, Kitten, tapped her black high heel on the floor in an impatient rhythm that matched her agitated stance. Tonight she wore a sparkling black cocktail dress that went well with her dark good looks. She also wore a matching mask that made her look like a cat. "Master Liam, Master Rory," Kitten said in a cordial tone. "Why the fuck aren't you going to train Goddess?"

Rory gave her a sharp look. "What?"

Dove took a step forward, her hands on her rounded hips. "If you didn't want to train her, you should have told her to her face instead of just not showing up."

Liam set his beer down, the need to paddle some sub's arse making his palms itch. "Woman, you will watch your tone with us. You're being rude, and you're not being clear."

Now it was Kira's turn to yell at them. And yell she did. "She's crying her eyes out right now because you bastards left her waiting. She's been wandering around for the past twenty minutes trying to find you. No one knew where you were. Only that you'd arrived, then vanished. She thinks you're with another submissive right now."

Both men stared at Kira, and Rory sputtered out, "Why the hell would she think that?"

From around the room came hushing noises, and the girls all blushed.

Dove lowered her voice. "Because the competition for your attention among the subs is fierce now that you're in-between trainees. Word spread that Rhi—er, Goddess met with you, and the claws came out. More than one bitch tried to scare Goddess off. A few members said some shit that was nasty enough that I would have beat the crap out of them if they said it to me. We didn't find out what was going on until Mistress Onyx clued us in. Said she couldn't intervene but asked if we would find you and let you know."

Kira actually began to tear up as she spoke. "Poor Goddess. She's so sure that you don't want her. Do you have any idea how hard it was for her to seek you out? How many hours we had to spend with her convincing her that you wouldn't think she was dirty or used or all that other fucking evil bullshit that tears away at her self-esteem? You probably don't know this, but she really is kind beneath her bitchy exterior, and you just flat out avoiding her is tearing her up. How could you, Master Liam?"

"Where is she?" Rory asked through clenched teeth.

Kitten handed Kira a tissue while she looked at the men and asked, "Are you going to train her?"

"That's between us and her, girl. Now where is she?"

A man's deep voice cut through the air behind him. "Well, well, well. What do we have here? Three little brats causing a ruckus when they told us they were going to the ladies' room?"

Master Isaac, Master Jesse, and Master Bryan all came around into Liam's field of sight, and their submissives blanched. Their shocked and guilty looks would have been funny if Liam wasn't so fucking pissed at himself and Rory for misjudging the time and at the people who had been verbally attacking Rhiannon. He wanted to hunt the offenders down and let them know how it felt to be hurt like that.

The three girls began to babble out apologies, but Master Bryan raised his hand, then said in a low voice, "Master Rory, Master Liam, I apologize for our submissives' behavior.

Gentlemen, I assure you it will be addressed and our girls will have a renewed respect for minding their own bloody business."

Kira paled, but Kitten lifted her chin. "We were just trying to help Goddess."

Master Isaac, dressed in a black tux that gave him a James Bond look, shook his head. "Did she ask you to yell at and scold Master Rory and Master Liam?"

Kitten gulped. "No."

Master Jesse took a step closer to Dove, and the small woman trembled. "Did you politely inquire as to what was going on, or did you come in here mad and yelling?"

"I wasn't yelling," Dove said in a whisper as tears filled her eyes.

Master Isaac pulled a ball gag out of his pocket. "Come here."

While Kitten was being gagged, Master Jesse had Dove's braid in his grip. By her pained expression, he was pulling hard enough to hurt. "The road to hell is paved with good intentions, baby. But you know better than pulling a stunt like this. Next time talk to me before you decide to go off in the quiet bar at Wicked."

Dove stopped struggling. "What do you mean the quiet bar?"

"Notice how nobody is talking but you? This is where the Dominants of Wicked come to relax. Not to hear you harpies shrieking. You pissed off a number of Tops tonight. Better be glad I don't share or your ass would be paddled until it bled."

Liam stood and focused his gaze on the trio of submissives. "Where is Goddess?"

Kira blew her nose, then said, "She's in the glittery safe room on the third floor. Master Hawk is making sure no one goes in there."

Jealousy and anger made Liam lose control of his tongue. Yes, she'd said she didn't have any romantic feelings for Hawk, but she'd trusted him to keep her safe. Liam wanted her to trust him like that. "Then shouldn't he be looking after her instead of us?"

Kira shook her head and leaned in to whisper to Liam and

Rory, "Absolutely not. She's terrified of him. Don't you know? Master Hawk is a dead ringer for the man who kidnapped her."

Chapter Seven

Too impatient to find out what the hell was going on with Rhiannon to dawdle, Rory took the stairs two at a time as he moved quickly through Wicked with Liam at his side. They hadn't exchanged a word, but Rory could feel his best mate's tension and frustration. It practically boiled off the other man and was doing nothing to help Rory calm down.

Hawk, who was standing outside the door of the safe room, watched them approach with a dark stare. His sharp Native American features could look downright intimidating when he chose. Unfortunately that glare only made Rory's protective instincts flare to life. Knowing that Hawk shared similar physical characteristics with the man who had brutalized Rhiannon made Rory's blood boil. It had probably been a major trigger and thrown her into a terrible flashback. He'd have to talk to Hawk later and find out what frightened Rhiannon so much. They needed to make sure that her life was filled with nothing but comfort and security while they trained her. She had to know that she was an impossibly precious woman and any Dom should treat her like a princess. In fact he wanted to give her something to let her know how important she was to him, how much she mattered, and that she wasn't alone anymore.

He gave Liam a quick look. "We're going to need to take her to the jeweler's soon to get her training collar."

Liam gave a short laugh, and Rory's shoulders eased as some of the tension left his friend. "You mean if she doesn't kick us in the bullocks first?"

"Well, there is that."

Hawk looked at each of them with a dark frown. "What happened?"

Giving Hawk a curt nod, Rory said, "The Florentines happened."

"Brought us up for a private chat about Rhiannon."

Hawk moved away from the door. "So you know you need to be gentle with her, right?"

Liam shook his head. "No, we'll be firm with her, and it will help her relax more than any gentle touch ever will."

Hawk grinned and backed up. "And that, gentlemen, is why you are the best trainers to ever grace the lovely halls of Wicked."

"Piss off," Rory said, trying to hide how much the other man's compliment warmed his heart.

With a laugh, Hawk waved and strode down the hall.

They looked at each other, and Rory gripped Liam's shoulder. "Nothing but positive around her, got it? I know I'm a fucking annoying bastard, and you want to pound my face in, but we need to shelve that shit."

Liam looked irritated, and Rory was afraid they were going to have another fight. But to his surprise, Liam merely shrugged his shoulders and rolled his neck. "Right. I won't be think'n about noth'n but lollies and unicorns."

Using the small dose of humor to fortify himself, Rory opened the door and took a moment to appreciate the room even as his inner caveman winced at being surrounded by such excessive femininity. Being in this space was like being inside a giant glittery soap bubble. Some kind of light show threw shimmering and ever-changing patterns on the walls. In the center of the room there was a giant circular bed covered in mounds of lacy pillows. A submissive could snuggle among all those pillows and have the sensation of being held.

The walls began to fade to green and gold sparkles, giving the bed a rather surreal look. Rhiannon sat curled among the pillows like something out of a fairy tale. Tonight she wore a lovely black silk sheath dress that dipped down in the back all the way to the top rise of her bum. She also wore a black G-string that hooked together in the back with a pair of miniature handcuffs. Around her wrists and ankles were silver cuffs that had tiny padlocks on them. With her long hair loose around her, bits of her body peeked through the curtain of dark locks and her dress.

Rory wanted to kiss every perfect inch of exposed skin on that woman's body.

Liam made a low, pained sound, and Rory sighed.

She slayed him without any effort.

He knew she heard them come in, but she wouldn't turn. "Rhiannon, love, we lost track of time."

Liam took a step closer to the bed. "Yeah. We don't like to wear watches while we're here."

Still nothing, but she began to wiggle her toes. She'd painted her toenails with some kind of shimmery red nail polish. On her second toe she'd placed a silver ring that made her look even more feminine. Everything about her was worn to tease a Master, to tempt him to think about putting bondage cuffs on her or suck on her toes while he fucked her.

"We feel like right bastards. Hate us if you want, yell and scream, but don't shut us out." Liam ran his hand over his head in a frustrated gesture.

She curled her toes again and turned her head just the slightest bit. "Why are you here?"

Liam stepped forward and brushed her hair off her face. "I want to see you when I talk to you, lass. No hiding those lovely eyes from me."

It hurt Rory's heart to see the evidence of her tears in the form of black streaks down her cheeks. "How did you know I was here?"

Liam snorted. "The terrible trio decided to find myself and Master Rory and make known their opinion about our inability to tell time."

Taking a cue from Liam's teasing tone, Rory added in an exasperated voice, "In a very loud, abrasive manner, I might add. Felt like I was getting scolded by my mum."

Rory couldn't stand how sad her gaze was when she looked at him. Her mouth opened and closed a few times before she said, "I'm sorry. They overreacted. Please, return to whatever you were doing. This was a mistake."

"Lass, we didn't mean to hurt your feelings."

"No, I'm okay—"

Rory placed his hand over her mouth hard enough to let her know he could make her be silent. Liam moved closer and began to run his hand in a possessive manner over her exposed leg. By the saints, she had the softest skin he'd ever felt. Made him want to rub himself over her, bare naked. She'd be so warm and wet for him.

The give of her lips against his hand tempted Rory to kiss her. "Don't lie to us. You can say you don't wish to talk about it at this time and we'll respect your wishes."

Liam added with a low growl, "But don't fucking lie. We know when you're doing it, and we don't like it."

Rory removed his hand. She licked her lips, then turned over so she was kneeling among the pillows on the bed. The front of her top was almost transparent, and Rory went rock hard at the sight of her tight fucking body and large breasts. No doubt Rhiannon had been put on this good earth to show men how easily a female could reduce males to the rutting beasts they were. Her stomach clenched, and the cute dangling emerald strand she'd put on her belly button ring trembled against her taut flesh.

"I'm sorry. I thought you were busy with someone else."

"Why would you think that?"

She flushed and looked down. "Someone said they saw you doing a scene with another submissive."

"Why would you—"

Liam gave him a look that made Rory swallow his words. "Lass, who said that?"

"I'd rather not say." She firmed her lips, and he got a glimpse of the steel in her spine. It was nice to know she'd stand up for herself if need be. "So why are you here? Do you want to win the bet?"

Confused, Rory frowned at her. "What bet?"

Her harsh laugh startled him. "Oh, come on. You know what bet. I hear the prize is up to two hundred and fifty thousand dollars for the first Dominant at Club Wicked that manages to fuck me."

Rory stared at her, not sure if he was more offended that she'd think that of him, or more hurt that she thought so little of herself. "I would never, ever make that kind of bet or participate in it. You aren't an object to be won, Rhiannon."

With an obvious effort to remain calm, Liam said in a low voice, "I'm not going to say I'm surprised to hear the wager—there are bloody arseholes that'll bet over anything—but if there is such a bet, we've never heard of it."

Rhiannon's lower lip trembled. "I knew I shouldn't have believed them, but it...it's hard to believe that you would want me."

"Want you?" Liam groaned. "Lass, I've been counting the minutes until I got to see you again."

She sighed and tried to wipe the tears off her face, smearing her makeup further and lending to the vulnerable look that tugged at Rory's heart. "I'm sorry I messed up your night."

He exchanged a glance with Liam. "Well, I wouldn't consider this evening a loss. Right now we're alone, with a beautiful woman, and a huge bed. Sounds like a pretty good way to spend the rest of my night to me."

She blinked at him and said in a soft, almost scared tone, "Would you please hold me? Both of you?"

Without answering her, the men took off their shoes before climbing on the bed. Liam slid behind her, then pulled her feet into his lap. Not that Rory was surprised. Liam had a bit of a foot fetish, and Rory had to admit she had really cute feet. Not giving her a chance to react, Rory moved to her other side and arranged her between them until they were all surrounded by pillows. In an odd way it was almost like being in a nest, but he knew it would bring Rhiannon comfort. At first Rhiannon was stiff in his arms, but he began to pet her in a nice, easy rhythm, and she slowly relaxed. He kept his touch gentle, not sexual. He'd found that sometimes the body knew what it wanted long before the mind came to a decision. He wanted to encourage Rhiannon to embrace the pleasure they could offer and trust them, and so far it seemed to be working.

As he touched her, he tried to keep his mind from returning to the revelations about her past they'd learned from the

Florentines tonight. To say he was angry about what happened to her when she was an innocent teenager was like saying a hurricane brought a nice breeze inland during the summer. Desperate to think about something else, he forced himself to appreciate the perfection of her skin and how nicely she fit against him. His only focus was Rhiannon—her happiness, her joy. Negative emotions did not belong here. He'd deal with the anger that threatened to break his self-control after they were done.

Liam played with the ring on her toe, and Rory noted his best mate had a rather healthy erection tenting his kilt. One of Rory's reoccurring fantasies was to reach beneath that kilt and jack Liam off while they kissed. God, he was hot for both of them, each his perfect fantasy in their own way. At some point she had parted her legs, and he could see the cleft of her pussy covered with those tiny panties. The slightest bit of dark pubic hair showed around the edges, and he couldn't wait to eat her. Fuck. He was salivating at the very thought, but that was a treat for a later time.

Tonight was all about making up for causing her to doubt both them and herself.

Rory caught Liam's gaze, and, after checking that Rhiannon's eyes were closed, he mouthed the words, *Tell her about training?*

Liam nodded; then Rory said, "Beautiful girl, we'd be honored to take you on as our trainee."

Her eyes opened, and her gaze shot to him; then she tried to move out of his arms. "Really?"

Liam laughed. "Yes, really. You are a lovely woman, inside and out. We want to help you learn how to show that to the rest of the world."

A tender emotion that Rory didn't want to acknowledge rolled through him as he cupped Rhiannon's chin in his hand. She had such an expressive face without her ice-queen mask on, and he gently brushed her smeared mascara from beneath her eyes. Her gaze widened; then she gasped.

"Oh no! I must look like a raccoon!"

"A sexy one," Liam agreed.

"A sexy raccoon?" She stared at Liam, then began to giggle.

"I think you need to see a therapist."

"Cheeky lass," Liam growled. He sat up and kicked a few pillows out of the way before dragging her across his lap.

"What are you doing?"

"Reminding you of the price you pay for pissing off a Dom."

When she wiggled, her dress rode up, and Rory groaned at how fuckable her ass looked. Smooth and a light brown color that made him think of bronze. "You're not my Dom yet."

Liam patted her bottom. "Don't be coy, lass. Either I'm your Master or I'm not. Am I your Master?"

She wiggled beneath his hand, and Rory tried to fight down his jealousy that Liam got to touch her.

"Yes, Sir," she whispered in a barely audible voice.

"What was that?"

"Yes, Sir."

"And what about Rory? Is he your Master as well?"

A small shudder ran through her, and she answered in a husky tone, "Yes, Sir. You are my Masters. If you'll have me."

Rory couldn't help but laugh. "Darling girl, we want nothing more in the world than to have you. As many ways as possible, over and over again."

Rory exchanged a grin with Liam as elation filled him. They would help her, they would heal her, and Rory was pretty sure they would fall in love with her. He could only hope they survived the loss when she left them to find her true Master.

Feeling the need to connect with Rhiannon, he gently pulled her into his lap and out of Liam's arms. "Such a good girl." She glowed at his praise, her smile warming him from the inside out. "I think you've had enough excitement for the night, and Master Liam and I have to discuss your training. But we'd like to hold you for a few more minutes. Touching you is a pleasure that we greatly enjoy."

She let out a long, deep sigh that made her melt into Rory's arms. When she snuggled into his chest, it felt natural to hold her close and rub his lips over her head. The bed dipped when Liam slid up from her feet. Liam wrapped his arms around Rhiannon and set his head almost near enough to Rory's to kiss. They stared at each other as the woman between them hummed with happiness and seemed to try to get as close to them as she could. He pulled back a bit and caught Liam's gaze. The determination he saw there mirrored his own and the weight on his shoulders lightened. He knew his best mate well enough to know that Liam was falling for the sweet girl in their arms as well.

One of the things he loved most about Liam was his compassion. The man was everyone's friend and made those around him instantly comfortable. Rory was so used to talking to high-society ass kissers and backstabbers that he marveled at Liam's ability to let people into his life. It took a good deal of time for Rory to allow someone to get close.

Well, it used to.

With Rhiannon, from the moment he saw her without her mask on, he wanted her. All of her. Now that he knew the woman beneath her bitchy exterior, had a glimpse into her wounded but still generous heart, he would destroy worlds to make her happy.

Shaken by the intensity of his thoughts, he untangled himself from Rhiannon and stood. She looked up at him with such hope that he felt like he was ten feet tall. While he liked subs to be bratty at times, obvious devotion filled a place in his heart that always seemed empty. It was like some primitive instinct told him that this woman was the female for him, his perfect mate.

It wasn't love—not yet—but it had potential, and that scared him. He was already fucked-up enough in the love department with Liam. At the same time, however, he really wanted to see how far it could go with Rhiannon. Not that he was planning on doing anything to manipulate her into being his permanent submissive, but he would give her such amazing satisfaction, both sexual and emotional, that she would never desire for anything else. In a perfect world, Liam would fall in love with her as well. It was selfish, and it was stupid, but he couldn't help but hope that if he could get Liam to love Rhiannon, somehow his relationship with the other man would improve.

Chapter Eight

Rhiannon looked into the private dressing room mirror adjoining the "classroom" at Club Wicked. Her Masters had given specific instructions what to wear. She'd loved the gleam of lust in both their gazes as they'd described the outfit. So here she stood, looking like an insanely slutty schoolgirl, and she couldn't be happier.

All day she'd anticipated beginning her training. Master Rory would be out of town late tomorrow for business, and he wanted to make sure that they started before he had to leave. She'd spent the day pampering herself, making sure every part of her body was scrubbed and buffed until it glowed. She loved having two men to dress up for.

While feminism was great, and she sure as heck was grateful for all the things she could do because of the women before her fighting for their rights, Rhiannon's wishes were very simple. She wanted a man worthy of her love so she could give herself to him 100 percent and trust him to take care of her. The thought of someday having her own family with her Master, of filling their house with laughter and love, made her heart ache and tears burn in her throat. She missed her family immensely, but since she couldn't go back in time and change the past, she'd have to work on making a family of her own someday. And she would never abandon her children no matter what they did.

In an effort to keep her mind on the present, she turned and looked at her outfit with a critical eye.

She wore a teeny-tiny plaid skirt that sat low on her hips and barely covered her sex. The men asked her to put on a pair of transparent white panties. It made the dark hair on her mound stand out from the dusky pink of her shaved pussy lips that pressed against the fabric in an indecent way. Her top consisted of a small white shirt that tied beneath her breasts, and because she wasn't wearing a bra, her hard nipples pressed at the fabric. She wore a small red leather tie around her neck.

To complete her look she'd donned a pair of knee-high white stockings and her shoes were what Dove called "fuck me" stilettos. Shiny black leather with a steel spike on the tips of the heels. They were hard to balance in, but Rhiannon had to admit they firmed the muscles of her legs all the way up to her ass. She smiled and gave a little twirl. From the accessory table she chose a simple white plastic headband. She'd taken off her makeup and just put on an ultrawet-looking cherry-red lip gloss and a hint of sparkly eye shadow.

She inspected herself and almost didn't recognize the woman looking back at her. For one thing she hadn't stopped smiling since the Masters had told her they would take her on as a trainee. She'd been so *sure* they didn't want her. It was stupid—she knew it was stupid—but when she trusted someone, it was all or nothing. If there was a way to hold back her emotions, she hadn't been able to figure it out yet. Which was why she only dated extremely gentle, kind, and almost submissive men who were wonderful but completely vanilla in the bedroom, leaving her sexually dissatisfied.

She had to hold some kind of record for faking orgasms.

But that wasn't going to happen tonight.

The inner muscles of her sex did an involuntary clench, and she closed her eyes. Her Masters told her that no matter what, they wanted her to be a brat tonight. Some Doms loved it when a sub bratted out, so she had to be proficient enough in it to satisfy both Master Liam and Master Rory.

She'd been e-mailing back and forth with both Masters, answering their questions and asking some of her own while talking on the phone with Kira. The other woman was a well-known brat and took pride in it. She'd given Rhiannon tips on how to act. The men had been very honest and open with her, and she'd even gotten Master Rory to admit one of his fantasies. Just the memory of what he said was so scandalous that it made her blush. Who knew that a man would find it arousing to eat another man's seed from a woman's freshly fucked pussy?

She walked as quickly as she could to the door. She'd dithered around in here, wasting time until she was sure the Masters would be irritated. They wanted a brat, they would get a brat. Having a role to play made this so much easier. Now she could lose herself in her character without any guilt about being slutty or a whore.

Those terrible words had been the last ones she'd heard from her father before she was kicked out for running off with an outsider and bringing the attention of the police and the media to their community. Hard, cruel words that had destroyed the last vestiges of innocence in the young girl she'd once been. To make matters worse, her entire family had been there to witness her being kicked out, and no one had stepped in to save her. Not even her mother.

She forced herself to open the door and step through into the school-themed playroom. She wasn't a slut, but she could pretend during role-playing.

Her heels hit the polished wood floors with a decisive *click* that made her Masters look up from where they were standing at the front of the mock classroom. On either side of her two rows of school desks lined the aisle. Directly before her Master Rory stood behind a podium, dressed in an impeccable gray three-piece suit. He also wore a pair of glasses with thin silver frames. The color set off the coldness in his gaze. A delighted shiver went through her.

She'd tried to role-play with one of her ex-boyfriends. It just seemed like Fred dressed as Superman in bed with her, not Superman himself. That wasn't going to be the case with Rory. He held himself differently now, and there was a dismissive turn to his generous lips that made him seem more imposing, more stern than usual.

Master Liam had exchanged his leather kilt for a plaid one that matched her plaid skirt. He wore a white button-down shirt and a black suit jacket over it. The suit jacket had a patch of some kind on it, and as she sauntered down the aisle toward them, she could make out the words Club Wicked Training Academy on it.

"How good of you to finally join us, Ms. Rhiannon," Master

Rory said as he studied her from the other side of the podium.

She slouched against the side of one desk and crossed her legs slowly, making sure each man was looking as she shifted enough to almost give them a hint of her sex. "Sorry. Had stuff to do."

Master Liam slammed his hand down on the desk. "We are here as a favor to you. Without our tutoring, you will fail your biology exam on the human anatomy. I will not tolerate such disrespect from a student."

Blinking rapidly, she tried to force her mind to think about something other than the kinky things they could do with a class like that. "Sorry, Sir."

Master Rory raised an eyebrow, and she quickly corrected herself, remembering she was a brat. Curling her upper lip, she sneered at them. "I'm here, so let's get this over with. I have a party I need to go tonight. You know, people to see, guys to do."

"Sit down," Master Rory said in a low voice that made her sex clench again.

Goodness, she wanted him in the worst way.

With a huff, she took a seat in the front row. Because of the height of the desk she had a hard time crossing her legs. Finally she just gave up and sat with her knees pressed close together. Both men watched her, and she grew a bit nervous. They were so big, so strong. They could do anything they wanted to her. Unease tried to worm its way into her heart, but Master Liam chose that moment to move from around the table.

He sported an erection that pushed against the fabric of the kilt in a way that should have looked silly, but instead Rhiannon found it really, really sexy and it turned her on something fierce. She wondered what his cock looked like up close, how thick he was, how much he was going to stretch her. Her sex continued to throb with the beat of her heart, and she couldn't remember a time when she'd been more aroused without having even been touched. Even hours of sex with one of her ex-boyfriends hadn't led to this desperate craving.

Master Rory gripped the lectern and leaned forward. "When asked on your final exam what the name of the female sexual organs were, you replied 'a cunt.'"

She flushed and looked down at her hands. Swearing was one of those things that made her uncomfortable yet aroused. "What? You wanted me to call it a pussy?"

Master Liam picked up a ruler off the table and hit it on the surface hard enough to make her jump. "Watch that insolent mouth."

Feeling bold, she stuck her tongue out at him and grinned when he gave her a wink. Master Rory was very intense in his role-playing, which she liked, but Master Liam also made it fun. Sometimes laughter was even better than sex.

"Girl, eyes on me."

She immediately gave her attention to Master Rory and swallowed hard. He looked so darn good in his suit; she wanted to rip it off him in the worst way. More than that she loved how possessive his gaze was, how commanding and in control. She loved men who were strong, both inside and out.

"Ms. Rhiannon, since you're such an expert on the female anatomy, why don't you tell me about the G-spot."

"Um..." She tried to remember what little she knew. "It's a place inside a woman that can be stimulated during sex."

Master Liam scoffed, "My grandmother could give a better answer than that."

"Do you talk about sex with your granny a lot?"

Instead of being amused, Master Liam gave her a stern look that sent pleasurable little shivers through her. Her pussy ached with the need to be touched. She parted her legs and slowly slid her hand down the front of her panties.

Let's see how they liked a little bit of teasing.

"Hold on. Let me see if I can find that spot."

Holding Master Liam's stare, she widened her stance farther. His gaze moved between to the juncture of her thighs, and passion flared in those hazel depths. When he glanced back up at her face, she took in a small breath at the desire suffusing his features. He captured her with his eyes, enchanting her will to his, making her want to serve him, to make him happy, to make him come.

He shifted and gave his cock a leisurely stroke through his

kilt, and she gulped in a huge breath of air.

"Sir, I know I haven't studied as much as I should for this class." She began to stroke her pussy through the thin panel of transparent fabric. "But I really do need to pass it. Is there any kind of special credit I could do?"

Master Rory cleared his throat. "Actually, there is. I've been researching the G-spot, and I need a volunteer to experiment on."

Not sure exactly what he was talking about, she shrugged and removed her finger from her panties, then licked it before answering him. "Anything's better than having to sit here and listen to you ramble."

After standing abruptly, Master Liam cleared off the books and papers from a desk with one sweep of his large arm. "Get over here, lass."

She rose on unsteady feet and took a deep breath. They were going to touch her now. Keeping her gaze focused on Master Liam, she made her way to the desk and stood before them with a cocky strut to her hip. She loved how they devoured her with their gazes as if she was the most desirable woman they'd ever seen. Being wanted like this made her feel so damn good, almost powerful.

Master Liam took off his jacket and shirt, then laid them down on the table. Every muscle in his body was firm and delicious. From his sectioned abs to his rock-solid chest with his tiny brown nipples, he screamed virility. A man fully in his prime. She wanted to smell him, to rub her face on his neck and just inhale.

"Take your skirt off."

Master Rory came over to her side and held out his arm. He steadied her as she took off her skirt. Once she'd put it up on the desk, he moved around and turned her so she was facing him. For a moment he just looked down at her, then very slowly, and with great intent, he slid his hands up her ribs to her breasts and filled his palms with her mounds.

He let go of her, then reached up and tore the shirt from her in a violent motion that sent moisture rushing to her pussy. She was so wet that her inner thighs were slick and she could smell her desire. Master Rory gently caressed the tips of her nipples with a maddeningly light touch. She swayed on her heels, and Master Rory laughed.

"Come on, darling. Up on the table with you."

He lifted her by the waist, and as soon as her butt made contact with the edge of the table, Master Liam helped her lie back. They adjusted her until most of her body was on the hard surface. Then Master Liam leaned over and began to suck her left breast. The sensation of his full lips pleasuring her had her reaching up and running her hands over the spectacular musculature of his torso. His smooth, dark skin was a few shades deeper than her own skin tone, and she loved how they looked like honey and chocolate together.

Master Rory spread her legs and starting at her right ankle, began to kiss his way up her leg. Wonderful, amazing sensations unfurled in her blood, and she writhed beneath them, wanting more, needing more. When Master Rory reached her panties, he took an audible breath and groaned. His obvious pleasure felt almost as good as Master Liam now biting her nipples.

Her desire-fogged mind cleared for a moment, and she tried to kick Master Rory and push Master Liam away. "Get off me! You guys stink like old man."

Both men froze, and Master Liam said in a low voice, "What's your safe word?"

"Mercy."

"Are you using it?"

"Are you as dumb as you look?" The Masters had ordered her to be as bratty as she could in this scene. She gave Master Rory another kick, making sure she didn't hit him. "I bet your balls are as wrinkly as a bulldog's face."

Master Liam was off her, and Master Rory had her flipped over onto her stomach. He jerked her down until her legs were hanging off the table and her ass was prominently displayed. Master Liam grabbed her wrists and held them to the table. His hands were so big that he could easily hold both wrists with one hand, leaving the other free to smooth her hair back. The gentleness of his touch was in marked contrast to Master Rory's rough movements as he moved her around until her position met his approval.

"I won't take your sass in this classroom, girl." Master Rory leaned over her back so she could feel his erection between her ass cheeks. He felt so good. She moaned low in her throat, wishing he would take her. "Five lashes with the cane ought to curb your wicked tongue."

"Why don't you—"

The first strike came down on her butt. It was a line of fire that really hurt! "What are you doing?"

"Do you need mercy, lass?" Master Liam asked in a low voice.

"No!" She struggled against his hold. The fact that he held her tighter, kept her from moving more than an inch sent shivers of fear and arousal through her. He could hurt her—*they* could hurt her—but she had to trust them. They weren't like...him.

Master Rory picked that moment to lay four more blistering lines across her ass. The pain drove all thoughts from her mind. Her ass stung, throbbed, and burned. That ache merged with the need to fuck and be fucked, making her restless and wanting more.

With a soft laugh, Master Liam leaned down and whispered in her ear, "Fight all you want. You're not going anywhere until Master Rory does his experiment."

God, he was so fucking hot.

Arching her back, she then spread her legs farther apart, no doubt giving Master Rory a nice view of her pussy. "Get on with it already."

Master Rory slid his fingers along her sex, his pleased murmur sparking her nerves. It was hard to fight him when he was touching her like this. Master Liam kept his firm hold on her. The knowledge that she couldn't get away flipped every switch inside her. She was on fire with passion as Master Rory continued to pet her pussy through those scandalous panties.

Master Rory made a low, delicious groan before he said, "You don't get to tell us what to do, Rhiannon. When you gave up control, you also gave up the right to call the shots. Right now, this is our pussy, our arse, and we will do whatever we want to it."

He moved behind her, and a moment later, his soft, wet tongue traced one of the burning lines on her bottom, sending a confusing mixture of pleasure and pain through her. She tried to think of some bratty comment or a way to please them with her naughty behavior, but the sensation of his mouth on her skin had her arching into his touch with a needy little groan.

Master Liam kept his secure grip on her wrists, pinning her to the table, but he swept her hair back so he could see her face. "There's a good girl."

Her eyelids fluttered shut as the joy from his compliment raced through her like a shot of good whiskey. This is all she ever wanted. To be someone's good girl.

Before Master Rory's mouth reached her pussy, he pulled away, then gave her stinging ass a slap. "On your back."

All too eagerly she complied, clad now in only her panties, stockings, and high heels. As she looked between Master Rory and Master Liam looming over her, she seemed to sink into the table. Ever muscle tensed, then released. With a slow, deliberate care, Master Rory teased her panties down her legs. Once she was completely nude, Master Liam growled low in his throat.

"You were made for a man's pleasure, little one."

Master Rory grunted in agreement. "Time to show you what your body is capable of."

He spread her legs wide, then had her put her feet on the table so her knees were in the air and her pelvis tilted slightly up. He ran his hands down her torso, then briefly gripped her hips before moving over to her sex. He tugged at the hair on her pubic mound and smiled.

"I like this. Don't shave it."

"Yes, Master." Her voice came out breathy, but she was surprised she could talk at all.

His pleased smile deepened as he slid his finger between the folds of her sex. "Mmm, so wet."

Master Liam trailed one of his fingers over her face, drawing delicate lines across her cheeks, her nose, her forehead, and her lips. His touch made her skin tingle, but it also made it hard to concentrate. Slowly, bit by bit, they began to overwhelm her with sensation until her mind shut down further. Everything felt good—from her sore ass on the table to Master Liam's surprisingly delicate touch to Master Rory manipulating her pussy.

He played with her clit, making her squirm and cry out; then he pulled away, and she whimpered. Their breathing deepened, grew rougher as her own quickened. She inhaled and swore she could taste their pheromones in the air. All the attention, all the stimulation, had her thrusting her hips in a silent plea to be filled.

Master Rory slapped her thigh. "Be still."

She softened after the blow and moaned when Master Liam began to play with her right breast. He took it into his big hand and squeezed hard, then tweaked her nipple until he had that little nub in a rough pinch. When he didn't release his grip—instead increasing the pressure—she arched into his touch and struggled to breath. So much, too much, not enough. They had her spinning between sensations in a way that should have been alarming.

Between them, she felt safe.

Master Rory gave her stomach a pat. "Can you hear me, Rhiannon?"

She forced her eyes open, not really sure when she'd closed them. "Yes, Master."

"I'm going to stimulate your G-spot until you ejaculate."

"What?"

She tried to sit up, but Master Liam chose that moment to release her nipple, then hold her close. Blood rushed painfully back into the abused nub. Her first instinct was to touch her breast, to rub away the hurt, but she was unable to move due to Master Liam's grip.

"No, lass. You don't get to do anything we don't let you do. Now, Master Rory is going to put his fingers into your delicious cunt, and he's going to make you come."

"Oh, God, please," she begged.

Both men laughed, and Master Rory said, "Inside you there is a spot that when properly stimulated will make you ejaculate."

"I don't understand." Master Liam had switched to her left breast now and was tormenting her in a delicious way.

"Don't worry. I'll take care of you. All I want you to do is bear down when I say, like you do when you're peeing."

She tried to sit up again, but Master Liam pressed her back to the desk. He abandoned her breast and held one of her hands in each of his, further restraining her. She had no hope of breaking away from him. Still, the thought of urinating on someone made her ill enough that she used her safe word.

"Mercy, Master. I don't want to urinate on you, Sir."

Master Liam chuckled. "You won't be urinating on anyone. When a man comes, is he peeing on you?"

"Well, no, but that's different."

Master Rory began to stroke her slit in a smooth up-and-down rhythm that had her tilting her hips up to meet his touch, urging him to go just a bit higher so he would touch her throbbing clit. "Yes and no. What will be coming out of you is just sucrose and water. Sweet water if you will. Many Masters love to give their submissives G-spot orgasms."

"Because," Master Liam picked up smoothly, "not only is it visually stimulating to watch a woman squirt, but the orgasm that you're going to get is going to be a lot more intense than just a clitoral or vaginal stimulation orgasm. And you can easily have multiple orgasms."

Despite her discomfort at the idea of anything squirting from her body, she had to admit the men made it sound intriguing. It wasn't like this would be the first time they'd seen a woman do it. They must have made hundreds of women squirt.

The thought sent an unexpected spike of jealousy through her. For Pete's sake, it wasn't like they were her real Masters. They were her trainers, and as such, she expected them to know what they're talking about. With all that experience came a great deal of skill. Still, she didn't want to think of them pleasuring another woman.

Giving her a small smile, Master Rory winked. "Besides, it's good for a Dom's ego when his submissive can no longer walk on her own."

She tried to keep the disbelief off her face, but by Master Liam's chuckle, she didn't do very well.

"Don't worry, lass. I'll be helping him out. Getting you in the right headspace will be a bit of a trick. In order to please us, you must try your very best to do what we ask. We will expect you to work hard, but I promise you will be well rewarded."

She looked up into Master Liam's eyes and relaxed. There was nothing but passion and kindness in his gaze. Well, that and a whole lot of attitude. The man was just shy of arrogant, and she found it incredibly sexy. If he had the skills to back that arrogance up, she was going to be a very, very happy woman.

Sharp pain to her right nipple slammed her out of her thoughts and shifted her focus back to her body. Another pain came a moment later, this time on her left breast. When she opened her eyes and looked, she saw two pretty gold thumbscrew nipple clamps embellished with sapphires and diamonds. They were gorgeous, and they hurt.

Master Liam moved so he was looking at her more from her side than overhead. He kept his hand on her the whole time, touching her shoulder, her arm, back up to her chest where he lightly tapped the left clamp. Immediate pain made her hiss out a breath, and he smiled.

Sadistic bastard.

"There we go. You need to stay with us, Rhiannon. Right now you belong to Master Rory and me. That means all of you is ours. No negative thoughts allowed."

Master Rory began to massage her clit. She let out a rather nonsexy grunt that made the men do that deep chuckle which shivered through her bones and sent a renewed flood of moisture to her already wet sex. "That's it, love. Stay with me. I want you connected to us, to what we're doing to your body, to the pleasure that is yours for the taking."

Good God Master Rory could tempt a nun. She stood no chance, especially when he massaged around her clit, bringing more blood to that sensitive nub. She was weightless, suspended in a shimmering soap bubble. Like a bubble she floated on a hot wind generated by the men touching her.

She could smell them, their musk, that blend of both men's scents that drove her wild with need. Without thinking, she reached out and palmed Master Liam's cock. He froze, then let out a low groan. He was so thick, so wide, that she couldn't even come close to circling her hand around him.

Swearing beneath his breath, he removed her hand. "No, lass. You don't get to touch until we tell you."

She started to pout at him, but Master Rory picked that moment to press two fingers at her entrance. Right away her attention snapped back to her body and she wanted to snarl in frustration. She wanted to touch Master Liam, to hold and taste him, but Master Liam wouldn't let her. Being denied made her want to do it all the more, made her arousal harder, made her want to please them.

She relaxed and allowed Master Rory to slide his fingers deep into her pussy, drawing a long and low groan from her. The delicate tissues of her sex were so swollen from his massage that the sensation of being filled pressed her into the table. Contentment mixed with rough desire buffeted her mind until she floated again.

Master Liam began to gently play with the clamps. He must have been watching her reaction, because he'd vary his technique, adjusting to what she liked and avoiding what she didn't. She wished she was able to open her eyes, but she seemed to have forgotten how to make her muscles move. Every inch of her skin was buzzing with energy, and she could barely breathe past the sensations.

Master Rory hooked his fingers and pushed against the top of her sheath. He moved slowly, rubbing on the inside of her sex, making her sigh and moan. Then he found...something, some place that seemed to be right behind her clit and when he manipulated that spot made her back arch with pleasure.

"Oh, God!"

"Bingo," Master Liam said in a low voice.

She fell into a maelstrom of sexual arousal.

With firm, rapid strokes Master Rory manipulated her, slamming his fingers into her hard enough that the desk rocked slightly with his movements. Master Liam chose that moment to unscrew the right clamp. She screamed, then cried out as his pillow-soft lips enveloped her tender nipple. It seemed like each soft suck went directly to her clit, then to that spot deep inside where Master Rory was touching in that maddeningly intense way.

She began to plead with Master Rory, her whispered words almost incoherent even to her own ears. The needs just spilled from her, begging Master Rory to make her come, begging Master Liam to let her touch him, and begging them to take care of her. To protect her. To keep her safe.

Master Liam moved his lips from her breast to her face and began to gently kiss her cheeks. "Let go, lass. We have you. I swear to you no one will ever hurt you while Rory and I are around. Be a good girl and come for your Masters."

"Shit," she whispered and gripped the edges of the table.

With a soft chuckle, Master Liam captured her mouth in a demanding kiss that shot her right over the edge. The next thing she knew Master Rory had removed his fingers and was urging her to bear down. It was such an odd request that she had to focus on what he was saying. When she did, embarrassment chased away a bit of her desire. Then guilt that she didn't do what he wanted had her trying, but nothing happened.

Her lower lip trembled while Master Liam kissed her and pulled back until their lips were barely brushing. "Easy, little one. This isn't a race. Take as much time as you need. Rory doesn't care if he gets arthritis. He'll finger bang your tight cunt until you give us what we want."

There it was, that dirty word that made her all tingly. Unable to help herself, she wrapped her arms around Master Liam's shoulders and returned his kiss, hoping that he'd allow it.

"Keep your hands there," Master Rory said from somewhere to her left.

The next thing she knew he was unscrewing the other nipple clamp. Oh, damn. This was going to hurt. As soon as the blood rushed back into her abused tip, it brought a pain with it that had her screaming. Master Liam ate her cries from her lips as if he could taste them. His hungry growl further undid her.

Master Rory slid his fingers into her aching sex and began to firmly massage her again. She clutched Master Liam's shoulders, loving how he dwarfed her. He sucked on her tongue, and her legs trembled.

A moment later, Master Rory began to suckle on her clit as he picked up the pace of his licks. Everything tightened from the tips of her toes to her hair, and she fought to move enough to kiss Master Liam back. After a few seconds, she gave up and tore her mouth away with a gasp, trying to ease the blinding need to come. A continuous chain of soft moans fell from her lips as she tried to process the demand on her overloaded nerves. It felt almost like Master Rory was stroking her clit from behind while he sucked on it.

An amazingly delicious sensation that had her sinking her nails into Master Liam's shoulders.

He bent his head to her neck and began to nibble on her, little stinging nips that had her hips snapping. She wanted...she needed...

Master Rory removed his fingers. "Come for me, Rhiannon. Bear down and give me your climax. I demand it as your Master. Now."

This orgasm was different, way different.

She thrashed on the table as the first wave slammed into her, her limbs jerking as if she had no control over her body. Master Liam lay his torso on hers, pinning her to the table. He whispered wonderfully dirty things against her neck about what he was going to do to her, how he was going to do it, and how much she would come. Warmth cascaded down her bottom, but it was such a *good* sensation that all she could do was whine as her body trembled and shook. It lasted for a blissfully long time, the intensity slowly lessening until she felt as if she'd been coming for hours. At last the contractions gentled, and she throbbed all over, utterly spent.

Master Rory eased his fingers back into her, and she gave a feeble groan. He ignored her protests. Soon she was squirming beneath Master Liam, scraping her nipples against his chest. Hell, he was going to make her come again.

No sooner did she have that thought than a fantastically terrible tension stiffened her limbs. Master Rory had to put her legs back into position because she didn't have the ability to do much more than exist and writhe against the increasing pleasure. She wanted them in the worst way. Their grunts and growls made her aware that she was saying the words aloud, but she didn't care.

They were her Masters, and her pleasure was theirs.

The more she talked, the more the intensity built until Master Rory removed his hand.

He didn't even have to tell her what to do this time.

She bore down, and that wonderful warmth spilled over her bottom again. Nothing mattered except feeling so amazing she wasn't sure she could survive the intensity.

Master Rory made her come two more times until she was a pile of twitching nerves on the table.

Master Liam lifted himself off her, and she shivered at the loss of his body heat.

The firm, gentle voice of Master Rory penetrated the postorgasmic fog surrounding her mind. "Rhiannon, open your eyes."

She tried to, but all she could manage was to lift her eyebrows. It struck her as incredibly funny, and her giggles resumed. Both men sighed, and that only made her laugh harder.

"She's sub drunk."

"Drunk as a skunk sub," she agreed before bursting into laugher.

Master Liam made a mock scolding sound. "I think we broke her."

"No. She had at least six or seven more orgasms left in her."

"Not unless you wanted to hook up an IV to battle her dehydration. Look at the lass. She's soaked the table and the floor. She needs some electrolytes in her."

At the mention of soaking wet, she realized that her lower half was damp. Once again she tried to look, but it didn't work. A man's strong arms lifted her from the table, and a soft, incredibly warm blanket was wrapped around her. Her feet wouldn't support her at all, so when she sagged, she heard Master Rory chuckle, and he caught her.

"There's my good girl. You did so well, Rhiannon." He cuddled her into his arms, and she snuggled into his chest, taking in deep breaths of his chest.

"Smell good."

He laughed; then the world shifted as he walked with her in his arms. "And you taste like cinnamon and honey."

"Mmm."

"You have a delicious pussy."

"Want to taste you."

His grip tightened. "You will but not tonight."

She stuck out her tongue and blew a raspberry.

"Why is the lass spitting on you?"

She turned her head to the sound of Master Liam's voice and managed to open her eyes just the tiniest bit. "Will you let me taste you?"

His eyes widened. "Little one, you have no idea how badly I want to say yes."

Master Rory shifted her and sat down on what looked like a brass daybed. She blinked in the mellow lighting and glanced around at the Victorian-patterned cream silk wallpaper. They had left the classroom, and she let out a giggle as she realized she had no idea they'd even moved. Her gaze traveled left, and she found Master Rory looking down at her with an unreadable expression.

"Rhiannon, we have as much time to train you as you need. Don't try to rush it. Sit back and enjoy your training. Each scene we have, each time we're together, we're trying to teach you something."

The reminder chased back some of her fuzzy feelings. They weren't really her Masters, just her trainers. She wondered what it would be like to be theirs; then she reminded herself that Master Rory and Master Liam were notorious for never settling down with a submissive. They weren't going to change their ways just because she wanted to be their one and only.

Master Liam sat on the bed next to them and handed her a sports drink with a straw in it. "You lost a lot of fluids. Drink up."

Obediently she sipped from the straw, the cool fluid rushing down her throat and making her aware of how parched she was. The more she drank, the thirstier she became until more than half the bottle was gone. She handed it to Master Liam with a sigh, and he put the lid back on before tossing the bottle to the foot of the bed. When she leaned back, she burped and flushed scarlet.

"Pardon me."

Master Rory laughed. "That was the daintiest burp I've ever heard. Then again I've been living with that heathen for the past twelve years, so my idea of what constitutes a good belch has vastly changed."

"Wow. You've known each other that long?"

The men exchanged a glance loaded with meaning and emotions she didn't understand. Master Liam broke eye contact with Master Rory, and she swore she saw sorrow and regret in his gaze. "Yes. We went to the University of Leicester over in England together."

She moved out of Master Rory's arms and rearranged herself between the men so they were all leaning back together with their legs intertwined. Then she grabbed one of each man's hands and held them in her own. Her need to touch them was almost a compulsion, but as soon as she was snuggled between them, a great contentment settled over her.

Rubbing her thumb over the light hair on the back of Master Liam's hand, she rested her head against Master Rory's shoulder. "It must be nice to have such a good friend."

"Do you have many friends, lass?"

She shrugged, discontent trying to steal away her peace. "I guess. But nothing like what you have with Master Rory."

Master Liam asked, "What do you mean?"

"Just that it's like you are two halves of the same whole." She toyed with their fingers, trying to put her thoughts into words. "It must be nice to know that there is someone who cares about you."

"We're more like an old married couple constantly bitching at each other."

She looked up at him and saw the yearning in his gaze. Her heart urged her to comfort him, to take his sadness away, so she turned and knelt between them before placing a gentle kiss on Master Liam's cheek. "Well I think it's sweet."

Suddenly Master Rory leaned forward and grabbed her ass with one hand. "I think *this* is sweet."

He pressed on a mark from whatever he spanked her with,

and that little bit of pain jangled down her nerves until it settled into a warm burn between her thighs. "What did you spank me with?"

The grin he gave her was positively wicked. "A ruler. Did you like it?"

She reached back and fingered the welts on her bottom. "Yes, I think I did. I mean, I do."

When she looked back at Master Liam his attention was focused on her nipples. The hungry way he stared at her made her want to purr. "How are your tits?"

Brushing her palms over her sore nipples, she winced, then squeezed her thighs together. "They sting."

Master Liam licked his lips, but before he could lean forward, Master Rory captured her right breast in his mouth. Master Liam then nuzzled her left breast. She looked down at them. Their heads pressed together, cheeks scraping as they suckled on her tight nipples. Master Liam wrapped an arm around her waist on one side, Master Rory on the other. They moved with such a synchronized rhythm that she quickly fell under the sensual spell they were weaving over her.

She ran her fingers through their hair, liking how Master Liam's short dark hair was rough like lamb's wool while Rory's bronze blond locks were a little bit longer and smooth. Together the men made low rumbles of pleasure as they lavished her breasts with attention. The sight of their heads touching as they licked at her chest fulfilled her on a very primitive level. She vaguely wondered how she would ever be satisfied with one Master after she'd been with two.

Chapter Nine

Liam stood on one of the lower steps leading to the Smithsonian Natural History Museum and glanced at his watch for the third time in less than two minutes. A glittering throng of DC's brightest and most powerful flowed up the stone stairs to attend the exclusive Emerald Gala. He normally didn't attend galas, but the Smithsonian had allowed Rory and Liam access to their vast mineral collection for research when they first arrived in the States to start up the US division of their oil and gas company.

He loved this museum but dressing in a tux and shaking hands for five hours while making inane conversation was not on his list of top one hundred things to do on a Tuesday night. Before Rory had left on a business trip late this afternoon, he'd informed Liam that Rory was sending over a business associate who would accompany Liam as his guest. He wouldn't say who she was, only that she was high maintenance. So now Liam stood in his tux with his platinum and rare Columbian emerald cuff links gleaming as he checked his watch...again.

The woman was late, and Liam had just about run out of patience. After he left here he'd be heading straight for Club Wicked. Tonight he was going to be alone with Rhiannon while Rory was out in North Dakota checking on some of their drilling locations. He found himself not only eager to see the woman but pleased that she would be all his for the evening. He'd never had possessive feelings about a trainee—hell, any submissive—and it worried him, but at the same time he couldn't deny how right it felt to have Rhiannon in his life. Like she was the final piece of the puzzle he'd been looking for. But fuck, nothing could ever be easy or uncomplicated.

Worse yet, he knew Rory also liked Rhiannon more than the usual trainee, and it irritated him. If it was even possible, he was jealous of both of them. Rory wanted Rhiannon, which made Liam envious, and Rhiannon got to do everything sexual and relationship-wise with Rory that Liam couldn't because of his fucked-up homophobia. Rhiannon seemed to care for Rory just as much as she cared for Liam and that also made him resentful. That last thought had Liam's temper rising, but he bit it back. He needed to go inside and make nice with all the good people who bought products from their company and helped fund their research. Beyond that, he genuinely enjoyed hanging out with the scientists. The men and women who worked for the museum were among some of the most brilliant people Liam had ever met. At the very least he needed to spend some time working the crowd, but bloody hell, he was eager to be out of here and on his way to his woman.

His woman.

Fuck.

He was fucked.

Rhiannon pushed every one of his protective instincts that demanded he take care of her and make her happy. It was almost like a compulsion to dominate Rhiannon because she was so obviously happy when she was treated as a submissive. That didn't mean she didn't have a temper—he'd seen her almost snatch another server bald one night after the other woman had slapped Rhiannon—but she was just so feminine and sweet.

And fucking hot.

Really fucking hot.

He looked down the steps once again and had to blink hard. Either he was more obsessed with the lass than he'd thought, or Rhiannon was making her way up to him. His gut clenched, and he tried to remember that she didn't know he was going to be here. She was probably on a date.

That pissed him off.

She took another step, and he drank her in. Dressed in a flowing deep gold beaded gown that hugged her in all the right places, she made every man who saw her do a double take. The front of her elegant dress was cut low enough to showcase her magnificent cleavage without being vulgar. Her hair was swept up off her neck, and she wore a choker of emeralds and diamonds, paired with matching teardrop earrings. They sparkled as she took the steps, heading in his direction. He wanted to kiss the skin beneath those jewels.

The need to take her threatened to overwhelm him, and he struggled to control himself. "What are you doing here?"

His words came out rougher than he intended, and she flushed, dipping her head so she was looking at the stairs.

"Mas—um, Rory thought you might like to have some company at the event." She clasped her glittering gold clutch. "I'm sorry. I shouldn't have come. I knew this was a mistake. I'll see you at the club."

He stared at her, his mind racing. Rory had said he had some errands to run before he left DC for North Dakota. Evidently one of the errands had been spending time with Rhiannon, getting her ready for what amounted to a date with Liam. Why the bloody hell was Rory doing this? Liam knew his friend, and he was more than aware of Rory's fascination with Rhiannon. Yeah, they'd shared women in the past, but this was different. Rhiannon was different.

She started to turn, and he gently clasped her small wrist in his hand, amazed again at how delicate and fragile she appeared. "I'm sorry. That came out wrong. You surprised me. Need to warn a man before you show up in a dress like that or all you're going to get is stuttering and drooling for a few minutes."

The way she smiled at him, the joy that lit her from within, washed over him like the warm waters of the Caribbean. He had a sudden, vivid fantasy of showing Rhiannon around their island. She would love it. If anyone deserved a getaway to paradise, it was his girl.

"Thank you." She quickly licked her lips, and he noticed her shoulders tense. "I've never been to anything like this before. Heck, I've never even been to this museum. I'm not sure what to do."

He took her hand and pulled her until he had her arm entwined with his. "The only thing you have to do is have fun. And don't worry about being embarrassed. We're like Beauty and the Beast together, and they'll be sure that anything you do was somehow my fault."

Her posture remained perfect, but the tight lines around her amazing green eyes softened. Leaning closer, she whispered, "All these people are so fancy, so out of my league."

"Lass, these are a bunch of people who enjoy mucking around with rocks for a living. Trust me when I say they're far more intimidated by you than you are by them."

She smiled up at him, and his heart swelled. "I doubt that, but thank you. Just please help me not make a fool of myself, okay?"

"You're safe with me." She arched a brow, and he grinned. "Well, at least in public. You said you've never been here before?"

"No. I don't get out much."

He hated the sad, slightly ashamed look on her expressive face. "You're in for a treat. I don't know if you're aware of it, but Rory and I are huge nerds, and we've spent a lot of time here. I'll bore you to death."

"I highly doubt that, but thank you for trying to make me feel better." She smiled up at him and joy filled him in response. "Shall we?"

They took the steps slowly as he switched the conversation over to Jesse and Dove's wedding plans before they entered the museum, giving her a chance to relax. With Rhiannon next to him, he tried to see the museum as it had looked the first time he saw it. At 1,320,000 square feet, the Smithsonian Museum of Natural History was stately and huge with massive amounts of artifacts stored inside. He'd like to show her the geology portions of the museum and wondered what part she'd be interested in. "So you let Rory dress you up?"

"Yes, he met up with me this morning before he caught his flight. Poor Mas—man. He had to sit through me trying on at least two dozen dresses. I don't think he had any idea what shopping with me meant." A sudden flush filled her face, and she looked away.

He had an idea of why she was blushing. "Hmm. Did Rory finally put an end to you playing dress up?"

"Yes."

The squeak in her voice amused him; then his stupid jealousy kicked in, and he was suddenly furious that Rory had sex with her before he did.

She must have noticed his silence because she cleared her throat and gave him an apprehensive look. "He spanked me until I made up my mind about which one I wanted to wear."

Shaking his head, calling himself a bloody moron, he gave her hand a light squeeze. "Sorry. I was distracted by the thought of all the things I'd do to you in that dressing room."

Her giggle lightened his heart. "Did I mention that one of the women who worked at the boutique walked in while he was spanking me? I thought for sure she was going to pass out."

His roar of laughter broke loose, and everyone looked in their direction. Rhiannon gave him a bemused smile, the red of her blush still burning her cheeks.

"Is he in jail?"

"Um, no. I was begging him to spank me so it was obviously consensual."

He swallowed hard and willed himself to not have an erection as they came to the entrance. There were photographers here, and he didn't want his picture showing up with a raging hard-on. Though if he had his picture taken with Rhiannon, there wasn't a man in the world who could blame him.

In an effort to cool down, he lifted his chin to the entrance. "So you've really never been here before?"

She shook her head. "No. I've been wanting to. I just never got around to it. I'm more of a homebody."

"Really?"

"Yes, really." She gave him a slightly annoyed look. "Why are people surprised that I enjoy staying at home? I have more hobbies than I have hours in the day."

He wanted to kiss the scowl off her pretty pink lips. "Like what?"

"I read, I practice dancing and doing my Aikido, I watch movies, I crochet, I—"

"Is there anything you don't do?"

"I didn't have time when I was growing up. I had to help my mom take care of my dad and my six younger brothers and sisters."

"Was your dad ill?"

"No. It's just that in my family, the women take care of the house and the men make the money." She shrugged. "I don't mind that part. What pissed me off is my brothers never had to do any housework. They'd go out and play while me and my sister scrubbed floorboards."

They reached the entrance, so he made sure to keep her close to his side. As predicted, once they reached the top of the steps, they had to pose as the cameras around them exploded with flashes of light. He'd never had this much attention getting his picture taken before, and he grinned at Rhiannon, who was giving a rather stunned smile. It wasn't his ugly mug they were so eager to capture on film.

He led them through the entrance and provided his invitation along with his ID. They were soon ushered into the massive four-story rotunda with the great African bush elephant in the center. That always made him smile. It never failed to amaze him at how big the majestic creatures were. He idly wondered if Rhiannon would like to go on a safari someday with him.

Next to him, Rhiannon gasped. "Holy moly. This is amazing."

Green, purple, and orange lighting set the mood, and there were dozens of tables arranged in the rotunda around the elephant. Each table was decorated with snow-white linen while giant raw emeralds were displayed as centerpieces. The lights slowly changed, giving the room a different feeling but in such a subtle way that he was barely aware of it.

Rhiannon looked up at him with such wide eyes that he couldn't help but grin. Slipping her arm through his, he said, "Come on. I want you to meet some people."

For the next two hours, they wandered the rotunda, and he introduced her to his friends in the geology department and brought her with him as he talked to various business associates. Rhiannon had been charming if a bit quiet. They left a group of jewelers, and as they walked away, Rhiannon pulled him over to one of the archways. She touched her neck. "This is real?"

"What?"

"That jeweler we were talking to from New York commented on the quality of these emeralds. Is this real?" She removed her fingertips from the necklace as if she'd been burned.

"Of course." He frowned. "Why does that upset you? Rory wouldn't send you to an Emerald Gala in fake emeralds."

"It's..." She looked around nervously. "Someone could steal this!"

He laughed and gathered her into his arms. She felt so good, so warm and soft against him. "Trust me. You'll be fine. The security here is insane, and I would kill anyone who tried to get near you."

She leaned farther into him, and her lips went soft while her pupils dilated. Evidently she liked it when a man was protective of her. A lot. She pressed her hips into his and leaned closer, tall enough in her heels that her mouth was only a few inches from his. The scent of her honeysuckle perfume teased his nose, and he imagined he could almost smell her arousal.

"How much longer do we have to stay?"

The breathy way she said that made his cock surge against his pants. "Why? Are you bored?"

She smiled and curved herself against him, molding her body to his. "No. But Master Rory told me that tonight you'd spank me until I came for being a good girl."

"Did he now?" His voice came out gruff while his cock swelled at the thought.

"Mmm-hmm."

Without another word, he dragged her through the crowd. She protested at his fast pace, giggling as he plowed past small groups of people talking. As they made their way to the front, he called his driver and told him to be ready. Now he'd just have to keep his hands to himself until they got to Club Wicked. If he touched her once in the car, he wouldn't be satisfied until she was underneath him with his cock shoved so far into her that she cried out in pleasure and pain.

He clenched his jaw as he realized he couldn't have that pleasure yet. Rory had made Liam promise that he wouldn't fuck Rhiannon without him. It wasn't unusual—they were always together when they first took a submissive—but Liam hated he'd promised not to have sex with her. He'd just have to find some other way of making her come multiple times.

By the time he was done tonight, she would know to whom she belonged

But he didn't want to do it at Club Wicked. He wanted to take Rhiannon home with him. He wanted to see her in his bed and spread out that glorious hair around her as he ground her ass into the mattress. His need to be inside her bordered on obsession. Rory would throw a shit fit, but for the first time in a long time, Liam was considering a future in which Rory didn't play a part.

Rhiannon slid into the backseat of the black Bentley and snuggled up next to Liam as the driver shut her door. Tonight had been so beyond her expectations that she didn't know what to do with herself. She'd never been to an event with that many people before. If it hadn't been for Liam, she would have been petrified that they would somehow know her past and could see the taint left on her soul. But with him at her side, she'd been entranced by the Smithsonian. Everyone was so brilliant and interesting, she found it easy to just sit back and listen to what they had to say.

The entire time Liam had kept her close to him, his pride in her obvious. Knowing she made him stand a little bit taller did wonderful things for her ego. The way he'd smiled at her tonight sent a wave of warmth through her, like taking a shot of really good brandy. Best of all, their night wasn't over. She was starving for a man between her legs, and no amount of getting herself off had soothed the need. Now she sat next to one of the most amazing, devastatingly handsome men she'd ever met, and he seemed just as hungry for her as she was for him. As soon as the car pulled away from the curb, he began to run his hands over her thighs with a firm touch that made her sex clench. Possessive, heavy, utterly male, he touched her with the assurance of having had lots and lots of experience with women. A little thread of jealousy burned through her as she thought about all the women she personally knew at Club Wicked who'd slept with him. The idea of him touching them like this dimmed her joy a bit.

Liam shifted next to her. "I have a proposal for you, Rhiannon."

Noting the seriousness of his tone, she sat up. "Yes?"

He let out a little growl and gripped her leg harder. "Yes what?"

Her clit began to throb between her thighs, and she squirmed. "Yes, Sir?"

His pleased smile made her melt. "I would like to take you home with me instead of going to Club Wicked tonight."

She blinked at him, totally thrown off by his request. "What? Why?"

"Because I want to see you in my bed." He frowned at her, his expression almost confused. "I really want to sleep with you tonight, to hold you until we both drift off."

Trying to ease the butterflies in her belly, she grinned at him. "Are you sure you just want me in your bed to sleep?"

With a low groan, he gripped the back of her neck with his other hand and lifted her to him. He was so strong that he had her pinned against him, unable to do anything but relax into his hard frame. The muscular surface of his body had no give, and when his erection pushed against her, she bit back a moan. The warmth of his breath brushed her lips as he spoke, holding her so very close but not giving her the kiss that she craved. Her want for him increased tenfold until she practically burned for him.

"I want to fuck you in my bed, to eat your little pussy until you scream from overstimulation, then come all the harder for it. I want to make you yell my name, to have your fingernails tear up my back as I fuck you so hard you no longer know or care who you are, only that you are mine."

All she could do was whimper and try to lean closer, but he denied her. If she didn't feel his gigantic cock pressed into her body, she'd think he was totally unaffected by her. His voice was so controlled, so deliberate.

"Yes, please."

He groaned and released her, then set her back as far away

from him as he could in the car. "No, I shouldn't be doing this. Forget what I said. We'll go to Wicked."

The scene he'd painted with his words was so seductive she couldn't help but protest. "No. I want to go to your house."

"No." He hesitated, then shook his head again. "Rory would flip his shit."

"Why?"

He only laughed and ran his hands over his face. "I'm so fucked. Let's go home."

Confused and getting angry at his attitude, she drew her shoulders up and lifted her chin. "No, it's fine. I'd just like to go to my home, alone, please. If you'll drop me—"

Instantly he sobered and peered at her. His aggressive gaze should have tipped her off that she'd annoyed him, but she was still surprised when he grabbed the back of her neck and pulled her toward him. The move irritated her yet made her oh so aroused. She loved the way he manhandled her as if he owned her. It was so fucking hot.

He released her neck and studied her. "Don't put that icy-bitch mask on around me, Rhiannon. I won't tolerate it."

Emotions suddenly rushed through her, hard and fierce. The thought of not being able to put that shield between herself and the world scared the crap out of her. "You can't tell me what to do."

"Actually, yes I can." He leaned forward, not touching her but projecting such authority in his sexy tux that her mouth went dry. "I'm your Master, lass. You know it, and I know it. Now think very, very carefully about my offer."

She looked away, unable to handle the intensity of the moment. It sounded so...personal when he said he was her Master. Like she really belonged to him. She tried to tell herself she was reading more into it than was there, but her heart said otherwise.

"Have you ever taken a trainee to your house before?"

"No."

She took a deep, shuddering breath. While she had no delusions that a woman had been in his bed at some point, it made her feel good to know he didn't take trainees back there. Fuck, what was she thinking? Master Rory would be upset if she had sex without him there. He'd said as much when he was helping her get ready for the gala.

"I want to, I really do, but I promised Master Rory I wouldn't have sex with you tonight."

Suddenly Liam leaned forward and gripped her upper arms. "He did what?"

The tone of his voice was low and dangerous, making her nervous. "It's nothing. He said it was part of my training. That I had to earn the right to have sex with you."

Liam's face closed down until she couldn't read any of his emotions, but his hands still gripped her upper arms tight enough to hurt. She tried to pull away, and his hold tightened more before releasing. The look he gave her was filled with regret, and she wished with all her heart that she hadn't promised Master Rory she wouldn't have sex with Master Liam.

"Master, please." She moved until she was in his lap. Instantly he closed his arms around her and made her feel safe. "I would love to fall asleep in your arms tonight, to wake up with you next to me, but I don't want to break my promise."

"I swear, lass. If you come home with me, we won't have intercourse."

She peeked up at him through her lashes. "Promise?"

"Promise."

Part of her warned against going home with Liam, arguing that he could keep her at his home against her will, but that stupid voice was quickly squashed. He'd been photographed with her all over the place tonight. His trainees adored him, and he was considered one of the most eligible bachelors at Club Wicked. She knew deep down in her heart that he would never hurt her.

Her stomach growled, and she rubbed it with embarrassment. Master Liam smiled down at her. "Hungry?"

"Yes. I'm afraid I didn't eat much at the gala. I was too excited."

His gaze softened, and he stroked her face with his hand, making her aware of how big he was, how strong. But with her his touch was gentle. "I didn't eat much either. Hold on."

He shifted her slightly to dig his phone out, then pulled her back so she was cuddled into him. It felt so nice to be held. She breathed in his cologne, sinking farther into him until his heartbeat was the only thing in the world. Absently she listened to him order some food and talk to his driver, but mainly she just lost herself in the steady thump of his heart.

An hour later, she sat at an elegant rosewood dining room table that could accommodate sixteen people. She felt kind of silly perched on Master Liam's lap at the head of the table. He fed her the last bite of strawberry tart, then set the fork down.

"Better?"

"Very."

"Good. Now I want you to stand up, take off that dress, and sit on the table in your heels and whatever lingerie Rory put you in to torment me."

She startled and looked around the room. Master Rory and Master Liam lived in a mansion in the historic district that had been converted into two massive town houses. From the outside, she could see that the building was three stories high. She wondered what they did with all that space considering she was pretty sure they each lived alone.

The velvet curtains were drawn over the windows, but she still felt very exposed. Kinky things weren't meant to happen in a room this elegant. Plus someone could walk—

Her thoughts were cut off as Master Liam gave the top of her breast a stinging pinch. "I gave you an order, girl."

She blinked once, then slid off his lap and began to reach for her zipper.

Master Liam sighed. "Seduce me, girl. When you disrobe for your Master, you need to be conscious of your every move. Think about me while you undress. Think about ways to make me want you."

She flushed and had to resist the urge to turn away. Being scolded like this killed her arousal. As she took a deep breath, she forced herself to think about focusing on her Master. The ability to lose herself in Master Liam was like a wonderful drug that soothed her soul, and she was eager for her next fix.

"Yes, Master."

Turning slightly, she gave him a view of her profile as she slowly pulled the zipper at the back of the dress down. It hung open enough to show the white garter belt with its small pink roses. She wore a matching thong that had the crotch missing from it. White lace surrounded the slit and made her exposed labia appear even darker than normal. Master Rory had been ready to devour her when he handed her these panties to wear tonight, and the memory of his fierce arousal gave her the courage to drop the dress to the ground and step out of it.

Master Liam made a pained sound, but when she looked at him, his face was blank. His cock, however, was tenting his tuxedo pants. He'd taken the jacket off and at some point had removed his tie as well. A few buttons of the crisp white shirt hung open, and the glimpse of his soft, furry chest had her wanting to rub up against him.

He stood and cleared their dinner plates from the table with a sweep of his arm. The crash of broken plates made her jump, but Master Liam didn't even flinch. Instead, he held out his hand and said, "Come here."

She placed her hand in his and shivered. Achingly aware of his heat washing over her, dying to get him out of the tuxedo, she started to lean up for a kiss, but he stopped her by clenching his hand around her throat. "No, Rhiannon. You don't get to decide when I kiss you."

A tremble of harsh desire tensed her muscles, and her sex clenched. "Yes, Master."

His dark hazel-green eyes stared into hers until she felt like he was looking at her soul. Energy buzzed along her skin, and her nipples ached as they rubbed on his shirt. He took another step closer, then flattened her to his chest with one arm while continuing to hold her throat with the other. The thick shaft of his erection pressed against her, and she was dying for him.

But Master Rory had said no sex tonight, and she'd promised.

Something she deeply regretted, and she felt a bit resentful that Master Rory had denied her the pleasure of fucking Master Liam. And she knew it would be a pleasure. When she'd first thought about training with the Masters she'd sneaked into one of their public training sessions with Jessica. Master Liam had fucked the other woman with such strength and finesse that Rhiannon's panties had been sopping wet by the time she left, her body primed for the taking.

As she stared up at him, she tried to put into her gaze her need, her desire for him. Maybe he would take pity on her. His dick twitched against her belly, and he slid his hand down her back to cup her ass.

"You, lass, are entirely too much of a temptation."

He stroked the edges of the G-string and slowly smoothed his hands down her bottom. One of the best stress reliefs for her was to exercise or dance, so she was pleased that he appreciated her hard work to stay in shape. For a long, long time, she hadn't taken pride in anything about herself, believing she was damaged goods, and no one would ever want her. Instead of the old bad memories intruding, she drew in a deep breath of Master Liam's scent.

With gentle, almost teasing caresses, he awakened her skin to his touch, never releasing her from his gaze. A small measure of panic attempted to worm its way into her heart as she realized how intimate his look was. When he stared at her like this, she felt like she mattered to him, that he really cared. Of course he cared as her trainer, but this was something more. Something dangerous and intense and utterly terrifying.

Unable to take intimacy, she looked away, and he responded by bringing one of his hands up to her neck and forcing her to look at him. "Eyes on me, lass."

When she looked at Liam, he used his grip to push her back a step before releasing her throat. She took a deep, shuddering breath, strangely missing his hold on her neck. There was something very primitive about surrendering to a man so completely that he literally held her life in his hands, and she did nothing to resist him.

He sat in his chair and patted his lap. "I want you bent over my lap. It's time for your spanking."

The matter-of-fact way he said that made her tingle and blush. Taking a hesitant step forward, she started to worry about what was going to happen. She'd never been turned on by pain, and if Master Liam wasn't careful, he could hurt her. Her stupid fucking PTSD tried to kick in, to tell her that she was about to get the shit beat out of her, but she mentally shoved those thoughts aside. It was hard work, and by the time she'd made it to Master Liam, an incredibly kind and understanding look had come over his handsome face.

He gently grabbed her wrist and brought her to stand between the cradle of his legs. Because of his size, they were almost at the same height now. With a slow, firm touch, he began to stroke her arms, taking the time to make sure every inch of her skin had been caressed. He brought her fingers to his mouth and gently kissed each tip. A shudder of longing went through her as her battered soul drank up his easy affection.

"Have you ever had a hard spanking?"

She nodded, unable to think past the feel of his full, pillow-soft lips against the suddenly insanely sensitive skin of her fingertips. Then she flushed and shook her head, saying, "No, I got spanked by Rory earlier and during my training with you both last night, but I don't think either of those were hard."

His grip tightened for a moment before he let out a slow breath. "In that case, I'll be gentle."

That startled her enough that she almost snorted but managed to barely hold it back. Something must have shown on her face because Master Liam gave her finger a sharp nip. "Don't worry, beautiful girl. I'll make sure you get everything you need. Trust me."

He helped her fold over onto his lap with her legs spread wide. She tried to brace herself on the floor, but her arms weren't long enough. She felt unbalanced, and her desire began to fade as she worried about tipping over. Somehow falling off him wasn't exactly sexy.

Once again, Master Liam seemed to sense her problem, because he gave her bottom a soothing rub. "Hold on to my pants or the chair. I promise you, Rhiannon, there is no way in hell you're leaving my lap until I want you to. I've got you right where I want you, and I'm not letting you go."

She gripped his leg with one hand and the chair with the

other. Bracing herself, she took a breath and held it, waiting for the pain. When he did nothing more than carefully stroke her skin, she let it out. Then he pressed his nails into her, and she arched into his touch with a soft moan. And when he spread her legs far enough apart that she could feel the cold air on her hot, swollen sex, she groaned and wiggled.

Master Liam shifted beneath her and ever so slowly began to trace circles on her inner thigh. "You have a beautiful pussy, Rhiannon. I fucking love big clits, and you have a nice, swollen clit for me to suck on. Maybe we'll use a pump at some point and make it even bigger."

That mental image brought her out of the sensual spell he'd woven around her. Before she could ask him what hell he was talking about, he slid his finger between her slick labia and teased the entrance to her pussy. She let out such a guttural moan that made Master Liam laugh, and he continued to tease her.

"Mmm. That is a very wet pussy." He played with her but avoided her clit, making her try to arch her back in an attempt to get him to touch her where she needed it most. "What? Begging for my spanking already? I'd hate to disappoint such a good lass."

He removed his hand from her throbbing sex and brought it down with a loud smack on her bottom. She flinched, waiting for pain, but only a slight sting warmed the skin of her left butt cheek. He spanked her again, this time on the other side, and she let out a low breath, relieved beyond words that he didn't plan on beating her. With that relief came a deepening of her trust in him. It had been a long, long time since she'd felt this connected to anyone, and she fought with the emotions that threatened to overwhelm her.

Slowly he began to spank her harder, the blows now definitely stinging her bottom.

"Look at that pretty red bum." He traced his fingertips over her ass, making her at once uncomfortable and aroused. "You have such a tight little arse that I can see my fingerprints all over you. I like that. I like having my marks on you."

He slipped his hand between her legs and unerringly found her clit. At the first gentle rub of that sensitive bundle of nerves, she gripped his legs and pressed her aching sex into his touch. He stopped moving but kept his fingers on her clit, letting her grind her pussy against his hand as her orgasm drew closer. The slickness of her arousal covered his fingers, and he groaned.

Removing his hand, he then gave her ass a brisk slap that made her yelp. "Up on the table with you."

She stumbled against the table, and he laughed, catching her, then depositing her on the surface. The cool wood stung her burning bottom. "Ow!"

He began to unbutton his shirt, and she forgot everything but the handsome Scotsman looking at her like she was the most delicious dessert and he had a huge sweet tooth. Slowly his solid chest came into view with its light smattering of dark chest hair. Something about Master Liam was so exotic. He was such an interesting combination of cultures with his smooth chocolate skin and amazing hazel-green eyes. Add to that his sensual lips and huge frame, and he was any woman's fantasy man.

And right now he was all hers.

She shoved that possessive thought away. Fuck, the box of things she was trying to not think about was growing bigger by the second. Then Master Liam began to remove his pants, and she sat up for a better look. His pleased grin at her attention helped to ease her back into the moment. That and the pain from her ass as she shifted.

"You are the most beautiful woman I've ever seen, inside and out," Master Liam rasped.

He paused, clad now only in a pair of black boxer briefs that showed Master Liam was packing a very, very thick cock. Jessica had told Rhiannon that Master Liam loved to fuck women in the ass, but Rhiannon really, really hoped he didn't plan on that tonight. Master Rory's order about no sex didn't seem so bad right now if that included letting Master Liam's huge cock near her tender asshole.

Master Liam stepped closer, drawing her gaze to his chest. She wanted to lean forward and lick him. He was so fucking hot, and she momentarily lost herself in gazing at his body.

Placing his hand in the center of her chest, he pushed her back onto the table. "Here are the rules, girl. You will keep your body still from the neck down. If I move you, you will not help. Your only job, the only thing I expect of you, is to lie here and stay still."

Gazing up at the chandelier, she willed herself to relax and go pliant. This wasn't so bad. It might even be fun.

Then he stroked a hand down her inner thigh, and she gasped and spread her legs wider.

Immediately he slapped her breast. "I said stay still."

She clenched her teeth, trying to keep from glaring at him. It wasn't her fault she moved. The way she reacted to him, the sensations he made her feel, they all contributed to a complete loss of thought. Her body simply reacted to him in a way she'd never experienced.

She placed her palms on the table. She had more control than this. What if her future Master liked to play games where he tormented her like this? She would have to be able to give him her complete surrender. Or as much as she could. Besides, she trusted Master Liam.

He began to stroke her again, running his hands over her body, brushing past her aching nipples and skimming her sex. For a moment, his touch left her, and she felt the brush of his hip as he bent down, then stood back up. A second later, a very odd sensation traveled over her skin. She started to look up but stopped herself at the last second.

Cold, hard, with slightly sharp edges.

"Can you guess what it is, my beauty?"

She liked the way he said that. There was obvious affection in his voice, and she relaxed further. "I'm not sure, Master."

He began to brush it through the curls covering her mound. It almost felt like a comb. "A fork, Master?"

"Very good."

He moved again, and she tensed in anticipation. Pulling her slightly forward, he then spread her legs wider. "I cannot wait to get in that wet pussy."

She groaned and had to fight the urge to tilt her hips up. Never before had she realized how much she used her body to express her emotions. With Master Liam she just wanted to give in to her instincts and lose herself in him.

Then he put some ice on her clit, and she shrieked and tried to back away.

"Bad girl," Master Liam scolded.

She could only moan in protest as he manhandled her, turning her over and flipping her on her stomach, then jerking her to him until her feet hit the ground. "Take a good stance, lass, because you're getting another spanking."

"No! It will hurt!" She quickly cleared her throat. "I mean, whatever you wish, Master."

He chuckled and rubbed her bottom. "Sensitive, are you?"

"Yes, Master. I'm sorry."

"Why would you be sorry?" He curled over her, bracing his arms on either side of her head. The press of his warm, solid body on hers, covering her, protecting her made Rhiannon want to cry. He thrust his cock against her bottom, and she arched into him, rubbing her ass over him with a wanton moan.

"Because I'm not as good at taking pain as I should be."

"My beauty, never apologize for being born just the way you are." He placed a kiss on her cheek then rubbed his lips against her face. "I happen to like sensitive women. They feel every little touch, every sensation in a way most of us will never experience. It makes playing with you so much fun."

Moving just his lower pelvis, he began to push into her ass in a rhythm that had her scrambling for purchase on the table. She was sure the front of his boxers were totally soaked with her arousal by now. He scraped his nails down her back hard enough to sting. The lingering burn hurt, but it was nothing compared to the sensation of his cloth-covered cock rubbing on her. She wanted to taste him, to lick her essence off his cock, to have him use her however he wanted.

"Please, Master, let me suck you."

With a low groan, he pressed his face to her back. "Time for you to come."

He knelt behind her and began to eat her pussy in a way that had her moaning his name over and over. The long, rhythmic strokes of his tongue quickly drove her higher and higher until she ground her sex on his mouth, dying for an orgasm. He gave her ass a brisk slap. "Stay still or I'll start biting your clit."

"Fuck," she breathed out and tried to find something to hold on to, but only smooth wood met her fingertips.

"Mmm, like that idea, do ya?"

His evil chuckle should have been warning, but she still froze when he bit her clit below the sensitive tip. Her toes curled, and she lost her footing. Master Liam steadied her but didn't release her clit. Instead he continued to gently hold it between his teeth and suck. The excruciating desire tensed every muscle in her body. A few more seconds of that intense pleasure and she was trembling. Arousal built, built, built, throwing her higher until she could scarcely breathe past her need to come. Then he pressed his thumb into her anus, and she climaxed with a scream that hurt her throat. It was so good—too good—and the pulsing waves of her release tore her apart. White spots danced around her vision as she twisted and writhed, trying to escape Master Liam's tongue. He was relentless, stimulating her until she shook and begged him to stop. At last he gave her a final long, slow lick and moved away.

"Your cunt is delicious."

All she could do was twitch. Circuits had been blown in her brain, and she struggled to do anything more than lie there and smile. She felt amazing, so satisfied, and she began to giggle.

Master Liam chuckled and picked up her limp form. "Do you always laugh after an orgasm?"

Trying to stifle her giggles, she shook her head. "No. Only after the really amazing ones."

"I like it. The joy is so bright in your beautiful emerald eyes." The smile he gave her was that of a very pleased and proud male.

"I like pleasing you, Master."

He sat in the chair and slid her down between his feet. "Make me come, lass."

She arranged herself between his legs and ran her hands up his thick, solid thighs and gave in to an urge she'd had since the first time she saw him in a kilt. Placing her teeth into his skin, she bit the solid muscle of his thigh. He jumped and fisted her hair.

"Easy with the teeth."

She smiled at him and placed a kiss on the bite mark. "Sorry, Master. I've been wanting to do that for the longest time."

The hand in her hair gentled. "How long have you been watching me, lass?"

The question made her look away, and she began to run her fingers up his inner thighs, scraping ever so lightly with her nails. Maybe if she worked hard enough she could distract him from this line of questions. She enjoyed giving head, and the thought of giving Master Liam the kind of pleasure he'd just given her awoke the recently satiated heat between her legs. Arousal tightened her nipples as she leaned forward to rub her lips against the crest of his cloth-covered cock.

"A while."

His dick twitched against her mouth as she nuzzled him. "I had no idea."

"I know. It's not your fault. I watched you when you didn't know I was there."

Adding her hands to the mix, she began to gently massage his balls while sucking along his shaft through the boxers. "Stalker."

The word came out in a barely legible rumble, and she smiled against him. "Master, would you please lift up so I can pull your boxers off?"

He grunted and complied, revealing the long, thick, uncircumcised length of his cock. The tip was pink while his shaft was a few shades darker than the rest of his skin. He kept his pubic hair neatly trimmed, and his balls were shaved smooth. Men didn't usually shave that region unless they really liked a woman playing with them.

Eager to please, she leaned forward and drew his testicles into her mouth one by one. Master Liam grunted, then gripped the arms of the chair. She placed her hands on his thighs and held the solid muscle, enjoying how they flexed as she moved. Eager to taste him, she began to lick her way up from his balls, up his shaft, to the head of his cock. A nice drop of precum wet the tip, and she gently licked at it. Master Liam made a rumbling sound of pleasure deep in his chest, and she loved the fact that her efforts had drawn that sexy noise from him.

Holding him in her fist, delighting that she couldn't get her hand all the way around his shaft, she gently kissed the tip and moved the soft skin covering the head of his dick slowly back, licking at the revealed flesh. Suddenly his hand was in her hair, and he was pushing her mouth down onto his cock in a forceful motion that took all the control from her.

She struggled to keep up with his pace. She had to brace herself on his thighs as he fucked her mouth. Using her, he was using her body for his pleasure. That was so hot. Her desire flamed to life, arousal pinging through her system and making her wiggle as he shoved his cock deeper.

"Going to come in your mouth, Rhiannon. I want you place your lips just around the tip and suck as hard as you can while I come."

The strain in his voice, the tension in his thighs, and the scent of his musk filled her with longing. She wished he was inside her, soothing the ache he'd awoken in her body. The thought of him coming, of Master Liam filling her with his taste, had her moaning as he continued to move his cock in and out of her eager mouth. He groaned, his pelvis rising to meet her enthusiastic sucks.

He shuddered and slowly raised her mouth until the fat mushroom head of his cock spread her lips. She began to suck hard, and he shouted, gripping her hair tight enough to make her scalp tingle. A second later, the first spurt came, and she swallowed it as fast as she could. Another rush of his seed, and then another went over her tongue and down her throat as she swallowed. To her surprise, he gave her three more hard releases before he finally relaxed back into the chair.

She gentled her mouth and made sure he was totally finished before pulling away. Panting, she rested her head on his stomach and wrapped her arms around him the best she could. He let her nuzzle against him, petting her hair, stroking her face, but not saying anything. Eventually her arousal faded, and she became aware of how sore her knees were from being on the ground for so long and how her butt still hurt. She might have sensitive skin, but he had a really big hand.

Easing back, she slowly hobbled to her feet and rubbed her legs, trying to get the pins and needles out. When she looked up, she found Master Liam watching her with a smile she didn't quite understand. Feeling suddenly very naked, she looked around for her dress.

Before she could find it, Master Liam stood up and grabbed his white shirt from where he'd flung it. Walking closer to her, with his erection once again starting to grow, he slipped his shirt over her shoulders. The hem fell below midthigh, and the sleeves completely covered her hands. He grinned and rolled the shirt up until her hands where free, then cupped her face and placed a kiss on her forehead.

"Will you stay with me tonight? I'll have my driver bring you home in the morning. I'd take you myself, but I have an early flight to catch."

She looked up at him and studied his face. "Are you sure?"

"Very."

Trying to clear her mind and think, something that became difficult around Master Liam, she took a step back and attempted to fix her hair. The thought of sleeping next to him was incredibly intimate, and she couldn't find the strength to deny herself the pleasure. She knew that getting attached to him would only lead to heartbreak but the thought of sleeping alone instead of snuggled up to him made her heart hurt.

She gathered up her clothing, trying not to flash Master Liam. "Do you snore?"

He laughed. "I don't know."

"Well, have any of your trainees ever complained about you snoring?"

The warmth of him pressed up against her back as he moved behind her, then turned her around, holding her in his arms as she leaned back into his grip. "No, but I've never slept with a trainee."

She blinked at him, unsure of what to make of that statement. The stupid part of her that believed in knights in shining armor wanted to take that as a declaration of Master Liam's undying love for her, but the practical part, the one that had brought her through the hell, quickly reminded her that she was just another trainee to Master Liam. One thing Jessica had been adamant about, and that Kira, Dove, and Lucia had echoed, was that Master Liam and Master Rory never, ever fell in love with their submissives. In fact, as soon as a submissive started to show signs of falling in love, the men would politely but firmly send her on her way.

The thought of being rejected by the men had Rhiannon's emotional walls falling back into place and helped to clear her mind from the seductive spell that Master Liam had woven around her. This was just temporary, the men were just a means to an end, and to them she was nothing more than a trainee. To hope for anything more was emotional suicide.

Keeping that thought in mind, she stepped away from Master Liam and firmed her shoulders. "If you don't mind, could you have your driver take me home? I have a lot of work that I need to do before I see Master Rory tomorrow night."

He frowned at her, nude and aroused but somehow managing to not look vulnerable. "Of course."

She slipped off his shirt and wished she could change without him watching her. The way he looked at her gave her the distinct impression that she'd hurt his feelings. She was tempted to give in to his obvious desire to have her stay with him that night. Then she thought of all the women he'd sleep with after she was gone and it helped to firm her resolve. It wasn't fair that he was making her feel things she shouldn't feel. Some bonding with her trainers was totally expected, but she couldn't fall in love with them.

If they left her, if they made her go away after her training, it would destroy her heart if she allowed herself to love them. She'd worked too hard, come too far, to give up on her goals now. She wanted a man who would not only be her Master but also her husband. Something she didn't think Master Liam could ever be. While they'd agreed to only see her during her training, she knew Master Liam would want an open relationship where he could have sex with other women. Already the thought of him kissing someone like he kissed her, making those rough sounds as he came for another submissive, made her stomach fill with acid.

She slipped into her dress and zipped up the back as much as she could. Master Liam fastened it up the rest of the way. He placed a series of gentle kisses along her shoulder. "Stay with me."

Oh, he tempted her, especially with the trace of

vulnerability in his voice. "I can't."

"He abruptly pulled away. "I'll call for my driver."

The silence thickened between them as he dressed, and soon he was on the phone arranging her ride. He led her out of the elegant dining room. This was the right thing. She was merely establishing the boundaries she would need to keep her emotions out of the equation.

They waited in his foyer together, and she pretended to look at the paintings while he studied her. Headlights flashed through the windows around the front door; then Master Liam took a step closer to her. He held her chin in his hand and forced her to look into his eyes. After studying her for a moment, his gaze shuttered and grew cold. He released her and placed a kiss on her forehead.

"Good night, Rhiannon."

He sounded so sad and disappointed that her guilt surged and mixed with confusion and hurt. She quickly opened the door, afraid she would cry. "Good night, Master."

She practically sprinted down the steps to the waiting car. After giving the driver directions, she settled back into the elegant darkness of the plush Bentley and tried to pretend she couldn't smell Master Liam. Images from the evening played out in her mind, but she kept returning to one memory over and over again—the feeling of incredible satisfaction as she'd rested her head on Master Liam's lap after making him come. She'd felt so loved and cherished, and she wished with all her heart that she could convince herself that she wasn't falling for Master Liam.

Chapter Ten

Rory clenched his teeth as Liam met him in the foyer of his house. His private jet had just landed, and he was beat. Even though he'd slept on the comfortable bed in the jet, it was a broken and jagged sleep. Dreams filled with jealousy, want, love, and hate tormented him. He was so bloody glad to be home. His best mate, on the other hand, had his suitcase with him. Rory had just returned, but Liam was going off to Brazil for three days.

Rory stared at Liam and tried to see if he could tell how last night with Rhiannon had gone. The brazen smile he'd expected wasn't there. Instead Liam had dark circles beneath his eyes and tight lines around his mouth. It wasn't the face of a man who'd spent all night with one of the most beautiful women in the world, that was for damn sure.

His stomach sank, and he carefully leaned against the polished stainless-steel banister leading to the second level of his home. Though the outside of the home stayed true to its classic beauty, he'd decorated the interior with an eclectic mix of modern art and minimalist design. It might have been cold and forbidding without his priceless collection of comic book art displayed everywhere. The first thing to greet a visitor as they entered his home was a gigantic image of his favorite superheroes from the 1950s. It was an iconic image, but what Rory appreciated was how the artist had managed to capture the look of a Dom in the superhero's direct gaze. Every guest of his who happened to be a submissive would give a little gasp when they looked at that image, and that always made Rory smile.

Liam rubbed his face, and his shoulders slumped. "I asked

her to spend the night, and she turned me down."

All Rory's senses went on alert. "You did what? I purposely told both of you no sex. She isn't ready."

"I know! But once I was with her... Fuck, I lost my mind." He gave a bitter laugh and turned to face the superhero painting. "You don't understand what it's like to be around her. And I didn't try to fuck her. I asked her to spend the night in my bed so I could fall asleep with her in my arms."

The last part came out tightly, and Rory stared at Liam's broad shoulders. Jealousy tore through him as he worried that Liam had managed to seduce Rhiannon away from Rory. The betrayal of such an act hurt him, and he wondered when Liam had gone from loving him to hating him. They'd always shared a submissive—always. But Liam had never asked any submissive to spend the night at his home, and they both knew it.

"What did she say?"

"Why? You want to hear how she humiliated me?"

Hurt rang out in Liam's tone, and Rory tried to let go of his irrational anger. No matter what, Liam would always be his friend, and he didn't like to see him upset. "Hey now. Don't you go turning all soft on me. Do I need to go get you some tissues and a tampon?"

Liam laughed, and some of the tension left his frame, but he didn't turn around. "She's different. Special."

"What do you mean?"

With a low sigh, Liam finally turned and looked at Rory, his expression serious. "I know this is completely daft—I've spent all night telling myself that I'm a fool—but I can see myself spending the rest of my life with her."

Swallowing hard, Rory tried to mask his emotions. The thought that Liam might be severing their friendship for Rhiannon made his heart pound. "Are you asking me to step away?"

"Balls." Liam fisted his hands behind his head and looked at the ceiling. "Part of me wants to say yes, that I want her all to myself, but a bigger part of me wants you there. Needs you there. I— Fuck, I don't think I can give her everything she needs on my own."

The last part came out in a whisper, and it made Rory's heart ache. He wanted to go over and hug Liam, kiss him, reassure him that he would never leave, but he couldn't. Twelve years later, he still remembered the fateful night he and Liam had jerked each other off at their old university apartment. It had been so fucking hot, but their friendship had almost ended when Liam's homophobia drove him away. It was only after Rory brought his female submissive home for a ménage that they found a way to get what they needed without crossing the line between best friends and lovers. When he'd been younger, he'd thought that was going to be enough, but now he was ready for something more.

Time changed a man, and Rory had found himself envying his friends lately in a way he never had before. They'd all found the women they wanted to spend the rest of their lives with, and their joy was so intense it made Rory hurt with longing. He wanted a woman to look at him like Dove looked at Jesse. Or how Kitten smiled at Isaac, like he was her entire world. He remembered watching Bryan cradle a very pregnant Kira in his arms as she slept. The tenderness with which Bryan had stroked Kira's belly was enough to make a man want to get all misty-eyed.

Rory wanted a family of his own and would love it if Liam could be included in the equation. But he wouldn't spend the rest of his life with a man he couldn't admit he loved. Then again he also couldn't turn away from his friend's obvious pain. And now he had to factor in the idea that Rhiannon might not want them separately, and if he made her choose between them they could both lose her.

Taking a deep breath, he then blew it out and rubbed his tired eyes. When had his life become so damn complicated? "Don't be so fucking daft. You know her history. Evidently she doesn't have too much of a problem with physical intimacy, but emotional intimacy seems to make her shy away. So you asking her to sleep next to you, a very intimate thing, sent her running."

"Do you really think that's what it is?"

"Before you asked her to stay, how was your evening?"

"It was magnificent." He gave Rory that brazen grin of his that never failed to make Rory's breath catch. "Juiciest pussy I've ever eaten. The jet should be ready to fly again by now. I'm off.

Take care of her tonight."

Their gazes met and held for a moment, full of unspoken words and worries. Liam broke eye contact first and checked his watch, then sighed. His lips moved like he wanted to say something else, but instead he picked up his suitcase and headed out the front door without another word.

Rory studied the cut-glass panes around his black steel door. They threw beautiful refracted rainbows around the room. With a heavy sigh, he left his stuff in the foyer and went upstairs to his bedroom. By the time he reached his room, his eyes burned with lack of sleep, but the anticipation began to build. Tonight he was going to see Rhiannon, and he was going to make sure that if she had to choose between him and Liam that he would win. He felt like a bastard for plotting against Liam like this, but he was tired of living a lie.

So bloody tired.

That night he met Rhiannon at the local rugby field for the team he belonged to. He had a game to play, and he'd asked her to come cheer for him. While they were a minor league team, they were very good and always drew a crowd. Liam played on the team as well. Despite being in their thirties, they ran twenty-year-old men off the field.

"Hey, Rory."

One of his teammates, a nice kid named Walt from Georgetown University, came up and gave him a slap on the back. "Good to see you, old man."

Rory laughed and doubled-checked his shoes and pads. "Yeah, yeah."

"Where's Liam tonight?"

"He had some business to attend to down in Brazil."

"I swear, I want to be you guys when I grow up. Brazil one day; Paris the next. You're living the dream."

"I promise your imagination is much better than my reality."

Walt didn't answer, so Rory looked up to see what was

wrong. He found Walt staring at something behind Rory with his jaw hanging slightly open and his eyes filled with awe. Wondering what the fuck was going on, Rory turned and saw why Walt had been dumbstruck. He was fighting the urge to drool himself.

Rhiannon was making her way over to the fence. The late-summer nights were still warm enough for shorts, and the khaki pair Rhiannon wore made his blood boil. They weren't slutty, long enough to be considered almost modest, but she was so bloody hot that she could have worn a paper sack and made it look like lingerie. He quickly looked away from her smooth, tan legs and took in the white silk top she wore. It was secured over one shoulder with an elegant gold pin, leaving her other shoulder bare and begging for his lips. She wore her long hair in a high ponytail, and she could have stepped out of the pages of a fashion magazine. She slayed him where he stood without even saying a word.

Pride filled him that she belonged to him.

He'd have to get her a public collar ASAP.

And maybe a tattoo of his name on her ass.

"Holy shit," Walt muttered.

"What?"

"Who is that gorgeous creature?"

"My girlfriend." The words rolled easily off his tongue. He grinned at Walt, then caught the other man's very confused expression. "What is it?"

Walt flushed and looked away from Rhiannon. "Oh, nothing. I just, uh, well, you and Liam never have girlfriends, ya know."

It took him a second to figure out that Walt thought he and Liam were a couple. The instinctive reaction to deny any attraction came to mind, but today Rory shrugged it off. He was curious as to how many other men on the rugby team thought they were gay. "You thought Liam and I were a couple?"

Walt looked like he wanted to die. "I'm sorry, man. I didn't mean anything by it."

"No, no. It's fine." He took a quick glance around the field. "The whole team thinks we're a couple?"

Walt actually scuffed the ground with his cleats, looking far younger than his midtwenties. "I don't know."

The way he said it let Rory know it was a big yes. Funny. No one on the team had treated him and Liam any differently. Had he and Liam been living in such oblivious denial that they didn't notice their teammates thought they were gay? For a moment the realization that he could be with Liam and still have his life as it was stunned Rory. He'd always assumed they'd have to live in secret, that they would lose their friends or business partners if the word got out that they were gay, even though they weren't. He and Liam just never seriously dated any woman, preferring instead to train submissives.

You train them so you can avoid falling in love.

Walt cleared his throat. "Well, your hot-as-fuck girlfriend is looking worried. Sorry again. I didn't mean anything by what I said. I hope you don't think I'm a douche."

He gave the kid a quick one-armed hug. "Don't worry about it, mate. Now if you'll excuse me, I have a woman to woo."

"I'd woo the fuck out of her until she couldn't walk straight and I passed out," Walt said with a teasing grin and ducked the fist Rory jokingly threw in his direction. "That is one fine-ass female."

"Indeed."

Rory crossed over to her, conscious of everyone watching them. Were they staring because they thought he was gay? Shit, that certainly explained why the wives and girlfriends had stopped trying to fix him up with their friends and sisters. He'd always turned them down because he didn't get involved with anyone who wasn't a submissive, and he didn't get involved with any submissive who wasn't a trainee. Combine that with the way he and Liam did practically everything together, and he could easily see why his friends thought they were gay.

It made him angry that he and Liam could have been together—except Liam was too fucking chickenshit to even consider it. Resentment for his friend bubbled up, and he mentally shoved it away, forced himself to think only about the beautiful and so very fragile woman watching him from the other side of the chain-link fence.

Rhiannon smiled as he came nearer but glanced around

nervously. "Hi." She moved closer and whispered, "Why is everyone staring at us?"

"Well, the blokes are staring because you could make a dead man hard in those shorts, and the women are staring either because they wonder what the most eligible bachelor in Washington, DC is doing with you or if they need to kick their men." He leaned over the fence and brushed his lips against hers. "Or they are wondering what a gorgeous creature such as yourself sees in an old man like me."

She gave an uncomfortable laugh and backed away. He cleared his throat, realizing he was coming on too heavy. He'd lectured Liam about pushing her emotional comfort zone, but here he was doing the same bloody thing.

"I, however, am staring at you because I plan of touching every inch of your silky skin with my tongue tonight."

Her eyes widened, and she closed the distance between them. "Shh. There are children here."

"I missed you."

The honest words popped out before he was even aware he was going to say them. The truth of his statement rang through him, and when she smiled like it was the best news she'd heard all day, his heart lightened. Here was someone he could be with, someone he could care about, whom he didn't have to pretend was nothing but a friend.

"The things I'm going to do to you..."

Rory nipped at her fingers when she tried to cover his mouth, and she giggled. Rory's friend from Club Wicked, Isaac, waved from across the field, and Rory waved back. Isaac played for the opposing team. It was nice to see him so relaxed and happy, and Rory knew it was because Isaac was head over heels in love. The newly acquired gold wedding band on Isaac's finger had a lot to do with it, and Rory wondered what it would feel like to have a ring on his own finger, one that would forever tie him to the amazing woman who watched him with such shy trust that it made him want to protect her, cherish her, and love her until those emerald eyes were filled with nothing but joy.

Rory indulged himself by winking at her, making her blush. "Thank you for coming to watch me play. I know most women are bored to tears with sports."

"Oh, I don't mind." She gave him another bashful glance. "Thank you for asking me."

He brushed his fingers over her cheek, loving the satiny feel of her skin. "I would have asked you to meet me at the airport if I didn't know Liam had probably kept you up to the wee hours of the night."

Rhiannon blushed and looked at the ground, clearly uncomfortable at the mention of her time with Liam. Realizing he was moving too fast, he lifted her chin and made her look at him.

Before he could speak, Isaac came up and clapped Rory on the shoulder. "Rhiannon, please tell me you're not rooting for this tosser's team."

She laughed again, and as the big halogen lights came on she managed to look good even in their harsh light. "I have to cheer for my Mas—I mean, my date, er, my friend's team."

Rory stroked the back of his hand over her smooth throat, wishing he could touch lower and give poor Walt a stroke. Walt, along with most of Rory's team, tried to watch Rhiannon without being noticeable, but more than one man was seen adjusting his cup. A fierce possessive streak flared to life, and Rory traced his fingertips over her lips, letting them see he could touch what they couldn't.

"I like it when you call me your date."

A lovely flush stained her cheeks, and Rory exchanged a grin with Isaac. The other man pointed to the stands behind Rhiannon. "Lucia is up there. She asked me to tell you she hopes you'll sit with her. One of the women brought in some sangria, so they're up there getting toasted."

Rory quickly found Isaac's wife, Lucia, known at Club Wicked as Kitten, waving at them while holding a red plastic cup. Isaac was a lucky man because she was as sweet as she was pretty. Since she was one of the three women who had come to berate Liam and Rory about not meeting Rhiannon on time, he figured the women not only knew each other but were friends.

Rhiannon waved at Lucia, then let out a small sigh of relief. "Thank you. I was worried I'd have to sit alone."

The way she said it, as if it was one of the worst things that could happen to her, made Rory's Dom instincts rise to the surface. "I'd never leave you alone, darling."

She gave him a shy smile that moved him in an entirely new way, and swung her purse lightly. "I'm sure you have to get ready for the game. Good luck."

He laughed and motioned her closer. "If you want to wish me a proper good luck, you'll come here and give me a kiss."

Blushing more, she smiled softly as he brought his lips down to hers. He'd intended to make it a small, gentle kiss, but she stroked the tip of her tongue over the seam of his lips. It was all he could do not to grab her, so he held on to the fence instead hard enough to make his hands ache. Her lips were so incredibly soft and giving as she opened for him. When their tongues met, she sucked on his in a sensual move that was all slow heat and burning desire.

Isaac coughed. "Unless you want to pitch a tent on the field, I suggest you save it for after the game."

Rhiannon jerked back and gave a feeble wave before making her way up the stands. He didn't like how she avoided the eye contact of the crowd, as if she'd done something shameful. It was a kiss—okay, a heated kiss—but nothing he hadn't seen the other men giving their girlfriends or wives.

A shout cut through his contemplation. Isaac jogged backward and said, "Good luck."

"I don't need luck, mate. I've got skills."

"I was talking about with Rhiannon, not the game."

"Same thing applies."

They both laughed, and Rory began what was both the longest and shortest rugby game of his life. He was entirely distracted by Rhiannon's presence in the stands, but luckily his team picked up the slack. Not that he was a total waste of space, but if he noticed her watching him, he lost his focus on anything but Rhiannon and her lovely smile.

By the end of the game, Rhiannon and Lucia were with a bunch of the other player's wives, laughing and hugging as they celebrated the team's win. He got a lot of shit from the other players about his less than stellar performance, but he only listened with half an ear. It was time to follow Rhiannon to Club

Wicked, and he could not wait.

Rory tried to ease the hard pounding of his heart by taking a deep breath. The distinct scents of sex and perfume filled his nostrils as he waited near the women's dressing room of Wicked situated off the main entrance. Any second now Rhiannon should be coming out, and he was as nervous as a lad waiting for his first date. While he'd always cared about his trainees, he'd never felt this personally invested with one before. He wanted to make this one of the most amazing nights of Rhiannon's life.

"Master Rory!"

His name echoed through the three-story marble foyer. He followed the sound of that familiar woman's voice, and his smile grew wider at the sight of the pretty brunette beaming at him.

Kerry, a sweet submissive they'd trained three years ago, came running at him full tilt. A lovely girl with wavy light brown hair and sweet blue eyes, she was a plump and cuddly armful. With a bright smile she threw herself at him, he caught her and swung her around. As usual she gave a giggling shriek before wrapping her legs around his waist and kissed him soundly on the lips. "Guess what?"

"What?"

She pulled up her left hand and wiggled her finger, the diamond catching the light with her movements. "I'm getting married!"

"Congratulations!"

She hugged him extra tight, her legs still holding him close. She whispered, "Thank you so much, Rory. Without you I'd still be sitting at home, wishing I had the courage to talk to a man. You and Master Liam changed my life."

His throat actually closed up, and he hugged her back. "I'm so happy for you, sweetheart."

Suddenly she stiffened and thumped him on the back. "Uh, Master Rory, you might want to put me down before I have to fight that chick behind you."

He turned and found Rhiannon glaring at him. No, wait,

this was Goddess. The warm, giving, open woman who'd been at his rugby game was gone, and in her place was one very, very pissed-off female.

Clad in a flowing, transparent gown almost Grecian in style, Rhiannon had to be one of the most striking women he'd ever seen. Beneath the gown, she wore a tiny white thong that seemed to be made of ribbon, because the darkness of her pubic hair was peeking through. She'd swept her hair up and had woven some kind of gold rope through it.

From behind the golden mask shaped like flames, her green eyes glittered with anger, and her full lips were pressed into a thin line. Rhiannon gripped her hands into fists at her side and said in an icy voice, "Sorry. Didn't mean to interrupt. My mistake. Have a nice night."

Frowning, Rory let Kerry slide down his body. "What did you say?"

"You heard me!" Rhiannon trembled with anger, and the hurt in her voice physically pained him. "I'm sorry I interrupted. Please go back to fucking her in the foyer."

Kerry gasped and moved out of his embrace. "Oh, shit."

Ignoring Rhiannon, he turned and gave Kerry a very deliberate kiss, enough of one to let Rhiannon know that she wouldn't dictate what he did with a temper tantrum, not while they were at Wicked. It irritated him that she instantly assumed the worst, and he'd be damned if he was going to feel bad about hugging Kerry. He needed to set his jealous little submissive straight on a few things, like trusting him.

Rhiannon made some kind of muffled shriek, but he ignored it while he smiled at Kerry. "Congratulations again, darling. Tell Master Scott he'd better treat you right."

She nodded and turned on her heel, practically running in the other direction. A crowd had gathered now, probably drawn by the fireworks about to go down. He turned to Rhiannon and tried to get into her head. No doubt she wasn't pleased to find Kerry wrapped around him like that, but he'd had no idea how bad her jealousy was. She looked ready to go after Kerry, and while he knew her anger was from emotional pain, he couldn't have her wanting to beat up every woman who hugged him.

Her lower lip trembled when he pointed to the floor in front of him. "On your knees."

Blinking rapidly, she took a step forward, then stopped herself. "Why? So I can suck your dick and taste her on it?"

Shocked gasps echoed around him, and he slowly shook his head. She was just begging for a fight. He'd give it to her but not here. Why was she this antagonistic? Memories of her fight with Sunny over Hawk flashed through his mind. He had to resist the urge to growl with irritation.

Moving quickly, he picked her up and threw her over his shoulder, ignoring her screams, and she thumped her small fists on his back. He noticed that she wasn't really trying to hurt him, but oh, was she cussing up a storm. It might have been funny if he wasn't so worried about her.

"You fucking bastard! Let me go!"

"My mother might disagree with that statement."

He went into the first empty room he could find. It was a suspension room and held a variety of places to chain a submissive up, including a rather elaborate sex swing. It looked like the standard pull-and-release grid. He simply had to grab one of the manacles or cuffs hanging from the ceiling, jerk it down, and it would slide up onto the railing allowing him to position it as he wished. Another jerk and the chain would lock back into place, giving him a secure and strong restraint to bind his girl with.

The walls were a soft blue, and the floor was made of beautifully painted tiles with a drain in the center. While he didn't normally use wet play rooms, he knew what he needed to do in order to reestablish his bond with Rhiannon. She needed to know that she was the only woman he wanted.

When Rhiannon struggled against him, he gave her ass a solid swat. "I don't want to drop you, so cut the bullshit, Rhiannon."

She stiffened. "Let me go."

"No."

That set her off again, but he dumped her ass into the wide seat of the white leather sex swing. She tried to sit up, but the swaying of the chains and the lack of a good handhold stopped her. He pressed her back into the swing with his hand. "Lie still or

I'll put some stripes on your arse with a nice caning."

She blanched. "You wouldn't dare, you cheating asshole."

He had to hold his anger back. "I've never cheated on anyone, Rhiannon. Ever. Now I suggest you shut that pretty mouth and listen to me instead of having a tantrum."

"What the fuck do you call kissing that slut?"

He ripped off her mask and tossed it over his shoulder. "You will not call Kerry a slut. Am I clear?"

"Fuck you."

Grabbing her hand, he then pulled over a wrist cuff hanging from the ceiling. It was a big, solid white cuff lined with black rabbit fur. She gave a token struggle, so he leaned over and slapped her breast. "Stay still."

Her lower lip trembled. "I hate you."

He shook his head, moving around to secure her other wrist. "Keep your mouth shut. It's time you listened instead of just reacting."

She jerked her arms, but they were both hanging out to her sides. She couldn't reach him. That made her struggle, but the swing just absorbed the motion. He pulled a leg cuff. "Give me your foot."

"No."

She thrashed, but he was done fucking off. He looked around and quickly found the cabinet full of toys on the far side of the room. The whole time Rhiannon kept up her fussing, but the anger was draining from her voice. Now she sounded close to tears, and that made him only more determined. He couldn't have her doubting him or herself like this.

Making his way back to her, he showed her the zapper. It was a long object that looked like the lighter he used to light the grill. But instead of making fire, this device created an electrical charge that when applied to the skin felt like a rubber band being snapped. Unlike a rubber band it didn't leave any marks.

"Now why are you so angry with me?"

"Fuck off!"

He gave her a zap on the thigh, and she shrieked, then grew quiet for a moment before saying in a low voice, "What was that?"

"Time for one of your most important training lessons, Rhiannon. Honesty. I'm going to ask you questions, and you're going to tell me the truth. If you lie, you get zapped. If you're honest, you get rewarded."

"I don't want to do this!"

Keeping his voice gentle, he rubbed her stomach with a soothing touch, aware of how vulnerable it would make her feel to be caressed there. "Are you using your safe word, love?"

Her mouth opened and shut several times before she gritted out, "No."

"Good. Now tell me why your feelings are hurt."

"My feelings aren't hurt."

Zap.

"Ow!"

"Don't lie to me. I can feel your sadness."

Zap.

"Bastard! You didn't even ask me a question!"

"Stop playing games with me."

He held the zapper to the side of her left breast, and she sucked in a hard breath. "I fucking don't like you touching another woman. It makes me crazy jealous, you fucking asshole."

Leaning over, he then placed a series of soft kisses along her smooth thigh, inhaling the scent of her skin even as she tried to struggle away from his touch. "Why? All I was doing was hugging her."

"You kissed her!"

"That too," he agreed. "Kerry is one of the most touch-oriented people I've ever met. She can't be around people she likes without wanting to give them physical attention."

Rhiannon struggled fruitlessly against the chains. "Why don't you go fuck her?"

He sighed and put the zapper down on her stomach so he could cup her face with his hands. "First off, I trained Kerry three years ago. We've remained friends, and I enjoy having her in my life. That does not mean I want to fuck her or that she wants to fuck me. She's a comfort submissive. Touching and holding is as natural to her as breathing."

The tremble in Rhiannon's lips hurt his heart but not nearly as much as the pain in her gaze. He stroked her cheek, studying her.

"Then why was she kissing you?"

"Like I said, Kerry is very physical, and tonight she's exceptionally excited because she just got engaged."

Confusion crossed her face, making fine lines appear around her expressive eyes. Her hair had been messed up during their struggle, but it only made her more appealing. Moving slowly, he kissed every inch of her face from the delicate skin of her eyelids to her lips. She whispered against him, "I thought you didn't want me."

"Darling, I want you more than I've ever wanted any woman, and I'm sorry I hurt your feelings."

She let out a shuddering breath. "I'm sorry, Rory, I mean Master Rory. I'm fucked-up."

He pulled back just enough so he could see her. "Talk to me. I promise anything you say here will be kept strictly between us, but I need to know why you became so jealous. I've seen you do the same thing with Hawk. Talk to me, Rhiannon. I swear I won't betray your trust."

She searched his face. "Promise?"

He nodded. He had a feeling that whatever she was about to tell him wasn't going to be good. Suddenly he wanted her out of this room and in his arms. "Hold on a second."

He began to unbuckle her hands, then her feet.

"What are you doing?"

"This isn't the right place for this. Trust your Master, girl, and don't argue."

He helped her to her feet and kept his hold on one of her hands, then laced her fingers with his to maintain the contact between them. After putting her mask back on, she followed him out the door. He ignored everyone and everything as he took her through Wicked as quickly as he could. They reached the massive glass back doors leading to the side gardens, and he took her outside into the cool night air. Looking back over his shoulder to make sure she was okay, he was struck by her beauty.

The night seemed to embrace her, and the white of her gown glowed in the moonlight. Tamping down on his libido, he led her into a grove of old growth trees. They passed a few couples on the way, but they were no more than indistinct shapes among the trees. The first couple hammocks were occupied, and the sound of a woman orgasming not too far away made his cock fill with blood. He told his body to calm down, that Rhiannon needed his mind more than his cock, but he couldn't control his reaction to the delicious sound of sex.

When he found an empty hammock, he tumbled them into it, landing on a down comforter and a mass of velvet pillows. With a smile, he pulled Rhiannon closer, and she giggled as he hauled her around and rearranged her and the pillows until he was comfortable. Immediately he relaxed as Rhiannon snuggled into him.

This was right atmosphere for Rhiannon. He didn't know how he knew that, but it was true. Rhiannon blew out a low breath and began to toy with the edges of his T-shirt, so he settled back and let her get comfortable. Since she was in therapy he knew she'd had experience talking to someone about her problems, but he still worried that he'd push her too far too fast. Yes, he'd talked with her therapist and had been assured that he was doing just fine with Rhiannon, but he worried.

To soothe both her and himself, he continuously touched her and indulged himself in the pleasure of being next to her. "Ready to talk now, love?"

She groaned and buried her face against his chest. "I'm sorry. I just get so...angry sometimes."

"You were angry, but you were also very jealous and hurt. Why?"

"Well, you were kissing her!"

The last word was loud enough to make his ears ring. "I understand that part. But you didn't even think to ask for an explanation. You immediately assumed the worst."

She was silent for a bit, still playing with his shirt. "Look, I know you're not really my Master—"

He tilted her chin up so he could see her as best he could in the dim light. "No, Rhiannon, I am your Master. We agreed that during your training neither Master Liam or myself would be with anyone else. What have I done to indicate that I'm a liar?"

"No, it's not you. It's me. You don't understand. I'm fucked-up in the head, Rory."

Due to the nature of their discussion, he didn't bother to make her call him Master. "Explain it to me. Help me understand."

"I can't."

"Why not?"

"Because you won't want me anymore."

Her words came out so soft that he barely heard them. How such a beautiful woman had such low self-confidence was something he just didn't comprehend. "Aside from confessing that you're a serial killer, I can't think of anything that would make me leave you."

"The man who abducted me liked to play mind games with me."

Trying to keep his heart rate normal because she was lying on his chest, he took a slow breath and willed himself to relax, afraid she would mistake his anger as being directed at her. "Explain."

"I-I... This is hard to explain. How much do you know about the gypsy culture?"

"A bit. The drummer for my father's band is a gypsy, or like we call them in the UK, a traveler."

"Your dad's in a band?"

He froze, wondering how she'd react when she found out his father was a rock and roll legend. "We're not talking about my family, love."

"Well, in the gypsy culture I was raised in a girl is raised to be a wife. Her purity, her virginity is of the utmost importance, the key to her value as a bride. That's not to say it's that way with all gypsies, but for my people it is. No Roma boy wants a gypsy girl who has a bad reputation, and girls with bad reputations are often shunned by their families if not kicked out of the community. It's the girl's family's job to make sure her reputation stays intact and that she remains a good girl."

He wanted to say how strange that was but stopped himself. This was her culture, her people, and he didn't want to insult her by telling her he thought that was bullshit. She needed him to listen, not react.

"Were you raised like that?"

"Yes. I couldn't go anywhere without a chaperone, and my parents really hated me going to a public school. They were so happy when I dropped out in the tenth grade that they threw me a huge sweet sixteen party as my coming out. What they didn't know was that I had dropped out so I could run off after my party to be with...him."

"The man who abducted you?"

"Yes."

"But if you were so secluded, how did you meet him?"

"On the Internet. When I did have some free time, I liked to read, and I belonged to a chat room where I'd talk about a popular book series about a girl and her unicorn. My parents didn't mind because they had this software that was supposed to keep our computer safe, and a few of my female cousins belonged to the group as well. I mean, it was a bunch of young girls talking about unicorns, for fuck's sake. Or at least it was supposed to be. He was there as well, and at first, we just talked about books and life and stuff. He was so nice to me, but I should have realized then that no decent man would be hanging out talking with teenage girls. At the time, I was just flattered that he'd taken an interest in me, that he thought I was special." She took a shuddering breath. "Latisha, Mistress Onyx, says that he was an expert at grooming me, at bending me to his will. We talked for months online before he showed me how to hide my phone calls on my cell phone from my parents."

"How old were you when all this started?"

"Fourteen."

Rage washed over him. "And how old was he?"

"Thirty-six."

"So he talked to you for two years before he convinced you to run off?"

"Yes."

Rhiannon's abductor had been four years older than Rory was, stalking a little girl. The thought made him completely ill. He swallowed hard, twice before he could get his words out. "I see."

She curled in on herself, but he wouldn't allow it. Instead, he gathered her into his arms as much as he could, curving himself around her much smaller frame, wishing he could go back in time and kill that motherfucking pedophile who'd spent two years mind fucking Rhiannon.

"He used to make me jealous." Her words held so much shame that he wanted to tell her to stop, that she didn't need to torture herself like this, but he had to hear this, had to know what he was dealing with. "He'd send me pictures of himself on dates and forward the e-mails the women would write him about how much they enjoyed having sex with him. He'd tell me that he didn't really want these women, that he was just using them for sex until I was ready to become his woman."

"How could your parents miss what was going on?"

"My mom didn't know much about computers, and my dad was always traveling on business. It was pretty easy once I learned how to set up secret accounts. Greg, that's his name, worked for the government doing top-secret computer stuff in addition to being an artist. He knew computers inside and out and hiding our conversations from my mom was child's play to him."

"You were the perfect victim."

"Yeah. Young, sheltered, and painfully naive."

"I'm so sorry."

She stiffened, then leaned up on his chest so she could look at him. "Don't feel sorry for me. I hate it. I'm not weak."

"Let me rephrase this. My heart hurts for you, Rhiannon. I want to go back in time and slit his throat, to stop him from ever having caused you one moment of pain. It fucking kills me to see you sad like this and hurts me even more to know that I made you feel this way."

"No, no. Please don't say that. It's not your fault I can't handle my jealousy. I just... I saw you touching her, and my mind immediately went to him."

"What can I do to help?"

She was quiet for a long time, tracing her fingers along his chest in a way that soothed him. "Please don't kiss anyone else, okay? I know she's your friend and you didn't mean anything by it and you're just my trainer, but I can't take it."

He wanted to tell her that he wasn't just her trainer, that he was falling in love with her, but he managed to keep those notions to himself. It was way, way too early to be thinking those thoughts, let alone voicing them aloud. "I promise. No kissing other people."

"Swear on your word as a man?"

"I swear, love."

Her body slowly relaxed against his, and she let out a long breath, further softening in his arms. They swayed slightly in the hammock, and he gently stroked her back, praying that he was doing the right thing with her. She looked up at him and smiled, her teeth a bit of light among the shadows of her face as she lightly tickled his ribs. "Well, you can kiss Master Liam. That would be hot."

He laughed. "The sight of us kissing would turn you on?"

She giggled and moved so she was lying flat atop him. The cradle of her hips and her soft belly pressed against his cock, and he became suddenly aware of how good she felt. Soft limbs, smooth skin, and a layer of toned muscle that gave her a lovely shape.

"Mmm-hmm. I know lots of guys have a thing for watching two women together—it certainly seems to be popular here at Wicked—but I have a thing for watching men."

"Well, sorry to disappoint, but Liam would never kiss me."

The words didn't come out quite as he intended, because as he spoke, she pressed her breasts between her arms and completely distracted him. The sight of her magnificent tits sent a rush of blood intended for his brain to his cock instead.

She tilted her head to the side just the slightest, reminding him of a puppy with something that caught its interest. "Do you want to kiss Master Liam?"

He swallowed hard, the urge to confess his feelings for the

other man on the tip of his tongue. Never had he felt this comfortable with someone so quickly, but he had a bond with Rhiannon that was undeniable. He wondered if she felt it, if it would be enough to convince her to stay with him. "I want to kiss *you*."

He gripped her by the back of the neck and brought her mouth to his, licking at her lips, tasting her, and groaning as she wiggled around so her legs straddled his hips. It was hard to find purchase in a hammock, and he put his hands beneath her knees for her to brace herself. She smiled against his mouth; then she began to kiss her way across his cheek and down his neck, her soft lips branding him like an iron.

"Master, may I touch you?"

"You can do anything you want to me." The sassy grin she gave him made him give her arse a sharp slap. "Within reason."

To his shock she didn't mess around. She wiggled down his body and went straight for his pants. He grunted as she squeezed, then pulled his pants down enough to free him. The happy sigh she made had him smiling as he watched her stroke the head of his cock in this little twisting motion that drove him crazy.

His balls drew up tight, and before he knew it, she was jerking his dick hard, just how he liked it. Then she flicked her tongue over the top. He realized instantly that Jessica had told Rhiannon about how he liked to be touched. That was Jessica's signature move, and it drove him fucking crazy.

He sighed, thinking of all the ways he would make Rhiannon come after she sucked him off. The list of things he wanted to do to her was enormous. If they spent every night together for the next seven years, they wouldn't get to all the ways he wanted to take her, possess her, own her willing submission.

"Hmm." Rhiannon looked up at him and licked her lips, a creature of velvet shadows. "You taste good."

She sank down on his cock, then sucked hard enough to make him see spots. She was so eager to please, and he loved it.

He'd never been this turned on by a submissive before. Oh, he'd experienced things that were so good they had to be a sin, but with Rhiannon, his arousal seemed to go to a previously unknown level. Up and down her slick mouth went on his cock, pausing now and again to lick his balls.

Finally she sat back and loosened the top of her dress enough that her breasts spilled out. He grabbed a handful of one and squeezed hard, indulging himself with the feel of her tit. So soft, yet firm and warm. He tweaked her nipple, then held that tender nub and pulled her down by her nipple to bring her mouth back to his cock. He wanted to come and get it over with so he would calm down enough to play for real.

She spit down the crack of his ass, then began to work a finger around his anus. The nerve endings flared to life, and he groaned. While he enjoyed playing with a woman's bottom, he didn't often allow a woman to touch him there, but with Rhiannon, he was willing to indulge her in however she wanted to touch him. It was a very intimate thing, not only because of the taboo associated with it, but because he imagined Liam playing with his ass all the time. He had to admit that more than once he'd wished it was his ass Liam was pounding into instead of their submissive's.

At the thought of his darkly handsome best mate, Rory's bullocks drew up tight. But this wasn't the time. Instead, he reached out and brushed his hand over Rhiannon's hair. Then she added some teeth, and he once again lost himself in her efforts to please him. And she was making an effort. Right now, Rhiannon was doing everything she could to make him happy, because in her heart of hearts, she was a submissive who loved to please her Master.

"That's it, my darling girl. You look so bloody sexy taking my cock in your mouth."

She moaned and pressed her thighs together. He'd bet that right now her pussy was as wet and swollen as could be. If his cock hadn't been in her mouth, she'd probably be begging. She took him deep in her throat and finger fucked his ass.

The combination of the feel of her hair, the wet, hard suction of her mouth, and the way the nerves of his anus were being stimulated sent him over the edge. He grabbed on to the hammock, afraid he would rip her hair out as the first surge burned through his spine and into his pelvis. She pulled her lips up to the tip of his cock and let his cum spill out of her mouth as she jacked him off, squeezing more seed from him until he was ultrasensitive to her touch.

Then she began to lick him clean like a cat. He was pretty sure his eyes rolled back in his head. The delicate, gentle touch of her lips and tongue were the most exquisite torture, but he endured for her. He chuckled as an odd thought came to him. This was the closest he'd come to vanilla sex in forever. He couldn't remember the last time he'd done something sexual with a woman that hadn't involved any kind of kink. Yeah, they were outside but isolated, so that didn't really count. There'd been no clamps involved or sex toys or bondage or anything other than just the two of them touching each other.

She tucked him back into his pants, then gave him a shy look. "Did I do okay? Is there anything I could do to perfect my technique? I'm sure whoever my Master ends up being he'll appreciate it if I learn all I can about what has to be one of men's favorite pastimes."

He stared at her, insulted by her brazen reminder of this only being a training session. It was time to remind Ms. Rhiannon who held the control around here. "I'm going to finger you, then eat you, then fuck you, then eat you some more."

She almost fell out of the hammock, and he grabbed her with a laugh, his anger forgotten by her stunned look.

"This is so not fair!"

Bemused, he pulled her next to him, but she remained stiff. "What's not fair?"

"Master Liam made me promise that I wouldn't have sex with you or anything else. He said he wants to test my ability to attend to only my Master's needs. Plus he said he wants me hungry for when you both see me in two days."

Anger burned through Rory at Liam's audacity. True, Rory had forbidden Rhiannon from having sex, but it was for...her own good. Fuck, he couldn't lie to himself. He'd forbidden Rhiannon from having sex with Liam because he was jealous. Just like he was right now. God bloody fucking dammit. Both Liam and he were messing this up. Rhiannon needed them acting as a united front, not subtly trying to tear each other apart.

He'd respect Liam's request tonight, but they had some plans to make as soon as Rory came home and got that bastard on the phone. He suddenly wondered if Liam would call Rhiannon but decided not to ask. No matter what was going on in his head, he had to keep his shit straight for her.

"You aren't going to be able to walk this weekend at work."

She laughed, the young and free sound carrying through the grove. Her laughter certainly warmed him inside and out, strengthening his resolve to be the Master she deserved.

Shit, he must be in love.

His dad had told him the one true way for a man to know if he was in love was that the woman would make him want to be a better person. He wanted to meet all Rhiannon's needs so well that she'd never want to live without him.

He was so bloody fucked.

She leaned forward so her elbows were on his chest. "Oh, I forgot to tell you. I managed to get Saturday and the next two weeks off from work. I have about six months in vacation time built up."

"Six months? Don't you ever take time off?"

Looking away, she then pulled a pillow over and rolled off him with the grace of a cat. "Not really."

"Why not?"

"I don't know. I guess I really just have nowhere to go." She smiled up at him. "Well, I used to have nowhere to go. Going to your island will be the first time I get to use my passport."

Blinking, he tried to keep his expression smooth. Evidently Liam had invited Rhiannon without his knowledge. She grew quiet, and he forced himself to respond. "What day will you be joining us on?"

"Oh, I'm going to fly out with Liam on Saturday. He said you wouldn't be able to join us until Monday."

That motherfucker was trying to get Rhiannon alone. Liam knew Rory had a business meeting in Texas this weekend. Well, Rory *used* to have a business meeting in Texas. That shit was getting canceled the moment he had a chance to speak alone on the phone.

"Actually, I'll be able to fly out with you as well."

His heart lightened when she beamed at him. "Awesome! I

can't wait to see your island. I mean, I've never even been to the Caribbean. All day today I was looking at different websites, learning about the islands and the history. Oh, and the food! I can't wait to eat my way through the island. Do you have fruit trees growing there? What about a vegetable patch? Or is it too sandy? It is such a—"

He gently placed his hand over her mouth. "It's just a house on an island. No big deal."

She snorted and moved his hand. "I don't know what kind of world you live in, but in my world that is a huge deal."

He tugged her close and gave her a slow, melting kiss. Little did she know that his world was her world now. Pulling back, he nibbled on her lower lip. "It's getting late, darling. I don't want you driving home tired. Would you like to come home with me?"

She stiffened and jerked back. "No, thank you."

Turning lightly, she then rolled out of the hammock and smoothed her hands down her dress.

He tried to brush away his disappointment. It didn't matter if she wasn't with him tonight. She was going on vacation with him, well, with them. Even if he had to share a bed with Liam and Rhiannon, he was going to sleep with her.

Chapter Eleven

Liam sighed wearily but wasn't surprised to see Rory waiting for him at the airport instead of their driver. He should have known Rory would want to tell him face-to-face how he felt and, judging by his expression, he wasn't happy.

Liam wondered if Rory knew about his attempt to secret Rhiannon away. By the anger flashing through Rory's blue eyes, Liam would have to say yes. In fact, he couldn't remember the last time his best mate had looked this pissed. Tension radiated off Rory, and Liam wondered if he'd get his face punched in the middle of the airport.

Rory shoved his hands into the pockets of his jeans, the T-shirt he wore revealing the muscles in his arms. "Nice of you to let me know our plans had changed."

Trying to pretend he had no idea what Rory was talking about, Liam tossed his suitcase into the trunk and began to take his suit coat off. "What plans would that be?"

"Don't be fucking coy with me, you bloody wanker."

Liam cocked his head to the side. "Fine. You want to have it out here in front of these good people trying to get home after a long trip, by all means, let's go."

If steam could have come out of Rory's ears, it would have. "Get in the car."

Liam slid into the passenger seat of the car after throwing the rest of his luggage in the trunk. He looked straight ahead when Rory got in and wished he wasn't such a fucking bastard. Rory didn't deserve to be lied to. Hell, Liam prided himself on always telling the truth, yet here he sat, lying with every breath he took. He didn't like himself like this and had been unable to sleep last night because of his guilt.

Even worse, he couldn't respect himself.

Giving in to a rash impulse before he chickened out, Liam looked at Rory. "I think we should collar her."

The car swerved slightly as Rory looked at him in disbelief. "What?"

"She needs to know she means something to us, that we're serious about her. Despite the fact that she's an amazing woman, her self-esteem is shit. I don't like it that she still thinks of us as her trainers, like we're going to leave her at a moment's notice. I want her to have some physical proof that she belongs to us."

Rory said in a low voice, "I'm surprised you bothered to include me in your plans. What's with the sudden honesty?"

He winced but knew he deserved Rory's reprimand. "I was hurt that she rejected me and pissed that you got to see her when I didn't. She's...she's the most captivating woman I've ever met, and I'm acting like a complete asshole."

"Yes, you are."

"Well, you started it with that 'don't have sex with Liam' bullshit."

Rory merged into traffic and shot Liam an angry look. "You wouldn't have done the same thing? Be honest, Liam. You don't like the thought of me fucking her first any more than I like the idea of you fucking her first."

"Then why did you send her to the gala with me?"

"Because...because—fucking hell—because I wanted to see if you could love her."

"Why?"

"Liam, I haven't spent twelve bloody years with you to throw away what we have now. Besides, Rhiannon adores you."

He decided to avoid the sticky question of what he and Rory had in favor of the more pleasant idea of Rhiannon returning his affection. "She told you that?"

"She didn't have to." Rory gave a sour grunt. "When she talks about you, she lights up."

"Jealous?"

"Yes." Rory's honesty surprised him. "Very. Which is why we need to do this together. No more solo bullshit."

"What if she doesn't want both of us? What if she doesn't want either of us?"

"Then we make her want us."

"Oh, yeah. That'll work."

"Don't be daft. I think you were right about her needing both of us. Even if she hadn't been abused in her past, I think Rhiannon is the type of woman that will need lots of love. With our travel schedules, she would be alone more than I'd like. But with the two of us loving her together, that wouldn't be as much of an issue."

"Let's not get ahead of ourselves. Don't you think she'd freak out if we asked her to be our submissive?"

"Maybe, but we'll never find out if we don't at least try."

He sighed and tapped his fingers against the window, wishing Rory had put the top down despite the early morning hour. "Did she come last night? Wait, no, you don't have to answer that. Sorry. It's the fucking jealousy talking. I've never had to deal with this before. Balls. I can see why so many crimes are committed in the name of envy."

"Evil emotion," Rory agreed. "Rhiannon gets insanely jealous. Last night she almost beat up Kerry."

"What?"

Rory told him the story, and Liam rubbed his face with a groan. "Come on, man. You know better than that. Until you know how a submissive feels about you touching anyone but her, you keep your hands off."

"I know. I feel like an asshole, but Kerry is just…Kerry. I can't be around her without wanting to hug her. And not in a sexual way."

"Probably why she makes such a great comfort submissive. I'm glad she's finally found the right man for her."

"Yeah." The yearning in Rory's tone was clear. "Must be nice."

The freeway passed by in a blur as Liam stared out the

window. "I think offering Rhiannon a collar, letting her know it's there if she wants it, would help her."

"I don't know. What if it scares her off, and she finds someone else to train her?"

"No, I don't think that will happen. She sought us out, and despite the rather crappy job we've done giving her any actual training, she picked us for a reason that I believe goes beyond her desire to learn the art of submission. I talked with Jessica last night about Rhiannon."

Rory turned and raised his eyebrow. "What did she have to say?"

"That Rhiannon has a huge crush on both of us, and we would be idiots to let her go."

Laughing, Rory switched lanes to pass a semi. "I forgot how blunt Jessica is."

"Yeah." He smiled fondly at the memory of her spirit. "She also wanted to let us know that she's found a husband-and-wife couple that she really likes."

"Good for her." Rory grinned at him. "I had a feeling she'd end up with more than just a Master."

Silence stretched between them, but it wasn't as tense as it had been. Rory shot Liam an angry glare. "By the way, fuck you very much for telling Rhiannon she couldn't have sex."

"Me? You wouldn't even let her have an orgasm." Liam ruefully shook his head. "She must be pissed."

"I managed to try to explain it off as a lesson, but when we fuck our girl tonight, I want her to orgasm until she cries."

Liam suddenly had an image of Rhiannon pressed between them, their collar on her neck. "Think we should take her to Juno's first?"

Tapping his fingers on the steering wheel, Rory took their exit. "To buy a collar?"

"Yes, but we won't tell her that. Let's say that we're there to buy her some cuffs. Then we can go into the private gallery and see which collars she likes. From there we'll play it by ear. I have the hardest bloody time reading her, and I don't want to mess up…again."

"Good plan."

"But I swear to God, if I don't get my dick in her sweet pussy tonight, I'm going to get violent."

Rory nodded. "I'm in one hundred percent agreement. Do you think between the two of us we could get her to spend the night?"

"I sure hope so."

Rhiannon sat on her screened-in back porch, admiring the way the honeysuckle she'd planted last year was climbing against the side of the house. Soon it would be fall and the garden would go to sleep, but for now, she could enjoy the luxury of her room. The original back porch of the farmhouse she owned was a massive affair made to accommodate the large amount of people it took to run a farm.

Now it was a feminine oasis, a place Rhiannon was drawn to when her heart and mind were troubled. The shabby-chic theme of her home extended to this room as well with its mint-green-painted wicker furniture and cream floral cushions. A rug hand braided by Ms. Althea sat beneath a white-painted coffee table with a fairy carved into the surface. Crystal wind chimes hung near the breezy parts of the room, and they tinkled gently as a warm summer wind washed over her.

On the coffee table, next to two tea cups and a tray of cookies, sat Rhiannon's open laptop. Kira had been put on bed rest as she neared her due date, and she was going stir crazy. In an effort to help ease Kira's boredom, Rhiannon was video chatting with Kira while Latisha nibbled on a cookie as she lounged in an oversize papasan chair. Dressed in a red tank top and jean shorts, the lovely African American woman looked very different than the cold, demanding Mistress Latisha became at Wicked. Then Rhiannon looked up and found her best friend studying Rhiannon with those all-seeing eyes of hers and amended that thought. One could take the Mistress out of Wicked but not the Wicked out of the Mistress.

On the computer screen Kira started to sit up but grimaced and stayed put. While they'd been talking Master Bryan kept coming in to adjust her pillows, offer her a drink, and bring her snacks. Finally Kira started whacking him with a pillow until he left with the promise to give her thirty minutes without fussing over her.

With a sigh, Kira tossed her long hair over her shoulder and sat up as much as she could. "God knows I love that man more than anything, but if he fusses over me like this for the next six weeks, I'm going to lose my mind. Okay, spill. How's your training going?"

Latisha took a sip of her tea, never taking her eyes off Rhiannon. "Yes, I'd love to know as well."

Fiddling with the edges of her frayed jean shorts, Rhiannon looked away. "Do you want to know as my wannabe therapist or friend?"

"Both," Latisha said in a teasing voice. "But mostly as your friend."

"I want to know as a sex-deprived nymphomaniac who is on pelvic rest," Kira added.

"Fine." It took Rhiannon a moment to compose herself, to debate how much she should share with the other women without breaking trust with her men. "It is nothing like I expected."

"How so?" Latisha asked in a soft voice.

"First off we haven't even had sex yet."

"That's not so unusual," Kira said. "Maybe they want to take their time with you."

Rhiannon thought about it but shook her head. "No, I don't think so. I mean, they're not trying to rush me, but they keep forbidding each other to have sex with me even though I'm dying for either one of them, or preferably both, to fuck me until I can't see straight."

"Explain," Latisha said in her Domme voice.

Rhiannon launched into abbreviated versions of her solo dates with both men. And that was what they were. She knew from having talked to Jessica and Gloria that the men never met their trainees outside of Club Wicked for anything but private play parties. And they'd certainly never mentioned having a sleepover. What she couldn't figure out was why Rory and Liam were doing this.

When Rhiannon finished, both Kira and Latisha were silent. Nervous that she'd somehow fucked up, Rhiannon wiped away a tiny dusting of crumbs from the table. Kira stared at her through the computer screen while Latisha was unreadable. "Well, what do you think? Am I crazy or are they trying to date me?"

Latisha tapped one long red fingernail on the edge of the papasan chair. "I've known both men for about three years. In that time I've never seen them date any of their submissives. To be honest I thought they might be a private bisexual couple who enjoyed having sex with women but didn't want to bring one into their family unit."

Kira gasped. "Do you think that's what's going on? They want Rhiannon to be in their family unit?"

"Wait, wait, wait." Rhiannon held up her hands. "First, they're not gay, second they're supposed to be my trainers, and third, they know I'm on the hunt for a permanent Master."

"I never said they were gay," Latisha said in a mild voice. "I said I believed they were bisexual."

"Maybe they both want to be your permanent Master," Kira said as she practically bounced on the bed. "They're both at that age where most men are thinking about marriage and babies. Like a guy's version of their biological clock ticking. They want to breed, and honey, you're prime breeding stock."

"Thanks, that's flattering."

Kira giggled. "Even if they're not together, they both obviously want you. And let me tell you, I've seen Master Rory and Master Liam in action. You could do worse."

Inspecting her nails, Latisha then nodded. "I agree. While I don't like the string of broken hearts they've left behind, if you have a chance to land one of them, you would be set for life. Rich, handsome, and the kind of Master women dream of having. The question is, which of them makes you laugh?"

"Well, they both do. Why?"

"Because, baby girl, this is a laugh or cry world, and you want a man who can bring you joy even at the direst of times."

"Then grab both if you can and one if you can't." Kira slumped back in her decadent mound of pillows. "Damn it, now I'm horny."

Rhiannon needlessly straightened the table, avoiding looking at either woman. "How do I keep from falling in love with both of them if I only end up with one of them?"

Neither woman spoke for a long time. Birds argued with each other in a tree nearby, and the sunlight illuminated one of the crystal wind chimes, throwing rainbows around the room. She watched the beautiful colors dance and managed to relax a little bit. No matter what happened, no matter how much someone tried to break her heart and spirit, there would always be beauty in the world.

It made fighting for the good stuff bearable.

Finally Kira stretched her legs out and wiggled her toes. "You want my advice? Just go with it. If something happens, great, if nothing happens...well, you walk away as a fully trained submissive. The Doms will be beating down your door."

Rhiannon looked over at Latisha. "You're being unusually quiet."

"I'm not sure I approve."

Anger flared in Rhiannon, but she tried to keep it under control. "I'm not sure it's your place to approve."

"Hear me out before you flip your shit." Latisha pointed one long finger at Rhiannon with a stern look. "They know about your past, and they know how vulnerable you are. To two Doms who are driven to help vulnerable subs, you are irresistible."

"You mean they only want me because they think I'm broken?"

"That's bullshit!" Kira yelled. "You are not broken, and any man would be glad to have you."

"Simmer down there, Red. That's not what I meant. I was merely warning Rhiannon that she needs to get her head out of the stars and back down to earth. I can see how much you care about Rory and Liam, and I worry about you getting hurt." Latisha closed her eyes and blew out a harsh breath. "I'm sorry. I've just seen a string of submissives they've trained dismissed without a backward glance once their training was done. If they plan on doing that to you, Rhiannon, you need to make sure that you get some actual training from them. I know their teaching protocol, and they've never done anything like this."

"They must really like her then."

Hope warmed Rhiannon, and she looked over at Kira's image. "Do you think?"

"Absolutely. Those were public events that they took you to where their friends and coworkers would be. Men don't take you to those kind of things if they're not serious about you. What I don't understand is why they're forbidding you from having sex."

Latisha pursed her lips. "I think it's jealousy."

Rhiannon looked over at Latisha. "Really?"

"Yes. The behavior they're exhibiting indicates they're feeling territorial over you. The upping of the stakes with Liam forbidding you from even having an orgasm shows that he was not only trying to get even with Rory but to add an extra dose of revenge."

"But they said it was part of my training... God, I'm a dumbass."

Now that she looked at her time with the men not as a training session but as two men going on dates her, she wanted to smack herself. It was so obvious. Mentally she went through each night, picking up clues here and there. While she'd gotten that tingly feeling a few times before she'd actually played with either man, they weren't in full-time Dom mode. She felt like she'd spent time with the real Rory and Liam as a normal girl going out with incredibly sexy men.

"You're not a dumbass. If anyone's a dumbass in this situation, it's Rory and Liam for fighting over you like a bone."

"Yeah," Kira added in an indignant tone. "If they're going to fight over you, they should have at least told you about it."

"They're not fighting over me," Rhiannon said as her stomach knotted. "But if they are, I should stop training with them."

"Why?" Latisha asked in surprise.

"I don't want to tear their friendship apart."

Kira empathetically shook her head. "No. You are not the

cause of their sudden inability to share. You came into this expecting to be trained, and they better get the fuck on board with the program."

"Do you want me to talk to them?" Latisha asked in a deceptively calm voice.

"No. This is my mess, and I'll handle it." Rhiannon caught the pitying look Latisha gave her, and her anger flared to life again. "Don't look at me like that."

"Like what?"

"Like I'm some kind of victim. Don't pity me."

"It's not pity, Rhiannon. It's love. I care about you, and I don't want to see you get hurt. You're like the little sister I never had, and I consider you my family."

Kira sniffled. "That is so sweet. I miss my sister."

As the redhead began to cry, Rhiannon couldn't help but giggle. Kira's emotions were all over the place. A touching commercial for cat food could set her off. Latisha met her gaze and began to laugh, her beautiful and husky voice echoing out through Rhiannon's yard and into the forest nearby.

Soon they were all laughing, and Rhiannon gave herself over to it, letting the joy fill her and chase back her depressing thoughts. "This is so screwed up. Why does this stuff always happen to me? I try to get training and end up falling in love with two Doms."

Latisha's laughter abruptly cut off. "What did you say?"

Even Kira quieted, sniffling and wiping her eyes.

Rhiannon cleared her throat. "It's just an expression."

"Uh, no. Falling in love is not an expression." Kira blew her nose.

"I didn't mean anything by it. Just that I have bad luck with men." Darkness rolled through her mind at thoughts of her abductor. "And I'm not just talking about the bastard. Every relationship I've had has ended because I crave having a Master. I've accepted it, and I'm ready to make that commitment. I just feel bad for wasting the time of so many great guys in the past."

"Please think about what you're doing," Latisha said as she reached across the table to clasp Rhiannon's hands. "You have such a beautiful, trusting heart. I'd hate to see it get broken. Just try to take things slow, at least emotionally."

Rhiannon grinned and tried to break the serious mood. "Good thing you added that because I plan on fucking those men's brains out tonight. I'm so wound up a soft breeze makes my nipples hard."

Blinking at her, Latisha grinned. "I think I might be jealous."

"I know I'm jealous," Kira piped up. "I'd kill for a good fucking right now."

Rhiannon laughed, then sighed and rubbed her face. "I could be blowing this all out of proportion. Maybe they've just adjusted their training to fit me, or maybe they do both want me. If they're going to make me choose between them, I want to spend time with both of them to figure out who I would want to consider being a submissive to."

Latisha squeezed her hands. "Sounds like you've got a good plan. You work tonight, right?"

"Yep."

"I'm going to pass the word around that you will be looking for a Dom in the near future."

"Why would you do that?"

"Because it will increase your tips, thereby also increasing my tips." Latisha winked. "And it will let Liam and Rory know that you have plenty of options. If they want to win your heart, you need to make them work for it. Men don't value what's easily given to them."

"Ain't that the truth," Kira said with a sigh.

Rhiannon's cell phone rang, and she picked it up to silence it, then froze when she saw the name on the caller ID. "It's Liam."

"Answer it!" Kira squealed.

She pressed Talk and held the phone to her ear. "Hello?"

"Hello, lass." Master Liam's voice coated her skin like honey. "How are you?"

"Good. How are you?"

She looked frantically between Kira and Latisha, mouthing

Oh my God.

"I just got back into town. Rory and I were wondering if you wanted to get some dinner."

Happiness mixed with worry as she bit her lower lip before releasing it. "I have to work the early shift today."

"Oh, I didn't know that." He sounded honestly sad.

"I'm sorry, Liam."

"No, no. Don't be sorry. It's your job. I'm sorry we forgot you worked the early shift tonight."

"Is Rory coming with you tonight?"

"Yes. Is that all right? If you just want me to come with you, we can leave that bas—"

Suddenly shouting came through the phone, along with the sound of something getting knocked around. The phone was dropped and more yelling filled the air. She stared at Latisha and Kira as she wondered what the hell was going on.

Latisha lifted an eyebrow, and Rhiannon shook her head. "I think they're fighting."

Sure enough, a few seconds later, both men laughed, and the phone made an odd sound before it was picked up by Rory. "Hello, darling girl."

She giggled. "Hi, Rory. Where's Liam? Is he okay?"

"He's fine. Do you mind if we hang out in your section while you work, or would that make you uncomfortable?"

"I'd love to have you there." Excitement and nervousness battled through her blood; then she imagined Rory and Liam watching her, and arousal blossomed in a sweet wave.

"Excellent. What time does your shift start?"

"I'm working five to ten tonight."

"We'll see you then." Liam said something in the background, and Rory replied with a distinctly sarcastic tone. Rory laughed, speaking into the phone again. "Liam asked you to wear some sexy panties that show off that excellent arse of yours."

Heat filled her cheeks, and she darted a glance at an avidly listening Kira and Latisha. "Okay. I have to run, but I'll see you tonight."

"I can't wait. The things I want to do to you... I have an actual list written up, and it's sixteen pages long." He cleared his throat. "We'll see you tonight."

She ended the call and took a deep breath, debating kicking Latisha out so she could go masturbate five or six times before work.

Kira laughed. "You look stunned. What did he say?"

"He has a sixteen-page list of all the different ways he wants to fuck me."

Both women laughed, and Rhiannon gave a weak chuckle. The hunger in Rory's voice traveled through her body like she'd been pinged with a tuning fork. And she loved that Liam liked her ass. She'd never done anal play, but Jessica had said Liam was very, very good at it.

Maybe she could take Rory in her ass and Liam in her pussy.

"Rhiannon!"

She snapped her head up and flushed. "Sorry. I'm distracted."

Latisha stood up with a soft laugh. "Girl, you are too much. Have fun at work tonight."

They hugged, and Kira said, "Bye, ladies. Have fun tonight, Rhiannon. Lick a submissive or two for me." She gave a mournful sigh. "I miss eating pussy."

Kira never failed to shock Rhiannon with her honesty. While Rhiannon admired that, it was also kind of weird. She stepped back from Latisha and took a deep breath. "Wish me luck."

"No need. You're in charge of your fate, Rhiannon. Never forget that."

Chapter Twelve

Rhiannon bit her lower lip and tried to ignore the snide giggles coming from two of the bartenders. They were talking about her, and the shit they were saying was downright rude. It made her want to go over there and put that bitch Sunny in her place, but she needed to get back to Rory and Liam's table.

Tonight she wore an outfit that consisted of a series of brief white straps held together by gold chains draping down her back and ass. She'd forgone the bikini top and had opted for a pair of glittering white pasties. One of the nice things about living in such an isolated area was she could nude sunbathe. It felt so relaxing that she did it at least twice a week and had a decent tan that deepened the tone of her already dark skin, leaving her tanline free. Though she dressed in revealing outfits, she'd never just walked around in her underwear. It made her feel very uncomfortable and vulnerable to be that exposed, so she'd thrown a sheer pink baby doll dress over it.

"Ignore those skanks," Wendy, a pretty brunette and Rhiannon's bartender for the night, said. "I don't know what's gotten into Sunny lately, but she's really mean. Brandy has always been a cunt. The last thing you want is to get in a fight and have Master Rory and Master Liam find out."

"What do you mean?" Rhiannon flushed at Wendy's knowing look.

"Honey, everyone knows you're training with them, and we couldn't be happier." She glanced over at Sunny and Brandy in disgust. "Well, most of us are. I know you used to get into it with

Sunny, but for the past few months, you've kept your cool while she runs her mouth. Don't think we don't notice it. But you're a big girl, and you don't need other people fighting your battles."

Rhiannon took a deep breath and let it out. "Thank you."

"No problem." She winked. "Now go let those sluts drooling all over Rory and Liam know who they belong to."

Rhiannon turned her head and saw that Rory and Liam did indeed have submissives drooling all over them. One was currently rubbing Rory's shoulders while Liam was laughing with a girl kneeling at his feet. The sight of her men with those women made her jealousy rear to life.

When Rory and Liam continued to flirt right in her section, she fumed, then remembered everything Wendy had just said. No, she wouldn't flip out. She needed to think this through. If she went over there right now, she'd cause a scene. Well, maybe she could still cause a scene, just in a different way. Since Rory seemed to be oblivious about how bad jealousy felt, maybe she'd give him a dose of his own medicine. Liam too. That bastard was currently admiring the back of a pretty submissive's thong as she bent over to show it to him.

After taking a deep breath, Rhiannon pulled off her dress.

Wendy let out a low whistle and reached over the bar to take Rhiannon's discarded clothes. "Damn, girl. If I had a body like yours, I'd be constantly naked. I'd fucking grocery shop nude if I had tits like that. And they're real. You're such a lucky bitch."

Scanning the room, Rhiannon tried to pick out the perfect man to flirt with and quickly chose her target. "Can I have Master Denny's order please?"

Wendy grinned and placed the beer onto another tray before sliding it across the bar. "There you go. I hope you know what you're doing. A jealous Master is no joke, and you'd get it times two."

"I can handle it. What I can't take is them touching other women."

Wendy gave her a sympathetic look. "You know they never date their trainees, right?"

Rhiannon gritted her teeth. "I know. Thanks again."

She turned and out of the corner of her eye found Rory and Liam staring at her. Knowing their gaze was on her, she put her best strut into her stride as she crossed the room to where Master Denny sat alone in a wingback chair by the windows. He was big, bald, and intimidating as hell but a real sweetheart to the submissives. If she wasn't falling in love with Liam and Rory, he'd be the kind of Master she would be interested in.

His dark eyebrows flew up, and his deep blue eyes widened. "What do we have here?"

"Your drink, Sir." She smiled at him. His slow smile gave her a little tingle. He sat back and inspected her in a way that made her feel warm and desired.

"Can I get you anything else?"

"Come closer."

She took a hesitant step forward, fighting the urge to look over her shoulder and see if Rory and Liam were still watching her. "Yes, Sir?"

"I've heard you're training with Rory and Liam."

"Yes, Sir."

He slowly ran his finger over his lips, and she noticed how full they were. Nice but not as nice as Liam's and Rory's. Hurt settled in her heart as she thought about the way Liam had been staring at that girl's ass.

"I would very much like it if I could talk to you after you're done working." Then he totally surprised her. "I'd love to take you on a date. Strictly hands-off. You know, like the vanilla people do, before we spent any time together here."

The teasing tone in his voice made her smile. "I'll keep that in mind."

"No, she won't," Rory said in an angry voice from right behind her.

Rory pressed up against her and put a proprietary hand on her waist. Heat rushed through her body, and she was ashamed at how much Rory turned her on even when she was still mad at him. Her clit hardened, and she was almost instantly ready for his cock. The attraction she felt for him was insane.

Master Denny sat forward, tension filling his big frame. "I

think she can answer for herself. Besides, what do you care? As soon as her training is done, you'll release her without a backward glance."

"Not this time," Rory said with a slight growl in his voice.

Rhiannon froze, wanting to believe what he said with all her heart. Unfortunately the memory of him letting that girl rub his shoulders still burned inside of her. "You—"

"Quiet," Rory snapped. "You're in trouble."

Master Denny studied them for a moment, then grinned and sat back. "Have fun, you two lovebirds."

Rory muttered a string of swear words, then gripped the back of her neck. "Come with me."

He marched her across the room to where Master Liam sat. The girl he'd been talking with was still at his feet, and she gave Rhiannon a confused look. Chagrin mixed with anger filled her as she recognized the girl as Kerry, the one she'd caught Rory kissing.

"You just can't seem to stay away from her, can you?" Rhiannon growled.

"I suggest you shut your mouth right now."

"Fuck you. I don't have to listen to someone who lets other women touch him after he'd promised to train only me."

Rory stopped abruptly and turned her to face them. All around people watched with open curiosity, and she wanted to cover herself from their stares. "Your lack of faith in me is astonishing."

Taken aback, she glared at him. "What are you talking about?"

Sunny's sharp laugh came from nearby, and Master Rory looked over her shoulder. Whatever he saw didn't please him. "Has Sunny been giving you shit? I've been watching you all night, and it seems like she's trying to pick a fight with you. Say the word, and I'll have her moved to a different bar."

Part of her wanted to say yes, but she knew Sunny didn't like the sexual atmosphere deeper inside the club. Plus Rhiannon was more interested in the fact that Rory had been watching her. "I didn't think you noticed me."

He let out a long sigh; then his hand slipped from her neck to her hand. "I'm a moth to your flame, darling girl."

With that he led them the rest of the way to where Liam sat. Kerry's gaze darted up, but she didn't say anything, and Rhiannon realized the other girl was scared of her. Not that she blamed Kerry after the way Rhiannon had flipped out on her the other night.

She paused and leaned down. "Sorry I was such a bitch."

Kerry peeked at her, and the relief on her face was evident. "I'm so sorry. I didn't mean to get Master Rory in trouble."

Master Liam cleared his throat, and Kerry flushed, then stood and smoothed her dress. Her plump curves were covered in soft pink velvet. Rhiannon had to admit she was adorable. There was something about her that made Rhiannon feel strangely protective. "I have to go. Thanks for talking with me, Master Liam and Master Rory."

Kerry went to hug Rory, then hesitated and dropped her arms when she glanced at Rhiannon. Guilt pierced her. She wanted to tell Kerry to go ahead and hug Rory, but she couldn't get the words out past the lump in her throat. Was she such a bitch that she couldn't tell who was a genuinely nice person anymore?

Master Liam snapped his fingers. "Eyes on me."

With a sigh, Master Rory sat down. "You can't keep doing this, Rhiannon."

"Doing what?"

"Assuming that because we are talking with women we're fucking them."

Liam added with a growl, "And you can't go flirting with other Masters right in front of us."

"Oh, you should talk about flirting." She fisted her hands at her sides and struggled for calm. Anger simmered in her blood, a preferred emotion over guilt. "I was just talking with him, not getting a back rub. How would you have liked that? How would you have felt if you saw me surrounded by Doms getting a back rub while one showed me his underwear?"

Both men remained silent, and she lifted her chin. "That's

what I thought." Hurt and rage burst through her until she couldn't stop herself from spitting out, "Besides, I'm gone in a month. Why do you care who I flirt with? It's not like I'm wearing your collar."

She hated how her voice broke on the last word and swallowed, refusing to let her tears fall. Her emotions had always been intense—it was part of who she was—but she hated angry crying. It made her feel so weak. The repercussions of what she'd just said hit her. Hell, she'd been screaming at them, so they'd probably echoed through the room.

She glanced out of the corner of her eye and found that yes, everyone within hearing range was indeed watching them. Embarrassment cooled her anger, and she wished a piano would fall on her. She was about to get dumped right in front of the entire club. No Master could let a submissive go unpunished for an outburst like that. She knew the protocol and cursed her stupid mouth for running out of control.

Master Rory and Master Liam exchanged a look; then the big Scotsman, dressed in his usual leather kilt with a tight black T-shirt, nodded. "Go tell the bartender to have someone cover you. You're off the clock."

"I don't know if I can do that."

Master Liam raised his voice. "Isaac, we're making Goddess punch out early."

Humiliation crawled up Rhiannon's spine as she realized Lucia had probably witnessed her tirade. Now the tears that filled her eyes were ones of sorrow. Sunny's laugh rang out, and Rhiannon flinched at the biting sound.

Master Rory leaned forward and traced his fingertips over her belly, making her wiggle as it tickled. "Go into the dressing room and put on the smallest pair of panties you own. Then I want you to take those pasties off and bring me a tube of red lipstick if you have it. Or any other bright color if you don't. And I want you to be as quick as you safely can. Having you out of my sight right now is unacceptable so unless you want Rory and me storming the women's locker room I suggest you move."

Confused but grateful he wasn't sending her permanently away, she ran to do his bidding. There wasn't a doubt in her mind that he would do what he said, so she took off her heels to move quicker. Someone nearby laughed, but she ignored them and ran with her shoes in her hands, her long hair tickling her back.

She made it to the dressing room in record time. After stripping and sorting through her locker, she decided on a pair of nude-colored lace panties. They were so similar to her skin tone that she could wear them beneath a sheer dress and almost appear naked. With her breath coming out in soft pants, she ran her brush through her hair and sprayed some of her honeysuckle perfume on her wrists before grabbing her tube of cardinal-red lipstick.

This time she crossed her arms over her breasts as she ran to keep them from hurting as they bounced with her movements. A light sheen of perspiration covered her lower back, and she was out of breath, but she made it back to them in what had to be less than five minutes. The men looked surprised, and she handed Rory the lipstick. "Here you go, Sir."

For a long moment, they both inspected her, and she looked at each of them in turn, trying to figure out whom she'd rather have if it came down to choosing. She didn't want to choose. And she didn't want any other Master. She wanted them. After all, they were certainly acting like more than just her trainers. Master Rory's words about not releasing her after her training made her heart ache with want. She needed to please them, needed to show that she belonged to them and didn't want anyone else.

But what were they going to do? Wendy had been right. Making a Dom jealous was never a good idea...especially times two.

Master Rory uncapped the lipstick and motioned her forward. "Stand before me with your hands behind your head."

She did and became conscious of everyone watching her. Master Denny still sat in the corner, but now he had a pretty blonde sub who looked barely out of high school on his lap. He was whispering in her ear as he watched Rhiannon. Across the room, she thought she saw Dove with Master Jesse. Knowing her friend saw her public humiliation made it even worse.

Master Rory began to write something on her stomach. It startled her, so she looked down, but when she did, she couldn't really make out the words. When he was done, Master Liam smacked her hip. "Turn around."

He repeated what Master Rory had done, writing something on her lower back and ass. Her cheeks burned with embarrassment, but her panties were soaked. How sick was it that she got turned on by being publically chastised? Except this wasn't quite chastisement. The men weren't doing this to humiliate her; they were doing this to teach her. They weren't and never could be the kind of men who would get off on making her feel bad about herself.

When Master Liam was finished, he grasped her hips and squeezed hard. "Someday, not today but someday, I'm going to fuck this fine ass, and you are going to come so much you won't know your own name."

Abruptly, Master Rory stood. "Let's go."

Master Liam jerked to his feet and peered down at her. He cupped her cheek and brushed his lips over her trembling ones, his kiss infusing her with heat. She was still barefoot so he towered over her. "I missed you, lass. Don't ever doubt our intentions with you."

"What are your intentions with me?"

The fine lines around his eyes crinkled as he smiled. "Only the best."

Unsure what to make of that statement, she followed the men deeper into the club. It seemed like they took her everywhere, through every bar and public space. They would stop once in a while to speak with someone, but they'd make sure she was positioned so the room had a good view of her. She wondered what the fuck was written on her, because people would read whatever it was and grin. Well, except for a handful of submissives who gave her decidedly bitchy looks.

Not that she could blame them.

Master Rory and Master Liam were her wettest, hottest fantasy come to life. When she played with herself, she always thought of them. Always. And now they were here with her, making her feel so wanted and cherished. They constantly touched her, little caresses that left her straining for more, and when they spoke about her to their friends, the pride in their voices made her stand taller. Feel taller.

Eventually they reached a door to one of the private rooms on the second floor. She was curious which one they'd picked but didn't know what was behind this particular door. While she hadn't been in any of them for intimate reasons, she had delivered drinks there. But she'd never been in this one, so she tried to peer over Master Rory's shoulder as he opened the door.

The room was dimly lit, and she gasped in shock when she saw the bed beneath the waterfall coming from the ceiling. Like a gentle rain, water poured over a giant round white bed set inside a circle of smooth stones. An enormous mirror circled all the way around the room, and the only interruption in its perfect surface was a series of small lines that showed the door leading out. A warm golden light gleamed from somewhere overhead, positioned so it illuminated the water and made it look like liquid gold.

"Wow," she said in a low breath and took a step forward.

Master Rory chuckled, a warm and rich sound. "I'm glad you like it."

A metal buckle clanked, and she glanced over to see Master Liam taking his boots off. He'd already removed his shirt. She licked her lips at the sight of his massive shoulders flexing with his movements. He was sex on a stick, no doubt about it.

Master Rory began to undress as well, so she turned and backed up until she stood in the mist surrounding the bed. She had no idea what the mattress was made of, but when she touched it, the surface was wet, warm, and silky. Perfect for being screwed on.

That's what she wanted, needed. She needed them to fuck her, fill her up, and claim her as theirs.

Master Liam approached her first, his thick erection leading the way. He paused before her and glanced over his shoulder, waiting for Rory. The automatic way he did it gave Rhiannon hope that maybe they could make this work. Liam cared about the other man and wanted him to be with them. If she was being honest with herself, she wanted both of them, the package deal.

Now she just hoped she got to see them fuck each other.

A needy moan escaped from her, and Master Rory joined Master Liam, making a soft, hushing sound. "Easy, darling girl.

We'll take care of you."

She reached out, holding a dick with each hand and gently squeezing. Maybe if she made them as insane with pleasure as they made her they'd take pity on her. Or at the very least let her come.

Master Liam groaned. "Get your hand off me."

Stung, she jerked back and looked up at him in confusion.

He smiled and lifted her up, depositing her beneath the deliciously warm water streaming from above. "I'm fucking desperate for you, lass. If you jerk me off, I'm going to spray you like some virgin that's never seen a cunt before."

Her heart lightened, then filled with happiness when Rory joined them. He gently moved her wet hair to the side and bit her neck hard enough to sting. "Do I need to give you a collar of bite marks to let you know how serious we are about you?"

She shuddered, her mouth going slack as Liam began to suckle her breast. The strong, intense suction of his mouth had her rubbing her ass against Rory. He muttered something and reached around to her front before sliding his hands down her panties. When he pressed his finger into her slit, he groaned.

"You are so ready for us. Jesus Christ, you're soaked."

The only thing she could do was whimper in agreement. Master Liam reached between her thighs, and together he and Rory ripped her panties off. The violence of the move jerked her between them, and they both pressed tighter until she was trapped against their bodies. Almost as one they began to play with her pussy. Liam finger fucked her while Rory lightly toyed with her clit. She trembled hard when Liam curled his fingers and attacked her G-spot.

"I want you to squirt for us again, lass. You are so fucking sexy when you come. Remember, push out when you feel the need. We're already so wet it won't even matter, but I want to watch you come. Be a good girl and please your Masters."

She nodded, mesmerized by Rory's skilled touch on her clit. He massaged the little nub, making it so swollen with blood it throbbed to the beat of her heart. Sensation overwhelmed her, then she sagged, or at least she would have if they didn't each move an arm to support her. The way they moved together was something to behold, and she forced her eyes open so she could watch them in the mirror. Rory was rubbing his epic hard-on between her ass cheeks, entrancing her with the flex of his muscled ass and thighs. His precum anointed her lower back, and she could see smears of the red lipstick on all three of them.

Liam was toying with her breast, flicking his tongue over the surface. She looked so small and fragile between them, but she felt like she could eat them alive with her need. Never in her life had she been this ravenous for a man. She could catch just a glimpse of Liam's big balls between his thighs, and she wanted to play with them, but doing anything other than feeling was beyond her.

Master Rory began to work her clit by pressing his thumb down in a slow, firm circle that had her arching toward his touch. "You belong to us, Rhiannon."

"And we belong to you," Liam murmured against her collarbone before catching her mouth in a searing kiss.

Throwing her arms around him, she frantically kissed him back. That was what she'd wanted. They owned her, heart and soul, but she owned them as well. She surrendered, her spirit crying out in relief as she let their obvious affection for her ease some of the burden. Her tears mixed with the warm water from above, and her orgasm swept over her in a searing wave of relief. Through it all, through every massive release of physical pleasure, Liam never stopped kissing her, and Rory never stopped whispering how beautiful she was, how amazing and wonderful.

By the time she'd come down, she was sobbing, held between the two of them as she cried. Eventually she got control of herself and wiped her face. "I'm sorry. I don't know why I cried."

"I hope it wasn't because you only want us as trainers," Rory said in a soft voice.

She turned in his arms, seeking his gaze so he could know how sincere she was. "No, I want to roll with it."

"What?"

"I mean I want you, both of you. I'd like to see where this could go if that's okay with you. I-I'd like for you to be my Masters. Like for real."

Rory smiled and looped his arms around her and pulled her

close into a hug. Liam wrapped his arms around both of them and she thought she might die of happiness. They wanted her. They really did.

Master Liam shifted, and he pressed the tip of his cock against her anus with unerring accuracy. She squeaked and moved away, making him laugh.

"No worries, lass. I was just trying to figure out what size butt plug we need to start readying you for me." He leaned closer and bit her ear, making her moan. "And trust me when I say you are going to love every minute of me fucking that tight little hole."

"I want you, please," she whispered and rubbed herself between them.

Rory looked at Liam, then nodded. "On your hands and knees."

They moved and helped her arrange her stance to their liking. Heat flowed through her in a never-ending cycle of bliss until her eyes refused to open anymore. The rough scrape of their hands over her body, caressing her, teasing her, making her squirm, had to be some kind of sensory overload, because within seconds they had her back to the ravenous state she'd been in before she'd orgasmed.

Wiggling her ass, she then arched her back and offered herself to Liam. Then she reached out and pulled on Rory's thigh until he knelt in front of her. His beautiful cock, flushed to a deep red with arousal, bobbed before she grabbed it with her hand. He was so long that she needed two hands to grasp him properly but could only use one without losing her balance. Liam had moved into position behind her, and she could feel the heat of his skin as he moved closer. Any second the velvet tip of his cock would enter her pussy, and she ached for him.

Rory scooted forward and then ran his hand through her wet hair. "Suck me."

The rough and dominating tone he used had her obeying him without thought. The moment his shaft slid into her mouth, Liam began to push into her. She froze, then began to suckle just the tip of Rory's dick as Liam slowly entered her.

"She's so fucking tight and slick," Liam groaned out.

Rory gave a rumbling moan. "Such a sweet mouth."

Joy mixed with desire at the knowledge that she was serving them well. They were pleased with her, and she couldn't imagine being any happier than she was at this moment, filled by both of them. Her delicate tissues stretched to almost the point of pain as Liam's wide cock breached her, easing one ache and starting another. She dropped her head for a moment, releasing Rory's cock as she panted.

Rory scooted back and knelt before her. He captured her gaze and started to slowly fist himself, squeezing out a drop of precum. It was a struggle to keep her eyes open as Liam pulled out and pushed back in, but she managed. Rory was just too magnificent to not look at.

"So fucking beautiful speared on Liam's cock. I could watch him fuck you forever."

He held her regard while he stroked himself, and she moaned at the combination of stimulation. Liam worked her body like the Master he was while Rory worked her mind. His gaze kept her aware of her submission to them, of his dominance over her. She felt like a bird looking at a cobra ready to strike out at her any second.

Gradually Liam picked up the rhythm until it became too much for her. She slumped forward on her arms and keened at the way the new angle made him plunge even deeper into her. He grabbed her ass with both hands and began to slam into her rough enough that she had to clench her teeth together. Reaching beneath her, Liam then played with her clit, and she lost it. The tension built, spinning her tighter and tighter until she exploded in a series of gut-wrenching screams. Liam pulled her close and ground his pelvis into hers as he came with a roar.

His hips twitched against hers, the heavy weight of his testicles brushing against her oversensitized flesh. She smiled and began to giggle. Liam pushed off her. "You okay, lass?"

"Hmm? Yes. I just feel so good that I can't help giggling."

Suddenly Rory was lifting her and practically threw her on her back. "I'm not in a laughing mood."

Her smiled faded as she stared into his intense eyes and began to ramp back into full arousal. The fact that he could make her this turned on with just his gaze sent delicious shivers through her already buzzing nerves. He shifted, and for a moment, she saw doubt and hesitation in his gaze, along with a longing so devastating she could barely comprehend it. Without thought, she spread her legs and pulled Rory between them, the head of his dick slipping through Liam's seed. She felt momentarily embarrassed, like she was sloppy seconds or something, but then Rory gave a pleased growl and began to kiss her and nothing mattered but him.

He rubbed the head of his cock over her clit, holding himself up effortlessly on his arms in a move her yoga instruction would have admired. He was so strong, and she loved it. Her body urged her to mate with him, to have his babies, to entice him to be her protector and man. Massive surges of hormones swamped her, and she cried out against his mouth when he entered her.

After Liam's girth, it was a smooth slide, but Rory was longer, and she gasped when he hit her cervix. The feeling wasn't very comfortable, but then Rory pulled her legs around his waist and adjusted his angle. He pressed against her G-spot, and his slow, smooth rocking motion had her crying out over and over. Master Liam began to gently stroke her face while Rory fucked her. She found the combination both incredibly erotic and romantic.

Rory's pace increased, and she lifted her hips to meet him, dying for his touch, wanting to touch as much of him as possible.

"You are so fucking sexy," Liam murmured. "I love watching Rory fuck you until your pretty lips tense up and I can see that you're ready to come. Such a darling lass. So eager to please us. It makes me very happy to see you taking such good care of Rory, giving him such pleasure."

He leaned closer so that his cheek was against Rory's as he whispered, "Come for us, lass. Soak Rory's cock with your sweet arousal. Let him know how fucking good your tight pussy feels when it squeezes him."

She reached out blindly, looking for something to hold on to as her body geared up for her release. Liam caught one hand, and Rory the other, pinning her to the bed. Rory hammered his body into hers, and she broke for him. She must have snapped something in her mind because it was a long, long time before she came back to the real world. When she did, she found herself curled around the men beneath the gently falling water.

After opening her eyes, she traced a finger over Liam's flank, fascinated by the way the water beaded on his skin. Rory shifted behind her and began to stroke her upper chest in a soothing way that nonetheless made her arousal flicker weakly. She could stay like this forever.

Liam sat up, and she glanced down at his semierect cock, wondering if she could talk him into another round. He smiled down at her, and she couldn't help but grin back as he said, "What are you doing tomorrow?"

"Nothing much." Whatever she had to do could all be put off.

"We'd like you to come pick out a collar with us."

She tensed and gently slid out of Rory's arms. "I'm not sure I'm ready for that kind of commitment."

"Why not?"

Rory sounded slightly hurt so she faced him, trying to make him understand. "Because being collared is as serious as a marriage for me. When I do it, I want to be with that man or men forever."

Her cheeks burned with a hot flush, but Liam nodded. "I understand. But if Rory and I don't get something on you to show that you're our submissive, I'm afraid we'll get kicked out of Wicked for beating other Doms' asses. If Denny ever looks at you that way again, I'm going to knock his pretty white teeth out."

She thought back to her flirting with Master Denny and looked down on her stomach. Whatever they'd put there was long gone. "What did you write on me?"

Both men chuckled, and Rory smoothed his hand over her leg with a sigh. "What you need to worry about is what we'll write on you if you don't wear our 'seriously dating' collar."

She giggled. "They have a 'seriously dating' collar?"

Liam hauled her against him and gave her a sound kiss on the lips. "They do now."

Rory sobered and rolled off the bed, the flash of his ass making her hungry for him all over again. That man really had a world-class butt. Round and firm with two dimples at the top and only lightly hairy. Made her want to lick him all over.

Liam followed suit, and she gaped at his now soft cock which she was pretty sure was still bigger than most men's when they were hard. He caught her watching and winked. "See anything ya like, lass?"

Raising her face to the water, she then swept her hair back before scooting off the bed. Underneath there were fluffy and sumptuous white towels. Both men dried her, and she felt utterly content and pampered. Having this much attention on her after feeling alone for so long was wonderful. With a start, she realized that was what had been missing in her previous relationships. She'd been with someone but still felt alone. But when she was with Rory and Liam, she connected with them on a fundamental level that didn't make any sense but felt so right.

After they were all dry, Rory and Liam put their clothes back on but handed her a robe. "Wear this."

"Why?"

Rory pulled his shirt over his head. "Because you owe Kerry an apology. She's devastated that she messed things up for us with you. That's why she was over there talking with us."

She stared at him, then flushed and looked away when he raised a brow. "You're right."

Liam gave her an alarmed look. "She did mess things up with us?"

"No, I mean I need to apologize. I just get crazy when you pay other women attention."

Liam took a step toward her and snugged her robe tight. "No matter who we pay attention to, you will always be our priority. But we do have female friends, and we won't stop talking to them just because it makes you upset."

"But I will stop the causal touching," Rory added. "We've just been single for so long that it's second nature for us to have submissives throwing themselves at our feet while wailing for the use of our cocks."

He gave her a leering grin, and she tried not to smile. "You're terrible."

"I am. Now come along. Kerry should be close to finishing

her shift."

Rhiannon followed the men out into the hallway, the silence somehow heavy after the constant sprinkle of falling water from the room they'd just been in. "She works here?"

"No. She volunteers."

Confused, Rhiannon gave Liam a small smile when he grabbed her hand in his own. "She likes to use her skills as a comfort submissive."

"What exactly is that?"

"First, it's totally not sexual. That's not to say it can't be, and with some submissives, it is, but with Kerry, it's all about the cuddling. She has some kind of...I don't know...energy that makes it feel really good to hold and be held by her."

Rhiannon tried to understand it. "But how can you not become aroused holding a pretty girl?"

"Oh, I'm sure people get aroused, but if they want a fuck, they go elsewhere. If they want to be held and loved without judgment, to have someone touch them like they care, they go to Kerry."

Rhiannon had never known Wicked even offered something like that. If she had, she might have made use of that service. Cuddling was one of her favorite activities, but men just didn't seem as into it. They eventually fell asleep, and snoring ruined the mood. She wondered if Rory and Liam liked to cuddle and if they would train her in how to become a comfort submissive. The idea of being the one her friends turned to for hugs made her feel warm and happy inside. "Do you think you could train me to do what she does?"

Rory paused. "It appeals to you?"

"Well, I love to cuddle, and I know what it's like to be dying for someone to hold me." She took a deep breath, blinking back tears. What was it about being around Rory and Liam that left her in such an emotional state? For years she'd managed to bury her feelings in public, but they'd stripped away all her careful shields, leaving her feeling free but very vulnerable. "If I'd had access to someone like Kerry, I wouldn't have dated some of the guys I did."

"Anytime you want a cuddle, you just let us know," Liam

said in a serious voice.

More tears gathered, and she wiped beneath her eyes. "Thank you."

She grabbed Rory's hand, wanting the contact of both men as they came out into a more public hallway of Club Wicked. People raised an eyebrow as they strolled past, but Rory and Liam wore arrogant smiles that had satisfaction glowing in her chest. They looked as proud as peacocks to be seen with her, and that made her feel special.

Loved even.

Soon they reached one of the smaller bars within Wicked, the Library Pub. In what had once been the massive two-story library now sat a bar of sorts. Endless leather-bound books still lined the walls, but the upper balcony had been changed into a series of comfortable daybeds, chairs, and bean bags that were perfect for relaxing and reading in. The brass sign next to the door announced that no public sex was allowed in this room, so the atmosphere was very mellow.

As they entered, Rory and Liam immediately veered left and took her to a group of oxblood wingback chairs. Kerry was cuddled against a handsome man with dark chocolate-brown skin and a commanding aura. He was big, brawny, and tough looking. The exact opposite of his cuddly, plump submissive.

Rory approached him. "Dewan, good to see you."

Dewan smiled at Rory but gave Rhiannon a narrow-eyed look. "Is this your troublemaker who made Kerry cry?"

Rhiannon felt terrible and guilt twisted in her stomach. "I'm sorry."

Frowning at her, Dewan stroked Kerry's long hair. "Did I ask you to speak?"

She gaped at him, and Liam whispered in her ear, "Dewan is a high protocol Master."

Turning and leaning on her tiptoes, she whispered back, "I don't know what to do."

Liam pressed gently on her shoulder until she knelt before Dewan. The fire in the other man's gaze softened a little as he studied her expression. "What is your name, girl?"

"Rhia—I mean, Goddess."

Kerry gave Rhiannon a sympathetic look but did nothing to interrupt her Master. "Why are you here?"

She glanced at Rory, but he kept his expression impassive. She could recognize the dominant side in him rising, replacing her playful lover. It turned her on.

"I wanted to apologize to Kerry. I didn't mean to lash out at her like that. I...I have jealousy issues, but I'm trying to work on them."

Kerry touched Dewan's leg. "Master, may I speak?"

He nodded, and Kerry turned to face Rhiannon on her knees. "Please don't be cross with Master Liam—"

"Can we cuddle?" Rhiannon blurted out. Embarrassed, she covered her face with her hands. That wasn't exactly what she'd planned to say, but holding and being held by the other woman wasn't only appealing on a spiritual level. She wanted Kerry to know she was sincere about her apology. A person just couldn't cuddle with someone they were pissed at. Plus she wanted to know why Rory and Liam found Kerry so appealing. Well, other than her cute-as-a-button looks and generous breasts.

"Sure," Kerry said, her eyes wide with shock. Then she glanced up at Dewan with a guilty look. "I mean, if that's okay with you, Master."

With a glance in her direction Rhiannon couldn't quite decipher, Dewan nodded. "That's fine."

Rory cleared his throat, and Rhiannon swallowed hard. "Er, Master, is it okay?"

"Well, since you've already asked her and she's accepted, that's a moot point, isn't it?"

Liam pulled her up by the back of her neck and whispered in her ear, "Just because we're head over heels for you doesn't mean we won't be your Masters in every sense of the word."

He pushed her over the arm of an empty chair and lifted her robe to the side, exposing her sex and buttocks to the room. She shivered but held her position. They'd been treating her more like a girlfriend than a submissive, and she'd forgotten herself. Arching her back, she looked over her shoulder. "I'm sorry,

Masters. May I please be punished for my bad manners?"

Liam actually bit his lower lip, and Rory adjusted himself. They exchanged a glance, then stepped forward. She loved how they almost moved like one unit rather than two separate men.

Liam gave her a stern look. "Five spanks from each of us."

She braced herself, then swallowed hard as Rory cupped her pussy, rubbing against her clit with the heel of his hand. "I want you to come home with us tonight."

He stole her ability to think with how he was manipulating the sensitive bundle of nerves between her legs. "Yes."

Without warning he removed his hand and gave her a sharp slap that jiggled her bottom. Another slap followed, this one harder, and she guessed it was Master Liam by the angle of the blow. She tried not to cry out as they spanked her, the pain in her butt rapidly becoming more than she thought she could bear. The final blow landed, and she found herself panting as if she'd just run a race.

Conflicting emotions ran through her: shame that the spanking had made her wet, pride that she hadn't cried out, and embarrassment that her punishment was on display. When the men pulled her to her feet, she hissed as the robe slid over her ass.

"Such a tender bum," Liam murmured.

Rory gave her a kiss on the forehead. "I'm proud of you."

She smiled up at them; then Liam gently steered her in the direction of Kerry.

The pretty woman held out her hand. "Come with me."

Chapter Thirteen

Rhiannon took the stairs after Kerry, watching the woman's round bottom jiggle with each step. While Rhiannon was happy with her body, she had to admit there was something really appealing about a full-figured woman. It just made Kerry seem more feminine.

Pulling Rhiannon after her, Kerry guided them to a gigantic beanbag at the end of the room. From here, they could only see the second level where other couples cuddled and in some cases made out. Conversation rose from below, along with occasional laughter. The light was dim, and it made the atmosphere up here more intimate.

Spinning on her heel, Kerry turned and grinned at Rhiannon, her brown eyes sparkling. "Ready?"

"For what?"

"Flop back with me. It feels awesome."

Rhiannon looked around, unsure if she wanted to do such a childish thing in this very adult place. When she realized the other couples were only focused on each other, she relaxed. This wasn't a place to see and be seen. This was something different...gentler.

Giving Kerry a hesitant smile, she nodded. A moment later, they both fell back into the beanbag, and it fluffed around them like a cloud. Rhiannon gasped as she felt like she was bouncing on a waterbed and sinking into a foam mattress. The effect was amazing, and as soon as she stopped fighting it, she groaned. "Wow, this is nice."

"Mmm-hmm." Kerry rolled over onto her side and continued to hold Rhiannon's hand.

Suddenly, Rhiannon's eyes filled with tears, and Kerry made a soothing sound. "Hey now. It's okay. I'm not mad at you."

"I'm sorry. It's not you. I just... It's been a long day."

Without another word, Kerry enveloped Rhiannon into her arms, then pulled Rhiannon's head to rest on her shoulder. Inhaling the scent of vanilla cookies that came from the other woman's perfume, Rhiannon tried to relax. She really didn't know Kerry, and while she'd like it to feel like she was hugging her sister, it didn't.

To her surprise, Kerry pulled back and wiped Rhiannon's face. "Why are you so sad?"

"I have a lot going on." She gave a choked laugh at the understatement of the year.

Kerry brushed a stray lock of hair off Rhiannon's forehead. The touch wasn't contrived. Just an unconscious extension of the woman before her. "I'd say," Kerry murmured. She scooted closer and looked around before almost whispering, "Anything you say is strictly between me and you, and I expect the same. Okay?"

Confused but wanting to know what was going on, Rhiannon nodded. "Okay."

Kerry gave her a small smile. "Rory and Liam are head over heels in love with you. I can totally see it, and I'm so very happy they finally found the right woman for them."

She wanted to believe that was true, so much, but she didn't dare hope for it no matter how much she wanted it. "They love me? No, you must be wrong. They hardly know me. You can't love someone you don't know." Rhiannon swallowed hard, trying to keep her excitement under control. They didn't really know her, and they could reject her at any time. She knew that thought was stupid, and Latisha had said Rhiannon had total inability to see her own worth, but love was something that grew over time.

"Oh, they haven't told you yet? I was assuming by the way they were acting that they had." Kerry gave Rhiannon a grin that made her brown eyes twinkle. "I knew after spending one night with Dewan, my fiancé and Master, that he was the one for me. I just felt it in my heart."

Rhiannon thought back on her fascination with the men. She had to admit her initial reaction to them had been unusually strong. The first time she saw Master Rory and Master Liam together in the Hall of Mirrors bar, she'd been drawn to them.

Frowning, Rhiannon considered how the men had paraded her through the club earlier this evening. "You saw me tonight when they were hauling me around with something written on me in lipstick?"

Kerry snickered against Rhiannon's neck, her puff of air tickling the sensitive skin there. "I sure did."

"What did it say?"

"You couldn't read it?"

"No."

"On the front it said Master Rory's girl, and on the back it said Master Liam's lass."

Intense pleasure filled Rhiannon until she thought her heart might crack. That was about as bold of a statement of ownership as one could get. Maybe they really did like her.

Kerry began to stroke Rhiannon's back through the robe, and she sighed. What the hell was it about this woman's touch that made her instantly pliant?

With a soft humming sound, Kerry relaxed into the beanbag. "I've known Rory and Liam for five years. They're great guys, but you deserve to know something they might not tell you if they are bringing you into their lives permanently."

Apprehension twisted Rhiannon's gut into a hard knot. "What?"

Kerry's gaze grew wide with sincerity. "I'm going to level with you. Please don't freak out or tell them, okay? They'd flip, big time."

"Please just tell me."

"Rory and Liam are in love with each other, have been for as long as I've known them, but they are in complete denial. I don't know how much longer their friendship will last if they don't come clean about their attraction. Before you came along, I was pretty sure they were about to part ways."

Rhiannon stared at Kerry. Of course. It made absolute

sense.

While she found the thought of Rory and Liam having sex utterly hot and would love them regardless, she knew in her heart of hearts that if the men didn't fess up to their desire for each other, their relationship as a whole would implode. How could it not? She was committing herself to two men, who for whatever reason tortured themselves by being as close as two men could be without being intimate. It was a recipe for disaster. Unease churned in her stomach.

Kerry nervously licked her lips. "I'm sorry I had to tell you this. I really, really hope you won't break up with them, but I couldn't leave you open to hurt like that. I hope I'm not overstepping my bounds."

The other woman looked miserable, and Rhiannon didn't even think about it as she reached out and pulled Kerry into her arms. It was nice how Kerry completely relaxed against her. The tension drained out of Rhiannon as she ran her lips over Kerry's fine hair. It was a sensual pleasure, but not a sexual one. Holding Kerry, comforting her, felt just right. Like the woman had been created to be Rhiannon's own teddy bear.

Kerry made a soft, happy sound and hugged Rhiannon. "It's okay. No one would blame you for walking away, but I think if anyone can get through to them, it would be you. They've never, ever been this possessive of a woman before. I like to people watch, and I've seen the three of you staring at each other for a while now. I was wondering when you would get up the courage to approach them. Then when they were taking you through the club tonight, showing you off, I knew I had to say something before it was too late. It's one thing to fool themselves, but it's a whole 'nother thing to involve you in their denial."

"This is so screwed up."

"It is, but that's love. If it was easy, I don't think we'd value it as much." Kerry sighed and snuggled closer. "If you're going to confront them, you have to do it soon before they shore their defenses up. You're something new in their life, and they've had to adjust their worldview to accept you. Now is the time to push them just a bit further and get them to admit they want each other. If you can do that, I think you'll have a relationship that will be the envy of just about every woman at Wicked."

Silence lapsed between them, but it was an easy one. The background hum of noise soothed Rhiannon until she was a boneless puddle. She drifted off with thoughts of Rory and Liam kissing.

Chapter Fourteen

Rory carefully made his way up the steps of his house, an unusual nervousness entering him at the thought of Rhiannon entering his home for the first time, even if she was asleep. Liam followed silently behind and turned the lights on as they walked into the foyer, sliding the switch down to keep it on dim. It was just past three a.m., and Rory was tired all the way to his bones. Tonight had touched him on just about every emotional level, and his brain begged for sleep.

It must have been a long night for Rhiannon as well, because she'd slept the whole way home. Now Rory had the pleasure of carrying her, and as they walked through his house, he couldn't help ducking his head and smelling her hair. The warm smell of honeysuckle and woman filled him. Damned if he didn't find himself sighing with contentment as they reached his bedroom.

He had an insanely huge bed, so it was only natural they'd ended up at his place, though likely Liam would have preferred they were in his home. Once they were in Rory's room, he made his way across the smooth oak floor to his bed. Custom built, the oversize mattress was easily big enough to sleep six. While he didn't need that much room, he did have the occasional overnight guests.

However, when he set Rhiannon down on his silver silk sheets, his heart did a funny lurch at the sight of her in his room, on his bed. She shifted, and the robe gaped around her legs, revealing smooth, firm flesh that he wanted to grab and lick. His cock stirred, but Liam thumped him on the shoulder.

"Keep it in yer pants."

He grinned at his friend and lifted his chin to the bathroom. "You want to use it first?"

Liam nodded and went into the master bathroom. In the time it took Rory to get undressed, the other man had come back. Seeing Liam naked in his room made the same hard lurch go through Rory's heart that watching Rhiannon in his home did. Fuck, he wanted that man in the worst way. Observing Liam with Rhiannon tonight, feeling the love created by all of them, had blown away Rory's preconceived notions about what love could be. This intense emotion scared him in how good it felt, a sensation that he could easily become addicted to. But living without this feeling would kill him from the inside out.

With a sigh Rory tossed his clothes onto the chair near his bed. The room itself was done in shades of white, black, and gray with a few primary color art pieces here and there. He loved the clean simplicity of this space and was instantly soothed by it. After doing a quick cleanup, he returned to the room to find Liam cuddling a now naked Rhiannon.

She had a sleepy smile on her lips as she curled herself around Liam. His best mate appeared so happy that Rory hated to interrupt them. Liam glanced up at him, and his gaze brightened. He looked down at Rhiannon, then up at Rory and waggled his eyebrows in a leering way. Only Liam would do something like that right now. Rory chuckled.

As he slid beneath the smooth sheets, he thought about all the times he'd shared with Liam; then he thought about all the things they would do together with Rhiannon. His cock stirred as he curved himself around Rhiannon's firm little backside that still somehow managed to be soft and giving. She gave a tired moan. "Mmm, nice."

Liam and Rory met each other's gaze, and both men grinned. Rory sighed with relief. Somehow they'd done it. They'd managed to bring Rhiannon home with them. A surge of complete satisfaction settled in Rory's soul, and he knew without a doubt that these were the people he was meant to spend the rest of his life with.

A woman's soft moans woke Rory up, making his dick start to pulse to the beat of his heart. The delicious scent of feminine arousal hung heavy enough in the air that Rory swore he could taste it. The scent of her musk was intermixed with honeysuckle, and Rory came fully awake, realizing who he was smelling and hearing in his bed.

He rolled over and found Rhiannon with her wrists cuffed to her ankles, getting flat-out fucked by Liam. She must have taken a shower at some point, because her hair was still damp, and he reached out to curl a strand of it around his finger. This had to be one of the best sights he'd ever woken up to. She hadn't realized he was watching them yet, being too caught up in her pleasure. The way her face tensed let him know that she was close to climaxing. In a perfect world, he'd be able to slip behind Liam right now and ease his lubed fingers into the other man's ass, opening Liam for his penetration while the other man fucked their woman. Then his mind switched to the fantasy of fucking Rhiannon with Liam behind him, filled with cock while the world's hottest pussy sucked at his dick.

Liam paused his vigorous fucking and switched to long, slow strokes. He smiled at Rory, then winked. "Not going to orgasm on me now, are you, lass?"

"No, Master."

Rhiannon's voice had gone husky with passion, and she made a pitiful whimper that turned Rory on. He debated joining them but just watching was really nice. It gave him time to admire them together, to have a live porn show right in front of him. Sometimes watching Liam fuck a sub was more arousing than doing it himself. Rory wanted his dick deep inside their girl, but he'd wait his turn.

She flexed her hands, jerking at her restraints. "Please, Master."

Liam continued a slow in-and-out drag to and from her pussy. Rory laughed as her eyes rolled back in her head when Liam finally went balls-deep.

Her eyes flew open, and she looked over at Rory. For a second, uncertainty and guilt filled her gaze. He put a stop to those thoughts before they could take hold. "Good morning, darling girl. This is a nice way to wake up. More beautiful than a sunrise and twice as hot."

She started to respond, but Liam thrust into her hard enough that she grasped the sheets. All that came out was a moaning, "Master."

Her breasts shook as Liam moved against her, and Rory began to stroke her nipples. Rhiannon let out a wail of despair, then clenched her teeth in her effort to not orgasm. He really should take pity on her and leave her alone, but instead he took one of her dusky nipples into his mouth and sucked hard. She panted against his ear as he continued to torment her until she was out of her mind.

The clang of metal from her cuffs added a nice note to their fucking, and Rory wondered if he should up the BDSM aspect of their relationship. If she really wanted to be with them she needed to know how deep their need for control went. And one of their favorite ways to own a woman was orgasm denial. He loved the frantic look that came to a submissive's eyes when she was almost helpless against the urges of her body to come. Rhiannon loved to please them, so for her, this type of arousal would be doubly intense. Not only was she pleasing them, but she was also surrendering herself.

Rory slipped his hand down Rhiannon's stomach and trailed his fingers through her pubic hair. Splitting his fingers into a V, he then rubbed her pussy while Liam continued to take her in a relentless manner. Occasionally Rory could feel the slick slide of Liam's cock in and out of her pussy. Hoping his friend was too gone to really notice, Rory closed his grip a bit so that Liam was not only fucking Rhiannon, he was also getting the additional sensation of Rory's fingers.

Liam let out a low, deep, rough grunt that made Rory's dick ache. Rory could imagine Liam's seed filling Rhiannon's pussy, and he had a hard time not pushing Liam out of the way so he could fuck Rhiannon. He wanted Liam's seed coating his cock while he took their beautiful girl, but more than that, he wanted to look into Rhiannon's gorgeous exotic eyes as he emptied himself inside her. He bit hard on Rhiannon's nipple, and she let out a pitiful whimper.

Liam gave a few more jerking strokes, then collapsed on the side of the bed."Fuck, Rory. You really do sleep like the dead."

He looked up from lapping at Rhiannon's sore nipple, intent on making them so sensitive that putting a bra on would be uncomfortable to her. "Helps me sleep through your snoring."

With a laugh, Liam swung his legs over the bed and put his pants on. "I have to run over to my house for a few. Take care of our girl."

Rory looked down into Rhiannon's wide green eyes and smiled. "My pleasure."

He wasn't sure when Liam left, only that by the time he'd licked his way over to Rhiannon's other breast, she was wiggling her hot arse all over the bed. The restraints kept her immobilized, forbidding her from doing anything to alleviate her need.

Giving her left breast a hard bite, he then grinned as she screamed. He liked the sound so much that he did it again, then began to place feather-soft licks around the distended nub. Rhiannon let out a shuddering sigh. "Oh, shit. That feels so good."

"I'm proud of you for holding out as long as you did with Liam. He isn't easy to resist when he fucks like that."

Something flickered through her eyes, insecurity and maybe fear; then hot desire sank in, and she worried her lower lip before asking, "Do I get a reward, Master?"

Curious as to what was going on in that intriguing mind of hers, he decided to give her some room, to let her play a bit. All their couplings had been intense, but he also needed to show her that he could please her in any way she wanted. Images of a variety of dirty things went through his head, but he kept his attention fully on Rhiannon. "What do you want, sweetheart? Tell me, and it's yours."

She swallowed a couple of times before her voice came out, whisper soft. "Please eat my pussy."

His breath froze in his lungs as he held her gaze, wondering if she remembered how much the idea of tasting Liam's cum in her hot pussy turned him on. One of the submissives they'd trained had a huge fetish for licking the seed of other men out of a woman's cunt, and Rory had to admit he found it hot. Actually, more than hot. It made his dick throb, and the knowledge that it was Liam's cum that he would eat was the stuff of fantasies. Oh, he'd sneaked a taste here and there but nothing as blatant as licking it out of a woman. He couldn't with Liam still there, but Liam had left, and Rhiannon's hot pussy was flooded with the other man's release. Now he could finally indulge himself as he wished with a more than willing woman.

And not just any woman—their woman.

"You want me to clean your slick little cunt?"

Her lips parted in a gasp, and she slightly arched her back. "Please."

Trying to stall, to draw this out, he trailed his fingers through her slit, then pressed his thumb into her pussy. While he held her gaze, he pulled his thumb out and sucked it clean, the taste of their combined fluids going straight to his cock. A little growl escaped him before he could stop himself, and Rhiannon moaned.

"What turns you on about this, love?" She flushed, and he gripped her chin, forcing her to look at him. "No, I won't have you embarrassed about confessing your secret desires to me. I want you, all of you. Mind, body, and soul. There is nothing you can say that will get rid of me."

He gentled his hold and tried to get her to look into his eyes, but she kept glancing away. "It turns me on because the idea of two men together turns me on."

The saliva in his mouth dried up, but he forced himself to speak. "Really. Anyone in particular?"

Crimson painted her cheeks as she blushed, but she finally met and held his gaze. "The thought of you and Master Liam fucking drives me insane."

"Why?"

He was proud he'd managed that one word, his mind at once racing and totally blank. What was she trying to do here? Did she really want that? Had Liam said something to her? Had she guessed on her own? He felt like an idiot and released her chin, avoiding her gaze as he untied her.

"Because…because you belong together." She took in a deep breath. "We belong together."

The smooth skin of her wrists had been slightly abraded by the restraints, and he paused to kiss that tender flesh. "I would love to give you what you want, but I'm not the only one who has to make this decision."

For a long time, she was quiet, allowing him to untie her and kiss the marks left by her bindings. When she finally spoke, nervousness screamed in her every word, even though she barely whispered. "Do you love him?"

He thought about lying, he really did, but he was so fucking tired of lies. "Yes."

She traced her slender fingers over the side of his face, her touch a gentle balm to the painful emotions racing through him. "Have you ever been together? Just the two of you?"

"Once."

He gave her a rundown on the disastrous night in college when a very drunk Rory and Liam had a mutual masturbation session, and how close Rory had come to losing his best friend. Liam absolutely could not handle the idea of being attracted to a man, and Rory knew that if he pushed it, he would lose his friend. So instead he'd brought another woman home with him, and that had been the start of the road that led them here, twelve years later, with the same wants and needs but also an enormous amount of frustration and hurt.

"So since that night you've both been in a ménage relationship of one form or another."

"Yes."

Her voice thickened as she said, "That's so sad."

"What are you talking about?"

Blinking back tears, she shook her head. "You obviously love each other but are letting other people's opinions stand between you. I can't help but wonder if you'll do that with me. If I meet your family and they find out I'm a gypsy, will you leave me if they don't like me?"

His heart leaped at the trust she was showing by opening up to him even as it ached for her obvious pain and fear. He wasn't doing his job as a Dom or a man if he let her suffer needlessly. Besides, he was falling helplessly in love with her and would give the world to make her happy. "Darling girl, no one can take you from me. The only way you're getting out of my arms is if you leave me. I mean that."

Her sigh held such relief he couldn't help but cup her face in his hands, marveling at how fragile she appeared. His own bullshit got pushed to the side, leaving him clear-headed and in control of his emotions, at least for the moment. Healing her heart was the only thing that mattered.

"Promise?"

"I swear it." He took a deep breath and let it out slowly. "I'm falling desperately, madly, insanely in love with you, Rhiannon."

"You are?" Her voice came out soft and almost childlike.

"I am."

A sob escaped her, and he pulled her into his arms, trying to surround her with his body as if he could shield her from the past that had destroyed her trust. "Please don't cry, love. It kills me to hear your pain."

She moved enough that she could look into his eyes, her green gaze impossibly gorgeous in the morning light that burned through the sheer curtains. Even crying she was so beautiful it slayed him.

"What about Liam? You love him too, right?"

The worry in her tone made him adore her all the more as he realized she didn't want Liam to be hurt. "Yes, Rhiannon. My loving you doesn't take any of my feelings away from Liam, however fucked-up they may be. My dad likes to say that the heart has more love than all the oceans on earth, that love is our connection to the divine and limitless." He gave her a small grin. "Then again, my dad has been high or drunk for most of his life, so I take his advice with a grain of salt."

The light tone of her giggle made him even more aware of how feminine she was. His woman would always be what some considered too girly, but he enjoyed that she liked to look good, that she enjoyed taking on a more domestic role. Taking care of people made Rhiannon feel happy, and he'd be lying if he didn't admit that he liked being cared for by a woman who took pride in her appearance. It made him proud to be seen out in public with her, knowing she'd made an effort to look good for him just like he made an effort to look good for her. The mental image of introducing her to his parents made his heart thud. He could just picture the lecherous if harmless grin on his dad's face when he got an eyeful of his and Liam's girl.

The thought of Liam brought his mood down a bit, and he stroked Rhiannon's hair back from her face. "You know Liam would never accept me as a lover, don't you? Can you live with that, because I have to, or I'll lose him. And I don't think either of us wants that to happen."

"No, no. I don't want to lose him," she said quickly. "But Rory, how long can you live your life like this? The thought of you two breaking up hurts my heart, and I can't imagine what it's like to live a lie of this magnitude."

The knowledge that the lie had been killing him was a fact he kept to himself. Rhiannon had enough to worry about; she didn't need to hear his bullshit. He shrugged. "I love him, Rhiannon. If this is the only way we can be close, so be it."

She traced her fingertips over his face, reawakening his body after the seriousness of their discussion. "I just want you to know that if you need any help talking to Liam, I'll go with you."

"Will you hold my hand?"

She ran her fingers through his hair and grabbed a handful, then gave him a gentle tug. "I'm serious."

He removed her hand from his hair and gave the pads of each finger a nip sharp enough to make her yelp. "You're also a brat."

"I am not!" She leaned away from him. "Don't you give me that look. We're talking about serious shit here."

Yes, and he was fucking tired of being serious all the time. While he loved her endless compassion, he needed her joy. "What look?"

Mischief sparkled in her eyes a moment before she said, "Like you want to eat me."

A low growl rumbled out of his chest as she tried to scramble away from him.

Grabbing her by the waist, he then slung her back into the middle of his bed. She parted her legs without having to be told, and he let out a pained sound at the prettiest pussy in the world shining with an extra layer of cream. The knowledge that it was Liam's seed he was about to eat only added to the eroticism of the moment for Rory. It must have turned Rhiannon on something fierce as well, because she was writhing on the bed like someone was fucking her instead of looking at her.

"Easy, girl." He leaned forward and pinned her thighs with his hands. "Let me enjoy my treat."

She arched as best she could and gasped, "Oh, Master, you're so dirty. I love it."

Moving back enough that he was on his stomach while still gripping her thighs, he then lowered his face to her wet heat. "And I love you."

A soft, almost pained sound rose from her when he began to lap at her pussy with long strokes of his tongue. She had such a pretty little cunt, and the taste of Liam's cum mixed with her natural sweetness had Rory rubbing his cock on the bed for relief. He took his time cleaning her, giving little glancing licks to her hard clit that had her begging him until her voice broke. When he was certain that her pussy was cleaned of every drop of Liam's seed, he pushed himself up and over her.

She stared up at him with dazed eyes and wrapped her arms around his neck. "Please, Rory, take me. I need you."

Fisting himself, he slowly eased into her welcome heat, gritting his teeth as her strong inner muscles spasmed around his cock like they were trying to suck his dick deeper into her. "Then you'll have me."

With a snap of his hips, he sank into her, forcing her pussy to open for him, ramming himself into her as deep and hard as he could. She screamed and clawed at his back, coming around his cock as he tried to pull back out, clenching him with her pussy until he thought he might climax from just that one stroke. The sting of her drawing blood as she dug her nails into his back helped him to pull back a little, to still the tremors that shook his thighs and set a burn flaring in his spine.

Her cries eventually turned to little panting moans, but she continued to rub herself against him. He flipped her onto her stomach, then placed his thighs on the outside of hers, effectively trapping her smaller body beneath his. Her bum was worthy of worship, and as he sank deeper into her, he pulled her firm cheeks apart, giving himself a decadent view of his cock sliding in and out of her tight grip.

"There we go. Feel that? Feel my cock sliding in and out of you? You have the prettiest pussy I've ever seen, and right now it's sucking on my cock, trying to keep me inside your greedy cunt." He groaned as her channel did indeed clamp down on him like it was trying to suck his cum out. "God love a sinner, you drive me insane. So perfect, so beautiful, so mine."

Gripping her arse, he began to stroke harder, his body moving in a subtle wave as he gave her what she was begging him for in a ragged whisper. Her face was turned to the side, her eyes closed, and her midnight-black hair spread around her in silky darkness. She began to rock her hips back into him as best she could, chasing another orgasm as her muscles began to tense.

"That's it. Feel your body getting ready to climax. I bet right now your little clit is as stiff as can be." He moved her hips up so he could slip his hand around her waist and pet her sex. "Yeah, nice and hard."

He picked up his pace and moved deep within her, losing himself in her sighs, her moans, and the way she undulated against him. He'd never been with a woman who moved like Rhiannon, and the press of her delicate body against him filled him with a rush of possessiveness. This was his woman—*his*—and no one, not even Liam, was going to take her from him.

"Mine," he growled as he fucked her relentlessly, loving how she tried to both get away from him and get closer.

"Yours," she agreed in a breathless pant. "My Master."

The heartfelt devotion in those words undid the last threads of his control, and he roared as his orgasm ripped through him, locking up his muscles, then sending him into hard shakes as he emptied himself into Rhiannon. She bucked beneath him, making him lay his weight on her to hold her down as she moaned and cried out, her cunt rippling around his cock like a massaging hand and demanding every drop of cum that he had to give. When she finally quit, his dick was so sensitive he was almost afraid to pull out. The feeling of her pussy was just too exquisite to leave, so he carefully rolled them over onto their sides so he was spooning her.

Rhiannon gave a deep, contented sigh and burrowed against him like a puppy.

"Feeling good, beautiful girl?"

"The best," she murmured and pulled his arm over her. "I haven't felt this good in a long time. Maybe ever."

He lifted his head momentarily to kiss her cheek before lying back down, a delicious lassitude encouraging him to stay in bed with his woman. "Me too."

"It would be nice," she whispered against his hand, "if Liam were here as well."

His heart momentarily hurt, but he tried to keep it out of his voice. "It would."

"Do the bedrooms at your island home have big beds?"

"Why?"

"I'd like us all to sleep in the same bed, please."

"Anything you want, darling girl."

She was quiet for a few more seconds, but he could tell by the slight tension of her body that she had more to say.

"Rory, you really need to talk to Liam. I don't think your…need is one-sided. I see how he looks at you. He wants you."

"He doesn't know what the fuck he wants."

Slipping from her body, he tried to ignore her flinch when he left her. She said, "I'm sorry."

Guilt hit him, and he shook his head. "Don't be. I always want you to speak your mind around me. It's one of the things that I value about you. I don't want a doll; I want a partner, even if that partner makes me think about things I don't want to think about. You scare me sometimes with your honesty, but if I'm going to love you, then I need to stop running from the truth. I just hope you can deal with the potential fallout."

"I won't leave you, Rory."

Hating how fucking vulnerable he felt, he lowered his lips to her neck and gently kissed her. "How do I know that, darling girl? The only person that has ever stayed has been Liam, and I'm afraid I'm losing him."

She came to her knees and to his surprise grabbed him in a strong hug, her soft curves pressing into him. Contentment filled his soul. "I love you. Please don't hurt me."

How he could want to cry and smile at the same time he had no idea, but now it was her turn to hug her close.

"Quite a pair, aren't we?"

"We need Liam," she muttered against his chest. "He's the only sane one among us."

Laughing softly, he slipped his hand beneath her long hair and stroked her warm back. "If that's true, we're in trouble."

Chapter Fifteen

The chime for Rhiannon's front door rang, and she let out a slow breath. She'd put on a flowing white summer dress that had a modest sweetheart bodice line and was embroidered with daisies. It was short enough to hit midthigh. She'd have to be careful bending over or she'd be flashing the world. Just in case that happened, she wore a pair of lacy white boy-cut panties beneath.

She'd decided to wear her hair down with a simple white headband and had kept her makeup minimal. Added to that was her supercute white Jimmy Choo wedge sandals paired with a delicate gold anklet. She felt pretty. Looking nice gave her self-confidence, and she needed all she could get right now. Her nerves were shot, and she'd put on her extra-strong deodorant for fear of sweating too much.

Giving her reflection in the mirror situated on the far wall of the foyer another look to make sure she was ready, she took a deep breath and opened the door, then let it out in a stunned huff of air.

Together, in the daylight on her porch step, Rory and Liam were devastatingly handsome in different ways. Rory had the rakish good looks going on with his artfully tousled wheat-blond hair, and Liam was everything dark and delicious. Rory wore gray pants that went well with his hunter-green button-down shirt while Liam wore a pair of khaki pants that complimented his blue pullover. They both smiled at her, and she swore her heart skipped a couple of beats.

"Hello, Rhiannon," Rory said.

"Hello, lass."

Overcome by emotion, trying to yell at herself to not act like a stupid teenager on her first date, Rhiannon took a step back. "Won't you please come in? I just need a moment to grab my purse."

Liam came in first, then froze in the doorway. Rory followed, pushing his friend out of the way, "Move, you big..."

She cocked her head and watched as they examined her foyer.

Finally Liam swallowed hard and said, "Wow."

"Wow what?"

Rory looked at her with wide eyes. "You really like fairies."

"And sparkly shit," Liam added in a hushed voice.

She flushed and crossed her arms. "Yes, I do. What of it?"

The men exchanged a look, then came at her so fast she found herself backing up until she pressed against the banister at the bottom of the stairs.

"I think it's cute," Liam said with a growl in his tone as he stepped up on her right side.

"We didn't mean anything negative. It's just...a lot of fairies," Rory added as he pressed against her left side.

Sandwiched between the men and surrounded by their warmth, her ire drained away, replaced by arousal. Still, she didn't like the slightly shocked look that Liam got every time he looked around the room. "What's wrong with that? Don't you collect anything?"

Rory grinned. "We collect rocks."

Liam perked up. "Yeah, we have a pretty awesome collection between the two of us. We have it arranged in the basement, but I think we might need to get some kind of storage unit to house it all."

She giggled. "You collect rocks?"

Rory nodded. "When we first roomed together at the University of Leicester, we both put up some of our favorite rocks from our collection on our desks."

"I knew right then that we'd get along."

Liam smiled at his friend with such affection that Rhiannon was sure he loved Rory. She looked from man to man, noting their easy body language and how Rory's smile had gentled. Oddly enough she didn't feel left out when they looked at each other like that. If anything, she felt an echo of their love, and it was almost as good as them looking at her with such open affection. They were happy, so she was happy.

Master Liam cupped her ass in a proprietary manner that made her wet. "Go get your purse so we can get to the store. I know you have to work tonight so we're tight on time."

Master Rory stepped away but not before he ran his hand down her arm, leaving a trail of goose bumps behind. "You look beautiful, and I'd love to fuck you on those stairs while you sucked Liam off, but we have to get going."

She stared at him, her body ripe and ready to take him. He smelled so good, like lemongrass and bergamot. "I can call in sick."

Liam laughed and gave her butt a swat. "Tempting but no."

She gathered up her purse and wondered what the heck she was getting herself into.

Two hours later they were in the private showroom of an exclusive jewelry store in the heart of Washington, DC. The back room consisted of a set of comfortable dark leather couches along with an empty table and a few chairs. A beautiful auburn-haired sales associate had brought them a chilled bottle of champagne and strawberries, compliments of the shop. When Rhiannon leaned forward to look at the label, she'd been shocked to see it was a brand she knew cost over two thousand dollars a bottle.

If the store provided that kind of champagne for free to Rory and Liam, then the men must spend a shit ton of money here. She thought about the emerald choker that Rory had loaned her for her date with Liam at the Smithsonian and speculated if it had come from this store. If it had, no wonder they got the private viewing room with the good champagne.

A very handsome black man dressed in an impeccable navy suit came out with a wide smile. The way he moved, the energy he gave off, made her instantly aware that he was a Dom. It would make sense, considering he evidently made high-end BDSM gear. As he neared, she took in his exotic tilted eyes that reminded her of a cat's and his high cheekbones. Combined with his full lips and muscular frame, he was a man any woman would take notice of. Even Rhiannon, as in love with her Masters as she was, couldn't help but give him a nice slow once-over.

Rory and Liam stood, and she did as well, pressed between them. Both men put a proprietary arm around her waist, and she couldn't help the no doubt goofy smile that curved her lips. It just felt so...right to have them touching her like this. With their arms crossed over her, she felt so safe and protected.

Rory reached out and shook hands with the man. "Emershan. Good to see you, mate."

The other man smiled at Rory, then looked at Rhiannon. His voice held a smooth accent as he smiled at her, then said, "And who do we have here?"

"This is our girl, Rhiannon," Liam said with obvious pride in his voice.

A warm tingle raced through her, and she was pretty sure she blushed when Emershan took her hand and lowered his lips to it. When he brushed them across the back of her hand, her skin warmed. He looked up and winked. "It's a pleasure to meet you, Rhiannon."

She swallowed hard. "Thank you. It's a pleasure to meet you as well."

"If you ever get tired of these two idiots, please do look me up." He exchanged a glance with Rory standing to her left. "Though how these lucky bastards managed to find you before my brother and I did I'll never know. She would have made a beautiful bride."

Rory must have seen her confused look. "Emershan and his brother Demarco are on the search for a woman stupid enough to marry both of them."

She blinked. "Both?"

"Indeed," Emershan said with a purr in his voice. "It is the tradition of my family, so our diamond mine never leaves our blood line. Our bride-to-be is lucky that there are only two of us. My mother married four brothers."

Shock had her standing there with her jaw open. She couldn't imagine being married to four men. Two were more than she could handle as it was. "Wow."

Emershan's deep chuckle almost rivaled Rory's and Liam's in its ability to make her body react. "Indeed. If you ever decide these two are unworthy of your exquisite beauty, keep us in mind. I think you'd enjoy being our princess."

"Back off," Liam growled and tugged Rhiannon closer. "She's ours."

Liam glared at the other man, and Emershan took a step back with a grin. "You can't blame a man for trying."

Rory pulled her back down onto the couch with them, and Liam sat as well. Both men adjusted their hold on her but remained touching. Liam draped his arm over her shoulders while Rory put his large hand on her thigh and began to rub her skin beneath the dress with his thumb. They were obviously sending a message that she was theirs, and the possessive display delighted her. Yeah, women weren't supposed to like being owned, but she did. That didn't make her crazy or a doormat or a stupid. She just loved the warm, gratifying sensation of a man—in this case, two men—protecting her from the world.

Emershan folded his hands behind his back and smiled. "Please tell me she's here to be fitted with a clit and nipple clamps. Or an anal hook."

Her butt clenched. Liam must have noticed her flinch, because he laughed. "No, just here for cuffs today. Ankle and wrist."

Rory gently stroked her hand. "We'd also like to see your Catherine line."

Emershan's eyebrows rose in surprise. "Well, well, well. It's about time."

Confused, she looked to Rory, but he kept his attention on Emershan. "We want the cuffs in gold with the fur lining."

With a definite growl in his voice, Liam said, "And a pair in silver with the black leather."

Emershan nodded, but his speculative gaze returned to Rhiannon, and he studied her with interest. "Come here, girl."

He held out his hand, and Rory and Liam reluctantly let her go. Emershan brought her to stand next to him and pulled a roll of tape out of his pocket. He glanced over at Rory and Liam glowering at him on the couch. "Do you want me to measure her for full restraints?"

"You just want to an excuse to touch her," Liam muttered.

Emershan stood up to his full height. "Gentlemen, if you really think I'm the kind of man who would take advantage of any woman while doing my job, I'm afraid I've misjudged you."

Rory held up a placating hand. "Sorry. We're just a little...protective of her."

Turning back to Rhiannon, Emershan winked, the stern look gone from his expression. "Let's just do wrists, forearms, neck, waist, ankles, and thighs today."

Both men gave Emershan a warning look, and true to his word, the handsome black man took her measurements with a gentle and respectful touch. She relaxed as he looked at her with a detached expression, no longer seeing her as a woman but as a job. After he finished measuring her, he paused and walked around her once, examining her body from every angle.

Rory cleared his throat. "How long will it take you to make what we need?"

"The restraints I can have to you by this afternoon."

He said something in a language that Rhiannon didn't understand, but Rory evidently did because he responded in the same language.

Confused as to what they were doing, she made her way to Liam and sat on his lap. He immediately cuddled her close, and she whispered, "What are they saying? And what language are they speaking?"

"French, and if I told you, it wouldn't be a surprise."

Rhiannon had to count to one hundred at least a dozen times in an attempt to hold on to her temper with the bartender, Sunny. The other woman was being especially nasty to Rhiannon tonight, and despite her best intentions, she was getting to the point where if Sunny didn't shut up on her own, Rhiannon was going to shut her up. If it wasn't for Liam and Rory watching her work, she'd have planted her fist in Sunny's bitchy mouth an hour ago.

Oh, she knew what the other woman's problem was. Master Hawk was sitting with Liam and Rory tonight, and he'd been nice to Rhiannon all evening, smiling at her and joking with her in a way that probably looked like flirting. Rhiannon knew Master Hawk meant nothing by his behavior; he was merely relieved that Rhiannon no longer flinched anytime he looked at her. For the first time in what seemed like forever Rhiannon no longer saw the monster who had abused her when she looked at Master Hawk, just a nice man who was genuinely worried about her. His relief at her lack of distress would have been comical if she hadn't put the man through the emotional wringer before. Guilt still haunted her at the memory of Master Hawk's pain-filled expression as he tried to comfort her, only to have her strike out at him in mindless fear.

No, she wouldn't think about that, not now. Not when things were finally going right in her life. So far she'd managed to avoid any nightmares for five months, and she wanted to keep it that way.

The edge of her silver-beaded mask itched her face, and she twitched her cheek, wishing she didn't have to wear it but still unwilling to show Club Wicked her true self. Tonight she wore a ruffled and rhinestone-studded baby doll pink corset paired with matching boy shorts and nude fishnet stockings. The corset stays laced all the way down the back, and the shorts had a big pink bow on the butt. Both Liam and Rory had practically drooled when they saw her, and she couldn't wait to fulfill the promise of hot sex their gaze carried. Only one more hour and her shift would be over; then she'd be all theirs to play with, to pleasure however they wanted.

As she carried her full tray past the men and onto another table the three Masters paused in their conversation and smiled at her. She had to look away, sure that her face hid nothing as the love she felt for her Masters overwhelmed her. All night people had been complimenting her on how happy she looked, how different, and it finally began to sink in that over the years that she'd worked at Club Wicked she'd made friends even if she hadn't realized it. Friends like Mistress Alice and her wife, Shy.

The two women were cuddled together on one of the couches, and Shy had bright red stripes covering her thighs and buttocks visible through her sheer cream dress. The sweet blonde submissive looked up at Rhiannon and grinned. "Congratulations."

"Yes, congratulations," Mistress Alice said in a low, husky voice. "I'm assuming the reason you're floating around the bar tonight is Master Liam and Master Rory. I heard about their little display of public branding of you the other night."

Flushing, Rhiannon nodded. "Yes, Mistress."

It seemed that everyone knew that Liam and Rory had finally taken a submissive, and she'd been receiving congratulations all night. Well, congratulations and ill-concealed jealousy, but she was ignoring those bitches, refusing to let them ruin her night.

"About time." Mistress Alice glanced behind Rhiannon in the direction of her men. "I was beginning to worry about them."

"Why?" Mistress Alice raised one fair brow, and Rhiannon cleared her throat. "I mean, may I ask why, Mistress?"

"They'd lost their spark. Training for them was becoming a chore. Oh, don't get me wrong, they did wonderful work with their girls, but…I think they were very lonely before you."

"Lonely? How could they be lonely with women throwing themselves at them all the time?"

Mistress Alice laughed softly. "Men are odd creatures. They can have sex without emotions being involved, unlike most women. But you, you're good for them. You've brought that spark back, and then some."

Out of the corner of her eye, Rhiannon noticed Mistress Onyx signaling her from the bar. The club was busy tonight, and she could quickly fall behind on her orders if she didn't get a move on. "Thank you, Mistress. May I please be excused? I'm afraid Mistress Onyx may beat my butt if I don't get back to her."

Shy giggled. "I've had Mistress Onyx beat my butt. She has a hand that could break brick walls."

With an indulgent sigh Mistress Alice pinched one of the red marks on Shy's thigh, earning a squeal. "You are such a pain slut. Maybe I need to beat you harder."

"No, Mistress," Shy squeaked with equal parts fear and

arousal.

"Off with you, Goddess," Mistress Alice said as she turned her attention to her squirming submissive.

Rhiannon made her way back to the massive bar, exchanging smiles with another harried server who moved past her with a full tray of drinks. By the time she reached the counter, Mistress Onyx had her next order ready.

"Here," she said, sliding the tray across the bar. "I have to take a break for a minute. I'll be back by the time you've filled this order. The champagne needs strawberries still. Can you throw those in there for me?"

"Sure. You go do what you have to do."

"Thanks."

Out of the corner of her eye, she noticed Sunny watching her. Tonight the woman wore a black latex catsuit, and her short black hair was in artful disarray. Her black mask conformed to the upper half of her face like it was painted on, and her lips had been colored with black lipstick. The overall effect was striking, but Rhiannon couldn't help a bitchy thought about how all that black made Sunny look like a pretty corpse.

Mistress Onyx bolted to the back entrance of the bar, and Rhiannon busied herself with arranging the drinks and carefully placing each strawberry in the glasses of champagne. At six hundred dollars a bottle, the champagne was practically liquid gold, so she took her time, careful not to spill a drop. She was almost done with it when another tray slammed into the edge of hers, pushing it over the side and sending it crashing to the floor and covering her in beer, champagne, and what smelled like whiskey.

Stunned, she looked up to find Sunny smirking at her from the other side of the bar as conversation halted around them.

"Oh, sorry. My bad."

"You bitch!" Rhiannon seethed, the liquid from the drinks chilling her skin as it seeped through her clothing. "You did that on purpose!"

The other servers and bartenders stared at them, but Rhiannon was beyond pissed. Sunny merely shrugged. "Clumsy me. You better stay away from Master Hawk if you don't want any more accidents. You may have fooled Master Rory and Master Liam, but I know you're just using them to get to Master Hawk. Your manipulation won't work, and Master Liam and Master Rory will realize what you are. Nothing but a used-up piece of trash. They'll figure it out soon enough; then they'll see that you're nothing but a filthy whore and leave you. I'll make sure of it."

Heartbreaking pain seared through Rhiannon as Sunny spat out the last words Rhiannon's father had ever said to her. For a brief moment, she was transported back in time, being shoved out the front door of her home by her father while he railed at her for bringing the attention of outsiders to their community and called her a filthy whore. She could actually feel the cold rain and the pain of falling down the front steps of her home as her father, the man whom she'd adored and worshipped beyond question, disowned her with what seemed like her entire family watching.

"That's right," Sunny said in a nasty voice. "You're nothing but a dirty slut. I can only hope you didn't give Master Liam and Master Rory a STD."

Rhiannon lost her mind.

With a scream, she launched herself across the counter at Sunny, then grabbed the momentarily stunned woman around the throat with both hands as she slid over the bar to the other side. Sunny shoved Rhiannon before she could get her feet under her, breaking Rhiannon's grip on her throat. After that everything became an enraged blur as she kicked out Sunny's feet, making the other woman fall back. Throwing herself at Sunny, Rhiannon then pinned Sunny and hit her right in her bitchy mouth, smashing her lips against her teeth. Glass broke, and people were yelling, but Rhiannon's rational mind had left the building.

Strong hands lifted Rhiannon off Sunny, but the second the other woman was unpinned she threw herself at Rhiannon, getting in a good blow to the side of Rhiannon's face that sent a bright explosion of sparks across her vision.

They were screaming at each other, calling each other every bad name in the book as they were hauled through the back entrance of the bar and down the hallway. Rhiannon tried to tear herself away from whoever held her, to get at the woman who was still saying she was going to make sure Master Rory and Master Liam knew what a whore Rhiannon was, that they would never want her. The need to make Sunny feel the pain that was eating Rhiannon alive blocked out everything happening around her until someone shoved a ball gag in her mouth and someone else locked her hands together with what felt like leather restraints.

"What the fuck!" she screamed from behind the ball gag. Or at least tried to scream it. What came out was an undignified garbled mess.

Sunny was receiving a similar treatment, but instead of a ball gag, Master Hawk was tying a cloth gag between Sunny's bleeding lips. Master Liam moved to assist him and quickly bound the other woman's hands and kicking feet with leather restraints. Before she knew it, Rhiannon was tossed over Master Rory's lap, and through the veil of her hair, she watched Sunny pinned on Master Hawk's lap.

Master Hawk's hand rose up and made contact with Sunny's exposed ass the same instant someone hit Rhiannon's ass—really hard. She screamed out and tried to writhe away, but Master Rory's voice stilled her. "Have you lost your bloody mind?"

The crack of his hand against her ass had her screaming out behind her gag, but Master Hawk's voice rose above both women's voices. "I'll forgive you for just about anything, beloved, but harming another out of misplaced jealousy is beyond my limit."

The blows kept on coming until Rhiannon was sobbing, everything but her burning ass forgotten as she was spanked harder than she'd ever been spanked before. When she was nothing but a blubbering mess, Master Rory finally relented and hauled her off his lap. She became aware that they were in what had to be an office. Probably a man's by the deep, rich burgundy and dark wood decor. Currently she was sprawled out on the carpet, still bound and completely drained. Sunny joined her on the rug; the other woman was sobbing like her heart was breaking behind her gag. Someone had taken Sunny's mask off, and Rhiannon realized hers was missing as well.

The three dominants moved to the side of the room and looked down at them with impassive expressions. Shame tore Rhiannon apart, and she tried to wiggle her way over to them, to somehow show them how sorry she was. She'd lost it, plain and simple, and her actions might have cost her the love of her Masters.

"What is wrong with you?" Master Hawk said to Sunny. Instead of being disgusted, his voice was filled with hurt.

"I thought you were stronger than this," Master Liam added to Rhiannon.

Master Hawk shook his head. "You can't keep doing this, beloved."

Sunny sobbed, and Master Hawk leaned down to work the gag from her mouth. The sight of the blood from her split lip made Rhiannon nauseated, and another wave of shame filled her that she had caused that damage. Sunny looked so frail in the bright overhead lights that Rhiannon was afraid she'd really hurt the sobbing woman.

Sunny whispered, "I'm so sorry, Hawk."

"It's not me you need to apologize to. I heard what you said, and you couldn't be more wrong. You know you're the only woman I love."

"Then why did you go to her?" Sunny sobbed. "Why did you fuck her when you said you loved me?"

Master Hawk's expression turned pained as he glanced over at Rhiannon, then back to Sunny. "You know I can't discuss what happened between myself and Goddess. I promised what happened in that room would stay in that room, and I never break a promise, not even for you."

Master Liam crouched next to Rhiannon and removed her ball gag before helping her onto the couch. "Lass, it's up to you to tell her what happened. This animosity between you can't continue, and it's hurting Master Hawk."

Moving the other woman as gently as he could, Master Hawk placed Sunny on the other side of the couch but didn't untie her hands. "And you need to listen, really listen to what she has to say."

Sunny turned her tear-filled gaze on Rhiannon. The pure agony Rhiannon saw in the other woman's eyes gave her the courage to speak. "We didn't have sex, Sunny."

"I'm supposed to believe that? I see the way you look at him. You want Hawk." Sunny gave a bitter laugh. "You can give him what I won't."

"We didn't have sex." Rhiannon took a deep breath. "Can someone untie me please? I promise I won't hurt her, but I can't talk about this while bound. I might...I might trigger."

Liam and Rory immediately untied her, and Liam crouched next to her, then held her hand while Rory placed his hands on her shoulders, securing her and giving her the strength she needed. She touched each man, reassuring herself that they hadn't left, that they were still here despite her terrible actions.

Master Hawk unbound Sunny as well, then sat on the couch and pulled her onto his lap. She stiffened at first, then clung to the handsome Native American man and faced Rhiannon. "I'm listening."

"Do you know anything about my past?"

Sunny gave her a confused look. "No."

"When I was sixteen, I was abducted, then raped and tortured by a man who bears a striking resemblance to Master Hawk."

Hawk flinched while Sunny gasped. "What?"

Rhiannon gave the other woman a brief rundown of what had occurred, and by the time Rhiannon reached the end, she was shaking. "That's why I was drawn to Hawk. Not because I wanted him, but because I thought that maybe if I could be with him, it would help erase the memories of that bastard. Even though they look similar, Master Hawk is a good man. When I asked him to do a bondage session with no sex, I didn't tell him about my past. I-I triggered big time before he'd even finished tying me up."

Sunny looked up at Hawk, then back at Rhiannon. "What do you mean you triggered?"

The shakes had gotten so bad now she could barely speak, spent adrenaline and intense emotions rushing through her as her body tried to cope with the overload of stress. Master Hawk must have seen this because he answered in a low voice, "She thought she was back with her abductor, that I was him. For a while there I didn't know if she would snap out of it. It scared me more than I've been scared in a long, long time."

Rhiannon was grateful that he didn't mention her screaming and crying, that she'd been so terrified she'd lost control of her bodily functions and had urinated on herself.

"Thankfully Latisha, I mean, Mistress Onyx, and Mr. Florentine were there and they helped her." His voice thickened. "It killed me, knowing that I'd somehow caused this to happen, that I'd probably damaged her on some fundamental level."

"It-it wasn't your fault," Rhiannon managed to stutter out as her jaw chattered.

Liam scooped her up into his arms and sat on the couch, holding her like Master Hawk was holding Sunny. Rory sat next to him and stroked her body, his touch helping the shaking to recede until she felt limp and emotionally exhausted.

Sunny cupped Master Hawk's cheek, then turned his face to hers. "I'm so sorry. If you'd just told me, but you couldn't. You never break a promise."

"No, beloved, I do not."

With a low sigh Sunny turned in Hawk's lap to face Rhiannon. "I'm sorry I've been such a bitch to you. There is no excuse for it, but I was so jealous that you'd been with Hawk. It drove me crazy."

Shame curdled in Rhiannon's stomach, and she leaned forward, then reached out to Sunny and grabbed hold of her frail hand. "I'm sorry as well. I shouldn't have let you continue to believe that we'd had sex. I was jealous of you too. The bastard that took me basically trained me to be. He'd tell me about the other women he was having sex with and manipulate me until I was crazy with anger. He got off on that, on mind fucking me. When I saw you with Master Hawk, saw how much he liked you, it made that fucking training kick in even though I didn't realize it at first."

"I'm sorry." Sunny squeezed her hand. "I haven't been thinking clearly lately. I've had these terrible migraines, and they've made me very…irritable."

"They've made you an evil bitch," Master Hawk said in a surprisingly gentle voice. "You need to take your medication."

"Not here, Hawk, not now. Please." Sunny released Rhiannon's hand and laid her cheek on Master Hawk's chest. "I'm so tired."

Rhiannon exchanged a confused look with Rory and Liam, but both men seemed equally baffled. Rory stood, then rubbed the back of his neck. "Come on. Let's get Rhiannon home and put some ice on her cheek. You're going to have a nice bruise there, girl."

She reached up and brushed her fingers over her sore cheek, then winced. "Ow."

Sunny touched her lips and gave an answering flinch. "Nice uppercut by the way. You don't fight like a girl."

That struck Rhiannon as really funny. She began to laugh. Sunny met her gaze and began to laugh as well, and soon the women were laughing so hard tears were running down their face. The men looked equal parts confused and wary as she and Sunny laughed like loons. Rhiannon couldn't help it; the stress had just piled up to the point where she needed some kind of an outlet, and she'd rather cry from laughing than cry from hurting. Slowly their laughter tapered off, and Liam passed Rhiannon to Rory before standing.

"You two will still have to answer to Mr. Florentine for the mess you made out there."

Sunny tried to stand, but Hawk pulled her back into his lap. "You're staying right here, beloved."

She pushed against his chest but quickly gave up with an irritated expression. "I need to get back out there and help clean up."

Rhiannon wiggled in Rory's arms. "Put me down. I can't leave Latisha, I mean Mistress Onyx out there alone."

"Girl, we've been back here for a good hour. By now your shift is over, and the damage cleaned up."

"Oh, God," Sunny moaned and covered her face with her hands. "I started the fight. I'm going to be fired."

"No, you aren't," Rhiannon protested and shoved at Rory until he let her go. She moved to where Master Hawk sat and crouched down next to Sunny. "I'll take the blame."

Sunny shook her head adamantly. "No way. I won't let you lose your job because of me."

Before Rhiannon could protest, Liam grabbed her and slung her over his shoulder in an undignified fireman's carry. "Neither of you are going to be fired. You will probably have to do some penance to make up for your little fight, but Mr. Florentine isn't going to fire either of you."

"It was actually pretty entertaining." Rory gave Rhiannon's ass a smack. "At least it was until you ducked behind the bar and we couldn't see you anymore."

"Would have been better if you were naked, oiled up, and wearing strap-ons," Hawk added with a chuckle.

"You are such a pervert," Sunny said in a shocked voice.

"Only for you," he replied in a low murmur.

The rest of their conversation was lost to Rhiannon as Rory and Liam carried her out the door and down the hall.

"If you put me down, I can walk," Rhiannon said as she tried to move her hair out of the way so she could see.

Liam smacked her ass, hard, bringing back the burn. "I'd watch yer sass, girl. Right now you're on very thin ice with me."

"Where are we going?"

"Home," Rory said with an audible growl of irritation in his voice.

"I can't go home with you tonight."

Liam came to a stop and slid her off his shoulder before roughly moving her against the wall. Both men closed in on her, Rory braced his hand on one side of her face and Liam on the other. Looking up into their faces, she tried to shrink into herself, taken aback by the anger there.

In a soft, low voice, Liam said, "If you think we're letting you out of our sight right now, you're crazy."

"I have to feed my cats," she whispered, a trace of fear skating up her spine.

"Then we're going to your house." Rory narrowed his eyes and pinned her to the spot with his gaze. "This is not up for debate."

"Okay."

"Now, I suggest you keep silent until we tell you to speak. Don't push us, Rhiannon. Not now."

She nodded and swallowed hard as the men moved away.

They made their way through the back of the club, and a

clearly worried Dove met them at the back door with Rhiannon's bag. "Are you okay?"

Rhiannon nodded, and Rory took her bag. "She's fine, Dove. We're going home with her."

"Oh, good." She went to hug Rhiannon, then hesitated and took a step back. "Take care of her."

Liam gave Dove a kiss on the cheek. "Go on back to your Master. We'll take care of our girl."

They went out the back door to the staff parking lot. Rory paused and looked down at her, his expression unreadable. "Where's your car?"

"I drove with Latisha. She's my neighbor."

"Call her and let her know we're taking you home."

"May I have my bag please? My phone is inside." A cool wind blew in from the surrounding forest, and she shivered.

"Son of a bitch," Liam muttered, then stripped out of his shirt. "You'll freeze in that scrap of nothing."

She lifted her arms so he could put his shirt on her, immediately snuggling it close as they took her through the lot to a big navy-blue SUV.

"You drive," Liam said to Rory. "I need to hold her."

"I need to hold her too," Rory said with a challenging look in his eyes.

Liam moved her to the side and took a step toward Rory, clenching his fists at his sides. "Don't be an arse. Just drive the car."

"Fuck you," Rory said in a low growl. "You got to hold her on the couch."

They proceeded to bicker over her until she was afraid they would come to blows. Seeing them argue over her like that made her heart ache. She stepped between them, having to force them apart. "Guys, please. I'm cold. Please just take me home."

Immediately Liam picked her up and held her close. "She's freezing, you jackass. Just get in the car and drive."

The look of anger in Rory's eyes directed at Liam scared her, but he nodded and opened the back door for them with a jerk.

Liam helped her inside, then moved in next to her and pulled her as close to his body as he could before burying his face in her hair. He took a deep breath of her scent and slowly let it out. She snuggled into his heat, conscious of Rory's gaze on them in the rearview mirror as he started the car. For the first time she saw true jealousy in his gaze, and that renewed sense of guilt came back, along with fear. Not that she was scared of Rory, but she could feel some fundamental shift starting to happen in Liam and Rory's friendship. A disturbance where she knew she was the catalyst.

Despite her best intentions, she was afraid she was tearing the men's relationship apart.

CHAPTER SIXTEEN

"Call Latisha," Liam reminded Rhiannon in a low voice, trying to get control of his anger. It wasn't truly directed at Rhiannon—well, part of it was for her being stupid enough to get in a physical fight where she could have been harmed, but the majority of it was for Rory. Right before Rhiannon and Sunny had started fighting, Hawk had jokingly asked the men whose baby Rhiannon was going to have first.

Both Rory and Liam had answered "Mine" at the same time, and when their gazes met, Liam saw a real challenge in his best mate's eyes. For the first time Liam saw Rory not as an essential part of his life but as a potential rival for the woman he loved.

Rhiannon dug through her bag and pulled out her phone. "Okay."

A few seconds later a woman's voice came from Rhiannon's phone, too faint for him to understand.

"I..." she glanced at Liam, then away again. "I lost my temper. Master Liam and Master Rory are taking me home right now."

She listened for a few seconds, then nodded. "Okay. Master Liam, she would like to talk to you please."

He took the phone. "Hey, Latisha. It's Liam."

"Like I could miss that Scottish brogue," Latisha said with a soft laugh. "Listen, she's going to have some nasty nightmares tonight. I don't know what you guys plan on doing, but please don't leave her alone. If you can't stay, let me know, and I'll come sleep with her. You'll also need to slip her a sleeping pill. She hates taking them, but if you don't, she'll get physically violent with you during her nightmares. They're in the cupboard to the left of her kitchen sink. Just dissolve one in a drink for her and make sure she finishes it."

"Do you have to do that a lot?"

"Not anymore. Did she tell you she lives close to me and most of my family?"

"She mentioned you were a neighbor."

"Rhiannon grew up in a very insular, tight-knit community. She was floundering on her own, so I convinced her to buy the old farmhouse next to my grandmother's property. Me and my three brothers live nearby, so we tried to give her that sense of community, of belonging again." She sighed. "Somewhere along the way Rhiannon went from being my friend to almost being like my sister, and my family pretty much adopted her. She needs to be protected from those that would take advantage of her innate kindness."

"I understand."

Rhiannon gave him a curious look, but he ignored her as Latisha said, "Rhiannon is a strong woman, but it took her a long time to get herself back together after her abduction. You need to be aware that if you stay with her tonight, she might relive some parts of her torture. She won't see you or hear you so you'll just have to hold her and be there for her. She may talk about it, she may scream, or if God is merciful, she'll sleep through the night. Can you handle it?"

He met Rory's gaze in the mirror and was knocked out of his own selfish anger by Rory's obvious concern for Rhiannon. He pushed aside his bullshit and tried to totally focus on Rhiannon. Trying to say his next question without tipping Rhiannon off was tricky. "Do you think Sunny will remember it?"

"Sunny? We're talking about...oh. She's right next to you, of course. Neither of you would let her out of your sight right now. No, she usually doesn't remember the next morning if she's had a sleeping pill. Sometimes with PTSD a person's mind can't deal with the horrors they've faced while they're awake, so the mind will try to process the past trauma through their dreams. It's not going to be pretty, but I need to know if it will change how you see her, how you interact with her sexually. She adores you both and loves being your submissive. It would kill her if you suddenly pulled back because you were afraid of doing some of the things that pedophile rapist did to her."

"What do you mean?"

Latisha blew out a breath, and he glanced over at Rhiannon, cupping her cheek and trying to give her a reassuring smile. The worry on her tear-stained face made him ashamed that he and Rory had been bickering about her right in front of her. They knew better than that, but he'd deal with their bullshit later. Right now Rhiannon was the only thing that mattered.

"Just don't be afraid to tie her up, spank her, do all those things your instincts tell you she wants. Rhiannon trusts you completely, and no matter what, you need to know that she does not think of her rapist when you touch her. You're the first men to ever win her heart, and I hope you realize what a precious gift that is. Don't fuck it up with your personal crap."

"I don't know what you're talking about."

"Yes, you do. Denial isn't only a river in Egypt, ya know. But that's between you and Rory, and now Rhiannon."

"I'm not discussing this." Anger mixed with shame at the thought that his perverted desire for Rory was so apparent.

"Don't get defensive with me. I'm not your therapist, so I can't tell you what to do, but as a friend, I can tell you that you need to think long and hard about what you want out of your future, who you really want to spend the rest of your life with, before you take things any further with Rhiannon. It would hurt her deeply if she felt like she was the reason you split up."

He wanted to argue, to yell at her, and tell her to mind her own fucking business, but both Rory and Rhiannon were watching him too closely. "Anything else?"

"I've pissed you off." She sighed. "I'm sorry. That wasn't my intent. Look. Just be good to her, okay? If you need me tonight, I'll be ten minutes away. Please call me if you think you can't handle it."

"We can handle it."

"You know, together I'm sure you can. It's what's going to happen if you let your homophobia tear everything apart that I'm worried about." She hung up on him, leaving him staring at the phone and feeling like he'd just been kicked in the gut.

After he gave the phone to Rhiannon, he was silent for the rest of the trip back. He kept on thinking about what Latisha had said about him being homophobic. He couldn't deny it, even though he hated himself for feeling this way. He wished he could just accept Rory's love, could move past his upbringing. But what if his parents found out? He'd be disowned, without a doubt, and he would bring shame to his family just like his friend Dayle had brought shame to his when he came out in high school.

Guilt ate at Liam's gut as he remembered his friend getting mercilessly bullied and beaten to the point where he'd finally been hospitalized. At first Liam had tried to protect his friend, but when his father had heard about it, he'd taken his belt to Liam and beat him until Liam could barely walk. After that Liam had avoided Dayle, ashamed that he was too much of a coward to go against his father's orders. Liam hadn't even been able to visit while Dayle was recovering from his injuries because if he had he would have been labeled a fag himself, and then his life would be the one turned into a living hell. Dayle's family had lived in their village for five generations, had been loved and accepted as respected members of the community, but even that didn't save them or their son. Their house had been burned down in the middle of the night while they were visiting Dayle in the hospital after a particularly brutal attack left him with a concussion and a broken leg.

Everyone knew it had been arson, but the constable had ruled it an accidental fire. Liam could remember his cousins drinking with his father the night the fire happened, all five of them smelling like smoke and gasoline as they laughed and congratulated one another on burning out the nest of wickedness from their village. Liam had listened from the top of the stairs to their boasting, sickened by their actions and heartbroken that his father was capable of such evil. Liam's mother had found him listening, and her only remark had been that the family got what they deserved for harboring such perversion.

The car slowing as it pulled down the drive to Rhiannon's home broke Liam from his bitter thoughts and brought him back to the present. A bright floodlight came on from the garage, bathing the yard in cold illumination. Rhiannon stirred next to him, and he realized that she'd been dozing against his side.

"You awake, lass?"

She looked up at him and nodded, then frowned slightly as she traced her fingertips down his cheek. "Are you okay?"

His heart grew heavy with guilt that he was thinking about himself rather than this beautiful girl who needed him. "I'm fine. Just a long night is all. Come on. Let's get you inside."

Rory opened Rhiannon's door and helped her out before Liam slid out after her with her bag. She looked so young dressed in his shirt, and he wondered what the fuck they were doing with her. Rhiannon deserved only the best, a man who could love her with all of himself, not a man haunted by his own demons. Hell, two men at that.

When Rory swung her into his arms and began to carry her to the house, a pang of envy went through Liam at how good they looked together. Her trust in his best mate was evident in the way she relaxed in Rory's arms and buried her face in his chest. And Rory's expression, his touch, left no doubt that he loved Rhiannon. As Liam watched them he couldn't help but think of what a good couple they made, and he wondered if Rory was the better man for her in the long run.

When they reached the top of the steps leading to the front porch, Rhiannon squirmed out of Rory's arms. She dug through her bag and brought out her keys, opening the front door to her home. Once they were inside and she'd locked the front door, she slumped against it with a rough sigh. "I'm sorry I ruined your night."

Unable to stand her pain, Liam moved with Rory, and they both cuddled her between them. "I don't want to hear that foolishness, lass. You go on upstairs with Rory and wash up. I'll bring you some tea in a bit."

She made a sour face. "I hate tea. Could you bring me some whiskey instead?"

Rory laughed and kissed the top of her head, but his eyes held a great deal of worry as he met Liam's gaze. "I think we could all use a drink. Come on, darling girl. Let's get you cleaned up."

With a heavy heart he watched Rory and Rhiannon take the

stairs to the second level. As he walked through her home looking for her kitchen, he was struck again by how feminine it was. He'd been living on his own for so long that he'd almost forgotten what it was like to see a woman's touch in a room. He wondered what it would be like to live with Rhiannon and how they would ever manage it if she wanted all three of them to live together. His family had accepted Liam's relationship with Rory as nothing more than friendship because they lived in separate homes, but if he actually lived with Rory and Rhiannon, they'd become suspicious.

Sure, he hadn't been home more than once or twice a year since he moved out, and if he was just losing his parents' love, he might be able to accept the loss, but the thought of never seeing his nieces or nephews again hurt him on a fundamental level.

He soon found her kitchen and set about making her a cup of hot chocolate. He also found the liquor cabinet, and the need for a drink himself had him pour a healthy amount of whiskey into a glass and slam it down before refilling another. He wanted his nerves dulled right now, his senses coated in the fuzz of alcohol. Anything to get rid of this feeling that he was failing everyone he loved. First his parents, then Rory, and now Rhiannon.

A chime came from the back door of the kitchen, and a brown-and-white cat with a belled collar slipped inside. The fat creature gave Liam a surprised hiss, then flicked its tail in his direction and ambled over to an empty food dish near the stove. After a quick search, Liam found the bag of dry cat food and filled the bowl. When he tried to give the cat a scratch behind its ears, the bloody beast swiped at him.

With the bottle of whiskey in one hand and Rhiannon's mug of hot chocolate with a sleeping pill dissolved in the other, he made his way upstairs. The sound of voices led him to her room, and he paused in the doorway, taking in the magnificent bed with its canopy of crystals that threw soft rainbows over the room. Rory had Rhiannon in bed partially beneath the covers and was curled up next to her, softly stroking her cheek and telling her in a low voice how much she meant to him. She'd pulled her hair back into a simple braid that made her look impossibly young and innocent. Rhiannon had also put on some kind of silky blue nightgown that shimmered in the low illumination from a fairy nightlight on the other side of the room.

It broke Liam's heart to see the obvious love in Rory's gaze. Jealousy mixed with the alcohol slowly working through his system. They were perfect together, and from the way Rhiannon looked at Rory, Liam could tell she loved his best mate. Suddenly he felt like an outsider.

Rory looked up at him and smiled. "Welcome to the land of fairy."

Trying to brush aside his negative thoughts for Rhiannon's sake, Liam plastered on a fake smile and moved across the room, then set the bottle and Rhiannon's mug onto the small side table. A small statue of a fairy kissing a frog sat on the table, and as he took a glance around the room, he let out a silent whistle. Everywhere he looked there were winged women.

"Wow."

Rhiannon sat up with a grumble and grabbed the mug, then took a sip and made an appreciative noise. "This is good, thank you. And I bet you nerds have more rocks than I do fairies."

Rory gave a forced laugh and gestured to the bottle. "Give me a pull of that, mate."

Liam took another hefty slug himself, enjoying how his nerves were slowly becoming fuzzy, then handed it to Rory. "Drink up."

Rhiannon did as ordered, then handed the almost empty mug to him. "You make good hot chocolate."

With a grunt, he settled back in her bed, then sank into the soft mattress while Rory smiled. "You should taste his Christmas hot chocolate. He uses real peppermint-flavored melted chocolate and homemade whipped cream."

"Really?" Rhiannon looked up at Liam with a smile that made his heart ache.

"Aye, lass, really." Unable to help himself, he stroked her cheek, relishing the feel of her fragile softness. "My mother makes it for us on Christmas morning."

Liam chuckled. "Though last year she finally admitted that Rory and myself were old enough that we could have peppermint schnapps in our hot chocolate."

Sadness filled her eyes, and she looked away. "That's nice."

"What's wrong?" Rory said as he moved closer, pressing her between them.

"It's...it's nothing."

"Rhiannon," Liam said in a low voice. "Tell us."

She sighed and lay all the way back on her pillow, then looked up at her canopy with that deep sorrow still lingering in her distant gaze. "It's just that my family did something similar. You're lucky to have a mom that will still do that for you."

The need to take away her sadness overwhelmed Liam, and he realized that he couldn't give Rhiannon up. He loved the wee lass, and the truth of his feelings slapped him like a splash of cold water. "She'd do the same for you."

"Really?" Her lovely emerald eyes met his, and his heart ached at the sight of tears filling them.

"Absolutely." He awkwardly leaned down and placed a kiss on her forehead. "She'll love you."

"And my parents will adore you as well, darling girl," Rory added in a low voice as he stroked her.

Resentment bubbled up in Liam's heart at Rory, and he took the bottle back from the other man before taking another healthy swallow.

With a soft sigh, Rhiannon snuggled between them. "I'd like to meet your families. I'm sorry you can't meet mine."

"Don't be sorry," Rory soothed, but his gaze was on Liam as he said, "It's their loss that they can't love you for who you are."

Liam frowned at his friend, knowing what the message there was but also more than aware that this wasn't the time or place for that particular discussion. He set the whiskey bottle down on the table next to her mug and tried to get hold of himself. Tonight wasn't about him and Rory; it was about Rhiannon, and he needed to get his fucking head on straight.

Rhiannon blinked rapidly, but a tear managed to escape and slide down her cheek. "I miss them."

"Hush now. Of course you do." Liam gathered her into his arms, ignoring Rory's glare as he effectively moved Rhiannon away from the other man. "But you have me now, and I love you just the way you are."

His chest tightened with apprehension as Rhiannon stiffened in his arms. For one terrible moment he thought that maybe she didn't return his feelings, but then she twisted until she could look at him with such joy that his heart melted. "You love me?"

"Aye. More than the sun loves the moon." He tried to smile, but the emotions filling him combined with the alcohol now flooding his system left him close to tears. Bloody fucking whiskey always made him an emotional drunk.

"I love you too," she whispered, then smiled bright enough that it felt like the sun was shining on him in the middle of the night. Then she glanced over at Rory and gave him the same smile. "I love you both so very much."

Jealousy bit at Liam again, an irrational anger filling him that she loved Rory as well. Even in his increasingly buzzed state, he knew better than to let those negative emotions show now, especially with Latisha's warning about Rhiannon's nightmares still fresh in his head. Fuck, what the hell was he doing drinking? His girl would need him tonight, and he was failing her by getting smashed because of his own inability to face his feelings.

Not wanting to upset her, he pulled her up on his chest for a long, slow, leisurely kiss. Her lips were so soft, and the sensation of the silk of her gown pressing against his bare chest had him growling with desire. Then she leaned back and let out a small, barely stifled yawn.

"Am I boring you, lass?"

She shook her head. "I'm sorry. I'm suddenly so sleepy."

Rory made a soothing noise and wrapped his arms around her, pulling her off Liam, much to the other man's discontent. "You've had a long day, darling. Just relax and let us hold you."

Abruptly Liam moved off the bed and ran his hand through his hair. "I need some food in my stomach."

He left Rory holding Rhiannon and snatched the whiskey off the table before going downstairs, then out the front door. With a sigh he sat on the steps of her front porch, admiring the flowers Rhiannon had planted around the house even as he hated himself for not having the courage to love as openly as Rhiannon did. For all his talk about family to Rhiannon, his family would never accept Rhiannon if she had two lovers who shared her. Eventually she would have to choose between the two men, and Liam feared she would pick Rory over him. There was no way they could make it work as a permanent ménage, no matter how much he wanted it to. In his heart of hearts he knew Rory wanted him as more than a friend, but because of his upbringing and what had happened to Dayle, Liam couldn't bring himself to admit his love for the other man. And he did love Rory just as much as he loved Rhiannon. He was too much of a coward to admit it out loud.

In a fit of anger, he stood and threw the whiskey bottle as hard as he could into the trees, hating himself more than he could bear.

"Well, guess I won't be having any more of that."

Rory's deep voice came from behind Liam, and he whirled around, snarling at the other man. "What the fuck are we doing here?"

"What?" Rory moved farther out onto the porch, looking as handsome as sin, tempting Liam with something he could never have.

"This. Us. Rhiannon." He gestured to the house with anger and self-disgust burning through him. "What the fuck are we doing to that poor girl?"

"Keep your voice down, you bloody fool," Rory growled.

"Fuck you." Liam stomped down the steps into the front yard.

"What the hell is wrong with you?"

Frustration ate away at Liam as he locked gazes with Rory. "This will never work between us. We're just stringing the poor girl along. You know one of us is eventually going to have to walk away, and I'll be damned if it's me."

"Oh, so you think that just because you can't handle loving me that we should all suffer?"

Stunned, Liam took a stumbling step back as Rory advanced down the steps toward him. "I don't love you."

"Yes, you do, and I'm fucking tired of pretending that I don't love you just because you're too much of a fool to admit it." He got right up in Liam's face, the anger coming off him in waves. "For twelve fucking years I've let you hide your feelings behind our friendship. For twelve fucking years I've endured your indecision, your fear of people knowing that you want to fuck another man, but I'm done. No more hiding, Liam. No more bullshit."

To Liam's shock, Rory grabbed his face and kissed him. Their lips met, and for one brief moment, Liam allowed himself the pleasure of touching Rory, of kissing the other man, before his fear welled up. He shoved Rory away, but the other man refused to be denied.

"Tell me you don't want me." He grabbed the back of Liam's neck, holding him until their foreheads were pressed together and their lips inches apart. "Tell me you don't love me."

"I don't," Liam managed to growl out while his cock filled with blood and arousal burned through him.

"Fucking liar," Rory muttered before he kissed him again, tenderly this time.

Fire raced through Liam's veins, sending desire speeding through his system and filling him with a need like he'd never known. Helpless against years of self-denial, he held still as Rory kissed him, Rory's firm lips moving over Liam's, seducing a response out of him that he couldn't afford to give freely. When Rory's tongue traced along the seam of his lips, he groaned and opened for the other man, his hands going from pushing Rory away to pulling him closer. With a desperation bordering on insanity, he kissed Rory back, loving the feel of the other man in his arms even as he hated himself.

Their tongues stroked against each other, and Rory's erection pressed into Liam's stomach, a testament to the other man's arousal. Liam reached between them, intent on doing something he should have done years ago when he first became aware of his attraction to the other man. He gripped Rory's cock through his pants, and Rory groaned into his mouth, his hips bucking into Liam's hand as Liam rubbed the hard length of his shaft.

"Want you," Liam whispered against Rory's lips. "Fucking hate myself for it, but I want you."

Rory grasped Liam's face between his hands, then pulled

back just enough so they could look each other in the eye. "I love you, Liam. There's no shame in that, no sin."

To his humiliation, tears burned Liam's eyes. But the look of gentle understanding from Rory undid him. He wrapped his arms around Rory and clutched him as tight as he could. The hot tears slid down his face and onto Rory's shirt while the other man held him close enough that he had a hard time drawing a deep enough breath. God, he wanted this, wanted Rory, and he wished with all his heart he could have him.

"We can't do this," he whispered in a broken voice against Rory's shoulder.

"Yes, we can. Who are you going to live your life for, Liam? How long are you going to let hate that isn't even yours fester inside you? Let it go."

"It's not that easy."

Rory's arms tightened farther, and he fairly shook with emotion. "It is, you daft bastard. I love you. I've loved you for years, and I refuse to pretend I don't anymore. Don't you know how much you mean to me? I've waited twelve bloody years for you to admit it."

"My family will hate me. They'll hate you."

"Who gives a fuck? I mean really. You are my family, Liam. You're the one I spend every holiday with. You're the one who I plan my life around. You and now Rhiannon."

"Does she know?"

"Know what?"

"About...us."

Rory snorted. "What do you think?"

"Probably. Not much gets past our girl."

"She knows, and she wants us to be together."

"Do you think she'll be put off by anything...physical between us? Not that I'm ready for that yet, but you know what I mean."

The vibrations of Rory's laughter moved through his chest and into Liam's. "I don't think that will be an issue. That little minx has some fantasies about us that'll blow your socks off. I'm pretty sure she thought we were a couple before she even approached us for training."

He sighed and closed his eyes, breathing in Rory's scent. "Sometimes I feel like she sees me more clearly than I see myself."

"She loves you Liam, just as much as I do. I know our relationship isn't conventional, but I want both of you in my life. However, I need to know what *you* want."

The need to take what Rory was offering—to admit his love for the other man tore at him—but he couldn't open his mouth to say the words. His courage failed him as he imagined the disgust on his mother's face, his father's disappointment, and how he would never be welcome in their home again. Then his mind switched to what their friends would say and how people would see them in public together. He'd have to start carrying a gun in case they were jumped for being gay. "I don't know what I want."

Rory made a frustrated sound. "Liam, for fuck's sake, think. You can have us, both of us, in your life. You can wake up every day no longer having to hide who you are or what you want. Most importantly you can forgive yourself for loving a man. It has to eat you alive to know that you love me when you've been raised to think of it as being a sin."

"What about our friends? Are you ready to lose them? Are you ready to lose business once the word gets out that we're queer?"

For a second he thought Rory was going to choke him, but the other man took a deep breath, then slowly let it out. "Liam, don't you know that most of our friends think we're bisexual? That the majority of them believe we're already in a relationship?"

He actually stumbled back a step, stunned by the idea. "What?"

"Hell, our rugby team thinks we're a couple, and you know what? They don't give a shit. Just like they don't give a shit about the other gay players on our team. Washington, DC isn't like where you grew up. Most of these people haven't been raised to hate others because they're gay. Of course there is going to be ignorance wherever we go, but for fuck's sake, gays can get married now. That has to tell you something."

Liam rubbed the back of his neck, the pleasant buzz from the whiskey burned away by his intense emotions, leaving him a little more clearheaded.

Rory grasped his shoulders and pressed their foreheads together. "Now, Liam, how do you really want to live the rest of your life? Alone and hating yourself? Or surrounded by so much love that you will never feel lonely again?"

"I want..." He took a deep breath and slowly let it out. Why not be honest? Out loud, to his best mate, to admit out in the open that he loved Rory. "I want us to be a family, a real one. I want to marry the lass, to have her waiting at home for us when we come home from work, to fill our lives with her joy. I want us to have beautiful babies with her, to make her our wife, but I don't want to rush her. She's so young. I want her to be sure that we are what she wants."

Rory chuckled. "Sometimes I feel like we're the young ones, but I agree. No need to rush her. We have the rest of our lives to make her see that we're all she'll ever need."

"I'm sorry for being such a coward."

"Me too, mate. Me too."

They stood holding each other for a long time in the quiet of the night, the chirp of crickets and rustle of the wind the only sound other than their harsh breathing. Rory began to slowly rub his back, and Liam sank into the other man's touch, his heart slowing, and the anger leaving him in small increments. Liam took a deep breath and began to accept his decision to come clean about his love for Rory, feeling better than he had in years. In his heart of hearts he'd known this day was coming, but he'd honestly never thought he'd survive it.

The relief that he felt swamped him, and more tears came, but they weren't bad tears. It felt more like he was crying away the hate and self-disgust that had been festering inside him. "I love you."

Rory's body froze against Liam, then softened as Rory let out a long, slow breath. "I know you do, you bloody wanker."

That startled a laugh out of Liam, and he pulled back, then roughly scrubbed his cheeks. "I—"

His words were cut off by a female shriek coming from inside the house. They looked at each other, then raced for the stairs. By the time they reached Rhiannon's room, she was full-out screaming, writhing on her bed as she let loose sounds of terrible pain and agony.

"Rhiannon!" Rory started to go for her, but Liam stopped him.

"Wait, she's having a nightmare. Latisha said she gets these. That it's her mind's way of dealing with her kidnapping."

"No!" Rhiannon whimpered as she curled up into a ball. "I'm sorry, please don't hurt me. Please stop. No more hitting. Oh, God, it hurts."

"What do we do? Do we wake her up?" Rory asked in a broken voice.

"Latisha said to let her sleep. She won't remember this in the morning. Come on."

He kicked off his shoes and climbed onto the bed with Rory following suit. Rhiannon flinched when he touched her, and the pained sound she made tore at his soul.

"Please, no more, please. I'll do anything you want, anything, just stop hurting me," she whimpered as she tried to move away in her sleep.

"Easy, lass," Liam whispered as he arranged himself next to her, sliding beneath the sheets with his kilt still on. "We're here."

For the next three hours they had a private window into Rhiannon's personal hell, and by the time she finally settled back into a dreamless sleep, Liam felt like he'd lived her memories. The torture she'd survived tore him apart, and he wished with all his heart that he could get his hands on the bastard who had done those terrible things to her. If Rory hadn't been there with him, holding him as they comforted Rhiannon as best they could together, he wasn't sure he would have survived the night without his soul breaking beneath the weight of Rhiannon's pain. Latisha was right; no one man could deal with this heartache alone. It was only with Rory's strength added to his that he could endure the agony of her past.

He loved the lass as much as he loved Rory, something that should be impossible, but it was true.

The soft sound of Rory humming filled the room, a soothing melody that helped wash some of the darkness from Liam's soul. He met Rory's gaze and reached over Rhiannon, then ran his fingers through the other man's hair before wiping a tear from Rory's cheek. In his own way Rory had always been the strong one in their relationship, the man who could be relied on to get them through whatever bullshit life threw at them. To see his best mate lose it like this reminded Liam of how much Rory needed him as well, how much his friend relied on him.

The ramifications of tonight were just beginning to set in Liam's mind. Part of him was still terrified of how his family would react, but the adult part of his mind really didn't give a shit. It was as if by allowing himself to admit his love for Rory, he was finally letting go of the past, of all those years living in fear that he would do something to make others think he was gay, that it would be his house burning in the night with him trapped inside. He was like Rhiannon dealing with her PTSD, but where she faced her past and refused to let it rule her future, he'd been too afraid to do the same. Not anymore.

He was done hiding who he was, done denying himself the love that Rory had to give, and done pretending that he didn't love and want the other man with all his heart.

With Rhiannon pressed between them, Liam made a vow that he would do whatever it took to make Rory his husband and Rhiannon his wife. It was fucked-up, it went against everything that he'd ever been taught, but he knew they were the people he was meant to spend the rest of his life with.

Chapter Seventeen

Something tickled Rory's lips, and he wiped his face with an annoyed grunt, causing someone nearby to make a soft, feminine noise of complaint. Startled by the sound, he opened his eyes. It took him a moment or two to figure out why he was looking at what appeared to be a canopy of crystals. The scent of honeysuckle teased his nose, and when he moved his hand, he brushed over a lush female curve.

Rhiannon.

He turned and had to smile at the sight of his girl curled up among her pillows like a bird in its nest. She'd pulled most of the covers off him, leaving his still leather-pants-clad ass hanging off the side of the bed. Her hair spread about her in an inky blanket, and a few strands were tickling his chin, stuck in the short hairs of his unshaven face. The bed was empty on the other side. He had a moment of panic when he feared that Liam had run off on him again. Then the scent of bacon reached him.

After carefully sliding out of bed, he answered the call of nature and made his way downstairs. Following his nose, he found Liam in the kitchen, bare-chested and still dressed in his kilt while tending to a pan full of what looked like scrambled eggs. Rory leaned against the door frame, taking in the sight of Liam standing in a bright beam of morning sunlight. His gaze travelled down the length of the other man's muscular back to the dip of his waist and finally over the top curve of his firm buttocks.

"You going to come help me with breakfast or stand there staring at my arse all day?" Liam said in a rough voice without turning to look at him.

"What do you need me to do?"

Liam turned down the flame on the stove and set the spatula aside before facing Rory. "I need you ta kiss me."

Rory was so stunned that he gaped. While he'd hoped Liam wouldn't hate him this morning, he never expected an actual request for affection. He was so flabbergasted that he just continued to stand there and stare.

"Never mind," Liam said with a flush staining his cheeks.

"No, wait."

Before the other man could protest, Rory had him pressed against the counter as he cupped Liam's rough cheeks. The scrape of whiskers over his palms reminded him of how different it was to kiss a man, and his cock came to full attention as Liam nervously licked his lips. Rory paused, giving Liam time to back out of the kiss, but when their gazes met, he saw passion mixed with fear in his best mate's eyes but no disgust.

Moving ever so slowly, he then brushed his lips over Liam's, and a long-buried and hurting part of his soul cried out in relief.

"I love you," Liam whispered against his mouth. "I'm sorry I've been such a fucking coward, but I'm done with that shit now. I promise."

"I love you too," Rory murmured back, enjoying the feeling of Liam's strong arms wrapping around him. While he loved Rhiannon's petite size and softness, there was something to be said about being with someone he didn't have to worry about breaking. Liam could physically take whatever he had to dish out.

Their kiss turned heated, a dueling of tongues that matched the way they rubbed into each other. He was tempted to reach beneath Liam's kilt and indulge himself in touching the other man, but he didn't want to push it. As close as he and Liam were, this phase of their relationship was still new, and Rory wanted to savor it. That became hard to do when Liam grabbed his ass with both hands and growled.

"I want you."

Raw desire tore at Rory's self-restraint. He was pretty sure his dick couldn't get any harder. The smell of Liam filled him; the scent of his musk combined with the faintest hint of Rhiannon's sweet perfume. He'd dreamed about this moment for so long that he could barely wrap his mind around the fact that they were really here, in their woman's kitchen of all places, in broad daylight, touching each other. Unable to resist the lure any longer, Rory did what he'd been dying to do for twelve long years.

Holding Liam's gaze, he reached beneath his kilt and wrapped his fist around the other man's cock. The immediate pleasure that suffused Liam's rugged face almost had Rory coming in his pants, and the feel of the other man's fierce, hot erection was everything Rory had dreamed of and more. With a vicious snarl, Liam jerked at the fastening of Rory's leather pants, then worked them quickly down Rory's hips enough to reveal the engorged length of his dick, gripping it in his fist.

Liam crushed his mouth to Rory's, their tongues rubbing together as they began to jerk each other off. Bright bursts of raw pleasure detonated inside Rory as his breathing sped up until they were practically panting in each other's mouths. Precum wet the tip of Liam's cock, and Rory milked him, squeezing out more until his hand glided up and down the shaft. Love and desire mixed in Rory, pushing him swiftly to the edge of his orgasm. He would have been ashamed of how quickly he was going to climax if Liam hadn't been about to come as well.

He knew his best mate's body, knew what he liked and how he enjoyed being touched after years of training submissives together. Evidently Liam had been paying attention to what Rory loved as well, because he worked Rory's shaft just how he liked it. The pleasure became so intense it turned into a hot burn that settled into the base of his spine, urging him to come all over Liam's stroking fingers.

"Going to come," he whispered against Liam's lips.

"Give it to me."

"Together."

The past and present merged becoming one as Liam growled, "Together."

A moment of fear struck as the memory of the last time they'd done this and how he'd almost lost Liam hit, but all those negative feelings were swept away by the raw carnality of fucking Liam's fist while the handsome Scot pumped his hips in time with Rory's strokes. A rough groan tore from Liam, vibrating through

Liam's lips and into Rory's mouth as the first hot splash of cum wet Rory's fingers. His own climax burst from him in a barely contained roar as he muffled himself against Liam's shoulder, then sucked and licked at the hot flesh beneath his lips.

Eventually their strokes gentled, and when Liam finally released him, Rory almost fell before the other man caught him.

"Holy fuck," Liam whispered.

"Yeah."

Rory leaned over and grabbed a bunch of paper towels, then cleaned himself as best he could while Liam did the same. In the aftermath of his orgasm the worry about Liam freaking out surfaced again, and he studied his friend, searching for some sign of an impending explosion. When Liam's hazel gaze met his own, the only thing Rory saw there was pleasure and relief. Liam studied Rory in return, then grinned.

"Thought I was going to run out on ya, didn't ya?"

"The idea may have crossed my mind."

Liam grabbed him in a bear hug and whispered in his ear, "You're stuck with me now, you limey bastard. You and Rhiannon both."

A floorboard squeaked overhead, and Rory moved back from Liam, looking up at the ceiling as more noises came. "Our girl's awake."

Liam reached out and cupped the side of his face, drawing his attention back to the handsome Scotsman. "I don't want her to know about us yet."

An ache filled Rory's heart, and he cursed himself for really trusting that Liam would ever be okay with them being lovers. For a little bit, he'd actually believed Liam, but he should have known better. "Fine."

"No, wait. Not like that. I don't give a fuck who knows that I love you, but she's had a hard night...hell, a hard life. I want the focus to be on her, and I won't be able to do that if we let her know I've finally stopped being a dumbass. I'd like to tell her on the island, in a way that lets her know that she's just as much a part of this as we are. I want to do things right and proper with her. Treat her like she deserves."

Rushing water filled the pipes overhead, and Rory sighed. "I agree."

Liam rubbed his hands over Rory's shoulders, the other man's calloused touch soothing Rory. "I'm serious. I thought a lot about this last night, and I realized that part of me is still that scared fourteen-year-old kid listening to his father talk about burning someone's home down because he was gay. Me allowing that hate and fear to influence the rest of my life would be like Rhiannon never allowing herself to fall in love because of what that fucking pedophile did to her. It shames me that she's stronger than I am. I won't let them do that to me, to us, anymore."

Footsteps sounded on the stairs, and the men stepped apart. Rory glanced down at their still hard dicks and chuckled. "Um, you might want to get back to the stove until you calm down."

Liam grinned and turned, then picked up his spatula again as he turned the stove back on and whistled a merry tune. Moving quickly, Rory then went over to the full coffeepot and poured himself a cup into one of the mugs Liam had set out. He'd just taken the first sip when he caught sight of Rhiannon out of the corner of his eye.

"Morning, darling girl."

She took a hesitant step into the kitchen, and despite the fact that he'd just had a ball-draining orgasm, his cock still punched against the fly of his pants. Today she wore a pair of worn jean shorts that made her smooth, tanned legs look a mile long and a pink tank top that dipped low enough in the front to give him fantasies about sliding his dick between her breasts. She took another step forward, the sway of her chest alerted him to the fact that she wasn't wearing a bra, and when she smiled at him, he swore he grinned back at her like a love-struck schoolboy.

"Hello, lass," Liam said, and Rory glanced at him, catching a similar besotted look on his best mate's face.

"Morning." She licked her lips, and he wanted to kiss her in the worst way, but something about her body language held her back. "Did I...did I dream last night?"

He glanced at Liam, and the other man slowly nodded. "Aye, you did."

Wrapping her arms around herself, she looked down at the tile floor. "What did I say?"

Unable to stop himself, he made his way to Rhiannon with Liam in tow. Almost as one they held her between them, and her soft shudder didn't go unnoticed. He met Liam's gaze over her head, and they shared a grief-filled look.

Liam replied in a soothing voice, "You talked about what happened to you."

She shivered again, this time hard enough that Rory tightened his arms around her. "How bad?"

"What do you mean, lass?"

"Don't lie to me, Liam. How bad was it?" Her voice grew thick with tears. "I fucking hate this! I hate that he still haunts me, that I can't forget about him. I'm sorry you had to listen to me."

Pain tore through Rory at the agonized sound of her voice. "I'm not. We love you, and part of loving you means being there for you, always."

"But I'm spoiled," she said in a soft whisper. "Used."

Liam moved back and knelt before her. "Never say that. You are the strongest, kindest, most beautiful woman I've ever met, inside and out."

"You just feel sorry for me."

She tried to turn away, but Rory wouldn't let her, instead holding her close and making her face Liam, making her see the sincerity in his gaze. "Believe him, Rhiannon. Believe us. We've never told a woman we love them before. I won't let you dismiss it as pity."

"But why would you love me?"

Liam wrapped his arms around her hips and put his face against her belly. "How could we not?"

She dropped her arms, and her hands shook as she lightly caressed his head. "I'm afraid."

"Of what? Tell us what it is and we'll take care of it."

Her harsh laugh held no humor. "I'm afraid that you'll leave me. That you'll get tired of my nightmares, tired of my issues, and leave. Or that you're only staying with me out of pity."

With a low growl Liam stood and picked Rhiannon up by the waist, then set her on the counter. Rory moved next to him and they loomed over her. "Enough, Rhiannon."

Her eyes grew wide, and she looked first at Liam, then back to Rory. "Enough?"

Rory nodded. "Yes, enough. I'm not going to sit here and listen to you belittle yourself."

She sighed, and her shoulders slumped. "But what's going to happen when you want to go back to training?"

He exchanged a look with Liam, and he could tell by the other man's expression that he hadn't thought of that as well. "You don't want us to train anymore?"

Tears filled her eyes as she looked back up at them. "No, I don't. The thought of you touching another woman...it would kill me."

"We'll figure something out," Rory said in a soothing voice as he realized that while he would miss the satisfaction that came from training shy submissives, he would give it up in a heartbeat for Rhiannon.

Rory reached out to touch her, but she jerked back. "What is there to figure out? I can't stomach you touching another woman sexually, and there is no way you can't touch a woman and train her. You're the best trainers there are, and you love training. I'd just be holding you back. You'd come to resent me, I know it."

Liam chuckled, and both Rory and Rhiannon gave him an odd look. "You're right that we do love training, but I think I can safely speak for both Rory and myself when I say that our needs have changed. I haven't talked about it with him yet, but I think we should move on to training couples."

She frowned. "Couples?"

"Yeah, couples. Many people are already in a relationship when they finally get up the courage to ask for what they really want in the bedroom. We get a lot of established couples that join Wicked who have only played together with what they can figure out from books and the Internet. While Wicked has classes for them, I was thinking of doing something more along the lines of weeklong intensive workshops."

The idea appealed to Rory immediately. He smiled at Liam.

"That's bloody brilliant. We could do maybe one every couple of months, kind of like an intro to BDSM."

"But we'd need you to do it with us," Liam added. When he reached for Rhiannon, she didn't jerk away, and the hopeful look on her face made Rory swallow hard.

"You want me to help?"

"Of course, lass. We'd need to show them all the wonderful things that are possible when a submissive truly trusts her Master."

"Or in this case, Masters," Rory added and began to stroke her silken thigh, excitement building as the idea began to take hold. "You do trust us, don't you?"

"Completely," she whispered and gave them a heartbreaking smile.

"Then believe us when we say that you are exactly what we want and need."

"Come on now, lass. Have more faith in yourself." Liam gave her a disgruntled look. "If anyone should be questioning their worth, it should be that beat-to-shit Englishman standing next to me."

Her lips curved into a small smile, and Rory gave Liam a mock punch. "Beat-to-shit? That's rich coming from an old man whose knees snap like gunfire when he gets out of a chair."

Now she did laugh and placed one hand over Liam's mouth and one hand over Rory's. "Okay, okay. You're right. I'm too good for both of you. Happy now?"

They each nipped at her fingertips, making her pull back with a giggle. The sparkle in her eyes lightened Rory's heart immeasurably. "I won't be happy until I've had my breakfast."

She peered around Liam's shoulder. "It smells amazing. I had no idea you could cook."

"That wasn't the kind of breakfast I was talking about."

She squealed when he swept her from the counter, then gently placed her on the sturdy kitchen table. "Rory! What are you doing?"

He ignored her and with Liam's help quickly stripped her of her shorts, grinning as she halfheartedly fought them. "Liam, be a good mate and hold her down for me."

"With pleasure."

A hard bolt of lust sizzled down his spine at the sight of Liam pinning Rhiannon to the table, then kissing her. Returning his attention to her legs, he stroked his finger along the blue satin of her panties, loving that there was already a little damp spot from her arousal. Their girl was so responsive, and he loved how she reacted so strongly to their touch. Her hips wiggled, and a soft moan came from her as Liam deepened their kiss. Rory almost moaned as well at the memory of what it was like to kiss the other man. He intended on reliving that experience again, and soon, but first he wanted to see Rhiannon lose herself in the pleasure that only they could offer her.

He hooked his finger into the crotch of her panties, then pulled them over to the side and clenched his teeth at the sight of her wet sex. He leaned down and scooted her forward until she was in the perfect position for his mouth. Instead of diving right in, he delicately licked her pussy, giving her clit a light tap with the tip of his tongue that had her squirming in earnest.

"Such a pretty pussy," he murmured against her thigh before rubbing his cheek on the soft down of her pubic hair. "So soft and wet."

Her strangled moan made him smile, and he glanced up to find Liam helping himself to a handful of her gorgeous tits as he kissed her. Happiness filled Rory until he thought his heart might burst at the sight of the people he loved most in the world enjoying each other. But Rhiannon was an orgasm behind them, and she deserved her pleasure as well.

Using his thumbs, he held her open for his intimate kiss, taking his time to rouse her until her cunt turned a nice dusky-pink color. Her clit was fully extended from its tender hood now, and he lapped at it, then stroked her until he found that spot that made her thighs stiffen on either side of his head. As her cries ramped up, he slid a finger into her tight sheath, groaning at the way her inner muscles clenched against him. It would feel good to just shove himself inside her, ride her to their mutual completion, but right now, this was all about her satisfaction. He wanted her to never have to look elsewhere, to let her know that she would always find pleasure with them, always find love.

"That's it," Liam said in a low, rumbling voice. "Give it to us, girl. Come for your Masters."

A second later, her clit quivered against his tongue, and he suckled it, then lashed his tongue against the exposed bundle of nerves until she broke beneath him and screamed out his name as her pussy clenched and released in pulsing waves on his finger. Ever so slowly he licked and nuzzled her down from her orgasm until she was a limp bundle spread out on the kitchen table like a sacrificial virgin on an altar.

"Would you like some orange juice?" Liam asked after he gave Rhiannon a kiss and stepped away from the table.

"What?" She opened her eyes, the beautiful green gaze shimmering in the bright sunlight shining through the windows. "What about you?"

Rory stood and wiped his mouth, then gave her a wink. "Oh, you'll take care of us once you get your strength back. We have plans for you."

She gave him a slow smile and stretched, unashamed in her nudity. "Mmm, my pleasure, Master."

He gave her hip a gentle slap. "Up you go, darling girl. We need to run back to our house in a bit."

She sighed and stood, finding her panties on the floor before slipping them on. "When will I see you again?"

Liam laughed. "You think we're leaving you here? Oh no. You're coming with us."

The happiness in her smile filled Rory with joy in return. "Okay. But at some point I need to go shopping for some things for the island."

In all the chaos of last night Rory had forgotten about their vacation plans. The thought of Rhiannon walking down the beach in some skimpy bikini, or better yet naked, at sunset had him wanting another taste of her delicious cunt. Then an idea came to him, and he casually said to Liam, "I'll take her shopping if you go pick up that stuff we ordered."

For a moment Liam looked confused; then Rory scratched at his throat with a significant look. Liam said, "I'll take care of it."

Chapter Eighteen

After waking from her nap, Rhiannon undid the seat belt holding her to the butter-soft gray suede couch. Her heart rate sped up, and she gazed out the window of the jet, anticipating her first sight of the ocean. Standing with a sigh, she stretched her arms and yawned, then turned back to the windows. They were still flying over land, but they should pass across the ocean soon. She needed to see that beauty for herself, to know if such amazing colors could actually occur in nature. Pictures of the Caribbean had always made her heart ache with a strange wistfulness because she'd never thought she'd be able to see it in real life. The thought of traveling alone scared her to bits, and being able to afford it had been another issue. Or at least it had before she fell in love with two billionaires.

Even though she was awake, she still felt like she was dreaming. That wasn't too unusual considering she was in a full-size private jet that had actual rooms and showers and other crazy shit she'd only seen in movies. It was opulent, lush, and made all the more amazing by the two men watching her with equally hungry gazes from the other side of the cabin. Oh, she knew that look. The fire in their eyes told her they had something special in mind, and her pussy grew soft and wet in an instant. They had her trained to respond to their moods, to anticipate pleasure, and she was totally on board for any naughty thing they wanted to do.

In the two days since she'd had her fight with Sunny, the men had barely let her out of their sight. They'd stayed at her home, spending the time talking, going for long walks in the woods together, and making love to her until she practically passed out from pleasure every night. Waking up with them holding her each morning, sprawled across each other on her bed, was the best thing she'd ever experienced. The men seemed easier with each other as well, and she wondered if something had changed between them. Neither of them mentioned anything, so she let it slide for the time being. She was so happy that she was afraid to do anything that would disrupt the newfound balance in their relationship.

A flight attendant was setting out a lovely meal of fresh fruit, yogurt, and cheese along with all manner of sweets. Her stomach rumbled, and she couldn't help but smile. With all the sex she'd been having, she must be burning the daily calories of a long-distance swimmer. The men had pampered, spoiled, and teased her until she couldn't even remember her own name. Her mind had been reduced to a base state where they filled her so completely that she lost herself in them. Total surrender like that was almost worth the emotional pain she'd had to go through in order to let them into her heart. She'd had some rough spots, but the crying had been cleansing.

If this is what love felt like, she now understood what the poets and philosophers had been going on for ages about. The warmth in her, the feeling of being complete, of being loved was doubled thanks to the amazing men who each fit into her life like the perfect pieces of a puzzle made just for her.

Suddenly she became aware of the men closing in on her: Liam at the back and Rory at the front. They laced their arms around her, and she let out a sigh of longing. All they had to do was hold her like this and she melted between them. The scent of their colognes combining with her honeysuckle perfume made her light-headed with the need to take them both, now. Damn them. She was so primed for sex by their constant touching that she craved orgasms now. And not just her orgasm. She wanted their cum filling her one way or another. But neither of the men had been allowed in her ass yet. They both wanted it—badly—but as silly as it sounded, she had plans for her ass. And by denying them that part of herself, each man had become somewhat obsessed with being the first to take her there.

Hopefully that would make her plan to get them to admit their love easier. She was going to make them a proposition they couldn't refuse, and she was interested to see how it would play out. Well, interested and nervous. Would they laugh her bold demands off, or would they be disgusted by what she asked of them? The thought of them doing dirty, wicked things with each other had her body moving against them, little grinding circles with her hips that they both loved. Last night she'd danced naked for them, and they'd made her climax until she didn't know her own name.

"Though it pains me to say this, you need to eat, lass."

Rory rubbed a soothing hand down her arm. "Food first. If you eat, we'll give you a reward."

"Aye," Liam agreed with a dark laugh. "I've got a big fat sausage for ya."

"Idiot," Rhiannon muttered and threw her elbow back into Liam.

They released her, and she ignored them in favor of sampling everything on the table. The flight attendants had left, and she watched as Liam casually strolled over to the door separating the passenger area from the crew berthing and locked it. With a dark look in her direction, he fisted his cock, then adjusted the hard length beneath his tan shorts in a way that made her breath catch in her throat.

"We'll see what you'll be calling me as soon as you've eaten your fill."

Instead of responding, she took a pastry and bit in with a low moan of pleasure. If she wasn't wrong, a hint of strawberry mixed up with all that buttery goodness. One had to live in the moment, and part of that living included appreciating good food.

Rory picked up a piece of pineapple and slowly chewed it as he watched her. "You know, I've never noticed how sensual a woman could be while she's eating something other than my cock."

Managing not to choke on a shocked giggle, Rhiannon took a sip of her water and cleared her throat. "You, Sir, are a pervert."

"Absolutely."

They ate in silence for a few minutes, but as the tension built, she lost her appetite. Deciding that she was full, she took a long drink of her water and sighed. "This is nice. Beats the hell out commercial jets, that's for damn sure."

Rory stood first and held his hand out to her. "Come here, darling girl."

A warm tingle rushed through her blood, leaving her body awakening to him in a sensual rush. The touch of his hand on hers had her nipples aching, and when he pulled her into his arms for a kiss she thought she might have a heart attack. His kisses tore her apart, ripping away her defenses until she was giving him everything she had.

Liam's voice came from nearby. "Careful with that pretty shirt she's wearing and that short skirt. Looks like every dirty old man's dream about a hot schoolgirl."

She giggled against Rory's lips as he sighed. "Though I resent the dirty old man part, I do find you hot as sin in this outfit."

"Did you know I'm not wearing panties?"

"I hoped," Liam quipped, and Rory gently gave her over to Liam's warm grip.

Liam looked down on her with his intense hazel eyes, and she melted further. She was so incredibly lucky to have two of the world's best Masters to call her own. Pride filled her that they'd chosen her, loved her, and she reveled in the feeling of making them happy. When it came down to it, this was all she'd ever wanted. With Liam and Rory, she'd found unconditional love, and it made her heart sing.

"I love you," she whispered as she gazed up at Liam, eyeing his full lips and licking her own. Kissing him was an amazingly soft experience, a decadent pleasure that slowly ramped up her desire. And when he wrapped those lips around her clit, she felt an electric jolt that was pure ecstasy. It would be nice if he'd just kneel down and eat her until she came without teasing her forever, but she knew she wouldn't be that lucky. They seemed to love to drive her as high as they could, until she was pretty certain she'd go insane from the need to come, then gift her with an orgasm that would indeed give her the little death. The world, for one glorious moment, would go dark, and she simply floated in pleasure.

Addictive, soul-deep pleasure.

"We love you too," Rory said from over her shoulder.

When they were alone with her, they seemed to like as little physical distance between them and her as possible, and she had absolutely no objections.

"So will you tell me about this island we're going to? Every time I ask we end up having sex."

"And that's a problem how?"

She lightly slugged Liam in his massive biceps, wanting to wrap her body around him even as he irritated her. Sometimes their interactions were like this. A bit of Domming, then easily shifting back into what she liked to think of as lovers mode. Just as good if a bit less intense, but other times it was nice to just relax and touch.

"I don't know anything about this place. I mean, yeah, I like surprises, but I like anticipation even more. Plus I'm curious. The way you guys talk about your vacation house, it must be paradise on earth."

Rory led her over to the couch and sat her on his lap. Then Liam moved next to them, close enough that he had to sling his arm over Rory's shoulder in a casual gesture that nonetheless heated her blood to the boiling point. Every touch between the two men drove her straight out of her mind, and if she wasn't mistaken, they seemed to be touching each other more.

"What was that look for?" Liam murmured. "What were you just thinking about, my naughty little sub?"

Crap, he was asking her in his deep, dark, Dom voice that hypnotized her into submission. It was really unfair that he held such control over her, but she'd given it to him willingly and now had to face the consequences of her actions. Like the fact that belonging to two Doms meant twice the pleasure and twice the domination. Not for the faint of heart, that was for sure.

"Your island," she whispered. "Please tell me about it."

"Well, it's actually islands."

"But only one is big enough to live on," Liam quickly added. "The others are just nice to look at."

"When did you buy it?"

"About"—Liam glanced at Rory— "what was it, six years ago?"

"Around there. The main house just got finished two years ago. Everything takes longer in the Caribbean."

"Plus they had to deal with pleasing both of us with the interior design. I wanted something mellow and comfortable while Rory wanted some kind of psychedelic color scheme that made my eyes bleed."

"He just has cow-shit farmer tastes. Ignore him."

"Ha, right. We had to call your mom about it, and she agreed that it was, and I quote, 'an abomination of color birthed from the writhing haunches of a foul beast slouching toward Bethlehem.'"

She grinned up at them, loving how they were sharing themselves with her. They'd done more talking about their lives than she had about her past, but it was harder for her. Things hadn't been nice or fun for too long, and she was living her life with joy right now. She didn't want to risk this newfound happiness, and as a result she tried to stay in the moment. Eventually she'd have to tell them more about her past so they would know things that might trigger her, but for right now, she was content hearing about them and building on her knowledge of who they were as men.

Lord help her, she'd ended up in a complicated relationship.

Growing up, she'd been raised since day one to be a perfect wife. For her, getting married, having a family, had been her goal for as long as she could remember. Now she'd have to give that up in order to love these men. She was sort of okay with that, but she would never give up the possibility of having a child.

Yet another conversation she'd been avoiding.

Rory noticed her slight frown first and rubbed at the little line between her eyebrows. "Stop thinking so hard."

The soft timbre of Liam's voice deepened the sense of her security. "We're on vacation. No thinking allowed."

She gave the handsome Scotsman a small smile and nodded. "Yes, Sir."

"Now," Rory said with a soft purr in his voice. "We have around two more hours of flying. While I'd like to pound into you, I also don't want you walking funny."

"Or getting weak knees." Liam laughed and dodged her punch thrown at his arm. "Oh, getting feisty, are ya?"

Whenever he was trying to get her riled, he seemed to slip back into his Scottish brogue. It annoyed her and made her horny at the same time. The only other time his accent thickened like this was when he was deep in the throes of lust and he would growl out his pleasure. Like when he'd been on top of her last night as Rory watched. Liam had fucked her right after Rory came inside her, and the thought of one man's cum slicking the other man's entrance to her body had made her so wild with desire that Rory had to pin her so Liam could fuck her hard and deep.

"What are you thinking about?" Liam asked in an amused voice.

She wondered if he was even aware that he was slowly stroking Rory's shoulder. It was almost as if his body was doing something his mind wasn't fully aware of. A gentle touch, a brief caress. They must have been used to doing it often, because Rory hardly noticed the small strokes of Liam's fingertips. But she did. They were so damn hot she was melting on their laps. No wonder she'd gotten hate from many of the submissives at Wicked about the men being her Masters now, exclusively. Though she wondered how she'd find the courage to submit to them for training purposes in public. They'd given up a great deal by no longer training female submissives and switching to couples instead, a small part of her worried that they would eventually tire of her.

Suddenly a sharp pain came from her nipple, and she yelped.

"We said no heavy thoughts. If I have to watch those emerald eyes darken to the color of a pine tree in the sun, I'll have to spank you."

Liam chuckled, but he watched as closely as Rory did. "I don't think she's in the right headspace for this yet."

Slowly nodding, Rory smiled at her, and her pussy clenched. "When you're on our island, you will be in 24/7 mode with us."

Her breath caught in her chest, and she tried to hide her small shiver. She wasn't sure if it was a nervous reaction to his words, or desire. "Whatever my Masters desire."

"There we go," Liam crooned, then stroked his big hand over her cheek. "There's my eager little submissive."

She placed a kiss on Liam's wrist while Rory watched them indulgently. "You will take care of us while we're there. Only you. Our home is your home, and we want you to be comfortable there."

A delight raced through her at being the only one to make them feel good. "Thank you, Master."

The men exchanged a smile; then Liam looked down at her. "Thanks, lass. You just won me a twenty-dollar bet."

"Pardon me?"

With a sigh Rory elbowed Liam. "He bet me that you would love the idea of taking care of us. I, in my obviously wrong opinion, thought you would want to relax and enjoy your time being pampered."

She chewed on her lower lip. "Can I have both?"

"Greedy wench."

Rory moved her until she straddled both of them with her legs around one thigh each. The motion left her wet pussy exposed to the air, and she groaned when Rory and Liam moved their thighs up, spreading her farther. She braced her hands on their shoulders and whimpered when Rory began to lower the straps of her dress down her arm.

"Such beautiful skin," he murmured. "You're already so tan. I wonder how dark you'll get out in the sun. We plan on having you naked the whole time."

"Well, naked except for one thing. Stand up in front of us, lass, and remove your clothes."

Her mind briefly skipped to the locked door between the crew and her Masters, and desire spread through her body, aided by her heated blood rushing to her clit. They were going to touch her, do things to her, wonderful things, and she couldn't wait. Already her heart raced like a junkie getting ready to depress a fix into her veins.

Once she was naked, each man stood and moved to their usual positions. The feeling of their clothed bodies against her naked one had her groaning in pleasure. There was just something so sexy about them being fully dressed while she was naked. A male dominance that stroked her just right. She loved the alpha male, the strongest wolf in the pack, and right now she had two of the best making her skin tingle and her nipples tighten into aching points.

"Making you wear clothes is a crime," Liam said in an affectionate and rumbly tone. "This body is made for a man's pleasure."

Rory reached around her and handed her a small blue velvet bag. "Once we're alone on the island, we want you to wear this and only this."

Her hands shook as she fumbled with the strings of the bag, hoping that inside she'd find the collar she'd been hoping they'd give her. Though it may sound weird to the vanilla world, she considered a collar just as binding as a wedding ring, and she desperately wanted that physical proof that she belonged to them. The men had mentioned collaring her in passing, but so far they hadn't actually done anything. When she pulled out a long gold chain embellished with diamonds and emeralds she tried to hide her disappointment.

"You don't like it?" Liam asked in a soft voice, studying her face.

She tried to plaster on a bright smile, pushing her disappointment aside. "No, it's beautiful. What is it?"

Rory smoothed his hands over the curve of her waist, sending pleasant tingles through her. "A slave belt."

She ran the gold links through her hands, admiring the fierce sparkle of the diamonds and emeralds. "A slave belt?"

"Aye. We want you to wear this whenever we're at the island. Once you put this belt on you become our willing slave, giving us permission to use you as we wish."

Some of her earlier excitement returned, and she leaned back on Rory's chest, looking up with a smile. "Aren't I already your slave?"

"More like we're your slaves," Rory said with a soft laugh as he cuddled her.

"Aye," Liam smiled and stroked her cheek. "And you're a hard Mistress to please."

"Well you could please me right now by putting your talented tongue to use."

"Greedy wench," Rory said before he nipped her neck hard enough to sting.

"Only for you, Masters."

Later that evening Rhiannon relaxed back on the soft padding of an enormous white terry-cloth-covered lounge chair in Liam's arms, watching the sun set over the ocean. Her pussy throbbed as Liam continued to tease her, gently stroking her nipple before giving it a harsh pinch that sent a cascade of tingles through her. She was nude except for her slave chain, and a light coating of perspiration covered her body as her unfulfilled arousal burned through her blood.

Liam wore a pair of black swim trunks that were still damp from his dip in the infinity pool at the edge of the terrace. The setting sun made the water droplets in his hair gleam as he smiled down at her, the soft sound of Rory playing the guitar a perfect accompaniment to Liam's slow seduction.

Her other Master relaxed in the lounge chair next to theirs, strumming his guitar as he watched Liam toy with her, his lips curved in a small smile that melted her heart. She had no idea Rory could play the guitar, but he was actually really good at it. If it was even possible, she found herself falling deeper in love with them by the moment. Then again she dared anyone to come to this island paradise and not be overcome by its romantic beauty.

The island itself wasn't that large, but the space was used to its fullest potential without destroying the natural beauty of the place. There was the main home, a dock, and a small forest surrounded by gleaming white beaches on the western side and rocky coast to the east. A ring of barrier reefs encircled the property to the south, and the waves crashed against them, throwing up sprays of water that burned orange and gold in the light. Taking a deep breath, she tasted the salt of the ocean combined with the heavy floral scent of the exotic plants growing nearby.

"This is the most beautiful place in the world," she

whispered as she looked from Liam to Rory.

"I'm glad you like it, lass," Liam said with an indulgent smile. "Tomorrow we'll take you to one of the northern coves where the dolphins like to play."

Rory took a break from playing to take a sip from his beer. "Or we could go to one of the main islands if you'd like."

"If you don't mind, I think I'd rather stay here and keep you all to myself." She let out a soft moan as Liam leaned down to take her aching nipple in his mouth, the soft rasp of his tongue over her stiffened peak driving her crazy. "Oh, please."

"Please what?" Liam murmured against her breast.

"I need you."

"And you'll have us, but not until you let one of us into that sweet arse of yours."

She stiffened when he began to lightly pet the curls above her swollen pussy, fighting the urge to squirm so his fingers would go lower, to where she needed it. Oh, how she wanted them both inside her, but she had a demand of her own that would have to be fulfilled before she let that happen. A demand that she was terrified to voice.

"Rhiannon, what's wrong?" Rory asked softly as he moved his lounger closer so the two pressed together made what essentially became one big bed.

"What are you talking about, Master?"

The innocence she tried to project sounded fake even to herself, and she cringed when Liam leaned back enough to examine her face. "What is it? You know you can tell us anything. Trust us, lass. We'll give you anything you need."

"I..." She looked between them, then back at the sky, which was now only a sliver of burning pink on the rapidly darkening horizon. "Well you're both big men, and I'm afraid you could hurt me back there."

Liam laughed while Rory chuckled. "Darling girl, I assure you that when we take you, it will be nothing but pleasure."

"But how do you know? Have you ever been taken back there?" She took a deep breath, then blurted out, "If you want to take me anally, then I want to watch you get taken back there first."

Tension filled the air, and she tried to blink back her tears, afraid that she'd pushed them too far. Yes, the men seemed more comfortable with each other than ever, but what if this was the one thing they would never do? What if her request scared Liam off, and Rory hated her for making his best friend leave? When the silence continued, a tear escaped, and she dashed it away.

"I'm sorry. That was just a joke. I—"

Rory placed his hand gently over her lips. "So if I let Liam bugger me, you'll let me take your sweet arse?"

Unable to face him, she nodded and closed her eyes.

With a soft sigh Liam shifted next to her. "Lass, you look terrified. Open your eyes."

She did as he asked, and Rory removed his fingers from her lips. "You have a deal."

"What?" Shock mixed with arousal sizzled along her nerves.

Liam's soft laughter eased her heart. "It's okay, lass."

"But...but you..."

"I what? Am a fucking idiot that let his fear of what other people would think rule his life? Am too stupid to see that everything I want is right in front of me? That you're afraid I'll go running screaming into the night like a scared virgin?"

All she could do was gape at him in shock as he leaned over her body, then clasped the back of Rory's neck, bringing the other man closer until she had an up close and personal view of the two men's mouths almost brushing against each other. Then the distance between them was gone, and she had the pleasure of watching the two men she loved more than anything in the world love each other. The kiss started out tender, a soft rasp of firm male lips followed by a groan from Rory as Liam licked around his mouth. She scooted higher, getting a better view of the men licking and sucking at each other's lips, and her arousal burst into flames.

The ache that settled into her pussy demanded release, but she didn't dare touch herself, afraid of disturbing what had to be one of the most erotic things she'd ever witnessed. Their kiss built until it became savage, teeth nipping and low male groans blending into the crash of the surf in the distance. Unable to resist, she reached out and traced their lips where their mouths joined, feeling the heat generated between them. Rory turned, then slanted his mouth against Liam's and grabbed the other man by the back of his head with one arm, a deep growl vibrating against her fingertips as she continued to explore them as they kissed.

When they finally broke apart, she was panting as hard as they were. When Rory slipped the fingers of his free hand between her legs, she cried out in need.

"Oh, darling, you are so wet. Liked watching me kiss this big bastard, didn't you?"

"So fucking sexy," she managed to whisper as his wet finger glided over her swollen clit.

Liam stood and smiled down at her. "Come on, lass. We need to get your arse ready for Rory's cock."

"Your cock?" She looked up at Rory and bit her lower lip. "Does that mean you'll...take him?"

A shadow of apprehension flashed through Rory's silvery blue eyes, but he nodded. "Yes. And then I'm taking you. We both are."

They made their way back into the sprawling home, bypassing the enormous kitchen and living area to the master bedroom. Once inside Rory led her over to the huge dark wood bed while Liam went into the bathroom. He helped her onto the tall mattress, then knelt next to the bed so they were eye level.

"I can see your worry, but let me assure you that we both want this."

She glanced at the still closed bathroom door and lowered her voice to a whisper. "Are you sure? It would kill me if this caused problems between you both."

"We're sure, darling girl." He suddenly grinned. "In fact it's been a right pisser to keep our hands off each other, but we wanted to share this with you."

"Why?"

"Because you are as much a part of my life as Liam is. It's because of your love, your strength that we both found the courage to love each other." He took her hand and placed a gentle kiss on her palm. "I don't think you understand how much you mean to us."

"Aye," Liam said from the bathroom doorway. "I'd probably still be hiding behind my hate and fear if it wasn't for you, Rhiannon. You showed me what true strength is."

Tears filled her eyes, and she tried to blink them back. "I love you so much, both of you."

"We know you do, darling."

Rory stood and made his way to the bathroom, leaving her with Liam who joined her on the bed.

"Lass, I feel like everything in my life has been leading up to this moment. That you came into our world at the perfect time, the answer to our prayers even when we didn't know what we were praying for. I love Rory with everything I have, but it was your unconditional love that gave me the courage to admit it. Without your light, your warmth, I'd still be hiding in the shadows of my own hate. You are my family, you and Rory both, and I can only hope that someday I'm worthy of your love."

"Oh, Liam." She started to cry in earnest, and he gathered her into his arms.

"Sad or happy tears?"

"Happy," she said as she leaned back enough to meet his gaze. "So very happy."

Liam took her lips in a gentle kiss that she felt all the way to her toes, the kind of kiss that reached her on a soul-deep level. "My Master."

Rory returned with a large black bag as she cuddled in Liam's arms. "Now that is a beautiful sight."

Liam gently released her and moved to stand next to Rory. To her astonishment and delight, the two men began to remove each other's clothes, quickly stripping until they stood nude. The hunger in their gazes when they looked at each other stroked her just right, and she crawled down the edge of the bed for a closer look.

Both men glanced over at her, and she studied them in the light of the full moon coming through the open doorway leading to the patio. Her heart thumped as she drank in their masculine beauty, the perfection of their heavily muscled bodies, and the bone-clenching sight of their rampant erections. Rory looped his arm around Liam's waist and gave her an evil little smile.

"Well, look what we have here. Such an eager, wet, little submissive. Attend, girl."

She immediately knelt and spread her thighs with her hands clasped behind her back.

Liam set the bag on the floor and dug through it before lifting out a set of black leather restraints lined with padded suede. Her body dampened anew with need as he swiftly cuffed her hands behind her back. When she gave an experimental pull, they held tight, and she bit her lower lip, trying to suppress a groan. She loved being bound and exposed like this, drowning in their pleasure as they examined her body.

"Such a pretty cunt," Rory murmured. "I think we should adorn it."

"Roll onto your stomach," Liam said in a rough voice.

She complied, and a moment later, strong male hands lifted her hips up into the air, exposing her pussy to them. They didn't say anything further, but soon two pairs of male hands were caressing her, stroking her, and driving her out of her mind with pleasure. Then something cool squirted onto her anus, and she tensed.

"Shh," Liam whispered as he massaged the lube into that tight ring of muscle. "Relax and let your Master in like a good girl."

A whimper managed to escape as he eased first one, then two fingers into her. The pain of being stretched was easier to accept with Rory massaging her clit until she was shaking beneath their onslaught. Brutal pleasure suffused her as Liam began to stroke in and out of her tight bottom before removing his fingers altogether.

She moaned, unsure if it was from the pleasure of Rory's touch or the pain of Liam's abrupt withdrawal from her ass. Her mind whirled with emotions that seemed too strong for her fragile human soul to endure. Love, pleasure, apprehension, and most of all desire. Instead of fighting the confusion, she gave in to it, sinking into their touch until Rory had to secure her hips to keep her upright.

"Stay with us just a little while longer, love," he whispered into her ear as something cold and hard pressed against her tender bottom. "You'll want to watch Liam prepare me to take his cock."

"Oh, fuck," she moaned as that hardness began to press into her anus, stretching sensitive nerve endings until she was crying out.

"There we go," Liam said with an audible growl. "Almost all the way in, sweetheart. The biggest part of the plug is almost all the way in, getting you ready for Rory's cock."

He pushed the butt plug the rest of the way in, and she screamed, arching against him even as she fought to get away. It hurt, burned, and the pain chased away her arousal. Before she could cry out her safe word, Rory flipped her over and dived between her legs, his lips wrapping around her clit, then sucked hard.

The pain turned to pleasure, her overwhelmed mind unable to process the sensory overload as Liam began to kiss her. She tried to respond, tried to kiss him back, but all she could do was tremble and cry out as they worked her to a swift and agonizing orgasm. Her body exploded with pleasure, the burn from her anus seeming to extend the orgasm while each man sucked and stroked her until she was begging them to stop.

When they finally relented, she was nothing but a shuddering bundle of nerves on the massive bed. The ability to think fled as the comforting balm of her postorgasmic bliss seemed to blanket her in contentment. She couldn't even respond as Liam and Rory moved her so she had a good view of them from her position on the bed.

The men's movements were aggressive, rough even as they came together in a clash of lips and tongues that had her gasping. Rory and Liam were so handsome, so masculine, and she had no idea why anyone would ever consider two men coming together in their passion as effeminate. There was nothing soft or sweet about the way the men touched, both grasping and holding each other as they kissed with aggression. The sight was so damn sexy that she forgot to breathe, then took in a gasping inhalation of air as the men broke apart and stared at each other.

Liam looked over at her with a slightly worried expression. "You okay, lass?"

"Don't stop," she whispered. "Oh, please don't stop."

"Like this, do ya?" Liam grasped Rory's ridged erection, making the other man buck in his grip.

Every thought fled her mind when Rory fondled Liam's erection and squeezed far rougher than she would handle the handsome Scotsman.

Liam wrapped his hand over Rory's, and together they stroked Liam's hard shaft, making Rhiannon moan with envy. She wanted to join them, to be a part of the erotic scene presented before her. The very fact that she couldn't touch them made her even more aroused and she squirmed on the bed, wishing her hands were free so she could pleasure herself. It wasn't just the carnality of the act that aroused her, but also the emotions behind it. Being witness to something that had been years in the making moved her soul even as the sight of Liam throwing his head back with a low groan of pleasure brought an echoing sigh from her lips.

Rory released Liam and made his way to her. He bent over her body and brushed his lips over hers. "Take me in your mouth, darling girl."

He helped her scoot forward until her head was level with his pelvis, then placed a pillow beneath her head so she wouldn't have to strain to reach him. With his legs spread she had a view between his thighs of Liam kneeling behind him, his face level with Rory's ass. As she licked the tip of Rory's cock just how he liked, she was sure Liam was licking at his ass. Together they worked her Master until Rory was grunting and shoving his cock deep into her mouth before pulling all the way back out. Liam moved away from Rory's ass, then grabbed a tube of lube and began to work it into Rory's anus.

"Watch," Rory said through gritted teeth as she tried to reclaim him to suck more of his delicious precum out of his dick.

She settled her head on the pillow, then leaned forward so she was almost between Rory's legs. Liam had grasped the other man's hip with one hand, and with his other, he was slowly rubbing his condom-covered dick along the crack of Rory's ass. Sweat blossomed on her body, and she cried out when Rory began to toy with her nipples. It felt so good, so decadent to watch as her strong Master began to gradually accept Liam's invasion.

Rory's breath froze in his lungs, and she leaned up again, suckling on his dick while he experienced having his ass breached for the first time.

Both men groaned in unison, and Rory's legs shook before he moved back and gasped.

"So fucking tight," Liam said as he pushed closer, their thighs almost flush now.

She released Rory from her mouth and strained to move high so she could tongue his tight balls while Liam slid in deeper. As big as the Scotsman was, she was surprised that Rory was still hard. The pain of being stretched must be intense, but her Master's cock throbbed, with the thick veins on the side standing out in sharp relief. Liam made a soothing sound and pulled back slowly, taking his time despite his obvious arousal.

Their musk filled her senses, and she rubbed her cheek against Rory's muscular thigh, looking up between his spread legs to watch the slow press forward and back of Liam's cock. Soon his pace increased, and Rory began to move as well. Placing her head on the pillow, she pressed her thighs together and watched Liam fuck Rory. She was incredibly turned on, with her pussy aching to be filled. She wanted them inside her, moving in her like this, completing the circle between them. Rory must have sensed her need because he began to play with her pussy, shoving his finger inside her in the same rhythm as Liam was now fucking him, harder with a low grunt every time the man bottomed out inside him.

"Stop," Rory gasped. "Going to come."

Liam froze and shook hard enough that the tremors vibrated through the mattress. "Fuck." He slowly withdrew.

Once he was completely out of Rory, the other man moaned long and loud. "Can't wait to be inside you, darling girl. Can't wait to fuck you, feel his cock rubbing against mine, feeling you come apart in our arms."

"Please," she moaned and tried to press her hips into his

clever fingers stroking the clinging muscles of her sheath.

Rory stood, and Liam removed the condom from his swollen shaft, an almost feral look in his eyes. "We'll try to be gentle, but right now, I'm dying to be inside you."

"Just take me, Masters. I trust you."

With a muttered oath, Rory turned her over onto her stomach and took off the restraints. While she stretched out, Liam crawled to the top of the bed and sat among the pillows with his head braced against the dark carved-wood headboard. "Come here. I want you on all fours in front of me."

She scrambled to him, and he cupped her face in his hands. "Relax while Rory removes the plug. Remember that what you're about to feel is what he just felt, a big cock going straight up that tiny little arse of yours."

Her response was lost in a long moan when Rory began to ease the plug from her clinging ass, having to fight her muscles as he removed it. He gave her ass a sharp slap. "Let go of it."

Another slap fell on her other butt cheek, and soon she was clinging to Liam as Rory spanked her hard enough to shove her into the other man. Oh, her Masters were deep into their dominant space now, using her body for their pleasure, letting her deny them nothing. Liam grasped her nipples and began to pull and squeeze them, sending shards of pleasure pain from both her ass and her breasts rocketing through her. The plug finally came out, and she yelled out, arching back at the fiery burn.

"Good, lass. Now I want your hot little pussy on my cock."

Liam hauled her up onto his lap and reached between them, guiding his thick shaft until it was poised at the soaking entrance to her body. He didn't give her a chance to draw a breath before he was shoving her down on his dick, fighting her body's hard clench even as her abundant wetness aided his rough possession. She clung to his shoulders, crying out over and over again as he thrust into her, ramming through her delicate muscles and forcing her to accept his invasion. Her muscles tensed while her mind completely surrendered.

"I love you," she said in between her moaning pants. "So much."

"Such a good girl," Rory said from behind her as he spread

what felt like lubricant over her anus; then the warm tip of his erection pushed against her sore bottom. "Relax and open up for me."

Liam slowed his thrusts, then stopped altogether, then tipped her hips up so she could take Rory into her body as well. The pain of being stretched by two cocks became intense, and she whimpered, trying to endure for their pleasure, but it was difficult to get past the discomfort.

"Easy, baby," Liam said in a soothing voice, and he began to stroke her body, his hands gliding over the light layer of sweat beading on her skin. "He's almost in. You can take us."

"Trying," she cried out as Rory breached the tight ring of muscle attempting to keep him out. "Oh, God! It hurts!"

Reaching between them, Liam stroked her clit while Rory placed gentle kisses on her back. Together they comforted her, loved her, even as her body struggled to accept them.

"Relax, love. The hard part is over. You've done so well, and I'm so proud of you." Rory's normally light English accent had thickened, and his fierce erection throbbed inside the tender passage of her ass. "You're so hot and tight, filled with your Masters. Our sweet submissive, our woman. Always and forever."

"Who do you belong to?" Liam said through gritted teeth as he slowly eased his cock into the overstretched tissues of her pussy.

Her voice came out broken, thick with the emotions that tore her world apart and put it back together again better, stronger. "Master Liam and Master Rory, always and forever."

"Now," Liam said as he looked over her shoulder at Rory.

Something cold slipped over her neck, and she reached up, feeling metal links of some kind. Following the links she found a round metal circle dangling from the necklace. No, not a necklace, a collar. Tears filled her eyes as a shivering rush of pleasure threw her back into heavy arousal.

"Ours forever," Rory whispered into her ear, moving slightly out of her body before sliding back in.

Liam leaned forward and kissed the tears from her cheeks. "You belong to us now, lass."

Words fled from her mind when they both began to move within her, and she gave herself completely to them, so overwhelmed with joy and a sense of truly belonging that even her sore body didn't hurt anymore. Instead a brilliant warmth built from inside her heart, merging with her pleasure until she was screaming out their names at the fierce crush of her first orgasm. Both men groaned while her ass and pussy contracted around them, and they increased their movements, plundering her willing body while she collapsed against Liam's chest, the strong beat of his heart against her ear a perfect counterpart to the rhythm of their possession.

There wasn't a single part of her soul that didn't feel owned by them, not a square inch of her flesh that didn't wear the searing burn of their touch. They drove her higher, Liam moving her slightly so her clit scraped against the hard muscles of his stomach. He groaned when she began to writhe against him, moaning out her pleasure as a feral state seemed to overtake her mind. She wanted to fuck them, to brand them like they were branding her, to take them into her body and drain their cum from them until they filled her with their seed.

"Shit," Rory said in a harsh groan. "Not going to last."

Liam growled in agreement, and he bit the side of her neck where it met her shoulder below the collar, effectively holding her still with his teeth while he slammed his hips into hers. A few moments later, or maybe a lifetime, she screamed and bucked between them as her climax hit, and both men shouted out. In her hypersensitive state she could actually feel the men pulsing inside her, both buried to the hilt as they emptied themselves. The pleasure went on and on, destroying her even as the press of her Masters' bodies held her together.

She'd never known such satisfaction, such bone-deep relief as when they finally collapsed onto her, barely giving her enough room to breathe as they panted and shuddered. Eventually she just drifted, only anchored to the earth by the feeling of her collar against her fingertips as she stroked it. Their heartbeats seemed to synchronize until she was so wrapped up in them she couldn't feel any separation between her body and theirs.

It was perfect.

Rory withdrew from her, and she whined at the stretching

burn. Now that the amazing endorphin rush of her climax began to fade, she hurt. Her bottom burned, and even her pussy felt abused, still filled with Liam's hard cock. That man wasn't even human. Her orgasm had practically killed her while he was once again ready to go. Then Liam began to rub her back, and she sank farther into him, trusting his body to hold hers as she gave up even the vaguest control of herself. They could do with her whatever they wished.

Rory eventually returned, and Liam pulled her off his erect dick, then handed her to Rory who held her in his arms. He took her into the bathroom, and she vaguely noted that he'd lit hundreds of candles and filled the massive white marble bathtub. Liam came in behind them, and soon the men had her maneuvered into the tub, cradled between them and blissfully content.

"Are you okay?" Rory asked as he smoothed his hand over her thighs beneath the water.

"Perfect," was all she could say in return.

Chapter Nineteen

Liam stared into the mirror in the dressing room of the Victorian theater at Club Wicked. They'd returned from their vacation three days ago, and this was their first visit to Wicked after the momentous changes that had occurred during their vacation. Now Liam wanted to make the next and final step in admitting his love for Rory by doing a public scene with him and Rhiannon. Nerves and excitement battled for supremacy while his attention wandered to the reflection of Rory kissing their woman.

Rhiannon was dressed like a princess out of a fairy tale, well, a dirty fairy tale. She wore an elaborate blue and silver ball gown with a tight corseted bodice that pushed her tanned breasts into impressive mounds just begging for his kisses. The gown had been constructed by their friend Laurel so that the massive skirt could be ripped off, leaving Rhiannon clad only in the corset top along with the garter and sparkly silver stockings beneath. Her hair had been pinned atop her head in a mass of dark curls and secured with glittering diamond pins. Around her elegant throat lay their golden chain collar with its owners' medallion proclaiming that she belonged to Liam and Rory.

His best mate and lover wore a groom's costume similar to Liam's, except while Liam wore a kilt, Rory wore a pair of dark brown leather breeches that fit his body perfectly, outlining the delicious curve of his ass. Liam's cock stirred at the memory of fucking the other man's ass, of the rough interplay between them, and how good it felt to take Rory while the other man fucked Rhiannon. Some people might think since Rory had taken Liam in his ass that Liam held the dominant role in their relationship, but that wasn't true. That didn't mean Liam would ever be taking on a submissive role, but he enjoyed the clash of wills with his lover. If it wasn't for Rhiannon balancing them out, Liam was sure he and Rory would battle for dominance until one of them killed the other.

Rhiannon made a sweet, sultry little moaning sound that had Liam's body clenching, and when it did, he was reminded of the plug currently in his ass, stretching him out for his best mate just like Rhiannon was wearing an even bigger plug to ready her for Liam's cock. His heart slammed against his ribs as he tried to imagine what it was going to be like when he was both fucking and being fucked in front of what had to be most of the members of Club Wicked.

A knock came from the door.

"Come in," Rory said as he cuddled Rhiannon close to him.

When the door opened, a group of smiling women came inside, their grins and laughter chasing away the last of Liam's apprehension. Kitten, Dove, and Latisha entered the room and immediately swarmed around Rhiannon. The submissives wore matching Victorian maid's outfits while Latisha was dressed like the fairy-tale queen to Rhiannon's princess. All three had agreed to help Liam and Rory bring Rhiannon's fantasy to life tonight.

"Oh my God!" Dove squealed when she reached Rhiannon. "You look amazing!"

Kitten grabbed Rhiannon's hand and squeezed. "Stunning. Absolutely stunning."

With a smile Latisha made her way past the submissives to Liam's side. "You ready for this, lad?"

Liam grinned at her good-natured ribbing. "Full crowd?"

"And then some." She gave him a nervous smile. "You're lucky I love Rhiannon so much, because the thought of performing in front of all those people terrifies me."

"You'll be fine," Rory said in a soothing voice. "Just a few lines and your part is done."

Latisha blew out a harsh breath, the glittering crown on her head gleaming in the low lighting. "We need to get ready to go out."

The submissives were already herding Rhiannon toward the door when Rory placed his hand on Liam's shoulder. "Ready, mate? Remember, you don't have to do this."

"Yes, yes, I do." He held Rory's gaze, letting his love for the other man fill him completely.

Rory's smile radiated with such joy that Liam wanted to kiss him, but if they started here, they'd never make it to the stage. "Come on."

The women's giggles hushed as they moved to the wing of the stage, and Liam caught a glimpse of Isaac, wearing a tuxedo, standing in a golden spotlight. The lights of the theater had already been lowered so Liam couldn't see much past the first row, but he had the impression of movement from the entire room. He knew they would have an audience, and while he thrived on that energy, it also brought up the unpleasant thought that now everyone would know he loved another man. Bad memories tried to surface, but all he had to do was look at Rhiannon, and he found the strength to push them back. If she could get over her past, then so could he.

On stage Isaac was setting the story for this particular scene, a tale about a bratty little princess and a queen who had lost her patience with her only child.

Rhiannon took a deep breath while Latisha was muttering beneath her breath an almost constant stream of swear words. It moved him that despite Latisha's obvious discomfort she was willing to do this for them. More than anything he became aware of the true love that surrounded them, the love of their friends and in some ways their family. He'd spent more time with the people of Club Wicked than he had with his own kin for the past six years, celebrating their highs and comforting them during their lows. Tonight's performance was their coming out to his true family, the people who loved him regardless of his sexual preference.

As Isaac moved off the stage, Rhiannon and Latisha walked on and began their part of the performance. Despite her nerves Latisha did a wonderful job as the irritated queen scolding her daughter for putting herself in danger by riding off from the castle without her escort. Rhiannon was the perfect brat, and he was proud of her for pushing past her fears to get into her role. Then

Latisha left the stage with a warning that Rhiannon was going to regret her impetuous decisions, and Rhiannon's maids came on, ad-lib gossiping with Rhiannon about her being so naughty and warning her that the royal grooms were angry with her for getting them in trouble.

The maids departed, and that was Rory and Liam's cue. The lights dimmed as they sneaked on stage while Rhiannon was ranting about being able to do whatever she wanted while in her icy-bitch persona that she did so well. The audience chuckled as Rory and Liam sneaked up behind her, then outright laughed when they stepped into the spotlight, and Rhiannon let out a little feminine shriek.

"Hello, princess," Rory said with a low purr in his voice.

Liam moved behind her and crowded her, forcing her to step closer to Rory. "What did we tell you about ordering the junior grooms to let you sneak out for a ride? What did we tell you would happen if you did it again?"

With an arrogant tilt to her chin, Rhiannon ineffectively shoved at Rory's chest. "How dare you threaten me. The queen—"

"The queen," Rory interrupted her in a loud voice, "has agreed that your actions warrant a punishment."

"And since the stables are our domain, my dear princess, the price for your insolence will be paid to us."

"What?" Rhiannon struggled between them, but they easily captured her. "Unhand me!"

Ignoring her, Liam reached around and fondled her breasts, loving the little catch in her breath as he manipulated those warm handfuls of flesh. "Should we gag her?"

"No, I want those pretty lips wrapped around my cock."

Rhiannon broke away from them with a shriek, but Liam and Rory grabbed her skirt and yanked it off her, the material easily tearing away and revealing her long, luscious legs clad in thigh-high sparkly silver stockings and matching blue and silver garter belt. She screamed and tried to cover her sex as whistles and catcalls came from the audience as the sight of her world-class arse was presented to them. A real blush heated her face, and a trace of unease entered her gaze.

Instead of comforting her, Liam decided to push her a little harder. If she'd been afraid, they would have stopped, but her discomfort was from being so exposed to the members of Club Wicked. When she tried to run away, he grabbed her around the waist while Rory brought over two chairs from the edge of the stage. Rory took a seat in one and unceremoniously draped a squirming and swearing Rhiannon over his lap.

Pretending shock, Rory pinned Rhiannon down with one hand between her shoulder blades while he played with the crack of her ass with the other. "Well, well, well. What do we have here?"

Liam took the seat next to him, then lifted Rhiannon up so her chest rested on his thighs. He reached over and helped hold open her arse cheeks so the audience could see the silver butt plug with its large glittering blue topaz end in her ass. "What a naughty little princess."

"But so considerate," Rory said with an evil smile. "How nice of you to ready yourself for my cock."

Liam growled. "If anyone is going to be fucking the girl in the arse, it'll be me."

"No one is fucking my ass!" Rhiannon yelled, then shrieked when Rory slapped her bum hard enough that the crack was audible above the good-natured laughter of the crowd.

"Liam, be a good mate and shut her up if you would."

"My pleasure."

He easily maneuvered a mad and fighting Rhiannon so he could lift his kilt and present his erection to her. He imagined how they looked right now, an erotic tableau that would raise the desire of anyone watching. His skin sensitized, and when he grabbed a handful of Rhiannon's curls and forced her to look at him, he lost himself in her eyes. Her gaze had gone dark, her pupils expanding with desire.

"Suck it good, lass, or Master Rory will spank yer ass until you can't sit for a week."

Trying to hide an eager smile, she opened her mouth and allowed him to position his cock at her lips. Instead of taking him right in, she placed little butterfly kisses all over the throbbing head of his cock. The smack of Rory's hand meeting Rhiannon's tight little ass sent a bolt of lust through Liam, and he began to lose himself in the pleasure of his lovers. While the passion of the audience was good, nothing felt as right as the energy building between the three of them, a vortex of desire that threatened to tear him apart.

They fell into the rhythm of their passion, Rhiannon doing her best to make him come in her eager little mouth while Rory began to pick up the pace of his spanking. Soon she was moaning around his shaft, making him thrust up into her throat while she struggled to take him. The scent of her arousal filled the air, and when Rory began to play with the anal plug, she let out a breathy moan that had Liam's balls drawing up tight.

There was nothing as beautiful as Rhiannon while she was in subspace. The audience must have agreed. Out of the corner of his eye he could make out couples engaging in their own play while they watched the scene, and pride filled him that he was part of the reason that their desire was flaring. That it was his girl and his mate who were driving them to find their release.

Rory watched Rhiannon suck Liam's cock with barely concealed hunger. "Is our princess being a good girl? Is she sucking you how you want?"

"Not quite." Actually Rhiannon was deep throating him with a skill that would have brought him to his knees if he was standing, but they needed to move on to the next part of their scene. He should be apprehensive about what was going to happen, but instead he was so eager for it that he had to grip his cock at the base to hold back the urge to come. He grabbed Rhiannon by the hair and dragged her off his dick.

"Show her how it's done."

Rory shoved Rhiannon off his lap, and she landed before them in a heap of silken limbs, her wet pussy momentarily displayed to the audience as she struggled to right herself.

Before she could protest, Rory knelt beside her and pulled her up. "Watch."

With a soft whimper, Rhiannon knelt next to Rory, forcing Liam to spread his legs wide to accommodate them. His girl began to kiss and bite at his thigh, hard enough to sting. Rhiannon loved to nibble on his thigh muscles, and he had to admit the little sting of her nips was arousing. But nothing compared to the look of pure desire that Rory gave him when he grasped Liam's cock.

He was vaguely aware of the crowd going wild as Rory began to suck him, but his main attention was focused on the hot slide of his best mate's lips over the crown of his cock. Unable to help himself, he groaned aloud as Rory sucked him, pleasure suffusing him, then doubling when Rhiannon stood and lifted her breasts from the low-cut corset, offering him her nipples. He eagerly latched on to one and grabbed the other, burying his face into her softness and suckling the hard tip of her nipple with firm pulls that matched Rory's mouth on his cock. Teasing her nipple, he flicked the distended nub, drowning in her scent, her moans, and the way she whispered his name over and over.

The throb in his cock ached like an open wound, and the hot, slick sucking that Rory was giving him had him thrusting into the other man's mouth. Rory cupped his balls and gently rolled them while he pulled back enough to just suckle the tip. On the edge of losing it completely, Liam removed his mouth from Rhiannon's breasts, admiring the way her nipples were now a dusky brown tipped with red from his ardent attention.

Liam let out a soft growl. "I want to taste this pussy."

Rory released him with a last swipe of his tongue, and when Liam stood, his legs did indeed shake. He gathered Rhiannon to him. "Undress us."

Then he grabbed Rory by the back of the head and kissed him with all his pent-up passion, all his need, all his love. Another cheer rose from the crowd, but he didn't pay them any attention, instead focusing on Rory while Rhiannon stripped them both. He had to break their kiss so Rhiannon could remove Rory's pants, but as soon as the other man was nude, he grabbed Rhiannon by the back of the neck and shoved her to her knees.

"Suck him like he sucked me."

Rory groaned into his mouth, and Liam enjoyed how wild Rory's kiss became, how the other man rocked with the motion of Rhiannon's attentions to his dick. He knew how good it felt to have her tight, silken mouth tormenting him. The need to fuck and be fucked roared through his blood like a bonfire, and his patience snapped when Rhiannon lifted his kilt and started to jerk him off while she licked at Rory.

Before he could move, Rory stepped back, his chest heaving. "Oh no. I won't be spilling myself down your pretty little throat. We have other plans for you."

Rhiannon knelt before them in her debauched finery, looking like every man's wet dream come to life. "Yes, Master."

At some point in their play a massive brass bed had been moved onto the stage. As Liam turned, the lights above it turned on, revealing the white silk sheets and gleaming silver cuffs attached to the headboard. A small table was set up to the side with lube and a few toys that he planned on tormenting Rhiannon with while Rory took him.

"Up on the bed with you, lass."

She crawled over to the bed, lifting her hips to give the room a tempting show as the jewel gleamed between her taut cheeks. As soon as she was on the bed, she went onto her hands and knees and stuck her bum in the air, a silent invitation that he was all too eager to enjoy. Before he could move Rory stepped up behind him and reached around to remove his kilt.

"Do you still want me?" he whispered against Liam's neck.

"Always and forever," Liam murmured back as his kilt was removed and the cool air caressed his cock.

When he shifted onto the bed behind Rhiannon, he knew the crowd was getting a good look at the silver plug in his ass, and their excitement washed over him. He knelt behind Rhiannon, and Rory shifted behind him, the other man's fingers tapping at the plug and sending ball-clenching vibrations through the tender muscles of his arse. They'd only done this once before, but Liam would never forget the bone-deep satisfaction of being fucked by Rory. Only now he'd have the added arousal of being in Rhiannon's tight little ass at the same time.

It would be a bloody miracle if he didn't spurt the second he entered her body.

Rory handed him some lube, and he squirted out a generous amount, swirling it around the warm metal where it pushed into Rhiannon's bum. His best mate did the same thing to Liam's ass. He groaned as Rory began to work the metal out of him. His hand shook while he spread Rhiannon's bum cheeks and began to pull the plug from her tight little entrance. The sight of her anus stretching as he worked the thick plug out had Liam ready to rut on her like a beast, but he tried to temper himself. Liam knew he needed to go nice and easy with their girl because her sweet little arse wasn't used to taking someone as thick as he was.

A chill raced down his spine and settled in his balls as Rory worked the last bit of the plug out of his arse.

"There," Rory whispered against Liam's neck, his warm breath teasing Liam's sensitized skin. "You're ready for me. Now let's get our girl ready for you."

With a low growl, Liam flipped Rhiannon over to her back, and when he met her adoration-filled gaze, a dizzying warmth stole through his body, mixing with the heat of his desire and tempering it. Her love for him made him want to care for her, make this as good for her as he could.

He reached down and stroked her cheek, delighting in the way she cuddled into this touch while Rory moved over to her side. They both unhooked and removed her corset, leaving her naked except for her garters and stockings, looking so good Liam swore his heart skipped a beat.

"Love you, lass," he murmured, and her delighted smile brought an answering grin from his lips.

"I love you too, Master." She reached out and stroked her hand down Rory's flank. "I love you both so very much. My Masters. My men."

The world around them faded away, the sighs and moans of the crowd, the sight of so many couples enjoying themselves in the audience. All that mattered to him was this man and this woman. His perfect loves. He was made for them as surely as they were made for him, three parts of the same whole. Finally, after so many years, he was balanced.

Almost as one, Liam and Rory moved down to her pretty, wet pussy and began to kiss each other as they licked at her swollen clit. Her back arched, and Liam had to hold her hips while Rory placed his hand in the center of her chest to keep her still. They licked at her clit, their tongues stroking together as their girl tried to thrash beneath them, her frantic pleas to let her come rubbing against his cock like the caress of her slender fingers. God, she was beautiful, and she was theirs.

Rory stepped away for a moment, and Liam concentrated on suckling her clit while Rory cuffed her to the bed. With her arms stretched above her, Rhiannon went wild, abandoning herself to the pleasure of Liam's mouth with a wail. Her sweet juices coated his face, and just when she was about to climax, he pulled back, earning a frustrated scream.

A low growl spilled from Rory, and he leaned over, then licked Rhiannon's desire from Liam's lips.

"Need to fuck you," Rory whispered against his mouth.

"Let me get inside our girl first."

Liam slung Rhiannon's legs over his shoulders, opening the tender star of her anus to his rampant erection. He held her gaze as he slowly began to push into her, loving the wince of pain as her tight muscles reluctantly yielded. No matter how much they stretched her first, she was always tight enough that the intrusion of a cock hurt, and the sadistic part of him loved giving her that little bit of pain, loved watching her take it for his pleasure.

With a grunt, he pressed the thick head of his shaft through the ring of muscles and the slick heat of her well-lubed arse enveloped him like a tight, hot fist.

"So fucking good," he panted out, slowly sliding into her until his balls touched her ass.

She moaned and squirmed beneath him, her bum flexing around his cock in a way that stole his mind. Then the hot press of Rory's erection against Liam's ass had him freezing. She jerked at her chains, no doubt trying to reach for him, and the fierce arousal in her gaze allowed him to relax and let Rory in.

His anus burned as Rory sank into him, filling him as he filled Rhiannon. The sheer carnality of the act tore him apart, and he gasped, his head falling back against Rory's shoulder while the other man worked his way into Liam's body, brushing against his prostate and sending renewed shards of pleasure and passion tearing through his mind, through his self-control. All around them men and women screamed and roared out their pleasure. Liam gave himself over to the moment, loving that their fucking was driving those around them into a sexual frenzy. Lust filled the air until he was drowning in it. Only the tight clasp of Rhiannon's arse and the burning pleasure of Rory's cock kept him grounded to this world.

Rory began to move behind him, and Liam fell into his rhythm, Rhiannon's sweet heat gripping his dick while his best mate picked up the pace. Soon they were all panting and moaning, each lost in the whirlpool of desire that was as unique to them as their love. He became overwhelmed by the love mixing with the raw desire, filling his hands with her perfect breasts as Rory began to fuck him in earnest, pounding Liam's body into hers and driving their woman crazy. She broke first, screaming out Liam's name as her hot little ass clutched at his cock in such a powerful sensation that he had no choice but to follow her into his own climax.

His balls clenched, and his world filled with a bright white light. Time suspended and filled with the roar of his release. It scoured him, drained him, and filled him at the same time as his mind struggled to cope with the massive rush of pleasure. Goose bumps broke out over his body as he emptied himself into Rhiannon with harsh thrusts made all the more powerful by Rory rutting behind him. With a muffled yell, Rory sank his teeth into the sensitive skin where Liam's shoulder and neck met, dragging yet another burst of release from Liam until he was pretty sure he was going to pass out.

The pleasure, the soul-destroying pleasure, went on and on until he collapsed onto Rhiannon, managing to catch himself just enough so he didn't crush the lass. Rory slipped out of him and fell onto his side, then gathered Liam and Rhiannon against him. Still locked inside their woman Liam groaned at the quivering contractions of her body beneath his. He had no idea how long they stayed locked together like that, but, after what seemed like an eternity, soft feminine hands gently helped him move off Rhiannon.

When he fell back next to Rhiannon, he opened his bleary eyes and found Dove smiling down at him, still dressed in her maid's costume and gently cleaning him with a warm cloth. He turned his head, luxuriating in the blonde's gentle touch, and found Kitten tending to Liam while—to his great shock—Sunny knelt between Rhiannon's legs and gently cleaned her sex with a white towel. Sunny was blushing, but the smile she gave Rhiannon was a gentle one.

He glanced up at Rhiannon and found his beautiful girl crying. Not wanting to break the spell of comfort and sensuality that the other women wove around them, he brushed away Rhiannon's tears while Rory did the same on the other side. Once they were cleaned to the women's satisfaction, they left without a word, and moving as one Liam and Rory rolled onto their sides, pressing Rhiannon between them. He caught a motion out of the corner of his eye and smiled when Latisha, still in her queen costume, placed a warm blanket over them. She met Liam's gaze and mouthed the words *Thank you* to him with a smile that let him know how proud she was of them.

The vague sounds of passion still came from the audience, but he scarcely paid them any attention. Right now, everything important to him was in this bed, and it felt so good, so right that he mentally berated himself for denying the pleasure of Rory's love all these years. Then again, if he'd faced his own fears earlier, they might never have met Rhiannon. Maybe everything really did happen for a reason, because he would go through every bit of bullshit all over again for a chance to fall in love with the most wonderful woman in the world.

"No tears, darling girl," Rory whispered against the top of her head.

"These are happy tears," she said in a husky voice. "I'm so happy my body can't take it, so I have to let it out somehow. I love you both so very much. You're my everything."

A burning sensation infused Liam's eyes, and he found himself blinking back tears at the heartfelt emotion in her statement. "And I love you, both of you, more than anything in the world."

Rory smiled at him, and Liam sank into the love in his gaze. "I love you both, always and forever."

They held one another and cuddled close, occasionally talking and laughing, but mostly just content to be with each other. As the room around them slowly emptied, Liam tried to wrap his mind around the changes that had taken place since their beautiful lass had come into their lives, and he marveled at how one woman's love was strong enough to make him face his own demons and how...good he felt. Yes, he'd have to face what would no doubt be an epic battle with his family when he told them the truth, but the idea didn't scare him like it used to. Either they would love him for who he was or he would have to accept the loss of their affection. Rhiannon had taught him that true love was unconditional, and he wouldn't give up what he had with Rory and their girl for anything in the world.

"Always and forever," he whispered against Rhiannon's cheek.

"Always and forever," Rory agreed with a small smile.

Holding their girl between them, Liam succumbed to the sleep tugging at his exhausted mind and body, knowing he was safe and secure in Club Wicked, surrounded by their friends and true family and filled with love.

The men laughed softly; then Liam let out a long, slow sigh. "Amazing."

"Indeed," Rory replied and kissed her forehead.

"Mmm-hmm."

Liam watched as Rhiannon reached up to her neck and trailed her fingers over her collar. "Mine."

"Yes, darling girl, yours."

"Love you, both of you," Liam added as he leaned up and gave first her, then Rory a gentle kiss.

Rhiannon closed her eyes and snuggled into their embrace, her voice holding so much tenderness it made Liam's heart ache when she whispered, "My Masters."

Ann Mayburn

Ann is Queen of the Castle to her wonderful husband and three sons in the mountains of West Virginia. In her past lives she's been an import broker, a communications specialist, a US Navy civilian contractor, a bartender/ waitress, and an actor at the Michigan Renaissance Festival. She also spent a summer touring with the Grateful Dead-though she will deny to her children that it ever happened.

From a young age she's been fascinated by myths and fairytales, and the romance that often was the center of the story. As Ann grew older and her hormones kicked in, she discovered trashy romance novels. Great at first, but she soon grew tired of the endless stories with a big, wonderful, emotional buildup to really short and crappy sex. Never a big fan of purple prose (throbbing spears of fleshy pleasure and wet honey pots make her giggle), she sought out books that gave the sex scenes in the story just as much detail and plot as everything else without using cringe worthy euphemisms. This led her to the wonderful world of erotic romance, and she's never looked back.

Now Ann spends her days trying to tune out cartoons playing in the background to get into her 'sexy space' and has learned to type one handed while soothing a cranky baby.

Loose Id® Titles by Ann Mayburn

Available in digital format at http://www.loose-id.com or your favorite online retailer

The Breaker's Concubine

The CLUB WICKED Series
My Wicked Valentine
My Wicked Nanny
My Wicked Trainers
My Wicked Devil
My Wicked Masters

The VIRTUAL SEDUCTION Series
Sodom and the Phoenix

In addition to digital format, the following titles are also available in print at your favorite bookseller:

The Breaker's Concubine

The CLUB WICKED Series
My Wicked Valentine
My Wicked Nanny
My Wicked Devil
My Wicked Masters

The VIRTUAL SEDUCTION Series
Sodom and the Phoenix

CPSIA information can be obtained at www.ICGtesting.com
Printed in the USA
BVOW02s0341090915

416813BV00001B/63/P